WHALE MAN

WHALE MAN

a novel

Alan Michael Parker

WordFarm

SEATTLE, WASHINGTON

WordFarm
2816 East Spring Street
Seattle, WA 98122
www.wordfarm.net

Copyright © 2011 by Alan Michael Parker

Cover Image: iStockphoto
Cover Design: Andrew Craft
Illustrations: Alan Michael Parker, Felicia van Bork, George Eddy Smith
Book text is set in 11 point Monotype Dante

USA ISBN-13: 978-1-60226-007-8
USA ISBN-10: 1-60226-007-9
Printed in the United States of America

First Edition: 2011

Library of Congress Cataloging-in-Publication Data

Parker, Alan Michael, 1961-
   Whale Man / Alan Michael Parker.—1st ed.
      p. cm.
   ISBN-13: 978-1-60226-007-8 (pbk.)
   ISBN-10: 1-60226-007-9 (pbk.)
   1. Mothers—Death—Fiction. 2. Mothers and sons—Fiction. 3. Inheritance and succession—Fiction. I. Title.
PS3566.A674738W53 2011
813'.54—dc22

                                                      2010043307

P 12 11 10 9 8 7 6 5 4 3 2 1
Y 17 16 15 14 13 12 11

*for Corinne Duchesne
and Rudi Gombert*

The Tomb of the
Unknown Mother

ONE

. . . .

IN THE DREAM, through the window of his late mother's house, Avi Heyer watched an older man, someone familiar and yet changed, pick up a hammer. The workman wore a tool belt, heavy-soled brown shoes, and jeans torn at the right knee. Even from here, at a distance of more than forty feet, the man seemed to be shining, deep in some kind of happiness, his gaze focused on nothing but the hammer and the nail and the board, his body synchronized with the rhythmic and musical pounding of the work. He struck, paused, wiped his forehead with the back of his forearm.

In the dream, the moment changed. The weather in the dream changed, the air abandoned to its powerful scents, the scene lined with memories like a book read once before. The workman laid his hammer on a table and climbed an enormous standing ladder—maybe thirty rungs in all—to the penultimate rung, leaned into the ladder for balance, and then reached upward, with first the left hand and then the right, to grasp one of the curved wooden beams. Once hanging fully, he kicked away the ladder, which fell like something mythic, slowly and without a sound.

There in the unfinished building, the older man hung from a rib—a beam that now looked very much like a rib—and swung. He swung just a little, as though stirred only by an imperceptible breeze.

Slowly the swinging man increased his motion, pointing the tips of his worn boots forward and then bending at the knees to curl backward, pitched maybe fifteen or twenty degrees each way from his plumb-lined weight.

As Avi the dreamer watched, he felt his emotions sway with the movement of the man swinging—and beset by a kind of anxiety that seemed too like envy, Avi the dreamer wanted desperately to feel with his body what the other man felt, pendulous, aloft and at risk.

Gravity softened. From the swinging man, his pockets turned out, floated a hammer, a handsaw. An electric screwdriver, its colors distinctive, bit whirring. More tools, a rasp, a file, and an awl deeply oiled with use. Then a diaphanous chamois, too light and so fluttery. Still, he swung. Other objects appeared—the man's pockets were bountiful—but these weren't all tools, and they seemed not to fall but to rise and to float into the rafters. A cricket cage missing its door. Loosed swatches of patterned cloth, a quilt undone. An old brown valise, peppered with travel stickers and tied with string, the holidays of a previous generation, the memories in black-and-white. A bulbous copper lamp, its cord stretched out like a kite's tail. A knobby bag of oranges—which burst, the oranges tumbling out and up into the air. Still the older man swung, and the oranges floated around his body like new planets.

Avi the dreamer could smell the oranges. It was a small smell, a piquant bite of citrus in which was caught a whiff of the Jersey shore and his own real childhood. He wanted one. He lifted one foot up, straddled the open windowsill, climbed through, and touched down gingerly and then fully upon a raw wooden sub-floor, the planks freshly laid.

Above him, the arched and vaulted ribs of the building curved. The ladder was gone, but a ladder could be found. The other man was gone. Buried in shadow at the edge of the scene stood someone else, another person Avi the dreamer knew, someone the wrong age or just wrong—she shouldn't have been here.

He felt a rush of feeling, too much.

Mom.

His feet set firmly upon the wooden floor that throbbed with breathing, Avi the dreamer spread his arms and reached into the emptiness and up toward the ceiling of the structure where he couldn't reach. He was standing inside an enormous living thing—somehow wooden and alive—inside the belly of a beast. His mom was there; his mom was dead. His mom was there.

. . .

Can a person choose to dream, to re-dream? Somewhere in the house, but certainly not nearby, a cell phone chirped, and Avi's thoughts rose to meet the sound, his dream sinking slowly back into its ocean, Mom and whale and oranges bubbling down into un-memory, inaccessible for now. He was awake enough to consider finding the offending phone, not to recognize the little *chirrup*, to want to have back the dream, and to choose to lie still. "Dolly, get the phone," Avi muttered almost aloud to his dog, camped across the foot of the bed where she wasn't allowed, her bulk dominion.

"Crap," he said to himself.

The phone stopped ringing. Dolly gave a little sleep-woof. "Okay," she said in Doggish, although she clearly wasn't going to comply.

. . .

In his new dream, when he sat down upon the chair, Avi Heyer knew that the chair was unhappy, and not only the chair. The scarred table, the blue vase of lilies, the lovely meal steaming under its silver serving lid, all the things of the material world had feelings—some happier than others. And he himself had none.

Across the room, angled away from the table, and hung too high to look into, the mirror might have something to add.

But inside and outside were different; a hammering could be heard out there, someone fixing a roof.

The dreaming man stood ready to investigate, and began to search his pockets—now where had he put it? He had lost it. What was it? His hands went into his breast pocket, his pants pockets, and then his shirt, against his skin—and then his hands were rooting around inside his own chest.

His reached in and felt through his skin.

Avi handled his own bones, his stringy arteries and spongy lungs.

The hammering: his heart. He touched it, tough and somehow both meaty and gelatinous, and drew back, surprised and ashamed.

Above the sink the open window filled with a stupendous animal eye, looming, wise and gentle. Would the animal forgive him? In that moment the dreamer wanted nothing else.

Avi's hands were out of his body again, and now he was walking toward the window and the enormous intelligence of the animal. It was a sympathy for which he yearned, some good grace from that profound being. He glanced to the side, cut his gaze to check how he looked in the mirror. He was there, but he could see through himself. He was gone.

. . .

"Wakie, wakie!"

"He's awake," said someone. "You woke him, Sister."

"You told me to, Sister," said the first voice.

"I did," said the second.

"Oh, Sister," said the first voice.

Avi opened his eyes. There were two young women in the bedroom, identical twins.

"We've got your dog," said one of the twins.

No, not identical, just similar: the two women were blond, pig-tailed, and

11

dressed bizarrely in matching yellow sundresses festooned with large poppies. The twins might have been Avi's age.

"What?" he said. "What are you doing here? Get out of my house!" Avi shook his head slightly, *buhhh*, and sat up—and then pulled up the sheet to cover himself.

"We've got your dog!" The other woman held up Dolly's empty collar. "See."

"I like you, Sister," said the first woman.

"What? Where's my dog? Dolly—" Avi said. "Get out of here!"

"*Woof! Woof, woof, woof, woof!*" Dolly jumped onto the bed.

"Told you. We've got your dog."

"Gimme that," Avi grabbed for Dolly's undone collar.

"No!" said the woman holding the collar.

"You don't have my dog. She's right here!" The conversation was unbelievable, he thought. "You're an idiot," Avi said. Dolly was right here.

SMACK! Before he could react, one of the women slapped him. Damn, his face stung. "What did—"

SMACK! She hit him across the other cheek.

"Oh, Sister," cooed the other woman. "My turn! My turn!"

"You can bust him up later," the assailant said as she turned and patted her sister's shoulder. "Next time." And then she returned to Avi. "Calling us names will hurt you."

"Who are you?" Avi insisted. "Stop hitting me," he said. Wow, his face hurt.

"We're going." The woman tossed Dolly's collar onto Avi's lap. "Put this on. The Camel wants to see you."

"What?" Avi said. He needed to pee. "The Camel? What the hell is wrong with you people?"

The violent one raised her hand as if to strike—

"Okay! Okay!" Avi didn't want to be hit again. "Okay already." He threw off the sheet and damasked blanket, and swung his legs out of bed—his dead mother's bed, the linens decent, the mattress pretty comfy. Naked guy, he stood and walked to the bathroom, half-erect and half-aswing, woozy and ringing from being cuffed. He would play along, then call the cops.

"*Ewwwwwwww!*" One of the women shrieked.

"NO! That's disgusting!" The other woman pointed and squealed. "Don't!"

Cool, he had freaked out his home invaders; he left the door ajar, then called over his shoulder as he peed. "Hey! Who the hell's The Camel?"

There was whimpering and whispering back in the bedroom.

He washed up. "So?" Avi said as he returned.

"Eww." One of the women scrunched up her face. "I don't want to see it. Help me, Sister." She looked, and tried not to, and looked again.

"Sister . . ." the other sister cooed. "It's okay. It will go away. Just cover . . . it."

"Gotcha," Avi said with a wink. He arrived at the dresser by the window, rummaged for clean underwear, reached for jeans and a T-shirt, thought about which color of socks. "But it might show. You two better be careful," he winked again and began to get dressed.

"Ewww," said a twin.

"I know," said another twin. And then: "Sister, that was gross. . . . Let's go," she added. "The Camel wants to see you."

"No," said Avi, pulling up his jeans and wiggling them on.

"He said no! I heard him!" The one woman began to bop a bit in place, bouncy. "I love when they say no. It's my turn, it's my turn—"

"Right," said Avi. "No."

"Right? No?" the calmer woman said. "Make up your mind!" She pointed two fingers at her own eyes and then at his: *I'm watching you.*

"Oh, crap," said Avi. These women were morons. Violent, too. And then he made a decision. "Look, you dopes—don't hit me, don't hit me!—I'm going to make coffee and feed my dog. Then I'll go with you to see your camel. But you have to wait outside; you're not allowed in my house."

"Sister? He called us dopes."

"I know . . . and he's the victim! Let me kick him!"

And before he could reply, *BAM!* She kicked him in the shin.

Back down onto the bed Avi fell. "JESUS!" Avi said. "No kicking!"

"No coffee, no names. Let's go now: The Camel wants to see you."

"Not if you're going to hurt me." Avi crawled away on the bed, out of reach.

A glare-off: the twins and Avi glowered at each other.

"Okay! We'll hurt you later," a twin decided all by herself.

"Fine," Avi agreed, lying his way out. "Then I'll go with you now, and leave before you hurt me. But I need to feed my dog first."

"I don't understand," said the dumber of the twins.

"It's okay, Sister, we're winning."

"What about my dog?" Avi couldn't believe he was negotiating. The twins clearly shared a brain, but probably not a whole one.

"Don't worry, Victim." The woman turned away to check her make-up in the vanity, and blew herself a kiss. "I'm pretty," she said.

"You're pretty," her sister said.

"It's only a dog," the first sister said. Then she and her sister held hands.

"Who are you people?"

Both women laughed. "Let's see . . . I'm Snow White," said one.

"Oh, goody!" said the other. "I love this game. I'm Rose Red!" She jumped up and down, once, twice. "Sister, Sister, you're my favorite! Now can I punch him? Now can I hold the gun?"

"*Woof!*" said Dolly, fed up with not having peed or eaten.

A gun? Avi looked at the two women; one's nose might be a little slimmer than the other's. Skinny Nose nodded at him meaningfully and then turned to leave. The other one's eye might be higher. Fat Nose / High Eye.

"Okay," Avi said to Dolly. "Let's go. . . . *Woof*," he said to his dog, which meant *be careful*.

Dolly joyfully and doggily led a little parade downstairs: pooch, twin, Avi, twin. The twins had apparently stopped speaking to him, but the one in front was humming something. The one behind didn't need to hum; she was carrying a gun. He had lost track again of which twin was which.

"A gun," he said to himself, fear the new day's caffeine. "A dream," he said to himself even more softly. If he closed his eyes, he could still see through the window of the dream: Mom, the ladder, the oranges. He had felt his own heart. If he closed his eyes, he might walk into something and hurt himself.

Avi let Dolly out the back door, put her water and kibble bowls on the stoop—the latter her favorite, the one emblazoned with screaming cats. If he were a cat, now would be a good time to scream. He was sweating. "Okay," he said to the freaky twins. He grabbed his keys. They had a gun.

. . .

The twins made him drive, one twin un-seatbelted in his little Toyota and another leading in a Lincoln. Out of his mom's neighborhood, two useless U-turns later, they headed down 53 to Samson Parkway and then made a left. Avi hadn't been in this part of Elsbeth, North Carolina, before—he had not visited his mother in the years she had lived here, their estrangement facilitated by distance. A mile or two further down the road, as the morning light settled upon the strip malls, the Lincoln pulled into the crowded lot of a bowling alley and parked, and Avi followed suit. All was peaceable so long as he cooperated. He patted the cell phone in his left pocket; he would call the cops as soon as he was alone.

Once out of the car the twins took up positions on either side of Avi. They marched three abreast up the wide walk until they reached the front door and couldn't squeeze through, which caused a momentary quandary until the phalanx could be reconstituted as a procession.

The crowded bowling alley almost shook with league fun, the early racket cacophonous: balls in lanes and gutters, pins clattering, machines purring, Bloody Marys sloshing, happy bowlers in happy shirts, victors shouting. Onward the snarly and tense twins urged Avi, as they wove through the 1950s. And then there she was, waving cheerily as she stood alone on a lane before turning back to her game.

The person named "The Camel" had two bright orange bowling balls and bright orange shoes to match. She was small, five feet and change, dressed in loose-fitting blue pants and a green sweatshirt that said *Foxy!*, the garment a disco relic. She alone occupied Lanes 21 and 22, bowling almost nonstop, an orange ball down 21 then 22 then 21 then 22. She seemed not to care about her electronically kept score. Maybe she was fifty; Avi couldn't tell. Her hair was brown, frosted or highlighted.

She made him wait. A strike on 22, from which she turned to greet her guests with a sweep of her hand, her wrist trussed in some kind of bowling brace; she ushered him to a seat and smiled. "Hello, girls. *Herr Visitor.* What size?" she asked, pointing to his feet.

"I'm an 11 and ½," Avi answered. "I have big feet," he said for no reason.

She nodded. "Please remove your shoes."

Her power, that's what struck Avi. The request was polite. So he did as he was told, for now, and handed his shoes to the twins, who scampered away. What a relief to see them go.

"Did they hurt you more than necessary? You look a bit Raggedy in the Andy Department."

"What?" said Avi.

"Your cheeks. They're a little red. And you're limping."

"They have a gun."

"I think not," she said. "Guns are too complicated for the poor dears." She spun away neatly. "*Segue!*" she called out. "So . . . don't you loathe middle class America?" The Camel asked, glancing back at Avi as she prepared to fling the garish polyurethane ball pin-ward. "Such banality. I throw this"—which she did with a series of stutter-steps and then a nifty toe point, quite adroitly, really—"to knock down those. How quintessentially American. Rage and disaster; the more disaster, the higher my score." The pins clattered, a strike, and a large X flashed on the hanging scoreboard. "It's a foreign policy," she added.

The Camel turned and sighed and then stepped to the curvy pre-fab banquette where Avi sat. "And it makes me proud to know Americans everywhere," she said, her narrowed eyes blazing. "Just look." She swept her arm grandly, a flourish to take in all the other bowlers here in Elsbeth, North Carolina, bowlers all over the country. "What makes you proud, Susan Junior?"

Who? Avi didn't know what to say, so he let his silence abide. The Camel bowled another strike and then a spare, a seven on the spare, the third frame open. She had called him Susan Junior: if he were Susan Junior, who was Susan? His mom? What the hell was going on? His mother's name had been Maureen.

Before long the twins returned with his rented shoes: each girl handed him one black-and-red shoe, their actions clearly the result of some contested negotiation. Each had a bottle of root beer into which a long straw had been inserted. One of the twins was Rose Red, Skinny Nose, Lower Eye.

"Your mother was Susan, yes?" The Camel had intuited his confusion.

"Yes," Avi lied as he tied his laces. Susan, he told himself. By agreeing, he hoped to flee sooner, a tactic that usually worked with his girlfriend, Mimou.

Slllurrrrrpppp, the twins drank noisily, in concert.

"So you have what she had," The Camel concluded. "And you're selling," The Camel instructed him.

Slllurrrrrpppp.

Avi waited a moment. "Yes," he said.

"Yes?" The Camel narrowed her already narrowed gaze. "Why, that's the spirit," she offered, in the most pleasantly menacing timbre Avi had ever heard. "We knew you were still in her house for a reason."

He could not resist: he pointed at Snow White. "She slapped me twice," Avi said. "Then the other one kicked me. If anyone does it again, I'm not selling." He rubbed his face. "Still hurts."

Snow White punched Rose Red on the shoulder. "Told ya'," she said.

"Didn't."

"Did."

"Ladies," The Camel intervened. "Go outside and play Chicken."

"Oh, fun!" piped Rose Red.

"You're meat now, Sister," squeaked Snow White. "Chicken meat!"

They put down their sodas, hooked arms happily and skipped away. Avi exhaled.

"Henchwomen," said The Camel, rolling her eyes. *"Oy gevalt."* She sat down on the bench across from Avi, leaned toward him, and rested her chin on her fist art-historically. "Let me think about this," she said, and winked.

Avi didn't know what to say or do, so he crossed his legs, which made his shin bark. He tried to rub the pain away. Say nothing, he told himself. Dolly was at the house, the twins were gone, Mom wasn't named Susan and was still dead, and no one had a gun.

"Susan, Susan . . . I'm sorry for your loss, you know. She was perfect."

"What do you mean?" he asked, unable to help himself.

"Mean? I mean more than I say. Always. It's my bane." The Camel squinched her mouth into a grimace. "Do you realize your disadvantage? Studies show that more people will be unwilling to leave a room if their shoes have been taken—as opposed to the removal of any other garment, that is, including their underwear." With this last point she gestured schoolmarmishly, one finger raised. "I'm less sure about the dainties, but I'm willing to try confiscating yours. . . . So, are you feeling discomfited egoistically? That's one of my goals. Unless, of course, you're going commando, which would embarrass us both."

Avi shrugged, no, yes, whatever.

"Susan. And now Susan Junior. You don't look like her, you know, but may well as you age. The long hair's appealing, if kept clean. Very Quattrocento. . . . Care to bowl a frame? It might be therapeutic."

"No, thanks," he said. His shin hurt.

"Can't say I blame you," The Camel chuckled. "My own obsession with indigenous American sports must seem a little pathetic. *Pathétique*," she added, amusing herself. "Do you mind?" She rose, took hold of her bowling ball, and stepped to lane 21, settled into motionless focus upon the pins. "Fooling myself into fitness helps me think."

Again The Camel bowled, her form elegant, her small frame contained, ergonomic and athletic. She left one wobbly pin standing—and again she seemed not to notice the result as she returned to Avi.

He sympathized with the pin.

"We knew you were here . . . but we didn't know—that is, I didn't know—you would sell. Not to mention The Lima Bean, of course." The Camel smiled, her teeth a little sharp. "I would hope, and not gratuitously, that you understand the wisdom of suspecting The Lima Bean's motives at all times, not to mention her affected spiritualism. Granted, she and I are rivals," she added, adjusting her sweatshirt with a series of little tugs. "But you and I, we are *simpatico*, compatriots. Friends?" She extended her trussed hand, the wrist-and-finger guard like some sort of arcane battle device rather than a bowling aid.

He hesitated. Someone was named The Lima Bean? Holy crap. Someone named The Camel was talking about someone named The Lima Bean? Should he capitalize the "T" in The Camel when he called the cops? Avi suspected so.

But shaking her hand wouldn't mean a thing, not if he didn't mean anything by it—which he wouldn't, since he was too confused—and besides, Avi had to get out of here, fix his headache, call all the cops in Elsbeth to report that an orphaned adult son of a re-named mother had been twice-slapped and then kicked—a mother whose circle of friends included a bizarrely chatty little psycho and twin attack bimbos.

The Camel thrust her hand ever so slightly forward, impatient. *"Vamonos!"*

What could this woman do to him anyway? He could take her.

No, wait: that was a stupid thought. He was in cooking school and she was clearly some kind of criminal. She had henchwomen.

He pulled back his hair from across his face. Her hand still hung expectantly mid-air. Then, as ever, full of shit and always at risk, Avi met The Camel's gesture, pressed the flesh with her flesh-and-Velcro-and-nylon.

Idiot, he told himself. It was just like Barcelona. It was just like Warrensburg. It was just like Warszawa. It was just like Schenectady—or maybe not like Schenectady, since he had left there on purpose. But it was just like Avi Heyer to agree to something he didn't understand.

"Friends? I don't think so," Avi said to The Camel. "I sell and you buy."

"Of course." The Camel smiled, a smiling camel, a camel who would certainly spit and bite. "We shall further the work of your late mother." She continued to shake his hand heartily, not letting go.

Susan Junior had apparently entered the family business.

"But you don't know what I'm talking about, do you?" She eyed him with one Camel eye as she let go of his hand.

"Not exactly," Avi said.

"Aha! And yet you hold that inter-personal violence requires civic redress?"

"Um . . . yes, if you're asking if I'm going to call the police."

"You have accepted my hand, Susan Junior. Keep your bond. We all live by a code, each to each, notwithstanding that the irritations of our daily lives remain at odds with our values. No police."

A woman on lane 24 bowled a strike; a bevy of beehived women squealed gleefully. Avi admired them all.

"I don't understand," Avi admitted, although he kind of did.

"Your injuries are nothing. Your body is nothing. You sell, I buy, and thus you shall return to your little life—your dog safe, your friends unbothered by my nationwide organization and accomplices, the twins once more recalled to the shop for minor adjustment, and you no wiser but far, far richer." She brushed an invisible something off of her blouse, even the flick of her hand imperious.

"I am not a violent person . . . unless provoked," The Camel said. "*Si?* We are as one. And, oh—that nice young police officer?" She pointed to a long-legged policeman perched akimbo at the bowling alley's burger bar. "He works for me. So find the list and set a price."

TWO

· ·

HE CALLED THE POLICE as soon as he got coffee, thank God, from the drive-through at the Coffee Bear.

"Sir, you're telling me that one of two identical twins slapped you and kicked you in your . . . left shin?"

"Left shin."

"—and then took you bowling?"

"No, I didn't bowl," Avi said. "She bowled." The Coffee Bear on the cup smiled maniacally, the result of too much Coffee Bear coffee. Bears had all the luck.

"She kicked you and then she bowled."

"No, The Camel bowled."

"A camel."

"I'm telling you, she got my mom's name wrong."

"A camel got your mom's name wrong. Your mom bowled."

"Officer!"

"Sir, there's no reason to be upset."

"My mom's dead, Officer. She just died." He took a sip right-handed, hot, hot, signaled to turn left.

"My condolences. . . . That would be upsetting. Are you calling to report a murder?"

"I'M CALLING TO REPORT A SHIN KICKING!"

"Sir. I said that I'm sorry about your mother. There's no reason to—"

"*OWWW!*" Avi spilled hot coffee on himself. "Damn, damn, damn, damn!"

"Sir, are you all right?"

"*Ow,*" he said more calmly. "I just spilled hot coffee on myself. My shin hurts."

"Sir, are you in any danger?"

Avi thought about the question. "No."

"The camel is not with you now?"

"No."

"No one's kicking you at present?"

"No. I'm driving home. I mean, to my mother's house."

"Sir, I would suggest that you not drink a hot beverage while driving, and certainly not in your state of mind. In addition, if you have a lower body injury, driving itself may pose hazards. Also, if you would like to file a report, please appear . . ." The rest of the conversation faded, the dispatch officer quick to dispatch Avi's complaint.

As he was relating the events, he understood how ridiculous his story had sounded. One Elsbeth Three, see the man spilling hot coffee on himself. One Elsbeth Three, see a camel bowling. A person named The Lima Bean needed to be eyed askance according to a very scary person named The Camel? Someone should run a flag up the bullshit and see what flew.

Because Avi also understood what it meant to bullshit someone: bullshit oiled the gears, eased the easeways, opened the exit doors, filled the coffers, and brought a smile to the face of the dourest assistant assistant. Avi had always liked to lie, reality more fun when embellished. Besides, lying was the new truth; lying was the way of all hope; lying had always set Avi free.

Well, food was no lie, the chef-in-training said to himself. And sex. Sex was good: good sex was no lie.

But no matter The Camel's lies, she was freakishly scary.

He turned onto the street where at the corner stood his mother's house, Avi's house, although he didn't feel anything proprietary about the property. Her house, her room, her furniture, her cookware, her crappy linoleum—everything still seemed Maureen Heyer's, even though she had died three weeks ago in a single-car accident, her body so shattered that identification had to be by dental records. The next morning, just six days after his twenty-ninth birthday, Avi had come to do the job of the only child, carrying in his suitcase the yet-to-be-worn yellow sweater she had sent by mail, the gift like some sort of ugly, fluorescent message from the Beyond, the sweater's arms folded across the chest. "I'm dead," the sweater said. Avi had arrived to arrange the funeral and inherit her meager possessions, including a house he was definitely going to sell, the corner lot undoubtedly attractive to someone else, the park across the way a cute little preserve. A house to sell for nothing, the bank the real owner, Avi named in a will that apportioned an unfair bit of change to Amnesty International, which shocked him, the notion of Maureen Heyer's being charitable new to her son.

Susan Junior, he reminded himself. He would have to unshovel that load of crap. A full-of-crap camel—what did she want, a list of what?

Three weeks, and he couldn't seem to leave, to get everything done and get back to D.C. for good. Once more Avi Heyer had slept alone last night, his lover, Mimou Watteau, in all probability traipsing about her loft until four a.m. in her furry green slippers and Bugs Bunny T-shirt, a snifter of Argmanac in one hand and a book in the other, singing badly as she paced and drank. Mimou, like most night people and restaurant workers, would hate this time of day and even more so the banality of the burbs, Elsbeth and its *cuisine de merde,* a world reconstituted and reheated, indigestible. Mimou, whom Avi had realized he had yet to miss—another surprise, of sorts. There were far too many surprises in Elsbeth, North Carolina, he thought, and then, by mistake as he pulled into the driveway, he gave the horn a little *blart.*

Dolly came bounding to the fence, good Doll Face. Every reunion was a first for her. Once inside and thoroughly greeted, she flopped near her squeaky squirrel toy, one big paw on either side, a hug.

There was a message on the machine from Jack Markins, Maureen's attorney and the executor of the estate, asking Avi to call the office. He would do so later.

There was a different kind of message in the house now, too. The blinds were drawn as they had been left, the morning light slatted, lines on shapes, visual incoherence; the air in the living room floated with fuzzy nothingness, the shadows filled with shapeless apparitions.

Avi stopped at the foot of the stairs and glanced up toward the bedroom. He knew that he had dreamed an important dream. Standing here, he could still picture the dreamed structure—the fantastic ribs. When he unfocused his open eyes, to see nothing and concentrate on those ribs, they pulsed slowly in long, deeply heaving breaths. He could feel himself asleep-and-awake, as though naked once more in the bed upstairs.

Most of the dream was still available, an unusual phenomenon for Avi. He realized, though stunned by the idea, that the dream was one he had dreamed incompletely last night, and perhaps the night before, and who knows how many nights in a row before that—and that he might have finally finished redreaming if the twins hadn't slapped him into the day and shin-kicked him to the bowling alley.

The dream might be a question he had yet to ask. Isn't that what a dream must be, if the dream recurs? He would have to Google, and then hit the bookstore and look up dreams and dream analysis, subjects about which he knew very little. His mom was in the dream, and a whale; Avi had been inside the whale, and astonishingly happy there.

A whale. Exactly. Sort of.

Something beeped somewhere upstairs.

At the top of the stairs, he followed the beep toward the guest bedroom, down the hall, and then to the sewing room on the left, where Maureen Heyer's legacy—twenty boxes of useless sewing materials—stood stacked in inexplicably neat stacks, each box labeled "Sewing Supplies," one box no different from any other. Decisions, decisions, left, right, and where was that sound coming from? *More coffee,* Avi ordered from the waitress in his head. *Black,* he added. "Buh," he shook himself. The phone was somewhere in the sewing room.

The sewing room had no chair on which to sit, only the wall of boxes and a bizarre exercise machine, something pterodactyl-ish, a contraption that might be carnivorous. The phone could be in one of the boxes. Then the beep beeped again, the sound near the window. On the sill behind the eyelet curtain lay a plugged-in flip phone.

Avi pressed MESSAGES. Nothing happened. He went into the Options Menu and pressed MESSAGES. Nothing again. He selected MEMO. The phone connected somewhere, out in space where phones connected, then a voice came on, a voice in storage: "Hi. This is Susan. I'm not here right now, so please leave a message, and I'll call you back."

Susan? The intonation was clear, and the voice too—Maureen Heyer. Now he was freaked out. He hung up, and repeated the process, selected MEMO again.

"Hi. This is Susan. . . ."

Oh, God—he really was Susan Junior.

And then the cell phone rang, which made Avi jump. Okay, why not? He stared at the little thing, and then he pressed TALK. "Hello?"

"Is it safe?" asked a woman with a heavy accent.

"Hello? Who's this?"

"Susan Junior?"

"Who's this?" Avi asked again. Was she Australian?

"Oh, fuck," said the woman, and then she hung up.

Avi stared at the phone in his hand. The display read "Unidentified Caller." The phone rang again. Why not, Avi thought. He answered, "bye-bye," and then he hung up.

He waited. The phone rang again. "Wot, that wasn't nice, mate."

"So I'm not nice," Avi said. He actually thought he was pretty nice.

"She wouldn't like that, she wouldn't."

He began to wonder, hungry, what was for brunch. "She who?"

"She anyone. She the Queen of Fuck-all."

"Who is this?" Avi asked.

"Right," the caller said. "Don't go anywhere."

"Don't give me instructions. And don't say 'Fuck-all,'" Avi added, and hung up again. "That's enough of you. Oh, and I'm going to the kitchen," he said, then he pressed OFF.

Downstairs once more, he looked around and shook his head. In the undistinguished suburban town of Elsbeth, North Carolina (birthplace of Chanticleer Vee, the self-named VJ extraordinaire, and home to three pretty good Moravian bakeries, but host to little else of note), his late mother's house had a banal uselessness.

It was almost ten. The morning sunlight fired up the dining room on one side, the murkiness of the early hours dazzled into visual sense. Avi needed better coffee, eats, and an explanation for the cell phone, Susan, The Camel, the list—or maybe just coffee, coffee, coffee, a shower, and then he might try to think. He rubbed his shin. Like a little kid, Avi pressed his boo-boo to see if it would hurt, and it did.

• • •

For a family the house could use another full bath, the real estate agent had noted, and then gnawed on a thumbnail. Avi had nodded. Would it be best to reno the upstairs bathroom before selling? That might work, she had agreed, her brass nametag askew, the angle un-jaunty. Although, as Avi and the lawyer Jack Markins had concluded, the lack of equity in the house made a reno kind of stupid, and the soft real estate market made every estate a little less real. Faux black shutters framed each window, two of which, on the main floor, faced front and south; the yellow vinyl siding had apparently been recently installed. Upstairs were the two bedrooms, the sewing room, a half-bath, and the master suite with its own full bath; on the main floor were the kitchen, living room, dining room, parlor and another half-bath.

From the side door, past the good-sized driveway and carport and all the way around, the overgrown backyard was fenced—nice for Dolly. She liked to dig holes and roll in them, her coat and nose dirty, her lolling joyful. But she loved the woods behind Elsbeth Regional High School even more, where a scum-pond always had to be jumped in, for some dog reason; Avi had found the scum-pond his third day in Elsbeth, the streets so New Urbanized as to be cartographically unintelligible. Elsbeth from the air looked like a snowflake, here where it probably never snowed. Every turn eventually led nowhere; Elsbeth was a collection of dead ends.

. . .

"Susan," said Avi as he put Susan's cell phone on the kitchen counter. He wondered if either Maureen or Susan had taken her coffee or tea outside, and which Maureen had preferred in the morning, coffee or tea, and which drink Susan had drunk. He seemed to recall that when he was fourteen or so, the year his mom had left, she had switched from tea to coffee and then back again—but what kind of person switches twice? Someone unreliable, of course; a person with an alias, concluded Susan Junior.

He remembered one of the first times he had tried coffee, and how his mom had laughed when Avi had recoiled from the taste. A guy not grumpy or shin-kicked might have smiled to recall the scene.

He didn't want to be like her—which didn't just mean dead. Her house was a combination of indifference and fussiness. The living room upholstery was worn to a sheen, and he had found a wizened, rotting apple stuck between two sofa cushions, the odor sharp, along with the boxes of nothings doing nothing in the sewing room, all those boxes meticulously stacked. It was all too famil-iar . . . because Avi had to admit his apartment was like this too, a jumble of contradictions. He was neat about his long hair and hygiene, the jeans clean, and careful always to towel off Dolly's wet fur and paws, and tidy and orderly when he cooked, and yet totally capable of ignoring accumulated stuff others might find overwhelming. Fussiness and indifference: maybe fussiness came first, to Avi, but he and Mom shared more characteristics than he had known, and certainly more than he wanted to admit.

He wasn't sure if he had ever really liked his mother—she was a mystery, as obtuse to him as the porcelain puppies in her dining room breakfront. He did not *not* like her; more precisely, Avi had never known what to feel about Maureen except resentment, which he thought was a legit feeling to have, given her behavior.

But being in her house had screwed him up. In Maureen Heyer's guest room upstairs, two large, awful prints, a seascape and an urban skyline, both out of whack palette-wise, leaned against a wall. In Avi's apartment in D.C., two of his ex-girlfriend Sandy's paintings leaned against the wall of the living room. Sandy's work was okay, and kind of meaningful to Avi, remnants of a sweet romance, before Sandy had found her husband, Bo Lee, a good dude with a dumb name, and she had given birth to her cool baby, Ziggy.

The coincidence of The Leaning Artwork of the Heyers had unnerved Avi. He had hung up Mom's prints, so there.

Avi resembled Maureen in other ways too, with a fear of commitment that an angry teen inherits from a woman who would leave for an afternoon and ask her kid to cook a dinner that she didn't return in time to praise. Then there was the day Dad had turned the lights off at dusk, his wife's disappearance final; she had left them both for good.

Fourteen had not been a good age for Avi, or fifteen. His late teens hadn't been much fun, and some of his twenties. Twenty-four had really sucked.

Over all those years he had fought himself, and occasionally known that he was doing so: drugs and partying in high school until partying made more sense than school, and then dropping out after only a year of college and tying himself up with a string of bad jobs and no apartment, as he flopped on other people's sofas until he couldn't mooch anymore, not in good conscience. He had never gone back for his bachelor's degree, and hadn't regretted the decision yet. He had bummed his way all over the world; he loved to travel, and traveling had taught him food; back in the States these last four and one-half years, working for increasingly finer restaurants, sometimes in the front of the house but usually in the kitchen, food came to matter to him.

But now, just when he had made a better move, and had agreed to try cooking school, thanks to Mimou's relentless "encouragement," Mom had to go and die, and prove to him what a failure he still was. That's what her death felt like: Avi's failure. Her timing stunk as usual. Thanks, Mom.

At least she had attended his father's funeral a few years ago, and stood quietly at the grave next to Jane, Dad's second ex-wife.

One thing he knew about himself: Avi was not a man who resented others without becoming more unhappy; resentment to him felt like something poorly saved, a costly harboring of virulence. Which was why he had stayed out of Elsbeth, and kept Maureen Heyer in a little mental box that might as well have been marked "Sewing Supplies." He was safer at a distance.

One thing he didn't know: what was a dream? Was a dream a memory or a prediction, renewal or pre-newal? Should he feel sad or excited? Mom had been there, and she might have been someone or something solid in the dream, sharp as a pair of scissors, a vision who had a face and a body and ribs rather than an other-dreamly apparition; because of course her presence connected unmistakably to the whale, to swinging inside the beast, to the hammering of Avi's heart. But Mom was dead.

So a dream was a lie, too.

He made himself a nice little omelet: three eggs, cremini, a dollop of goat cheese, chives. He ground, dripped, and drank coffee. Then he assigned himself a task, and cleaned out the hall closet downstairs. Damn dead Mom, Avi thought, a thought that lasted for hours—a thought, in fact, that might not ever end.

At a few minutes before one, Avi remembered the call from Markins, found the attorney's phone number plainly printed on the envelope of the death certificate, and headed back to the kitchen phone.

"Mr. Heyer, great, I'm sorry I didn't get back to you—"

"No, no, you asked me to call."

"Right. Sorry. Did I? Oh. Okay, so let me just get . . . hold on a sec . . . sure, yes. . . ."

Avi stood in the middle of the kitchen, over-committed, the umbilicus of Mom's phone keeping him from dialing and wandering, his preferred telephone routine, a meandering man who thought better untethered and on his feet. He liked to meander: maybe he would go to Mexico in the fall.

"Okay! Here we are. Mr. Heyer, are you there?"

"You bet," Avi said brightly. "Shoot!"

"Okay. I've found something: it's, um, remarkable. As in, something to be remarked upon? That kind of remarkable. I have never seen anything like this, I don't know—"

"Mr. Markins," Avi gently interrupted.

"Right. Of course. There's a little note and then a codicil, duly witnessed. Here we go, I'll read it to you: *To my son, Avi Heyer, I offer an apology. My own affairs have kept me away from you for much too long. I'm sorry that I missed most of your teenage years and that we have not been closer. I'm sorry that you have to read this note.* Mr. Heyer, are you there?"

"I am," Avi said softly.

"Right, then," Markins said. "I'm afraid this is never easy. It's tough," he added. *"But not being with you was the cost of my ambitions."* Markins paused. "Okay, so here's the crux. *As a result, I am leaving you $500,000. It's a good amount of money, and you should be able to do something valuable with it. But the money won't be yours unless you earn it under the following conditions: one, that you do something you have never done before; two, that what you choose to do has no monetary or commercial value; three, that whatever you do to earn the money must be fantastic. . . .* Mr. Heyer?"

"Yes," Avi answered. He might have been crying.

"There's more. I'll read you the codicil, if you like. There's a bit of legalese."

"Yes, please," Avi said.

"Okay, here goes: *I add a new Paragraph B to Article I of my last will which shall read in its entirety as set forth below and I re-designate Paragraph B*—hold on, I'll find it. Here. *I give my accumulated funds to my son, Avi Heyer, if he survives me for his use during his lifetime upon the following conditions. 1. Jack Markins or his attorney-in-fact shall act as Trustee for such "Gift of Residuary Estate"; 2. The estate shall not otherwise be discharged until such time as Avi Heyer has completed the following: A . . .*"

Avi spaced out as Markins read further. Mom had left a lot of money. Mom had left a lot of money. Avi had to earn the money.

Mom had left a lot of money.

But something was off, in the expressed expectation that Avi do something fantastic and financially worthless. Did that mean extravagant and useless? What the hell did dead Mom want from him?

Markins was still talking: "*I, Maureen Heyer, the testatrix, sign my name. . . .* And then the document is signed, duly witnessed and notarized. She also wrote on the bottom, *Love, Mom.* And there's a postscript: she wrote *You'll know the list.* I'm afraid I have no clue what that means."

Markins paused. Avi said nothing. Markins was an okay guy.

"Mr. Heyer? I've read this to the County Clerk, and checked with another estates specialist. It's all most unusual, and nice."

Yes, Avi thought. No, Avi thought. Mom was never nice.

Markins had been saying something else: "—which means it looks like I'm to evaluate your . . . well, whatever it is you do, along with a named executrix who will participate in the evaluation. I've dug into the legal issues, as you might imagine, in case of default. The money will go to Amnesty International if you fail to meet the stipulations. It looks to me like you've got a year. Mr. Heyer? I'm sorry about this, really, it's most unusual. Mr. Heyer? Are you there?"

· · ·

He had filled two green trash bags with junk from the downstairs hall closet. Absurdly, Avi noticed that the bags looked like they might have bodies in them, one each. He had decided to dump the bags at the Salvation Army drop-off, hit the bookstore for dream info, do a Total Wine run, stop at the supermarket to squeeze the inorganic and genetically engineered peaches fresh from cold storage, and aim for a dusk walk with Dolly. To hell with the news, The Camel, the sports, the weather. To hell with Mom and her money.

But he made a mistake, not realizing whose phone was whose, and turned on Maureen's cell once more.

"Hello," Avi answered the phone's chirp as he started his car.

"Don't hang up!"

So Avi hung up, which was kind of fun.

The phone chirped again. Avi pressed TALK but said nothing.

"Right, mate. Wot."

"What?"

"Susan Junior?"

"Speaking," Avi admitted.

"Right, then. I'm the one named Ramona."

"You talk funny," Avi said. "Use your real voice." Then he hung up again—and waited a little while but Ramona didn't call back. Too bad, Avi thought, he was enjoying being on the giving end of the bullshit, and not just being kicked, the victim of the twins, and of Mom.

· · ·

One errand always begat another: Avi needed to price a new iPod, his old one lost somewhere in the house-cleaning. Or, as Dad used to say, one errand always meant three. Dad, who was never very funny, but liked to try.

The Camel wanted a list. Maureen had thought Avi would know what to do about that, so said her P.S.

He had yet to process the notion of the $500,000, half a mil, so much money it was an idea rather than a sum. $500,000 would be enough to buy ten comfy years around the world, or two years of cooking school and partial ownership of a mid-sized boat, to cater berth-to-berth somewhere in southern Spain, *Avi's Tapas*, specializing in *pulpo*.

A whale eats octopus, right? Avi didn't know.

With $500,000 a man could become a cowboy, rope an emu, wear a rhine-stoned toque, beef jerky on the house!

With $500,000 a man could buy a little house and some property in the middle of his imagination and go live there. He couldn't really think of where—Avi had been too busy choosing everywhere and nowhere for most of his life, even D.C. and his current digs more current than permanent; he was a migratory dude at heart.

Avi was rocked by the idea of the money, something to which he had never committed a lot of his energies, except when nearing the end of his supply;

money was made to be spent to be made to be spent, the universe of money a closed system, a school from which one never graduates, like an ant farm. Not that he was particularly prol, or class conscious, but having less money had usually meant liking less the Haves—a notion he understood as socially convenient.

He got out of the car in the parking lot of the bookstore, and jauntily arranged the brim of his favorite hat—a souvenir from a pretty good restaurant, City Grocery, where he had eaten rainbow trout in a surprisingly delicate caper-butter sauce, the sauce wholly capable of drowning the flavor of the fish but holding off, reserved. Mom and money and whales. Even with the prospect of so much cash, Avi still found himself beset by sub-marine visions, the whale-in-Avi just below the surface, a beast whose podmates must be pictured in picture books in the Nature section. The man with the brimming vision of a personal whale had a short-term goal: to wander the nonfiction aisles, excitement doubling for nonchalance, check out dream theory, and then *eine kleine whale musik*. Maybe he was sick. He rubbed his forehead, no fever, just a little giddy. Maybe it was the money, he thought.

No, he decided. Damn whale. Fucking dream.

And here was nonfiction, where ideas go to die. . . .

"Excuse me."

Avi stopped, startled: a young woman in a multi-colored long skirt, a T-shirt, and a baseball cap had decided to occupy the middle of the aisle. She had plopped herself right in front of the Warplanes shelf, as around her on the floor, eight or ten books were spread, some open to pictures of bombers.

She pointed at her own hat. "See. City Grocery, Oxford, Mississippi. I've been there too. Good food."

"I beg your pardon," Avi said. They were wearing the same hat.

"Lamb shanks," the woman said. "Port wine sauce. A reduction."

And then the cell phone in his pocket trilled.

"Better get that," the young woman said.

He was too surprised to do anything else. "Hello?" he said, staring at the woman. She had the same hat on as he did—what the heck?

"Susan Junior!" It was Ramona.

"Yesssss. . . ."

"Pill here. Wot, wot. Is it safe?"

"That's just a dumb question. What do you mean? And who's Pill?"

"Safe, mate?"

"Crap," said Avi. "Sure. It's safe."

"Pill, then. Wot. The Lima Bean wants to meet you, luv. In the bookstore."

He looked at the woman sitting on the floor; she smiled up at him. Crap! They were wearing the same hat. This had to be The Lima Bean sitting on the floor in front of him. Shouldn't a Lima Bean be in Gardening? he wondered.

"I . . . I see," he said. "Say, you're not Australian. You're not even a Brit," Avi said.

Ramona Pill laughed. "*Touché!* And you're Susan Junior, the sharpest bulb in the drawer. Ay."

"That's a bad Sean Connery imitation. Really, just once, use your real voice," Avi said.

Gazing up at him, The Lima Bean smiled a bigger smile.

"Me real voice?" Ramona Pill sounded stumped. "No such thing." She hung up.

Avi snapped the phone shut. He looked at her. "You're The Lima Bean," he said. "Shouldn't you be in Gardening?"

"I am she." She seemed pleased. She extended her hand to greet him, but didn't rise, her legs crossed lotus-style. "L.B.," she said. "You can call me Bean. And that's not funny—'shouldn't you be in Gardening.' Are you funnier than that?"

"That's a goofball name," Avi said.

"Don't say such things," she said with a smile. "Be polite. You'll get karma bucks."

He squatted and shook her hand. In a book open on the floor between them, a B-2 released its payload, good-bye, Vietnam. The picture was grainy and beautiful.

Bean tilted her head. "You're more than you let on," she said. "Our intermediary pegged you wrong, Susan Junior."

Avi laughed. "Ramona? She's our intermediary? Sheeee-it," he swore in fake Texan, and then felt self-conscious. Susan Junior was already a lie; Avi didn't need to be from Texas too.

"Help me up," she said.

He did. What small fingers she had. She stood, and gave a little hop as she gained her balance.

"What else did Pill say." Avi's question was more of a statement.

She took off her cap. Short brown hair casually ruffled, maybe with some kind of gel, pretty features, the sparkle of tiny solitaires. A small nose that came to a cute point. He wanted to see her figure, but could tell only that she was petite, her spangled, sequined long skirt a whole lot of batik. She was shorter than he by quite a bit.

"She said that you're Susan's kid, through and through. She said you're tough."

Avi chewed on his lip, trying not to talk. That might be the best strategy with these people, the sane ones and the wackos: let them talk themselves into compromising situations. But he could always ask: "What do you think?"

"Me? I don't think you're so tough. I think that someone as open as you could get hurt. I think that you probably don't know what you're doing, but you believe that if you let me blather on, I'll reveal some important detail, and you'll figure out what to do. I think that you probably act that way around women a lot. . . ." Her hands were on her hips. "I think that The Camel scared you because she's scary. I think that there's a totally astonishing amount of yellow in your aura—it might be gold, but that would be off the charts. *And* I think your aura's leaking. *And* I think that you have something I want. . . ." She pointed to him, her finger aimed at his chest, determined. "Coffee? My treat."

Avi smiled yes, dazzled and fearful, smarts and craziness always a bad combo.

"Let slip the dogs of war," she said, indicating the various aeronautical terrors splayed on the floor.

"What?" Avi said.

Bean smiled. "Leave the books there," she said. "A political statement. I hate war."

They sat at a café two-top watched over by an ill-drawn Dickens, his head big as a fridge. The poster hung slightly askew, perhaps to compensate for the dude's misshapen expression. She put two sugars in her latté, Avi one, a latté not black coffee, the steamed milk and coffee better when doctored. Bean paid for their drinks, and an enormous oatmeal cookie that lay untouched on a paper plate between them, the visibly mealy treat pocked and nubbly as the moon. He had to remind himself to be Susan Junior, son of she who was perfect, so said The Camel, a liar's truth. Susan Junior was a role to play. Susan Junior was a start-up, 500K invested in a brand.

On her left wrist Bean wore a bracelet, something onyx and silvery, its design a bit Bauhaus and expensive, an accessory that clashed with her outfit.

"The Camel told me not to trust you," Avi said. For no reason, he wanted to say "la, la, la," but didn't.

Bean laughed, her mouth wide. "Oh my God. That's too much."

Avi sipped the hot cup two-handed. "Should I trust you?"

"Of course not!" She slapped the tiny round table, and her cup jumped, splashing the saucer and the cookie. "Oh no, I'm sorry. Excuse me," she said, pushing around the spill with a paltry napkin. "Oh my God," she laughed. Then Bean's wiping knocked over the empty creamer. "Oops," she said.

"Wow," Avi said. He leaned away to be safe.

"You can't trust me," she said. "Plus I'm a klutz. But that's too funny, coming from The Camel. Talk about having a dangerous aura. And there's nothing written in her Soul Diary, not one word."

Avi scratched his noggin through his cap lefty, happy not to have Bean explain herself. A Soul Diary? "At least you didn't break into my house. Or threaten me," he said. "Or kick me."

"She kicked you?" She leaned forward. She was his age, in her twenties, and a lot of body, all kinetic and dynamic in the small space she occupied; happy eyes and an endearing nose. He hadn't known that he liked noses.

"One of the twins slapped me twice," he said. He held up two fingers. "Then I think the other one kicked me in the shin," he pouted.

Bean's expression dropped. "She's using the twins. That's not good. This is white collar crime. The twins bring bad *chi*."

Avi kept silent. White collar crime? What did she mean?

"Susan Junior?" Bean reached across the table and touched Avi's forearm. "Will you promise me something?"

"That depends."

"Of course it depends. But let me ask. Will you promise me that whatever you do, you treat right the memory of your mother? Susan was good people."

How could he make that promise? Avi had no memory of the person named Susan, and the person named Maureen was too dead—Maureen, who in a movie would have probably been killed by The Camel. Besides, it wasn't like he had treated his mother well; and even as her posthumous lies grew exponentially, they would never match what he had done.

Avi's lie was bigger, and permanent. A lie stuck in history.

She was having an affair, Avi had told his dad.

Avi? His dad had been devastated.

She was having an affair, Avi had insisted, the lie inescapable already. I saw her. It's why she left.

Avi? No. . . .

"Susan Junior?"

Avi was silent. The memory burned.

"I can see that you're moved," Bean said. She reached for her drink, sipped, and promptly jabbed herself in the right cheek with the stirrer. "*Ow*," she said. "Promise? You'll be true to your mother?"

"Promise," Avi lied.

. . .

From where Avi sat in the café, chatting amiably with someone cute and nuts, he could see the Natural Sciences aisle, and one particular book facing out on the top shelf, an oversized picture book of whales, the image poorly reproduced. He wanted that book, anything with whales. Even a toy rubber whale made in China would be something to want, a fetish to complement his dream life.

Avi wanted to run, to throw open the Toyota's door for Dolly and head back to the placid ennui of his life a month ago, to being yelled at by Giacomo at the Blue Egg for not plating the ravioli right. The past always seemed so harmless. But the dream of the whale had Mom in it, and the dream of Mom had a whale in it.

"You've seen *The Maltese Falcon*, right? She thinks she's a female Peter Lorre."

"Who does?"

"Why, Ramona." Bean laughed. "Well, not literally, silly. But someone like that. Of course, Ramona's not her name. Of all the people I deal with, she's the sketchiest—even The Camel, who's wicked-evil, has her ethics. Think about it: Ramona sold you to The Camel and then to me, didn't she, Junior?"

"Sold?" he asked.

"Sold," she said. "An expense of spirit every time."

"You paid her money to find me?"

"I *pay* her money for information. She would sell that information to anyone. She would sell you to the Feds for a Twix bar. Remember all the Peter Lorre films? Ramona Pill's the go-between, and the one person no one trusts. Ever."

"So where is she?" Avi looked around, played along. "What's her disguise? And where's the Fat Man?"

"Ah!" Bean said, satisfied. "That's just it! No one's ever seen Ramona Pill. But don't be obnoxious, please. Don't be mean to Bean."

Her top lip was full and glossy. She had a tiny scratch on her cheek from the coffee stirrer; Avi wanted to rub the little red mark with his thumb. Across the railing, just one aisle away, the whale in the picture might be singing—Avi had the impression that he could hear the song. Avi looked up and away: Dickens scowled down upon them. Maybe he wasn't Dickens but P. T. Barnum.

"I feel so used," Avi said with a fey shrug.

Bean laughed. "Uh-oh," she said. "Poor Junior. So how long have you been into food?"

"Food?"

"You're a chef, right?"

Avi paused. Bean knew stuff about him. Danger Bean. He wanted to change the subject: "No, not yet. So how long have you been a klutzy criminal?"

Bean laughed again. "I told you not to be rude," she chastened him. "Although I'm not really a klutz, not exactly. I've got a homunculus problem."

"A what?"

She repeated herself, maybe—but Avi felt like he couldn't hear her. . . . Something else was making noise, a singing, a keening up the register, and Avi felt a small shiver at the top of his spine. What the hell was going on? A dream, and now he could hear the sounds from the dream? Whale sounds? He rubbed his forehead under the brim of his cap, to check for aneurysms.

"Homunculus," she said. "Okay," Bean added. "I know that you're distracted, and that better be an awfully pretty girl you keep looking at, but try to pay attention. In the brain, there's this thing called the somatosensory cortex. In there, we think that there's a kind of map of the body called the homunculus. That means little man. And the map is what coordinates sensory understanding. It's a geographical representation of what your touch receptors experience. Mine's off," she said.

"Off?"

"Well, not turned off. But *off*. When I was younger, the doctors thought it was inner ear stuff. Now they think it's a badly drawn map—and that's all the science I know!" She laughed, and then settled into seriousness once more. "So I reach for things and get confused by where my hands are. My homunculus isn't so homonkey."

A homunculus. He bore down, made himself concentrate. "I'm like that," Avi said.

"You are?" Her face brightened even further. "You too?"

"No, no." He waved his hand. "I mean I don't have that problem. But . . . this is hard to explain. I feel like that," he confessed. "About life."

Bean stared at him, blazing and thoughtful. "Susan Junior," she said, "your mom was right about you. And all that gold in your aura, man, you're something. Have you ever had your Soul Diary read?"

• • •

Bean was cute but he had to leave. He had a dream to think about, not some chick who was trying to charm a list from him. Avi had to be alone; he was imbalanced, off-kilter, the dream and the money and the image of Maureen all together setting his gyroscope on TILT. He chatted amiably with her, or almost so, and then told her, "Look, it's nothing personal, but can we have this conversation tomorrow? I really have to go home." His glance, past her shoulder, took in the whale book, his desperation building inexplicably. "Please?"

"Sure," she said, a little insulted. "But don't be like that."

"Like what?" Avi asked.

"That," she said. "Don't get all huffed out. You can just go whenever. It's not all about you. Page four," she added mysteriously. Her smile was slightly asymmetrical.

"My Soul Diary?"

She smiled even more. "Mine." she said. "But I like you. Let's do business tomorrow. If going home doesn't mean back to D.C. Stay in town, okay?"

• • •

He carried the whale guide like some sort of Disney character hefting a magical, singing sword. He had considered briefly buying a CD of real whale songs, but Avi was hearing plenty of whale noise by himself. His other errands would have to wait.

In the plastic shopping bag, the whales in their pods sang to each other, thin arias across species and chapter headings, tuneful and dreamy. Avi felt as though his hearing had been adjusted to hear what other people couldn't. The thought worried him, a bedrock intuition that might well presage delusional behavior. He was almost hallucinating. Of course he knew that the whale songs weren't really happening, even though they filled his mind's ear. He could tell that he wasn't thoroughly crazy yet.

But Bean was crazy. Tricky, too, as she had told him nothing—in retrospect, she had told him even less than The Camel had. Forty-five minutes of chatting, no business, and he knew only that The Lima Bean was a nickname bestowed by her father, and that her real initials were L.B. But she was a hottie. The fact that she used her feigned candor and her physical appeal to charm Avi seemed perfectly acceptable; after all, if one wants to be charmed by a charming woman, then being charmed would be a goal met, right? He would be happy to be charmed more tomorrow, he thought.

She insisted on calling him Susan Junior. Maybe Maureen had kept Avi's real name a secret. Probably a good idea, with The Camel to consider.

At the end of their conversation, in the parking lot, Avi and Bean had shaken hands. Bye. Bye. Seeya. Seeya. Next time, we'll talk price. Price? Price. Your mother's legacy? Oh, right, I forgot. How about dinner?

Or maybe Avi had imagined that conversation. The whale songs were louder.

He had felt like a stoned teenager again, starting the Toyota but not driving yet, stunned, opening his notebook on the front seat and misspelling "homunculus" for tomorrow's test, watching Bean swish away in her skirt. There, she had given a little hop, of course, for show or luck.

The whale sang in the bag, in the Toyota, in the air, in Avi. In the dream, from the dream, the dream here, Avi filled and wanting.

Maybe he could make a whale. Like build one. Then he might be able to hear what he could hear.

Okay, so he knew what was happening, and what was going to happen—or hoped he did. Avi would build a little whale, have Markins come see, collect the 500 large, find and sell the list to The Camel, save his waking visions from his hallucinations, spirit Bean from her life of white-collar crime, and have $498,397 left over to spend on wine and song, to make all the lies go away.

Whale song.

Ooooeeeeeeiiiiiiieeeee. Or maybe *Mmmmmmnnnnmmmwswsws.*

A little wooden whale, just a little whale should do it.

THREE

· ·

THE NEXT MORNING, Avi sat at his mother's kitchen table and doodled on page B1 of the newspaper, 11:30 a reasonable time to break one's fast alone. He was trying to draw the inside of the whale, and count its ribs, but he couldn't picture how many ribs there were, and REM sleep had been unaccommodating, the most recent dream twenty-eight hours old, the specifics fading. In the dream, standing inside the vaulted interior of the beast had felt like standing inside a kind of living cathedral, the dreamed structure architectural and religious, and although unfinished—only a skeleton—kind of alive. Had the breathing been Avi's own, in the dream, the deep susurrus of his sleeping body filling the whale with life? If only he could draw better, he would be able to depict the immediacy of the body he had dreamed, how when he had dream-climbed through the window and into the whale, all his senses had seemed to awaken. Then again, just a few drawings he had ever seen got right the physical life, the senses pulsing in the lines of the figure, 2-D somehow 3-. Maybe Rembrandt.

The best drawing Avi drew looked like this:

The worst drawing looked like this:

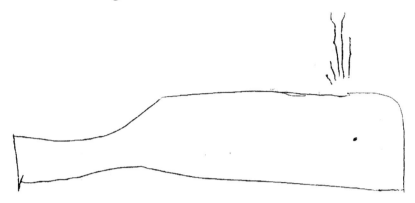

Now coffee and then coffee, wheat toast and raspberry jam, a chunk of Edam, and one of those oranges. "That was my cheese!" he said to Dolly with a little chuckle, a private joke between Avi and his pooch. Dolly lifted up her head obligingly from where she lay, thumped her tail.

Dolly liked people, and might yet like Mimou, as the doggy dog loved the treats Mimou would offer, those little bits of dough or scrapings of goose liver from the pan. Although Avi was sure Mimou would never like Dolly; and yes, there had been "The Revenge of the Cheese," as Avi's pal, Hans Hessel, the Blue Egg's former sommelier, had called the famous dust-up.

Dolly was gaga for raw broccoli, the stalks but not the florets, and had found some broc in a bag Mimou had forgotten on the floor as she worked one night at the large prep island in her loft. Avi had been in the shower, and had come out to find Mimou and Dolly squared off, the Irish-Frenchwoman on her knees as she wrestled the mutt for a broccoli bone, the gleeful Dolly thrilled to be at play.

"*Laisse tomber ce putain de broccoli, espèce d'abruti!* Drop it!"

Avi had stepped in, to help. "Dolly," he said. "Give."

"*Grrrrrr,*" Dolly had offered happily, shaking the stalk, Mimou's hand and arm whipped around by the pup killing the vegetable.

"Dolly! Give!"

The dog had been having too much fun. Pastry chef and pooch had glared at each other, and pulled and pulled until Mimou fell flat, forward, her chin bouncing on the unfinished concrete floor with an ugly little crunch.

That was enough. Avi had fetched a piece of cheese from the fridge and bribed the mangled broccoli from his bad friend.

"*Ce chien est très mal élevé,*" Mimou had said, her glare full of fury, a broccoli floret caught in her curly hair. She had rubbed her bloody chin. "*Oooh. We have no broccoli! And that was my cheese!*" Mimou had shaken her fist at Avi, and with a flourish flounced away—and then she had refused to speak to him for two days, her pout a full-fledged fit, un-cute.

Did she even like Avi? Sometimes he wondered.

Mimou did have a sense of humor, Avi told himself, her amusements born of irony and petulance. "*C'est vrai,*" Avi reminded Dolly this morning, who didn't speak Dog-French.

He returned to finishing his orange, and to his drawing. He was sticky. There had been oranges in the dream, but they had tasted like something else, and promised something else.

On the news-free pages of the News section of this week's *Elsbeth Herald*, Avi had already drawn five pictures of the whale, none exact; nevertheless, he wanted to save the sketches, and keep them free of juice, so he tore off the three pages that held the drawings, and wiped up. He would need better drawings, plans, and equipment.

He had seen some tools. Outside, at the rear of the carport was a storage area, more of a long closet really, in which Avi had found a hammer, saw, pipe wrench, and a rough workbench coated in dust. The mere presence of the equipment, hauled out of storage and laid out on the driveway to clean later in the day, led to a flash of anxiety. One wild dream was all it had taken to throw him off this cliff. *Aaaaaaaahhhhhh*, Avi said to himself, the noise that of a man plummeting.

The dream of the whale filled him. Avi felt his body to be suffused, like a peach soaked with brandy, the smell and the flavor of the dream more present than the corporeal self. But he himself was not a whale, of that he was sure; the dream wasn't about his body. Physically, he felt detached, connected only to the whale's breathing, one breath each. He wondered if human lungs might be whale-shaped. In their lumpy and elliptical form, maybe—or maybe he was making that up.

He began petting Dolly, who stood to be rewarded, and then who met his hand with head-butts that demanded more petting, purposeful nudges by which he was well-trained. The head-butts became insistent: Avi was distracted, so said Dolly, and yes, he had stopped scratching her back, sorry, girl. He looked at his hand, a real hand, impressed that he was really here.

Dolly gave up. If a dog could be disgusted, she was; she lumbered from the room and clumped upstairs to her first nap of the day. She would seek sunlight, choose a swath of brightness, and there she would snooze, her dreaming knowable by a kind of high-pitched, muffled barking, and a paddling of her big paws as she lay upon her side. Doll-Doll was too smart to do anything because of a crazy dream, even one in which Mom had had a cameo.

Avi snatched the drawings from the table, and followed Dolly up the stairs; he could hear her grunt and snuffle as she settled down on Maureen's bed.

He stepped into the sewing room. He ran up the blinds—sunlight, uh-oh, too much light—and then let the blinds fall once more. He would empty the sewing supplies boxes; if the contents of one box were combined with another, he could clean out the room without having to make too many trips to the carport garbage can to dispose of his mom's useless seamstressing and thus convert the room to a workshop or office—Whale Central, Whale HQ.

Wow, he felt jazzed. Was it just the money? Making Elsbeth safe for democracy?

Upper left corner, number one or twenty-five, the beginning or the end of Maureen's collecting: Avi slid the cardboard box, heavier than expected, from its perch. Odd that there were no chairs in the room, not even a place to sit by the sewing machine—and that the strange, pulley-and-weight exercise machine stood there, a kind of *Starship Troopers* thing, its own mechanical nightmare, a lethal contraption, probably the true cause of Maureen's death. He sat on the floor, set down his doodles and pen.

The box contained documents, not sewing supplies, stacked papers in folders all labeled in his mother's wild, unruly hand—which gave him a pang to see—that familiar, loopy script. And made his eyes feel fuzzy, not damp exactly, or teary, but fuzzy.

Avi wasn't sure he wanted to do this. He squinted at the file atop the pile, a brown folder labeled "Interbank Tickets."

· · ·

Upon first looking into Maureen's things and sorting her effects, he had given away great sagging green garbage bags of stuff, often without even going through the pockets of the clothes, but soon something had felt wrong. Which meant that emptying the house had slowed considerably; now Avi would spend hours going through a single drawer, say, wondering before acting upon the inevitable disposal of whatever meaningless items he had examined, whatever mementos that stood for memories he could never know. *Mourner at Work*: he wanted to make a little sign and take a cell-phone picture of himself as he lay there with his arms crossed, kidnapped by grief, and include a newspaper headline, proof of life.

At night, he would stay up late, drink reasonable wine and watch useless television, or read, or occasionally surf the Web, the Wi-Fi as predictably intermittent as his emotions. Avi was taking a working vacation, he told himself at first, the days directed toward the disassembly of his mother's life, and the nights rich with a kind of moodiness born of living in a stranger's house, and of grieving for a person he had never known. Days and nights apart from one another: the air in each felt different; the water after dark tasted more strongly of its treatment.

He was looking for his mom, of course. But surprisingly, Avi's new familiarity with her house and possessions, his immersion in the disassembling of her life, had only confused him more. Avi would re-open a bag of clothing from her closet, unball a blouse and hold it up, incapable of imagining the physical body that had filled its shoulders and sleeves. Emptiness seemed to blow through everything of hers he touched, the rooms full of falling dust motes and unintelligible mutterings—or maybe the rooms were breezy with the whispers of ghosts. Not that Avi believed in ghosts, or had any idea of who her ghosts could have been. The ghost of The Camel, he presumed. The Ghosts of Mommy Past. Susan Heyer's secret ghosts.

Today, all of the ghosts had changed to real ghosts, lies that had become real, although still untrue. Wow, Avi was turned around; he was trying to figure out what he meant when he said "Mom," a word he had avoided for years, "Maureen" the name of the disowned woman in the photo in his head. She had stopped deserving "Mom," he had reasoned, just as he had un-sonned himself at fifteen, an act of self-defense. But he couldn't re-will $500,000 to her, and he could never buy back Maureen's love.

The file folder marked "Interbank Tickets" was full of financial documents that had some passages inked over with black marker and others emboldened with a yellow highlighter. Avi flipped through the pages, uncomprehending. There was Maureen Heyer's handwriting, although the printed name as well as the signature clearly read "Susan Woodley." Of course, Avi thought: her white collar criminal alias. She was Susan Woodley and The Camel was The Camel and Bean was Bean. Crap, Avi thought. Who were these people? Why would they be so interested in bank documents?

He looked at his doodles. A man could make a whale just high enough so that when he swung inside, his pointed toes wouldn't touch the ground. While smaller than the dreamed structure, at least such a beast wouldn't be too difficult to build. So a little whale was possible, one that a man could build in his dead mother's driveway, given his slightly more than rudimentary carpentry skills. He would tell the neighbors he was building a boat. The ribs would look like a hull anyway, and boats are built upside down, after all, the explanation plausible.

He had to admit to being excited. The money was certainly appealing, sure, but the whale, the whale . . . Avi wanted to build the whale, and to swing inside, and to feel what the dude in the dream was feeling, and to eat one of those amazing oranges, and to make his dream life come to pass.

He had never before surrendered his waking life to a dream, at least not that he could remember. But what the hell; he'd build himself a smaller big-ass whale, sell the maternal manse, pay his tuition, cash a check rolling with zeroes, buy a couple of cases of wine to put down, and travel some before school started in the fall, meet Bean in the Juan Fernandez Islands for *escabeche* on the street.

Every time he closed his eyes, the whale surged inside him. Every time he daydreamed, the money spent itself.

He'd take apart the whale before putting the house on the market, of course.

With a black pen, he drew another whale on an Interbank Ticket, not a bad whale, if he said so himself, one with a little flair to its lines, and the hint of enormity, a whale bigger than a man.

Like the man in his dream, Avi was swinging forward and backward in time. Into a future he knew less about than ever before: rather than being able to say, unequivocally, that soon he would finish sorting through Maureen's life, put her house on the market, then drive home to D.C. and arrive and collapse and the next workday cancel the forwarding on his mail, reclaim his sad houseplants from the downstairs neighbor. . . . Avi had the feeling that his To Do list had suddenly been switched with someone else's, the priorities belonging to someone he wouldn't recognize, his old life vestigial. In a wild hand resembling his mother's, someone had written "Build a whale. Save a man."

What would Mimou think? "This is crazy talk," she would say, her syntax a non-English emotion, letting loose her Gallic pretensions; he sometimes thought she played the Frenchwoman just for effect.

There would be flour on Mimou's forehead. There was always flour on her somewhere, which Avi liked.

And he was also swinging into the past. Who was Maureen Heyer? Susan Woodley? When he looked back, over his shoulder, his mother was someone remembered by a thirteen-year-old, before he turned fourteen and she left, and before he had renounced her to Dad, the one big lie.

He had never admitted the truth to Dad: no, she had not been having an affair.

Maybe the whale was a dream, but guilt was a whale, too.

So he would reconstruct. One half of Avi's life had happened in the years since Maureen had left, one quarter of her life and who knows how much of Susan Woodley's. All was motion; he was moving backwards and forwards into his life, into Maureen's and the person Maureen had called Susan. Backwards and forwards, into the dream of the whale and its building, Avi felt himself already to be hanging mid-air and swinging his legs. But the happiness that the dream had offered, swinging from the rib of the whale, wasn't his; Avi still had to build the whale, and find that deep peace.

This was crazy talk.

· · ·

Driving to the building supplies store, Avi drummed on the steering wheel and dash. His cell phone was in the left front pocket of his jeans; her cell phone was in the pocket of his anorak (looks like rain) in case someone tried to reach Susan Woodley. Avi pictured himself answering another wacko's inquiry: "I'm sorry, she's unavailable, but I'm her son, Avi Woodley." He wondered if the name Woodley had come to Maureen in a dream. He repeated the name to himself, half-aloud—Avi Woodley, Avi Woodley, Avi Woodley—and then laughed, probably even aloud.

The tune he drummed had no melody, the changes a series of sputters and thumps. To accompany himself, Avi made small popping, puffing sounds with his lips, rocking a little and nodding his head, car cadences and road rhythms in time to a non-existent song. The feeling of being propelled by the engine and conveyed somewhere was one that Avi loved—in motion, free—and it often made him sing, and usually tunelessly.

Dolly's head hung out the back window on the driver's side; he could see her big dog tongue lapping up the wind, the absurd pink muscle twisted. Luckily, she liked the car, and would lie on the backseat and wait, and not eat the front seat.

Hailed upon entering the building supplies store by a smiling older woman, Avi returned the warm smile and hello but kept his hands stuffed in pockets. Past Lighting—all those fixtures dangling together, the soft whites, naturals, and halogens cosmological—toward Plumbing. There he made a right turn down the widest aisle, aimed himself toward Lumber. In the mirror of a marked-down vanity, Avi caught sight of himself, an average man, six feet and one-half inch tall, his hair clean and long and tucked behind his ears, his face darkened stylishly with stubble. Big feet, which a mirror wouldn't notice. A few pounds overweight, admittedly, especially this last year or so. He could lose the weight at any time, the gastronome told himself.

With its displays at intervals down the middle of the thoroughfare, the aisle widened into a boulevard, not the *Champs* but something grand in Building Supplies. He was greeted often, hellos and smiles he returned. What a happy place, he thought. Happy hardware, happy mulch.

"Hi." A red-shirted older guy in Lumber leaned on a pile of landscape timbers.

"Hi," Avi responded. Impressed by the warehouse-style rows of stacked lumber, the smell of sawdust and cured wood like the smell of a walk-in, like a special flavor, Avi said no more. He had come without plans, or know-how. Research the project, he had told himself, but now he didn't know how.

The other guy stood there too, trapped by his paycheck. He might have been in his late fifties, a guy with a pencil balanced over one ear, kept alive by working here.

"I need help," Avi admitted, trying to chuckle. "But I'm thinking," he said. "And that ain't easy for me."

The other guy nodded; the tiniest part of his mouth might have twitched. His demeanor said uncomplaining, his haircut was recent.

Avi gave a little wave. "I'll wander," he said. "I'll be back."

Strolling toward the larger palettes of lumber, deeper into the sharp smells of the store, Avi tried to decide what to do. A forklift turned the corner and came toward him a little fast, and so he stepped aside. The driver gave a chuck of his chin, the warning light atop the cab flashing, the beeping tinny.

In high school in Jersey, the summer between his junior and senior years, Avi had worked for a contractor, mostly hauling supplies and doing finishing work—and on occasion, a tear-down, the stoner's favorite. So he thought himself capable of learning the trade, having watched various crews build various additions; he knew a plumb bob from a chalkline, and could handle a table saw. Maybe he wouldn't have decided to build the whale otherwise, or even dreamed the crazy dream; perhaps the best intuitions trusted experience.

Notwithstanding Avi's modest carpentry skills, he understood that the only way to build something was to plan. From his pocket, he pulled the folded quarter-sheets of newspaper on which his doodles had been done, and turned back to find the guy with the pencil over his ear, Ear Pencil Guy.

"Um . . . excuse me."

"Yes?"

The dude had extraordinarily blue eyes. Small, light blue eyes that narrowed as he spoke. He was taller than Avi by a couple of inches but hunched in a tall guy's stoop. His teeth were a little gray.

"I'm starting a pretty big project, and I could use some help."

"Right," the guy said.

"Right," Avi echoed, and he unfolded one scrap of paper. "I'd like to build one of these."

"Right," the guy said again, as he accepted the paper and stared at the two drawings there.

"It's a whale," Avi said.

"Oh," said the guy. "How big?"

"Big?" Avi wondered along. Big enough to swing inside, he wanted to say but didn't. "Not so. Maybe like a little boat, and proportioned."

"Yep," the guy said, and he turned smartly and begin to stride away, down the wide last aisle of lumber.

Avi understood that he should follow, so he gave a little hoppity skip to catch up.

"What's it for?"

The question had been over the shoulder, but now the guy stopped in front of a stack of plywood, four-by-eight-foot sheets like huge layers of pastry, Napoleons without cream.

Avi felt suddenly shy. He hung his head slightly, and kicked a small wedge of wood near his right foot. "Nothing," he said. "Because," he added.

Ear Pencil Guy was silent. Was he thinking? Avi had long suspected that people who didn't say much thought deeply—maybe that was this guy's story too. "Eighteen of these," the guy said. "Make three big boxes, and then add curves. Wrap the sucker in something."

Now Avi felt stymied. What could he do but agree? He added up in his head how many sheets of ply would make three big boxes. "Eighteen," Avi said, to seem in control. "And two-by-fours, and one-by-threes, and a screw gun." He was almost at the end of his knowledge. "And bar clamps."

"Liquid Nails?" asked the expert.

"Yep," answered Avi, not knowing what that was.

"Safety glasses," the guy said, maybe condescendingly. "Two-and-one-half- and three-inchers. Thirty-six-inch Quick Grips for the clamps."

"Of course," said Avi, more foolish than ever. Two-and-one-half- and three-inch screws, he presumed, but he wasn't really sure. He held out his hand, glad to have the drawings returned, self-conscious about his neat fingernails and the various scars from cooking burns—not a carpenter, of course, his skin kept soft by applying lots of lotion, so that the wet work of the Blue Egg didn't chap. "Can I have it delivered?"

"Yep," the guy said. "They'll do that."

"Thanks," Avi said, and to explain himself, he wanted to say more, about the whale and how she needed to be huge and sturdy, or about that summer in high school he had worked a job for Anders, and the time that as they were laying parquet, Anders's uncle, George, keeled over right there, a stroke, and Avi had run to get Anders, who had come sprinting from the pickup, coffee splashing from a thermos he had forgotten to put down, coffee stains on Anders' carpenter's jeans. Or about Dolly in the Toyota, happy in the backseat unless someone came too close to the window. Avi wanted this guy, the stoic tool dude, to be glad to have met this bullshit dreamer with the dumbass hope, so that Avi might know that a pro approved of the craziest plan ever, to build a wooden whale in a driveway.

"Rick," the guy stuck out his hand.

But before Avi could meet the handshake and respond, Susan Woodley's cell phone in the belly pocket of his anorak began to thrum, someone else's second heart.

Neither of them moved.

The guy nodded toward Avi's midsection. "That's you," Rick said.

"Yeah," Avi said.

"Gonna answer?" Rick was almost smiling.

"I guess," Avi said, and so he did.

"Susan Junior!" Ramona Pill's voice was shrill. "Is it safe?"

"Aw, crap," Avi said. He smiled at Ear Pencil Guy, made an I've-got-to-take-this gesture, and turned his back to walk away. "Yeah, it's safe."

"Susan Junior, we are at an impasse."

"No shit," Avi said.

"Oh, oh, oh, oh, Susan Junior, don't you be taking that tone with Ramona, and don't—"

Avi interrupted. "Look, I'm busy. State your business. And don't call me Susan Junior; that's not my name."

Ramona Pill was quiet. "It's not? Then who the fuck, mate?"

"Yeah, yeah," Avi said. He looked around. "It's Rick. Me name's Rick, mate."

"Rick! Rick Woodley, then. Ay."

"So spew, girlfriend," Avi-Rick said to Ramona.

"Right. What's it going to be, eh?"

"What *what*?"

"The list. It's time to have a little auction."

"Right," Avi said. "Call me tomorrow," he said, and then hung up.

An auction might be fun, especially if Avi found the list. Would it be in the sewing room? The Camel had said that she had looked in the house, but she couldn't have looked everywhere; all of Maureen's things seemed in order.

Whatever the hell the list was. Damn Maureen.

Fine, then, so Avi would play a normal guy named Rick, and Rick would build a whale. Crap, if a man's dead mom were a mystery, her secret life more than just a penchant for the slots, then what about her son's secret life, along with his new career in whale-building? Unless . . . maybe Avi had no secret life, and the life he had been leading in public—twenty-something failure, wannabe chef, Dolly's person, Mimou's playdate, and now Susan Junior—had been all pretense and routine, the work of someone pretending to be Avi.

Maybe one of the ways to be happy was to cultivate a secret life, and then figure out how to lead a secret life as one's only life.

Avi paid the hefty cost of the lumber, agreed to be at home tomorrow morning to receive delivery, and smiled at the cashier in her blue smock, flattered that she had asked for his account number—apparently a number a contractor might have, as opposed to an unemployed restaurant worker. He used his credit card to pay, figuring that he couldn't come close to spending $500,000, and that if the whale passed inspection, well then, the money would cover the money. If the whale didn't swim, okay, Avi would be in debt again, and the Institute would have to wait another year.

He stepped outside to find Ear Pencil Guy, the real Rick, finishing a cigarette and grinding to death the butt beneath a boot heel. "Set?" Rick asked. He bent to pick up the cigarette butt and tossed it into a nearby trash receptacle, tidy guy.

"Yep," Avi said in Rick-speak to Rick.

Rick straightened to his regular stoop, and nodded. But then, oddly impulsive, he stuck out his hand. "Rick," he said again.

"Avi," Avi said, pleased. "A, v, i." They shook hands, let go.

"A whale," Rick said, his tone flat but the statement a question.

The handyman was intrigued: "Yes," Avi laughed lightly, flattered. "In a driveway," he added, as though the information mattered. "Moby Sticks," he said stupidly.

"A whale," Rick said, and gave a little *tkk* of his tongue. "Gotta come see that."

FOUR

AVI HAD RETURNED TO D.C. only once since Maureen had died, to quit his job. He had spent the weekend with Mimou, checking on his apartment half-heartedly, feeling like he was couch-surfing again. He and Mimou had enjoyed a pretty good three nights together, which helped, or confused, or both. Older than Avi by almost eleven years, Mimou slept no more than four hours a night, liked martial arts movies and licorice gumdrops and dirty martinis, made a marzipan that would melt a Republican's stone heart, and preferred her sex vigorous and before dinner, an *aperitif*. She was Cordon Bleu trained.

She had been in a good mood. On the Friday night, Avi and Mimou had attended an industry-only opening of a new fusion place at Dupont Circle that she thought nouveau and crass, which made her even happier. That was one very cool thing about hanging with Mimou: she was in the trade, so Avi had been able to attend events to which he otherwise would not have been invited, her connectedness generous, his professional aspirations part of her agenda.

Saturday, she was busy. Avi and Dolly hit a few of their usual haunts, including the dog park on N.W. Dorset, where Dolly romped with the poodle she had a crush on, a floppy-eared charmer named Tin Tin whose owner would sit with the crossword puzzle and chain-smoke. On the Sunday night, their last together, Mimou had made a simple meal, poached salmon and a hollandaise, a decent Pinot Gris; Avi had done a zesty cold rice salad, wild rice and wheat berries. Everything was ready for later, so before dinner, he and Mimou had taken a long, candlelit bath in her clawfoot tub, with lots of fun for both. Dolly had curled up outside the bathroom door, good dog.

Since coming to Elsbeth after Maureen died, he had been thinking a lot about Mimou, and he had found himself feeling guilty, the way he usually felt when he suspected that a relationship was going to end and he was about to do the ending. In a dumbass way, Avi was monogamous: being attracted to Bean, and flirting with her, meant nothing unless he meant something by it, which required that he first come to terms with Mimou, at least in his own head.

Sure, he was capable of being involved with more than one woman at a time, although doing so wasn't his first choice, mostly, unless there was sex involved. It didn't help that he was chickenshit, a chickenshit bullshit artist.

But before Avi could feel really guilty about the future, Bean had called and cancelled. *Poof!* went his plan, as she begged off.

"Do I believe your excuse?" Avi had asked rudely, surprised that his feelings had been hurt. The telephone could be a weapon.

"Really," Bean had said. "I've got to go out of town. I'll be back in a week. Consider this, Susan Junior: I want the list, and I'm leaving anyway, so my reason for traveling must be pretty good, yes?"

"All right," Avi mumbled. "Woulda been a nice meal."

"I know," Bean said. "Ramona told me where you shopped."

"Okay." He ignored that scary information.

"Okay? I'm hearing something else. Something's wrong. . . ."

"Tell me. . . ." Avi had said, not wanting to know. He took a deep breath. "Is there any chance The Camel killed my mother?"

Bean had gasped into the phone, *hmphed,* thought, *hmphed* again. "No." she had finally answered. "The twins were a late hire, and The Camel doesn't kill people. She might have hurt Susan, or set her up, but murder? No. . . . Listen, you should worry about The Camel, but not in that way. She will hurt you for a long time—that's more her style. Something more permanent than death."

Fine, sure, Bean's answer made sense; and so he listened to her advice and continued to worry. But more important, while Bean was beaning elsewhere, believing her singular beliefs—What was more permanent than death?— Avi built a little whale. He hammered and hauled and sawed and nailed and screwed and admired, his work day in daylight longer than usual, meals prepared and eaten and forgotten. On five straight mornings, Avi rose early and breakfasted heartily, a ploughman's feast, before donning the denim to labor in the driveway. Two huge plywood boxes, still probably too small, were now complete, looming in the dell. The third box was almost finished.

Each night for the past five, he had pored through the sewing supplies cache, three boxes per night before exhaustion set in, the banking documents incomprehensible, Susan Woodley's signature emblazoned at the bottom of numerous pages, distinct, cryptic, and flamboyant. He had uncovered no list to sell to The Camel, who had neither called nor sent her twin minions. He found their absence unnerving—especially as he knew that Ramona Pill was lurking about, disguised as an Australian Border Collie or a Cuisinart. Probably The

Camel's intent, he figured, to unnerve. Fuck The Camel, he thought, the literal idea even more unnerving, *ew,* the literal too often icky.

The neighbors had begun to slow down as they drove past. Avi would look up from his workbench and wave. The guy across the street had taken to peeking out of his front window a lot, like someone from another century.

Avi had learned to cherish the morning, grumbling through his first cup o' joe and then less begrudging as the work-week lengthened. This morning, standing at his workbench, safety glasses squeezed to the crown of his head, Avi paused before the day, the mist still threading through the foliage, the neighbors' cars dewy. He felt again the unreal sense of moving backward and forward in time.

But the whale was becoming even more real, a dreamed reality, its ugly body blocked out and almost whale-like. Cetaceous.

Avi had looked up "Cetaceous" in his mother's dictionary, for kicks, the word discovered in the new whale guide, and in doing so he had found four dried and pressed flowers: one between the pages of "clemency" and "clockwise," another between "escape" and "estimate," a third between *"missa cantata"* and "mob," and a fourth far in the back, between "thimbleful" and "Thorazine." The fourth pairing had made him laugh.

Detective Avi wasn't much of a detective, but a person who used a dictionary to dry and press flowers didn't play Scrabble every Thursday night. A person who used a dictionary to dry and press flowers didn't think of words as permanent. A person who used a dictionary to dry and press flowers had a nostalgic streak. A person who used a dictionary to dry and press flowers didn't plan to die in a car crash.

Unenlightened by his ignorance of Maureen's private drama, Avi had returned the flowers to the dictionary, no list there either, and amused himself by re-pressing them between different pages in the *Webster's 9th*, choosing to squash the blooms between "backseat" and "balance of payments," "dauntless" and "deathblow," "off-hour" and "old guard," and "serve" and "settle." But then Avi had wondered if the memories she had wanted enshrined in the pale bodies of the flowers might be associated with someone else. A lover? He had seen no signs in her belongings of Maureen having been intimate with anyone, and no one who had come to the funeral had grieved conspicuously.

The funeral had been small, a grim crowd of twenty, none of whom Avi had known, six or seven who had introduced themselves to the grown-up child while offering no particular consolation. Maybe The Camel had been there incognito, even though she hadn't looked familiar at the bowling alley; maybe

The Camel was searching the house while Avi was at the funeral. The twins surely hadn't come, as Avi would have remembered them, honking into their matching handkerchiefs and holding hands.

Maureen Heyer had lived here for eight years and her death had been barely noticed. More coverage in the local paper had been dedicated to the dangers of the street where she died than to the life the accident had ended, although Avi had paid for a standard death notice, *sans* photo. Luckily, the *Elsbeth Herald* decided not to run a ghastly picture of the car, the family-owned, small-town gazette not that sort of rag, even as its readership pointed and clicked the newspaper into oblivion.

He felt different this morning. Perhaps he could attribute the feeling—or feelings, really—to the nearing completion of the third box, the whale's body, and the sense that once he broke his back to lower the box onto a caddy, *ow, ow, ow,* heavy, and wheeled number three to number two, magic might happen.

The feelings came, too, from a drawing he had made in the middle of the night last night. Avi had awakened, his insomnia kicking in, even with all the physical labor, and had gotten up to pee. Dolly had been snoring loudly on the foot of his bed. Through the bedroom sheers, the moonlight had seemed to have a metallic quality, a shine, the room ignited with a deep blue color, mother-of-pearl. He had finishing peeing, washed, and then, naked, Avi had padded downstairs into the house that felt more asleep than he—a house always asleep, even during the day, its sole inhabitant, Maureen, gone.

The dining room table had been awash with dull moonlight too, like a desert or a sea. His new notebook, one of those Composition thingies, purchased at CVS for whale biz and Mom notes, had lain as though floating on the table, peaceful and somnolent, and he had doodled one little doodle right there: a man and a whale together in the honeyed moonlight.

The whale he had drawn was striated from its jaw to its flippers, and gnarled and spotted from flippers to fluke, quite decorative really, not so bad. He had attempted to render the baleen he had been reading about in *Whales of the World*, and those bumpy knobs some whales have atop their backs, near their blowholes. The whale wasn't lifelike, but its attributes were recognizable, even though Avi had been unsure of what kind of whale he might have drawn, and whether he had rendered the whale an impossible composite, like one of those absurdly cannibalized Chevy-Cadillac-VW-Hyundai stretch limos.

Accuracy be damned: the drawing of the wrong whale had been the best so far. Avi had drawn the whale he might want to build, a mutt of a whale rescued from the pound at the bottom of the sea:

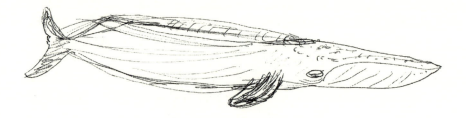

A naked guy in the middle of the night making yet another picture of a dream image—and always leaving out the little stick figure of his mom at the edge of the picture, the dead woman who made the dream real: he would have to figure out a way to apologize for the lie he had told his father. For fourteen years, he had known this, and successfully not done so. Now he was living in his Mummy's tomb—Lord, that was a bad joke, the naked man had chuckled to himself—and her spirit was restless, unburied. Shouldn't he carry her body to the cave, and gnash his hair and rend his teeth, do something mythic and priestly, the body of the son ravaged according to his corresponding grief, so said all that Greek mumbo jumbo? Not that he knew any good Greek stories about whales; not that his whale felt like anyone else's story. His whale was his own, a beast too unreal to belong to anyone else.

• • •

A man dreamed of building a whale, a dream that wouldn't let him go, that kept coming back, that wrapped itself around his sorrow. He had managed to construct a rough version of the whale's bulk, and with the use of heavy canvas straps, a jury-rigged plywood ramp, and a mechanic's dolly, wheel the three parts of the beast into alignment. He screwed them together, and then with a power saw cut out the top panel of each, close to the frame. The hole he made, *thus!* in the wooden vault of heaven was crossed with sticks. He paused and gazed upward. He then cut doorways between the three sections, the structure airy, and for the first time felt as though he might become the submariner he had dreamed, a man in a whale.

A long day of work, and at last the sun threatened to go down. The man fetched himself a brewski in a canski, the drink of whale-builders everywhere, and stood next to his boxes, leaned on one, unsure if the crude thing resembled the dreamed whale enough. Three cars came down the hill and passed—then a fourth, in which a moon-eyed child stared from a childseat in the back, and gave a little wave. The man with his hand on the whale returned the hullo. From the backyard, the man's dog barked; she had finished her dinner and could well want a dusk romp, the high-school pond stinking up her imagination, the freedom of the woods beckoning, the Elsbeth Jackals on summer vacation. The park across the street was lovely, but the man didn't trust his dog off-leash near traffic. One never knew.

He slugged some beer, crushed the can in one hand and then tossed the can aside, climbed up to lower himself down into the middle box of the tripartite whale. The man stood there and gazed upward. The ribs were thin, not at all the dreamed ribs.

He reached, braced his feet as he pulled himself up, and hung from a mock-rib, let his feet dangle. He pointed his toes, knees together, and began to swing. He swung. The sky was there, then gone. Sky, none, sky, none, sky, none, sky. . . .

When the first plywood wall twisted, torqued, and spit its screws, the structure teetered for two seconds—and in that precipitous moment the man understood that he should probably let go, and that he wouldn't. He didn't. The man knew he was a dipshit. So when the second wall pulled away, the rattletrap whale collapsed into itself with the man inside, his self-loathing matched only by pain as a sharp, large splinter from one of the snapped ribs pierced his right shoulder, lanced him as he fell, crushed inside the pathetic, ridiculous dream.

He closed his eyes. This was not a dream, so said his shoulder. He could lie here forever: he should bleed out. And would . . . and did . . . until he felt the beams and boards being ripped away from above, and a rough grip pulled him to safety—hauled him out and then mostly carried him—to lay him down upon the grass next to the driveway.

The wounded man was groggy, his shoulder felt as though on fire. His dog barked and barked, her anxiety annoying and familiar.

Dolly, shush, the man said, but not aloud. *Dolly, be quiet, I'm only dying. Take me, Lord.*

"You okay?"

Avi opened his eyes. "Yeah," he said. "I think. *Buh.*"

"Okay," said Rick, the guy from the building supplies store. "Not a good whale," said Rick.

• • •

Rick opened the first-aid kit on the kitchen table.

Avi shook his head, no. He would rather not speak.

"Doesn't look like your house."

Avi said nothing.

"Okay," Rick said. "Lemme see."

"No," Avi replied. He was woozy. Pride, pride.

Rick's hand stopped mid-air, just short of Avi's slightly bloody AC/DC T-shirt. "Aw," Rick said. He held a pair of scissors and a super-sized tweezers aloft, bandages at the ready.

The man's tone was respectful, disdainful, sympathetic, a little bit of everything Avi didn't want. "No thanks," Avi added, to be polite.

"Buddy . . . it's me or a medic, and I cost less."

A pile of wood waiting to be a bonfire stood in Avi's driveway. He considered how much he hated himself. This much, he decided, wanting to throw wide his arms, but unable to do so because his shoulder hurt, injury and insult, his pride ready for the bonfire. When would he stop being a failure?

"Your call."

Rick was a patient man. Avi looked up into the clear little eyes of the building supplies guy. "You just dropped by?" Avi asked.

"Yep. And yesterday."

"Didn't see you. You didn't say hello."

"Nope."

They were gazing at each other, thinking about the other. Was this what men did in Rick's world?

"Your call," Rick said again, and gestured toward Avi's shoulder, where the wound was visible through the torn shirt. "Gonna hurt."

"Hurts now," Avi admitted.

"Bet," Rick said. He waited. "Okay. Stop stalling," he said. "Got stuff to do."

"Right," Avi agreed, scooched back and braced himself. "Go for it."

. . .

Rick was mid-swab, the worst of the excision and extraction accomplished, the little wound throbbing, the injury actually not too bad, when Susan Woodley's cell phone chirped once more.

"Gonna get that?"

"Naw," said Avi. "Kinda stuck," he said, and shrugged his good shoulder. "Voicemail—" he began to add.

"Got it," Rick said, and reached over and did so before Avi could react. Rick pressed TALK. "Hello?"

Avi's jaw might have unhinged, for how agape his mouth felt.

"Yep," said Rick. "This is Rick."

Avi began to wave his good hand, no, no, no, no, no. . . .

"Rick? I'm Rick." Avi's rescuer and nurse was clearly puzzled. "Talking."

Avi pulled himself up to a standing position and gestured for the phone, a gesture met only with an impressively tiny, concentrated glare.

"*Ohhhhh,* the other Rick. Gotcha. Hold on."

They faced off, Susan Woodley's cell phone pressed to Rick's hip, on shirt-mute, Avi's heart beating loud enough for Rick to hear.

"That you?"

"Yes," Avi said. Embarrassment couldn't begin to describe how he felt. Utter humiliation was an understatement.

"You're Avi, right? A, v, i."

"Right."

"Got some extra names."

Avi nodded.

"One's mine," Rick said. Rick lifted Susan Woodley's phone to his mouth once more. "Ramona? He's here." He handed over the phone. "For you. It's Ramona." Reaching into the breast pocket of his short-sleeved denim shirt, Rick pulled out a pack of cigarettes and gave a flick of his chin to indicate the outdoors. "Be back," Rick said as he tapped a cigarette from the pack, then pulled the butt free with his teeth. "*Rick,*" he said, amused, the cigarette eased forward to rest between his lips, smokeable.

Avi waited for the door to close. "Hello, Ramona," Avi said to Ramona Pill.

"Who the hell was that, mate?" Ramona Pill sounded almost hysterical. "Is it safe?"

"Oh, shut up," Avi said. "That was Rick."

"I see," said Ramona Pill. "Everyone's named Rick."

"What do you want?" Avi asked, suddenly tired. "Talk."

"Talk?" Ramona Pill's voice rose from a whine to a screech. "Talk? The talking's over, Rick-shaw. I'm talking, see? It's time to sell: everyone's bidding. So name your place. Call the meet."

The woman wasn't stable, Avi supposed. But who could be? The whale was dead, and someone named The Lima Bean, along with her rival The Camel, wanted to meet someone formerly named Susan Junior, a.k.a. Rick.

"Nope," Avi said.

"Nope? Fucking shite, mate! What do you mean nope?"

"Nope, nope. Stuff to do. You've been spying on me, you know. Tell The Camel to . . . I don't know. Eat sand." Avi wasn't being funny enough, which he regretted.

"Eat sand."

"Bite someone."

"Bite someone?" Ramona repeated. "Wot, wot. That's a joke. She'll bite you, she will, you whingeing Pom. Aw, she bites, she does, and I—"

"I don't care," Avi interrupted her. "*Ciao,*" he hung up.

. . .

"What was that?" Rick exhaled.

Avi had joined his Samaritan outside. The evening steamed, a ruin of a day, just a big steam table with the trays removed. Avi and Rick stared at a pile of whale. Rick lit one cigarette from another. Behind the carport, Dolly could be heard snuffling at something in the grass. Across the street, a neighbor's porch light turned off, the sharp glow extinguished, not a message.

Avi didn't know how to answer. He waited. The truth seemed tellable. "Remember the call I got in the store? Same woman. But she wouldn't give me her real name, so when she asked for mine, I lied. Gave her yours."

"Gotcha."

The two men were quiet. A plane flew nowhere across a corner of the sky. Avi wanted to say more. The wreck of the whale defeated him.

"Three-quarter-inch ply's nothing. And you cut into your supports," Rick said. "And you used the wrong screws."

"*Hm?*"

"Things don't stay up like that."

Was Rick being philosophical? Avi couldn't tell. His shoulder burned, his ego more so.

"You wanna try again?"

Avi eyed Rick, who hadn't turned when he had spoken. "You wanna try again?" asked Avi. Rick didn't turn around. Avi eyed him. Who was this guy and why was he here?

"So?" Rick prompted Avi, the question an offer.

"Who are you?"

Rick smoked slowly to himself, no answer.

"I . . . I dunno. I guess," Avi said. The guy probably worked for The Camel; Avi mostly didn't care.

Rick nodded. "Tomorrow, first thing," he said. "The store at eight." He dropped his cigarette to the concrete, twisted out the ember carefully with the point of a shoe, and picked up the remains. He held two other cigarette butts. Avi remembered: neat guy, good haircut.

"Thanks," Avi said. "I'll be there."

Another long silence; another wasted moon hung above the horizon, about to rise, the light splashed and dreamy, the dreamer stupid as stupid gets.

"'Night, Rick," Rick said, his tone flat. He spun on a heel, agile and efficient, and strode toward a white pickup parked across the street.

"'Night, Rick," Avi called after him, unhappy and relieved.

• • •

His shoulder hurt. Stripped to the waist, the tape and gauze removed, Avi examined the wound. Rick had done a good job, the wound really not so bad, maybe not even a wound, nothing too messy. But people die from stuff like this, Avi reasoned, a little splinter of wood that swims the bloodstream to the heart, and *pop*, like a balloon, they're dead.

Rick hadn't said that, exactly, but he had said that there might be splinters.

Rick and Rick, Rick and his sidekick, Rick. Avi wanted sleep, so that he could meet his new partner in the morning, and a painkiller, something stronger than an aspirin, something to go with wine. Upstairs, he knew, Maureen's medicine chest held a small pharmacopeia, a little apartment of pills and liniments that Avi would never understand, another Mom mess, she with her boxes of lists and her Last Hint and Testament.

The dog was done for the night, the hope of a walk abandoned, her big head in her bowl as she slurped her bedtime drink; Dolly needed neither sleeping pill nor painkiller, just ritual, repetition, and Avi's love. How simple was that?

"You would eat whale meat, wouldn't ya'? Good dog," Avi said to his dog. "Blubber. Yum."

He moved through the downstairs, dazed and purposeful, hitting the lights until he hit one too many and left himself in the dark. Groping his way to the banister, Avi pulled himself upstairs toward pain relief, left-handed, tireder and tireder.

Toothpaste, Q-Tips, cotton balls, eye cream, nail polish, emery boards, ear plugs, fade cream, mascara, mascara, mascara, one blue earring, eyelash curler, liquid foundation, Jean Naté, rubbing alcohol, nail polish remover, *eau de toilette,* a bottle of expired Atarax. And three child-proofed prescription bottles of Zyrtec—which Avi knew was for hay fever, as Sandy, his ex-girlfriend, would pop the occasional tablet and then sleep nine hours. Mom had had bad allergies too, which Avi now remembered.

Take one pill, 10 mg., nightly, as needed.

Caution: may cause drowsiness, do not operate heavy machinery, do not combine with ineptitude, do not build a wooden whale without planning better, remember to remember that liars aren't good people, no matter how cute, and always hang up on Ramona.

Three bottles. Three names, the Zyrtec prescribed to one woman with three names—not two names, but three.

Maureen Heyer.

Susan Woodley.

Annie Morrison.

FIVE

· ·

THE HAY FEVER PILL RAN ITS COURSE in only five hours. He tried to get comfortable after that—kicked away a blanket, put on a T-shirt—and then gave up, read his whale book in bed for a little while before turning on the television. Up the channels, late night hucksters promised an end to every imaginable despair, and a few worth unimagining. Down the channels, the promises had price tags. The Food Channel featured some guy in a flowered shirt grilling pineapple. Off, click, off.

Outside, pre-dawn rain needled the roof, insistent upon the ruined whale, restless rain, fertile and warm and scented. Rain clicking and piddling in loops and swirls, planning next week's flowers.

Avi was full of feeling empty. Bean had said that he was too open, an idea Bean apparently found appealing, and that was how he felt, as though the rain could fill him.

The rain came harder, the sky gone noir. He threw on some clothes to go see, went downstairs, grabbed an umbrella, stepped outside, and walked to the carport to stand in the overhang of the eaves. His feet were wet. He felt like he needed a trench coat and a fedora, something to jazz up his duds. He was underdressed, Sam Spade gunned down at last in flip-flops. But Sam Spade never talked about his mother, and Sam Spade's mother never toyed with him posthumously.

Rain wiped the edges of the world smooth, softened suburbia, leveled the landscape to a sopped blur. If the rain rained all day, Avi would have to forego work, once he and Rick had conferred—which would allow more time to sort sewing supplies, oh, goody. He would have more time to spend with Maureen, Susan, and Annie.

Who the hell was Mom?

He watched the rain and its sixteen shades of gray, which made him think about the colors of whales, to be a whale. What would it be like to rise to the surface, and blow a gusty blast out through a blowhole into a downpour? Avi snorted. Not even close. How deep in the ocean would a whale need to be for her to lose awareness of a torrential rain above? Conceivably, the currents in the trenches might change with higher seas, the deeper movements of the water stirred from above by wind and rain. Would a storm on the surface matter to a whale deep below? What matters to a whale? Krill, singing, and babies; swimming really fast. Ice.

On the Internet last night, Avi had come upon an astonishing notion, with no means to verify its claim: whales sometimes rest in the water vertically. There among the blind, electric fish and bulbous, hypertrophic crustaceans, where tiny gribbles eat through shipwrecks, deep in the lightless depths, a fifty-foot long whale might hang, head down, serene. Or the idea was just wrong: the upside-down whale had been Internetted, after all, a crappy idea found in a virtual ocean of garbage. Avi didn't have much use for the Internet, except for email and downloaded music.

Rain, rain, no respite from the rain. He had better try to sleep a little more, before dawn didn't break.

He turned back toward the house and discovered the twins' big car idling in the street, headlights on, windows fogged. Crap, what time was it—six? The light was coming. He had not seen the twins in days, so what brought them? Fucking shin-kickers, wacko clothes monsters, henchwomen idiots, accessorized thugs . . . what could Avi do to change the unnatural order of things?

He slinked back inside. He mulled, brooded, and then he did what he did: Avi cooked oatmeal with dried cranberries, a splash of cream, brown sugar, and a thimbleful of whiskey, plated three bowls full—wiped the rims, presentation, presentation—inverted plates atop two bowls, and in a momentary break in the rain, carried the twins' their breakfast, his own oatmeal left covered and congealing in his mother's kitchen. His shoulder hurt a little, so Avi used his left hand more than his right, his balance askew, a dry rag tucked into his belt.

Knock, knock on the window of the Lincoln; the glass buzzed open a crack. He could smell perfume, sort of.

"Sister, look! It's The Victim."

"Why, Sister. Don't call him that."

"You said I could."

"Didn't."

"Did."

"The Camel."

"I'm not The Camel."

"I know that! I'm saying—"

"Ladies—" Avi interrupted. "Oatmeal." He wore a smile like a wet shirt.

"Oh, yay!"

"What is that?" asked the driver, Snow White. The window buzzed down another four inches. "Is it poison?"

"No," he said, a little pleased that she might think so. "It's got cranberries." The twins wore matching evening gowns, identical silver barrettes in their hair, and garish costume jewelry; their faces were slightly pudgy. "Nice dresses," he said. "It's a good look. Kind of debutante-with-a-gun. A little bit '80s."

"I am going to kill you," said Snow White.

"But I'm hungry, Sister. Can we eat it, can we, can we? Then we'll kill The Victim."

"Now you're calling him that." Snow White sniffed the gap in the window. "It's not poison?"

"No way!" Avi wouldn't smile, he wouldn't.

"Oh, goody! Breakfast!" In the passenger seat, Rose Red squealed. "Oh. Sorry, Sister," she offered. "It's your turn to choose."

Down came the driver's side window. Snow White glared at Avi. "If it's poison, I'm going to kill you," she said, and reached for the bowls. "Oatmeal," she growled.

"You're welcome."

"Wanna come sit between?" Rose Red said brightly.

"No . . . I'm okay," Avi said.

"Mmmm," Rose Red moaned happily, rooting around with her spoon. "Raisins."

"Cranberries," Avi said.

"Exthcuthe me?" Rose Red said, her mouth full, a little bit of oatmeal thhhtuck to her lower lip.

"Never mind," Avi said. "I've got to go now." To sneak out while you're eating, he should have said.

"Don't leave town," Snow White said. "Mmm."

"I'm just going back inside," Avi said, almost truthfully. "Breakfast."

"Fine," Snow White snarled. She reached for her napkin; the suddenness of the gesture made Avi flinch.

"Fine," Rose Red echoed. "Will you cook uth lunch?"

Avi faked a tight laugh. "We'll see," he said. He turned, waved, looked both ways, and crossed the street back to Maureen's. Actually, he could just poison them.

· · ·

He ate his own breakfast, tasty, waited, eyed the weather, got ready, and then when the rain came again, the sky rum-colored, he jog-crouched from the back door to the Toyota and pulled out (lights off) to his meeting with Rick. Drawings of the whale, the whale guide, the Composition notebook, a pencil, an eraser, Scotch tape, and his checkbook—all stuffed in a plastic bag. Avi wore his Smith's, hiking boots, a clean red T-shirt, the City Grocery cap, and a dark windbreaker.

He sprinted through the parking lot, rain slapping the macadam; there Rick waited outside the entrance of the store.

"You're three-and-one-half minutes late," Rick said, pointing to his watch. "Bad."

"I'm . . . what?" Breathless.

"Kidding," Rick said, not smiling. "Joke." He straightened. "How's the shoulder."

Avi nodded okay, a little lie.

"Not true," Rick said. "Should hurt."

The electronic double doors of the giant building supplies store parted. "Let's go," said Rick, as the two men strolled in side by side. They walked into the store, Neil Armstrong and Buzz Aldrin, Rick and Rick. Avi could feel the power in Rick's generosity, in the idea of the partnership, in whale-building as the possible work of just two men; two men could make a whale together, one man could hold the wood while the other hammered. Fuck the twins and The Camel.

"Got a plan?" Rick asked as they approached Customer Service.

Avi was deflated. "You . . . I . . . I brought drawings," he said, digging in the bag.

"Right," Rick said. "Gotcha," he added, a tiny lilt in his voice, like a wink.

"Hey, y'all. May I help you?" The woman at the counter wore a red smock over her sweatshirt.

Rick leaned in to read her nametag. "Hi, Keisha. In a minute, thanks."

Where was Rick's red smock? He must be off today.

"Okay," he turned to Avi. "Whatcha got." Rick said.

Avi looked around. At the end of one aisle, six unoccupied picnic tables and benches convened, arranged in a kind of open diamond and topped with brightly colored umbrellas. "Over there," Avi said, as he took off his wet jacket, gave it a little shake, and then led the way.

Upon reaching the first picnic table, Avi opened the plastic bag and spread out his things. Rick picked up the Scotch tape, looked at it, expressionless, laid it down again. Then he picked up the whale guide.

Avi started to object.

"Whales are big," Rick said, thumbing.

"I thought . . ." Avi began, surprisingly freaked out. He extended his hand, asked politely for the book. Rick handed it back. "I'd like mine to be very big. I'd like to be able to stand on this table and reach up and not touch the top."

Rick flipped open a well-worn pocket notebook and began to take notes. "Notes," he said. "Did some drawings too."

Avi continued, encouraged, his index finger pointed up to indicate elevation, his palm flattened to indicate the top. "Twelve, fifteen, sixteen feet," Avi guessed.

"I figured sixteen. What's height to length?"

"Good question," Avi said. He opened the whale guide, and used his thumb—nail to knuckle—to guesstimate the length of an illustration of a blue whale, and then its height. "Looks around four to one. Four knuckles to one."

Rick closed his eyes, opened them, and wrote something. "Wood. Big," he said.

Avi nodded. The caption under the illustration read, *The heart of the blue whale can be as large as a Volkswagen.*

"Okay," Rick said, thinking.

An employee scuttered by on a forklift, and gave a little wave, warning siren beeping; both Avi and Rick waved back. "Who's that?" Avi asked.

"Dunno," Rick said.

"Oh," said Avi. "Not your department." He was anxious to close the whale guide, and to do so without Rick noticing, to look carefully at the big blue whale, but at home, with no one else around. Maybe Avi shouldn't have come. Maybe the dream had to be his alone, and he should just call the police and have all of these crazies sent up river, where they would kick the shin out of each other.

Avi faked a sigh, stretched as a distraction, reached forward and closed the book, so smooth, on a first date. "New employee?"

Rick raised his glance over his note-taking, the light glinting on his glasses. What amazingly small and sharp eyes he had—flinty, really, or steely, or another kind of metal Avi couldn't name. Then Rick seemed to understand.

"Dunno," Rick said. "Don't work here."

It took Avi a few seconds to register the news.

"I'm retired. Contract work, mostly. You?"

Avi didn't know what to say. "I'm going back to school. To be a chef," he answered. "It's not C.I.A., but like that—"

Rick gave a little wave, a kind of cutting motion. "C.I.A.?"

"Culinary Institute of America. I'm with the competition. T.I.N. *The Institute Nouvelle.*"

Rick nodded. "Go on."

"But my mom died, so I moved here. That's her house. Three weeks ago, no, four."

"Gotcha," Rick said. "Couple of unemployeds. Welfare guys."

"Mid-lifers," Avi added, amused by the thought, at twenty-nine.

Rick paused. "I'm sorry," he said. "You know, 'bout your mom. My condolences on the loss of your mother," he said stiffly.

"Thanks," Avi said.

"And your whale. Coulda been a better whale. If."

"No kidding," Avi nodded. "Not your fault," he offered.

"Yep," Rick said. "But now I know how," Rick said. Was the guy excited? God, there was no way to tell. "Do it right this time. Shouldn't be hard. I'll show you. Always a better whale . . ." he added wisely.

Rick was scribbling more, lips pursed—had Rick ever said he worked here? Probably not: Avi didn't recall. But Rick seemed like a guy who said what he meant, someone who acted the way he felt. Always a better whale; Avi liked that.

"So, Rick. Can I hire you?"

"*Hmm,*" Rick hadn't actually answered.

"Hire, hire. You know. Can I pay you to be my contractor? Build the whale."

Rick stopped writing. He pressed the tip of a finger to his left ear—he wore a hearing aid, which Avi hadn't noticed. "Pal, that's too funny." He was shaking his head, giving what might be a Rick laugh. "Got any moolah?" Rick asked.

Avi nodded, lying. "Enough."

"I see," Rick said. "Well," he gave his ear a little poke. "I guess I'm your man."

"Hourly?"

Rick shook his head. He stopped, didn't say anything.

Avi waited.

"Naw. Project. Let me finish these figures, I'll give you a bid. I can build her. Got a whale to build," Rick said, amused. "You and me." He tore open the wrapper of a candy bar and took a big bite.

"Breakfast? Dude, you gotta eat better," Avi said. "And stop smoking. You take shit care of yourself."

Rick coughed. "What?"

"You heard me."

Avi and Rick stared at each other across the picnic table. Rick must be one of those people who counts to ten before he speaks. "Tastes good." Rick chewed. He wouldn't talk with his mouth full. "Right, my take'll be $2500. Materials should run six. Plus or minus tool rentals. Plus maybe two Gs for a crew at the end."

Avi did the math, rounded up: "So the project will cost thirteen or so?"

"Yep," Rick said. "'Bout that. Or more. Conservatively, maybe fifteen, sixteen."

"Okay," Avi said. "Let's say twenty. Here's my offer. I'll double your take if you quit smoking. Five grand. Plus I'll pay for the nicotine gum, or the patches or whatever, and all the rawhides you can chew. Double, plus the manicure after you've munched your nails. You can have your nails done, on me." Twenty grand was only twelve more than he had in the bank; maybe the whale could be rented out for Bar Mitzvahs.

"You're paying me to quit smoking?" Rick tapped his hearing aid. "Damn thing. Why?"

"Because I can," Avi said. "It's just stupid, is all," Avi added.

Rick thought for a long time. "No deal," he said. "I smoke."

Silence and more between the two men; Rick hadn't decided.

"Deal?" Avi stuck out his hand. "C'mon, dude."

"Still thinking," Rick said. "I like to smoke," he said. He drummed four fingers on the table; it was the first time Avi had seen him fidget. "But a whale. . . ." And finally: "Deal," Rick said, his grip enveloping Avi's. "Look. Plans," he said, letting go, and opening his notebook. "I drew some. A big whale."

· · ·

First Rick showed a drawing, sort of a gridded cucumber labeled *Whale Schematic Fig 3*:

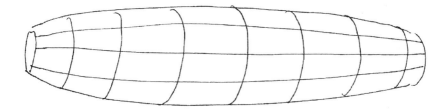

Then Rick explained how the cucumber would become a whale, and what steps would need to be taken to get that far, his explanation marked by organizational skills and construction acumen well beyond Avi's.

Step One: Six sheets of three-quarter-inch plywood, long side down, laid in three rows of two columns to make a large rectangle, sixteen feet by twelve feet. Glue three more sheets of ply, short side down, in the center of the rectangle, then cut two more sheets lengthwise, glued on either side, cross-grained top and bottom. Cut another sheet in quarters and fill in the corners. Add another layer just like the first, until the sandwich is two-and-one-quarter inches thick. Gallons of glue, Rick had noted. Lots of glue and screws. Glue, glue, screw, screw.

Cut enormous ovals out of the sandwich, one foot thick. Cut three more ovals inside each large oval, to make donuts. Make three three-ply sandwiches into four donuts per sandwich, twelve in all. These would eventually stand, so a few of them, the largest three, and two or three of the smaller ones, would need to be flat on the bottom.

Rick showed Avi another drawing, *Whale Sandwich Fig 5*:

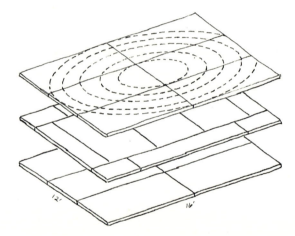

Step Two: To establish a 4:1 ratio of length to width, the whale would need a body sixty-four feet long. Lay eight sheets of ply end to end, along their short sides. Glue seven sheets of ply atop, but staggered. Measure and cut an eighth sheet to fill the areas left uncovered at both ends of the long strip. Fill in all gaps.

Avi listened, lost in the woods. Were there edible mushrooms somewhere, maybe next to the ogre's den? The fairy tale needed an ogre, he figured. Did an ogre have a den or a lair, or a grotto, or a cave? Really, he just couldn't follow what Rick was saying.

Lay another eight sheets atop, to make a complete third layer. Glue, glue, screw, screw. This three-ply hoagie would be two-and-one-quarter inches thick, four feet wide, and sixty-four feet long. Cut into strips, beams.

Step Three: Notch the insides of the ovals two and one-quarter inches to hold the beams. Stand up the ovals. With joist hangers secure the strips inside the Os, threading the giant skeleton with sixty-four foot long beams. "Like a fuselage," Rick had observed. "It's kind of like building a plane. Always wanted to build a plane," he had added.

Step Four: "Dunno about the exterior yet," Rick said, tapping his pen on the table. "Gotta research. But we should shop. We're buying seventy-four sheets of ply, so long as we don't mess any up, 'bout a tanker of glue, a big skillsaw, a Sawzall—probably one of the industrial ones, a reciprocating jobbie. A serious screw gun, one of those standing floorers. Rent that. I think we can do it ourselves except the assembly. Two weeks," Rick nodded. "Give or take." He looked toward the parking lot and the rain.

"Two weeks," Avi repeated.

"Step five," Rick said. "We'll need to put in some posts, so she doesn't roll. Then assemble her and raise her up. We'll hire a crew for that. Lots of hands."

"Raise her," Avi said.

"Look," Rick said, and there was one more drawing that put all the parts together, *Whale/Interior, Fig. 9,* an image that Avi stared at for a long time, the curves of the body too right:

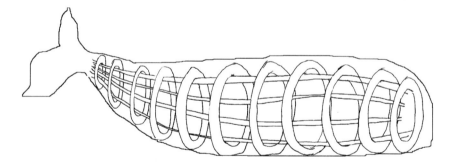

Avi couldn't believe it. The guy got it. The guy could do it. Holy crap: Avi had the right guy.

"Sure you got the money?"

Avi nodded, the lie bigger, the hole in his credit card widening. He was suddenly tired. He could hear a thin ululation, something in his jaw and ear. The whale guide was in the plastic bag. But something was singing: she was singing.

He had read in his guidebook that the humpback males were the ones who sang, but Rick had called her "she," and Avi had known too. She.

"But first, we gotta get that heap out of your driveway," Rick said. "Then it's a go. A whale raising," Rick said. "Ropes and a crew."

• • •

What they bought:

A Ridgid four-piece cordless tool kit that contained a skillsaw, hammer drill, Sawzall with carbide tipped blade, flashlight, and a charger with two batteries (thirty minute recharge rate).

One DuraSpin DS200-14 volt/SS-14 collated screwdriver, and the four foot extension that would allow for use while standing.

One Porter-Cable six gallon air compressor combination kit, including a quarter-inch Crown NS100H 18 gauge stapler/nailer.

One pack of half-inch staples.

Fifteen buckets of two-inch screws and one of seven-eighths-inch screws. 1,000 screws per bucket of the former, 800 of the latter. Square tipped.

Two cases of twenty-ounce tubes of Liquid Nails, twelve tubes per case.

Two one-quart smooth rod caulk guns.

100 Simpson Strong-Tie two-by-two-inch "A" Angle framing brackets.

One bucket of two-inch hot dipped galvanized nails, 1,000 per bucket.

One dozen packs of twelve-inch Quick-Grips, two per pack.

One package of 100 Catamount fourteen-inch multi-purpose ties.

Nine Stanley three-in-one workbenches.

One Stanley Max-Steel twenty-five-foot power lock tape measure.

One Johnson post level.

One Johnson sixteen-ounce plumb bob (contractor brass).

Thirty-two sheets of four-by-eight-foot dovetailed, treated plywood.

Forty-five sheets of four-by-eight foot plain edged, treated plywood.

Seven six-foot posts, six-inches around.

Two fifty-pound bags of Sakrete Ultra-High Strength Concrete Mix (half-hour setting, eight-hour walk-on dry time; just add water).

One Ames True Temper four-cubic-foot steel wheelbarrow.

One Ames Copperhead wood handle shovel.

One pack of four sponges.

Four pairs of work gloves.

Avi looked around at their loot and had to laugh amidst all these shiny things, each little patented item the brainchild of some weekend inventor and now flush retiree.

At the checkout counter, Avi read the delivery forms, which promised next-day, curbside service. The contract's final clause—regarding the delivery person's safety, possible damage to said delivered items, and how Avi agreed not to sue—made him hesitate: "By signing below, You acknowledge that You have read and fully understand the terms of this waiver and release, understand that You have given up substantial rights by signing it freely and without any compulsion. . . ."

The language was apt, and also wrong: building a wooden whale sure felt like a compulsion, and while giving up substantial rights, he was gaining too.

He had the right to be crazy, and to confuse a recurring dream with waking life, and to do so freely.

He had the right to build a whale.

He had the right to believe that he was honoring Mom's Last Will and Testament.

He had a right to Mom's money.

He had the right to spend the money before he got it.

He had the right to save himself.

He had the right to lie. His whale would be a lie, real but not a whale.

He had the right not to trust The Camel or Bean.

He had the right to find Bean attractive. To want to read her Soul Diary, whatever the hell that meant.

He had the right to live in his dead mother's house until his whale was built, and then to sell the house.

He hesitated, looked up from the page. The relentless rain on the roof of the building supplies store sounded like something composed and full of emotion, an unintelligible soundtrack. But the rain on the roof was on every roof, on everything, and everyone was connected somehow, and he didn't understand what he was feeling. "I just don't understand," he said to the rain, although he knew that he was buying happiness on credit.

He had another thought, a good one. When the rain ended, he would take Dolly mudding, one of their favorite pastimes, especially in a climate such as this, warm weather and lots of rain. They would both be slathered with mud, and Avi would fling mud-balls and Dolly would leap around and fetch and try to bite the flying mud-gobs mid-air, and bark and bark.

Really, he was thinking about Maureen and her three names. He supposed that the lawyer might be able to explain.

Names hurt, Susan Junior whispered to himself. Even the stupid twins knew that.

"What?" Rick was standing there.

"Nothing," Avi said. "It's just . . ."

Rick tapped a cigarette from a pack, stuck the butt between his lips, inhaled and began to fake-smoke the thing unlit. He had finished loading their take-home purchases onto a flatbed cart, the rest of the order on order.

"I dunno," Avi said. "Do you think we'll use all this stuff?"

"Yep. Plus."

Avi picked up a bag. "I guess. . . . Do you think I'm nuts?"

"Nuts?" They began to freight their loot outside, under the delivery awning; Avi would have to pull up the car. "Naw. But a fruitcake. Beyond all fruitcakes."

"I mean. . . ." Avi had almost missed Rick's sarcasm, it arrived so plainly. "Funny," Avi said. They were standing outside once again, facing the rain; he was feeling smaller now in front of the closed-down sky and all that water, the sweeping downpour angling into and across the vast parking lot. "It's just . . . aw, shit," he swore. "I mean, let's build her, you know?"

Rick lit up, and then sucked and sucked on his cigarette, a doubled or trebled drag, his relief evident. His gangly frame seemed to soften as he sighed. "Yep," he said, exhaling, as smoke poured from his nose and mouth. "A big whale."

"Hey," Avi said. "You quit smoking."

"Did not," Rick said, and took another deep drag. "Soon as I'm on site," he vowed.

"Lame," said Avi.

Rick stared at Avi.

"Put it out," said Avi.

Rick stared at Avi. "Fine," spat Rick, but then he put out the cigarette and tossed it into the garbage. "Happy now? Sadist."

• • •

"I am not your girlfriend! I fuck with you, and we go together, but this"—Mimou's accent took over—"this *thing* we do is not girlfriend and boyfriend. You are not there. Here, I mean. Shit!"

"I was only saying—"

"Yes, *mon cher*, you are only always saying."

Just back from the store, befuddled and resolute, he didn't want to fight with Mimou, that wasn't why he had called. "Please," he tried again. "It's complicated. I've met people who knew my mother, and they want something from me."

"But I do not want anything from you! I am going to be forty in two weeks!" Mimou was shouting into the phone. "Two weeks! FORTY! TWO WEEKS!"

"I know, I know. Please. Mimou. . . ."

"You do not know what a forty-year-old woman is like! You are not forty! You are only saying—"

"Oh, shut up!" Avi yelled back. "Really," he said in a lower tone.

Silence. And then, *"Comment?"*

"I'm sorry, I'm just a little tense. I didn't mean—"

"You are a bastard. I talk about my birthday and you tell me to SHUT UP!"

"Mimou, Mimou. . . ."

"Shut up, shut up! I AM FORTY! Okay, yes," she was telling herself to calm down. "Avi, I am coming to you there. On the Sunday. You will have a good wine, and put your dog in the other room. It is sexy, *non?* You shout at the phone like a Frenchman." She made a throaty, hearty sound, *"Grrrrr.* You better fuck like a Frenchman."

SIX

· ·

NYLON SHORTS, A RATTY SHIRT, his holey old Reeboks, once-white socks—Avi always wore the same socks for mudding, a pair of 99-centers that could be bleached back only to a miserable gray—the mudder's uniform was complete. Dolly couldn't believe her luck, bouncing and barking around the car like a wind-up dog, her ears flopping with each elated bounce.

He was cranking one of his favorite bands as he drove, The Rub Dubs, their new CD poached from Dwayne, the former med student now waiting tables at the Blue Egg, a kid who may have had something on Giacomo, or so the rumor went, the kid keeping his job despite a couple of brutal no-shows. *Gotta testify/not a drive-by/In a cop's eye/I'm a dead fly*: Rx, the The Rub Dub's lead singer, fairly spat the last line in her signature growl.

Avi wanted a signature growl. Dolly had one.

The Elsbeth Regional High School groundskeepers cultivated four fields of play lined for use, the first just beyond the stadium and track and each of the others down a hill, three hills in all. The bottom field had been recently tilled, or just dug up—at the foot of its approach lay thirty feet of gloriously churned dirt. On a previous walk, Avi had eye-marked the area for mudding, waiting for just the right warm, torrential rain.

Tap dancing in the back seat, Dolly sniffed until she snorted, snorted until she semi-barked, *how-ulled*. How amazing that a dog knows what she knows. Okay, so the extra towels were her Pavlovian signal, but still, his Doll was a brainiac of a pooch.

Not Avi. He was a dummy—to build a whale with a guy who had to be a Fed, or The Camel's accomplice? Rick with a hearing aid that was probably some kind of transmitter. Tomorrow Avi would try sign language, a test: Hello, Camel Central, this is Mud Whale One, over.

Dumb, dumb, dumb, moron, he told himself. It was just like Kuala Lumpur. It was just like Tottenham. Avi was always falling for everyone, until someone stole everything from him. Dummy.

But dummy or no, Avi was psyched. Mudding! Dolly's doggy glee was infectious, and the weather was cooperating, a perfect mist filtering down at the end of the storm, almost foggy, the springtime air-brushed, the colors blended. On his travels, Avi had come to think that, closer to the equator, the colors went together better, but now he wasn't sure about this theory. Elsbeth had screwed up a lot of Avi's theories.

Only a few cars remained in the lot after hours (no big Lincoln, the twins feeding elsewhere). He parked. Dolly was all joy. Not one jot of pathos, nor of fear, nor an awareness of her own mortality—a dog gamboling and gavotting about, ready for mud, may well be the essence of the universe, what unhappy people in their grumbling disenchantment miss. So why miss out: Avi was intent upon being the dog Dolly was being, or the man in a dream, or just a man. Well, whatever! He wanted to taste the world, to eat the world, as a dog does. To hell with the twins; *en garde*, Mimou! Mudding!

They ran together across one field and then slid down a hill, Dolly already nipping at his hand, running sideways at times, then across and down another hill, then to the third hill. Atop the last rise, facing the glory of the mud below, Avi stopped to breathe as the mist collected, the trees shrouded and fuzzy-limbed, the weather a bit sci-fi, the world solid and wet.

"Ready?" he asked Dolly.

"*Woof!*" she said. Her eyes blazed with glee, her tongue already hanging out, panting floppily, doggy mania.

"Ready!" he shouted. "Go, go, go, go, go!"

Avi sprinted down the hill heels first, short strides compensating for the incline, and bellowed the whole time, his soul poured into a crescendo of voluminous vowels. At the base of the hill where the true mud began, he launched himself—a kamikaze, comic-book, mock-Olympic dive, head tucked and arms first—and belly-flopped into the glistening, fantastic, eight or so inches deep, top soup of Earth.

What a slide! Ten, twelve, fifteen, twenty feet! This was real living!

From his belly, when he looked up, there was Dolly, all four legs deep in the muck and tossing her big head with glee. She had been barking the whole time.

"Again!"

He stood. Dolly gave a full body shake, beginning at her head and traveling down to her tail, launching gobs of mud skyward with each ripple. Avi put out his arms and shook too, his head, his shoulders, his hips, he shook it all; then he half-stepped and half-waded out of the bog and charged up the hill, laughing, gasping for air, slower toward the top, with his big ecstatic dog nipping at his sneakered heels. Avi and Dolly, Jack and doggy Jill.

Again, only this time better lubricated from chaps to nave, he managed to slide further. *"Ahhhhhhhhh!"* Avi came up with a mud-packed face, which he wiped with his mud-caked hands, rubbed his eyes with two fists. *"Pbbb,"* he spit.

"Again!"

"Again!"

"Again!"

He had lost count of how many times. Not counting but being, a man thrown to earth, a man renewed.

"Again!"

He sloshed out and angled himself up the hill, his dog running crazed circles around the man's more considered path. Oh, Doll-Doll. What a delightful, simple beast. She'd stink, and sleep for hours.

"Go, go, go, go, go!"

This time a butt slide, his body crooked, arms and feet up, less diving than splashing as he powered through the muck—and finally mud-tired, Avi lay back in the geological gumbo, and closed his eyes.

Dolly barked twice and bounded through the muck.

"Arghhhhh!" Someone yelled.

Avi sat up. At the edge of the bog, fingers splayed and eyes wide in disbelief, all carefully attired in what might once have been white pants and a deep-lilac top, was a mud-splattered Bean, around whom Dolly was racing excitedly. And then, *BAM!* Dolly skittered too close, banged into this formerly clean person, and—*WHUMP! SQUELP! PLISH!*—down went Bean, muddied.

The humans stared at one another. "Hi," Avi said, uh-oh.

"This better be fun," Bean said.

"It is," Avi said.

"Fine," Bean said. "But I'm charging you 100 bucks, off the top; these clothes are done." She picked up a gob and threw it at him. "And you better watch out. I like to tackle boys."

"Again!" Avi yelled and rose to his feet. "Dolly." He charged up the hill, Bean laughing close behind.

Rejuvenated, Avi mudded with Bean, three more good runs, Dolly friskier too, another friend in the pack. Then at the bottom of the hill, Avi and Bean fell upon one another, wrestled and jumbled, tangled in a knot of limbs, their bodies corruptible. He was aware of Bean in her wet clothes, of Bean's hand here, of his leg there, slippy mud, Bean's butt. Of Dolly's big head bumping in between the two mudders.

"Again!" Bean yelled.

"Again!" They climbed up together to the top.

Avi hurtled down face first, bulldozed the muck with his chin. He stood up: Bean had come tumbling after. She was right there—she pushed him and he fell. Avi laughed and grabbed her ankle, yanked so she flopped into the soup next to him, a butt-first *kersplash*.

She had a spectacular lump of mud on the left side of her head, like a potter's error. She had a giggle that seemed endless, a kind of happy crooning high in her chest and throat. "Maybe . . ." she tried to catch her breath and talk through her laughter.

"Forget it," Avi said, laughing too hard. "*Pbb*," he spit more mud. She had nice arms.

"Damn, I'm dirty," she laughed.

"Oh yeah?" He scooped a handful of mud, reached forward, and drizzled the guck down upon her head.

"Why, thank you," she cooed, her eyelashes batting. "You look like shit."

Then laughter took them both and they laughed together, a duet.

"Damn, Susan Junior. I haven't done this since . . . ever," Bean said more calmly. "You're a sneaky one."

Avi began to pack handfuls of mud to his chest, just because. "It's not Susan Junior," he said. "It's Avi. A, v, i."

"Avi?"

"Yes." His chest was covered; he had become a mud monster. He noticed too, now that the adrenaline had abated, that his shoulder was stinging a little in the wound where the splinter had been. Time for antibiotics and ale.

"That's a better name," she said, and followed suit, lumping her torso with mud packs. "Damn," she laughed again. "I'll never be clean. The dirt here is so red. . . . What does Avi mean?"

Avi felt self-conscious. "Lord of mine," he said, breaking eye contact. "It's Greek."

"Not Hebrew?"

"Naw," Avi said. "Dolly! Come!"

"Lord of mine," Bean repeated, slathered anew in mud, the Mud Woman of Loch Elsbeth. "I don't think so," she said.

• • •

"How did you find me here?"

They were done, not quite embarrassed, walking side by side up the hill.

"I didn't," Bean said. "Ramona did." The incline got steeper; Bean held out her hand for help, so Avi helped. "Avi Woodley," she said to herself, but aloud too.

"Right," Avi half-lied, unsure as to why.

They were both a little out of breath atop the last hill, the dull brick of the high school in view once more, and there was the Toyota, a return to civilization. Her hand was her own again.

"Are you ready to sell?" Bean asked.

Sell what? What was Bean talking about? Oh, right, he remembered.

"I mean . . . I'm sorry to do business now—I am, Avi, really—but I need the list. How much will you want? Avi?"

He was dazed, a little bit out of his feelings. "Look," he said, thinking sadly about Mimou, then happy. "I like you."

Bean blushed muddily.

"But this stuff with my mom . . . it's more complicated."

"Your whale," she said, smart.

"My whale."

"I see," she said, and reached out with her right hand to touch his cheek, missed by a little, adjusted her trajectory. Then Bean was touching his face, not even pretending to wipe him clean.

"How'd you know? Wait, let me guess. Ramona told you about my whale. She's always out there, spying on me."

"No, silly, you did. On the phone. When I called to cancel dinner."

"Oh," said Avi. "Right. Well that changes things, doesn't it?" He smiled at his mistake, having fun. "But I've made a decision. I think I've changed my mind, for now." Avi added. "The list isn't for sale."

"It's not?" She let her hand fall. "What? Wait, I see," she said. "I get it." Bean's voice became sing-song, her head bobbed side to side. *"You can't find the liii-iisssst."*

"Crap," Avi said. "That obvious?"

"Look at you! Your Soul Diary is *so* easy to read," she chuckled. "Shit, I'm muddy," she laughed. "But Avi, The Camel's in town and she's using the twins. You can't just screw around. Ramona called to say we're going to auction."

"I know," said Avi. He tried not to look down at her wet shirt. "They kicked me. . . . But she'll just have to wait. . . ." Avi said. "Until after the whale. Then I'll decide—or figure out something, or . . . I mean, hell, fuck The Camel."

"Fuck The Camel," Bean repeated. She put her hands on her hips, not his, oh well.

"Fuck The Camel," Avi said.

"Wow," Bean said. "Fuck The Camel. So you can build a whale," she added, shaking her head. "Fuck The Camel. . . . You sure are Susan Junior—'cause that's why we're here. She wouldn't sell either." Then Bean leaned forward, ready, ready, close, closer, closest, so slowly that he could guess what was happening, and *KAPOW!* planted one on Avi's cheek.

A kiss. She started it. . . .

He took hold of Bean's shoulder, lightly, and held her. Then Avi delivered Avi's special delivery: not a peck but a real one with tongue-tip and yummies, slow enough to relish, close enough to eyeball.

They pulled back, holding on. "Avi," Bean said. She blinked a few times. "But—"

"Wow," Avi didn't let her finish. And then in a higher voice: "I know. I feel so used. First the list, and now my body. . . ."

Bean laughed. What a nice laugh. Then she became serious: "That was a good kiss. But here's what I don't like: please don't interrupt me to say that you know. You don't know because I haven't said anything yet."

He thought about it. "Fair enough. . . . Dolly!" Avi called, unwilling to push his luck. "Dolly," he said as his dog galumphed into view. "Doll, go take a shower—and then pull up the car. I'll just wait here with the bank robber."

"*Woof!*" said Dolly. "*Woof! Woof!*"

Bean blushed again.

"Right?" Avi said, his blurted suspicion confirmed. "I'm right, aren't I? You're a bank robber."

She smiled.

"So all of you . . . The Camel . . . and Mom too? All bank robbers. . . ."

Bean smiled more.

"Mom too," Avi said again. "A bank robber."

"*Woof! Woof!*" said Dolly, which in Doggish meant *Holy Shit!*

"Holy shit," Avi said, on behalf of his dog.

Avi tossed the salad with the nuts and dried fruit and then put the greens in the fridge to crisp. He made the dressing, chopped the ingredients for his omelets, blanched the asparagus and removed the spears to a bowl of ice water and patted them dry with paper towels. He would drizzle the asparagus with truffle oil, fleck the asparagus with sea salt, and roast the spears for a few minutes, served warm *al dente*. But not yet: finish the veg and whip up the mushroom, shallot, and chevre omelet once Bean returned from wherever, and from the three consecutive showers she had announced she planned to take. He would dress the salad at table.

Avi was pleased that Bean had accepted his dinner invitation, offered only because he had shopped earlier in the day and knew his larder, as their spectacularly muddied clothes precluded even a quick stop on the drive home. Luckier still, he had a reasonable California chard chilled, nothing too oaky, a wine Mimou wouldn't like anyway, and the baguette could be freshened if need be, of course, although freshened wasn't the same as fresh.

The prep work done, his skin after-tingling with the scrubbing of a loofah found beneath Maureen's bathroom sink, Avi sat at the oak kitchen table with a nice-sized glass of wine and read his whale guide, the book propped. He could still taste mud.

"I hereby separate the whales from the fish," wrote the Swedish naturalist Linnaeus in 1776, and with this sentence, the whale was named a mammal. But long before Linnaeus, maybe sixty million years before, following the demise of the dinosaurs came the rise of the whale's ancestor, the condylarth. Originally terrestrial, the condylarth—bizarrely, the evolutionary predecessor of whales, hippos, sheep, and even deer—inexplicably began to live in the waters of the Tethys Sea, in what was now central Asia. As a result of this change in habitat, adaptation occurred, so said the fossils: forty-five to fifty million years ago, the condylarths had yielded to the archaeocetes, the first purely aquatic animals, which had become extinct themselves twenty to thirty million years later.

Avi ran his finger across the page. There on the timeline the order of archaeocetes or "ancient whales" divided, and two suborders of modern cetaceans appeared: the *Odontocetes*, or toothed whales, and the *Mysticetes*, or mustached whales. His finger reached the present. Of these whales, *in toto*, seventy-nine living species had been named, with debate as to overlap and error, and with the knowledge that some whales might remain unknown—including most poignantly the fabled Longman's beaked whale, *Mesoplodon pacificus*, an animal never seen alive in the wild, found only rarely, and only then beached and dead.

Avi thumbed through the book for the hundredth time since its purchase, hopeful, looking for his whale and knowing that he wouldn't find her here. A humpback, a gray, a sperm, a blue—none matched. His whale was definitely a whale, real in the way that the book, the table, and the salad were real, and unreal too. But that would change.

A humpback whale hunts by releasing a cloud or net of bubbles around (or sometimes below) a school of fish. Once the fish become trapped, the whale, a gulper, turns, returns, and swallows its meal. A trap made of air in the water . . . he turned the page. Some people believe that whales navigate by responding to the earth's magnetic fields. Some people believe that a dream is as real as an omelet.

Maureen was a bank robber, Avi said to himself. Everyone was full of shit, apparently, Avi's gift inherited—and now, crap, he couldn't even be proud of his better lies, Avi's one's true talent unoriginal. Thanks again, Mom.

Bean's face appeared in one window square of the kitchen door just as she knocked and his cell phone rang. Avi let her in, motioned, grabbed the phone: she was rosy, bright-eyed, wearing a quilted long skirt and a sleeveless vest, festive hippie bank-robber wear. Along with the diamond solitaires, her nifty bracelet. A clean, scrubbed smell, a little like apples.

"Hello?"

"Avi! *Mon dieu!* I call and call and you ignore me."

"I'm sorry. I was out." He made a face, sorry, and turned away from Bean, embarrassed. He had ignored her, true.

"See! You are out!"

"How are you, Mimou?"

"How am I? You little boy. I am forty!"

"I know, I know. Look, must you come so soon? I mean—" Oh crap, Avi thought. Bad thing to say.

Mimou sniffed. "Bastard."

"Mimou, please—" He really shouldn't have said that. "I've got something cool going on, and I want—"

"When I get there, I will be there!" And with a vicious click, and what probably was a spectacular full body twist and flourish, she hung up the phone, leaving Avi as always a bit amazed.

• • •

"Wow, that was good." Bean leaned back from the table. "You sure can cook."

"Thanks," Avi said, rising to clear the dinner and salad plates. He hoped so.

"Oh, let me help—," Bean said and reached forward, knocking over her water glass. "Shit," she swore, jumping up. "Sorry . . . don't let me help."

"No problem," Avi replied over his shoulder, as he hustled for paper towels and a sponge. "Really, it's fine."

"I'll just stand here and not touch anything. It's what my mom used to tell me to do," she added bitterly.

Avi began to mop up the water, moving around the items on the table, there, here, chess without rules. "That couldn't have been fun."

"It wasn't," Bean said tightly. "But I got mine."

He raised his head to look at her. "Revenge?"

Bean laughed. "Yes, revenge! What a funny notion. No, not revenge. That's not what I mean. I mean success—you know, daring to break the law in full view, and all that. And the money."

"You're such a criminal," Avi said.

"A criminal? A criminal?"

Avi couldn't tell if she were mad.

"I'm not a criminal," Bean's voice rose. "I'm a bank robber!"

Avi had to laugh.

"Your mother wouldn't have treated me like that, if I were her daughter. Susan was so . . . amazing. What a Soul Diary."

"She was," Avi agreed. "I mean"—he sat down again—"people seem to say so. But I didn't know her. She left when I was fourteen."

"Ah," Bean said. "That explains it."

He finished wiping the spill. He stood again. "Explains what?"

"Her pride in you," Bean said. "She would talk about you. . . . You were larger than life. You couldn't exist. You were never real."

"She talked about me? What did she say?" He almost sat, changed his mind, and stepped away to discard the wet paper towels. "But I'm real," he said to the air in his dead mother's house.

Silence. The air had nothing to say. So be it.

He returned to what he knew. "Coffee or tea?"

"Coffee, please," Bean answered. "I'm going to be up for a while. But maybe you don't want to have this conversation."

"I do."

"You do? Then how come you can't sit still? I mean, up and down and up and down."

Avi stopped what he was doing, which was nothing. "Fine," he said. "Be my shrink. But I have to go over here to make the coffee." He gestured. "Is this okay, Dr. Lima?"

"It's fine," she smiled. "Just make good coffee. Coffee for Bean."

He waited to ask more until his back was to her, his hands busy with the grinder, then Mr. Coffee warming up, the early evening far away, outside the kitchen window; Dolly was probably upstairs with her butt on his pillow, her stinky fur off-gassing into the fabric and polluting Avi's dreams.

"What was she like?" There, he had asked.

No answer. He stayed where he was, looking out the kitchen window, where a bird or something flashed across the dusk.

"Wow," Bean finally said. "A whole person."

More silence. Avi had to put something there: "I mean, you know what I mean."

"*Mm,*" Bean made a thinking sound. "I don't, really. I had only known her three years or so. She recruited me. She was amazing."

"So I hear," Avi responded more bitingly than he had intended. He turned without turning around, watched the coffee drip.

"Hey, you know something? In her Soul Diary—"

"Okay, okay. I give up." He turned once more, to face Bean. She had a little piece of something in her hair. "You've got a little bit of something in your hair." He pointed, and she found it. A bit of asparagus, most likely.

"Thanks."

"Sure. So what's a Soul Diary?"

Bean smiled. What did her smile mean? "Kiss me again, and I'll tell you."

Avi smiled back. "Okay. Blackmail."

"Not blackmail. Bribery."

He kissed her slowly.

"*Whew* . . . a Soul Diary. . . . Well, I have a very strong relationship to trees. . . ." She stopped to take a breath.

"Trees? Druids?"

"*Whew,*" she exhaled again. "No, don't be ridiculous. Only trees. Some day I'll tell you about my dad. He raised me when my parents split. And my other dad—but that's a longer story. I even have a third dad!" She laughed.

Avi scraped a chair away from the table, sat once more. "I'd like that," Avi said. "I mean, I'd like to know."

She looked at him, a funny little look. "Right," she reminded herself of something. "Soul Diaries. Everyone has one, it's not a real book that you can touch of course, but it's something real in that it's a coming together of the power of destruction with the power of creation, spirit and wonder, and it's where you can read your soul."

"Go on," he said.

"Well, it's not really your soul, not in the Judeo-Christian sense of the term. It's not like that. More *chi,* you know? Essence? And sometimes you can see what it says in your Soul Diary, if . . ."

"If . . ."

"Oh, well. Think about the symmetry of your body, right? The left-right division. The *spine*—just like a book, right? Anyway, learning to read your Soul Diary is a lifelong lesson. It's got to do with balakweneo meditation and the body and making your thoughts transparent." She smacked the table, laughed. "*Ow.*" She rubbed her smacked hand, laughed harder. "And sex!" She winked at him.

Avi didn't know what to do or say. He wanted to have sex with Bean.

"Paracelsus," she said. "The salamander. That's on the cover of my Soul Diary."

"What's on the cover of mine?"

Bean's smile changed to something more serious and twinkly. "Really. A fetish is always an animal. . . . Yours is a whale, you dope."

Avi shook his head. Oh my God, she was loony.

"Hey!" Bean said, standing up suddenly. "How about we look at her stuff? I can tell you stories about her, or make up stories. I'm good at making up stories," she said in a funny tone. "What do you say?"

"You're good," Avi said. He had to smile. "Coffee's ready."

"You're good yourself."

"No, I mean you're not bad. You're a pro. You say that you were raised by your dad just like I was, and then we kiss, and then you go into this riff on Soul Diaries, and you say "sex" and then, oh, yeah, you want to look at her things with me? Maybe see if a special little list might be taped under her desk drawer?" He was a little disappointed. "Nice move."

Bean was standing there, her palms open. She smiled and nodded. Her face shone, tilted at a charming angle. "You're not so bad yourself, Avi-Susan Junior," she added. "You cook too. But my dads and your Soul Diary, they're real. Anyway, yes. You can't fault a girl for trying. I want the list. . . . Besides, your mom wouldn't have left it out anywhere. And The Camel knows that too. Okay?" she said more than asked. She stuck out her hand. "So. Shake."

"Shake? On what?"

"Just shake. So I can touch your hand."

"Shake." They shook hands, her small hand in his, a little bit of touching and rubbing. "The Camel said that she searched the house, but I have my doubts."

"I see," Bean said. "And now you get to build your whale." She leaned forward. "I'm going to kiss you," which she did, *zounds*, deeply, the length of her small body at an angle, to keep his from too much contact, just lips and tongues. Then Bean pulled back. "Never con Bean."

"Con you? No way." Avi wanted more of her. He stayed near. "I'm not bullshitting you. I . . . In fact, I'm trying to quit. It . . . hurts people."

Bean's gazed widened. He could kiss her again.

"Avi, you're something," she said. "You're a new person, I think. But I'm not going to have sex with you yet." She put up her hand, stop right there. "You're too distracted. You'll just have to wait."

CHAPTER SEVEN

. . . .

"SISTER, HE'S AWAKE."

"No, I don't think so."

A long pause. "He's cute when he doesn't move."

"Cute."

"Do you think he's cute?"

"If you want one, Sister. . . ."

"I don't want one. Except for that little line in his chin—what is that called?"

"A cliff."

"Right. A cliff chin."

"I like that."

"Oh, Sister. Let us find a man with a really cliff chin, just for you."

He dared to stir, believing his sleep charade sufficient, rolled toward the voices, and opened his eyes. There they were, bedside: the twins and Dolly between them, his watchdog watching happily, bad dog, her head and shoulders wiggling as she wagged.

Dolly barked. "*Woof!*"

Avi reached out and patted her head. She licked his hand.

The evil henchwomen wore camouflage cat suits, black berets under which they had tucked their blond locks, and enormous camo earrings shaped like rifles; he couldn't see their shoes. They had matching—no, that wasn't right—corresponding black eyes, one right and one left.

"What happened to you two?" Avi asked, his voice gravelly from last night's wine. Crap, it must be before seven again: it was too fucking early to be alive.

"The Victim talks." Twin Left Eye bared her teeth in a smile. "We disagreed."

"Oh God," Avi exhaled involuntarily.

"We made up," Left Eye continued. "You're next."

"You're it," said Right Eye. "Tag. You're it." She punched her sister.

"No, he's it," said Left Eye. "Sister. . . ." She turned to her twin. "Remember?"

"Yes, yes, yes!" said Right Eye. "You're so wonderful, Sister. We want breakfast! The most important meal of the day!"

"But brush your teeth first," Left Eye said. "And no more of that—" she
pointed at his crotch underneath the bed linen. "*Ew.*"

"Break-fast, break-fast!" Right Eye chanted.

"No," Avi said. Damn dingbats. He moved to sit up. "I get coffee and you
have to wait."

Pow! Right Eye punched him on the shoulder.

"*Ow!*" Avi said. "No more hitting." He rubbed his shoulder as he sat up fully.
"Okay," he decided, "you asked for it." He threw back the sheet, the return
of Naked Dude, happy to watch the twins recoil. For their viewing pleasure,
once he got out of bed, he did a little dance—weight-shift one, cha, cha, cha—
swinging the thing as he left the bedroom to go pee. "You hit me again, I'll
tell," he called out.

The twins had huddled together for safety. One of them responded. "No, I
will!"

Jesus, what planet had they come from, Planet Imbecile? They probably
were kicked off their home world for being too stupid.

Avi came back into the room. "Coffee first, this time," he said. "And I assume
she wants to see me?"

"I don't," said Left Eye. She and her sister had turned so as not to watch.

"Not you," said Avi.

"Not me," said Right Eye.

"Oh, God," said Avi. "Not you. The Camel."

• • •

As soon as she could, having raced outdoors and done her business and then
trotted happily, emptily back, Dolly lay on her belly in the kitchen and ate her
kibble just like a dog, the enormous ceramic bowl pinned between her paws.
Briefly, Avi wondered what Dolly's head weighed; surely more than a twin's
gray matter. He pined for his coffee as the women sat across from each other
at the kitchen table and played Two Musketeers with a pair of butter knives
they had found.

"Stop that," Avi said. "I'm almost ready."

They looked up, mid-parry. "Victim . . ." growled Right Eye, whom Avi suspected to be Rose Red, the dimmer twin more prone to quick acts of violence.

"My house, my kitchen," Avi said, quoting Giacomo, who had last offered
the sentiment when he had fired Eva. Avi liked Eva. "Knives are not toys," he

told the twins.

"Sister," Right Eye said. "I'm hungry."

"Yes, Sister," Left Eye said. She threatened Avi with the round blade of her butter knife. "But not because you said so. So there." She stabbed the air— take that, Victim—and laid down the knife. The twins exchanged a look, Right Eye almost standing, Left Eye sneering. Then Left Eye laughed, so Right Eye laughed too. "Knives are too toys."

He filled three cereal bowls with muesli, mixed in some plain yogurt, a swirl of honey, Euro this a.m., spit, spot. The twins grunted as they ate, predictably messy. Avi sipped his coffee, a bright Kona, and watched their prison manners, their berets felted. What would he tell The Camel about the list? She hadn't found it either, so maybe he could just keep stalling. But if the twins hit him again, he would call the cops. No more, he told himself. Even though . . . calling the cops would likely mean the disappearance of Bean, her motive fleeing with the means.

Not before he slept with her, to see. He needed to know what that would feel like.

"Okay," Avi thumped the counter—which made Dolly start, and look around for her leash. "Sorry, girl," he said. "Dogs go out." He led her to the back door. "Okay," he said to the twins. "Lick your bowls and let's go Camel shopping."

Right Eye glared up at him.

Left Eye licked her bowl.

. . .

"My friend." With a flourish The Camel welcomed Avi to the batting cages. *"Mi amigo, mon frere, bù dǎ bù xiāng shí, aloha.* Would you care to join me, and swat the mock skull with an aluminum club?" She wore a Cubs baseball cap, a bright blue sweatshirt that said *Try It You'll Like It,* sweatpants, hightop sneakers with some kind of striated waffle tread, and batting gloves for batting. Maybe the C was for Camels. Avi glanced around at the other batting cages, all empty on a steamy morn, the smell somehow fetid.

"You look good in a cage," Avi said, caffeine a euphemism for courage.

"Now, now," she panted slightly as she leaned against the fence. The pitching machine hummed between feedings. "Don't make The Camel spit."

"Sorry," he said, and he was, The Camel not so easy to intimidate. "I just don't like being woken up," he averred. "Can we change our schedule?"

"Bad dad?" The Camel asked. "Substitution amok?"

"I'm not following," he said.

"Of course," The Camel said. She took a little practice swing with her dull silver bat, good form. "What are the work togs for?" She gestured toward his boots and jeans. "More reckless construction?"

Avi didn't answer.

"I see. Lima Bean got your tongue?"

Again, he kept quiet.

"Affirmative." She swung her bat a little more mightily. "Do you understand baseball as an idea? Quite fascinating, really. It's a game of failure, utterly impossible. Consider the batter who fails 70% of his career—he then makes the Hall of Fame as one of the best players ever. How quaint, don't you think? These Americans. . . ." Once more, with a sweeping flourish, her gesture took in the batting cages, the nearby Putt Putt course, the Go Karts, and all of the horizon. "The sport qualifies, too, as the only major American pastime in which the defense gets to hold the ball and initiate the action on every play. Sound familiar?"

Avi shook his head, no.

"You." The Camel adjusted her gloves with a precise, violent ripping of Velcro. "You're the defense. You've got the ball." She swung. The Camel's swing was smooth, her footwork agile: head down, powering through her hips, top hand coming off upon imagined contact, well-coached and/or practiced. She obviously pursued her obsessions diligently. "Now where are those challenged henchwomen? They're never around when I feel like threatening someone." She smiled. "Irony? Please be your mother's son."

He had to shake his head, almost amused. Maureen would never die.

It was time to feign nonchalance: "They're a pain. Two pains."

"Ah," The Camel said. "I can see that your wit persists, if only in limited doses. . . . Yes, they are. . . . But baseball! Let us return, then, you and I, and consider how many decisions might be made between plays—and how such strategizing renders useless that vapid sportscasting cliché, the color man who intones, 'And now a break in the action.' Insipid, don't you think? To miss the conceptual center of a sport appealingly decentered? A break in the action *is* the action." She dug into her pocket, pulled out a handful of change, stepped to the box, and inserted four quarters. "*Voilà!* The proceeds of criminal misdoings spread once more upon the economy. Sure you don't swing?" she added with a leer. "My treat."

"No, that's fine," Avi said.

"Be that as it may." The Camel approached the plate, tapped the insteps of her sneakers with her bat, swung twice, and then settled into her stance, concentration acute. The light on the pitching machine flashed green, out came a fastball, and—*DING!*—The Camel's swung bat met the pitch marvelously, a line drive back up the imagined middle of an imagined field. "Single," she proclaimed.

And again, and again: her form nearly flawless, her swing sure, The Camel took her exercise as Avi watched, almost every swing a hit, each accomplishment noted aloud. He wondered a little about that, what kind of bank robber needs to proclaim her deeds?

Fully breathless, finished, The Camel approached Avi, the fence between them merely chainlink. "Sell me the list," she panted.

"Maybe," Avi said.

"Ah." She took a slug of a neon sports drink. "Electrolytes." On one wrist, she wore a semi-fluffy band, which she now used back-handed to mop her brow. "Well, the list. How unfortunate that you have inherited an item useless to you and unavailable to me, but one that others want. . . . So upon what does the decision depend?"

Avi guessed that he should probably not hook his fingers through the fence, at least not so close to her. He tried to be subtle, offered a clearing of his throat meant to sound cough-like, and brought his hand back, safe at home. "Depends . . ." he said. "I need three weeks to decide," he said.

"Three weeks," The Camel echoed. "Three weeks! In three weeks, we shall all be three weeks closer to dying."

What did that mean? "I don't understand," he said.

"I know," she said.

"Three weeks is all," Avi said again.

"Well," The Camel swung her bat once more. "Three weeks is all," she mimicked him. "Would you mind squeezing that small towel through?" she pointed.

"Or not," he said. "Either I say no now, or I get three weeks. For my mom. I have to do something for my mom." He passed her the towel.

"Ah, the beloved *mater* gambit," The Camel said. "Thank you." She wiped her face, lay the towel down on a nearby stool, and resumed a batter's stance, but not in the batter's box. She pointed, aimed the barrel of the metal bat at Avi. "Impressive. Such stratagems deserve praise. I see," she mused. "Three weeks," she considered. "Ramona mentioned you had noteworthy *cojones*. But this tells me you have not found the list."

"You want the list, I want three weeks, is all. I'm not even looking for it unless you give me three weeks. And no twins. And no guns."

"No guns. But three whole weeks, each as arbitrary as the last. . . ? Did not the Cuban Missile Crisis turn in three weeks? If you were a bug, three weeks would be a lifetime. *Presto,* then! Three weeks you shall have, and we shall hope you are not a bug," The Camel added one last intimidating swing, the aluminum bat cutting the air between them, fence or no fence, a menacing swish. "Because bugs get squished. . . . We shall give you three weeks, for Susan Woodley!" The Camel declared. "We are not without sympathy, especially when plural." She paused a moment. "But, Susan Junior, the twins will need to be distracted. Upon you such obligations fall like rain."

"What?"

"Poetry."

"Oh."

As though hailed, the twins came striding down the walk.

"Girls, girls, girls," The Camel intoned. And then to Avi, "Maurice Chevalier, *non*? Or is it the late, great George Plimpton. . . ? Girls, we have a job for you."

"Oh, goody!"

"A job!"

"Do I need my crowbar? I'll get my crowbar."

"Sister, don't be silly. Jobs don't need crowbars. Jobs need *weapons.*"

"Spears!"

"Girls!" The Camel interrupted their babble. "Rick Woodley and I have a plan."

Left Eye stopped wiggling, closed her left eye, squinted at Avi, and sneered. "You and him?"

"Now, now," The Camel said. "Such posturing is unwarranted. Consider your assigned reading from *The Art of War,* IX: 41: *He who exercises no forethought but makes light of his opponents is sure to be captured by them.* A paraphrase," she added, and nodded to Avi. "Sun-tzu."

"You've got to suffer if you wanna sing the blues," Avi added. Why had The Camel agreed to give him three weeks?

"That's the spirit, Susan Junior." The Camel beamed, her smile toxic. "Be obtuse. Works for me."

"Job, job, job, job!" Right Eye threw out her arms and spun non-stop.

"Ah," The Camel noted. "Julie Andrews. Childhood. Song."

"Sister," Left Eye spoke up.

Right Eye twirled twice more, slowing down, her ditziness tinged with dizziness, and then, finished spinning, she hunched over slightly, winded, her body rocked with disequilibrium. "What's the job?" she panted. "Give."

"Yes, Susan Junior," The Camel chimed. "What's the job? Look, she has vertigo."

"The job?"

"The job."

"The job."

"The job. . . ." Avi crossed his arms, a gesture he hoped would seem definitive to the psychotic criminals. Lying to the liars seemed downright sensible, if not ethical. "The job . . . is . . . a woman-hunt."

"Yay!" cried Right Eye. "What's a woman-hunt?" she asked.

"Oh, dear," The Camel said. "Such a waste of a perfectly good physical specimen."

"Hey!" Left Eye said. "I don't think I like that." She closed her left eye to grimace at The Camel.

"Do I like that?" asked Right Eye.

"Girls, girls, girls," The Camel said. "Let us skip the *auto da fé*."

"Okay," Avi interrupted their bickering. "It's a hunt for a woman. We need you to find someone—"

"Because you don't know where she is!"

"My Sister," said Left Eye. "I love you."

"I love you, Sister." They extended their cat-suited arms and hugged.

Oh God. "Right. But we know her name."

"Indubitably." The Camel swung her bat, stayed loose. Avi admired how she had kept the fence between herself and her dimwitted henchwomen, probably more Sun-Tzu. The Careful Camel, who had other reasons for agreeing to wait three weeks, scarier reasons that Avi couldn't guess.

He turned, and waved both hands, one per twin, just because. "Her name is Annie Morrison," Avi lowered his voice to a conspiratorial rasp, looked to The Camel, and with all the stagecraft he could muster, to seal their agreement, he offered a knowing nod. "And she has the list."

The twins let Avi out, pushing him across the Lincoln's big front seat—with a few extra digs from Right Eye, the driver, who refused to slide out, choosing to make him climb over, and who giggled as she pummeled him lightly, one last slap on his butt for good luck. As he crossed the street, the Lincoln revved behind him, but just to be sure Avi turned to watch the enormous car rumble away, the henchwomen waving over their shoulders, their buh-byes synchronized.

And then a white van arrived, gliding into Maureen's driveway, a vehicle both sleek and square next to Avi's whale heap. Right, Avi thought. The wrong whale. Two men sat up straight in the front seat, who knows how many bank robbers slouched in the back—and then, from the van's passenger seat, out hopped Rick, his torso wrapped in a cloth lumbar brace, a gray T-shirt bulging almost ignominiously atop the corset. Amen, Avi exhaled. A man could only take so many circus acts before elevenses.

Without acknowledging Avi, Rick leaned into the van and slid an enormous toolbox from the bank seat, a silvery suitcase that could easily hold a submachine gun.

"'Morning," Avi rasped first.

"'Morning."

Wordlessly, Avi asked, who's the driver?

"Yeah, okay," Rick muttered. He dropped the heavy box in the grass, laid down the chainsaw more carefully, gave a little wriggle in his work girdle, straightened, and nodded toward the open door of the van. Rick had a splintered coffee stirrer pit-bulled between his teeth. "Avi, Henry. Henry, Avi. My truck won't start."

Avi waved hi to the driver, a large man with a cap pulled low over his eyes.

"Uh," Henry said, his gaze fixed elsewhere.

"Likewise," Avi offered. Henry refused to make eye contact, another not-so-happy-go-lucky guy. He was crankier than Rick, or merely paralyzed by a rare Far Eastern poison that only affects manners.

"Ready?" Avi said.

Rick stepped to the van, tapped twice on the paneled side, a motor pool signal, and Henry backed out. Avi waited. "S'why I'm here, dippo," Rick said, pained.

"Hey! No need to be nasty."

"Gonna be," Rick said. "I'm down four smokes."

"Oh my God."

"Live it." Rick munched the coffee stirrer, unlighted. "Doin' those two sisters?"

"Oh my God. Or say crap like that," Avi said. "Don't say crap like that. Don't be a jerk."

Rick's little eyes blazed, little lasers. "Sorry, Boss," he said, almost sincerely. "Five smokes counting now."

"Jesus," Avi said.

"Jesus smoked," Rick said. "Five," Rick said to himself. "Tango minus three. . . . Let's trash this trash—" he pointed to the heap. "Before the delivery.

Ten to two, they'll be here. C'mon, give me something to break."

"Right," Avi said. "Cool," he said to himself, cheered. "Let me get my gloves."

Back in Maureen's kitchen, he opened the back door: Dolly was happy to see him, happy to see him. "Okay, okay, *okaaayyyy*." Avi kneeled to receive Dolly's slobbery kisses, his own lips pursed to keep out the dog germs. "Wow, you need a Milk-Bone," he said, rising. "*Fyak!* Dog breath."

In the pantry, as he reached for the dog treats amidst the various foods he had stocked—the coconut milk, rice vermicelli, artichoke bottoms, good tomato paste, stash of excellent olive oils, Madagascar vanilla, wheat berries and *cous cous*—Avi caught sight of a cookie jar on the top shelf, a crude clay monstrosity befitting a 1960s tract house but apparently not too crude for the late Maureen. He had seen the jar, but never looked inside, not a cookie person. First, Dolly: Avi fed the poor dog a reconstituted meat-bone. And then, even though he was anxious to get outside and wreck the whale that had stabbed him—*Avast! Thus, ho!*—Avi took down the cookie jar and carried it to the kitchen table. He removed the lid: inside, he found a trove of snapshots and letters, rubber-banded mementos and the occasional keepsake (a rabbit's foot keychain, two shiny rocks, and a pair of granny glasses with yellow lenses)—all of which must have mattered to Mom.

He rummaged. There Avi was, in a snapshot with one corner ripped off; on the back, in her awful, extravagant cursive, his mom had written, "Farrington Lake." Avi remembered the trip, the newts along the shore that he had trapped with a plastic bucket, the sandwiches he had made—egg salad? olive loaf?—and stuffed into a grocery bag along with a cooler pack wrapped in paper towels. Maybe he had been twelve. He remembered Dad napping on a blanket in the sand in the sun, burned and bestriped and ornery, but laughing, too. Mom and Dad, as though they might have been happy. . . . Avi tried to remember how they had behaved toward each other at Farrington Lake, but he was pretty sure that the happy part of the memory was his own, and a lie.

In the photo, in an open and easeful, swaggering embrace, a kid grinned iconically, a toothy American junior bumpkin on holiday.

Now Dolly really needed to go out again, stamping and whining, and a bad whale needed to be dismantled: time to get down on it.

Avi lightly rubbed the image of himself with his thumb. He had surprised himself, feeling all that he was feeling. Mom's real stuff, and still no list.

BAM, BAM, BAM, BAM! Avi jumped.

BAM, BAM, BAM, BAM! "C'mon, c'mon!" Rick pounded on the kitchen door. "Time's flying!" *BAM, BAM, BAM, BAM!*

Dolly barked, *"Woof, woof, woof!"*

"Coming!" Avi called. He returned the photos and letters to their cache, for later, hustled to the pantry and stashed his sadness with the jar. Not his guilt, though: his guilt didn't fit in a jar.

BAM, BAM, BAM, BAM!

Unbelievable. To build a whale, he would have to work with a man paid to be a monster, the seemingly calm, stoic Rick undone by nicotine withdrawal, his personality split worthy of a Gothic novel. Avi couldn't believe what was happening: so far, the building of the whale had seemed a dream deterred, a series of trials or tests, poor planning parodied by the predations of psycho criminals . . . and now this, Avi's purposeful hiring of a nicotine-starved, demented foreman. What was a dreamer to do?

"Look. Sorry." The addled contractor opened the door and stuck in his head, owl-faced in a pair of safety goggles, still waggling his chewed-up coffee stirrer, breathless. "Just say go, and I'll chainsaw the sucker. Lemme at her. Green light."

"Go," Avi said. "I'll be right there."

"Yeah!" Rick left, slamming the door too hard.

"Yeah, yeah," Avi repeated to the rattled blinds. "Geez," Avi said to Dolly, who barked obligingly, doing her She Who Needs to Pee dance. "I know. Let's go out. I'll bite him and you bark a lot."

. . .

Work and sweat—Avi and Rick prescribed themselves a proper dose of chainsawing. One man, beset by nut-job criminals and compelled by the unpredictable elements of his dreamworld, whacked away at the wood with hammer and saw; the other, chemically deprived, chainsawed boards and beams whilst quietly cackling with glee. Then wordlessly they traded roles.

Avi felt better. He paused, and leaned on his push broom. In just an hour of hard work, the driveway was almost clean, the dead whale taken apart, pillaged for usable scrap but mostly done. How interesting that in only one week of a man's life, something can be built, a thing almost alive, and in a mere five seconds that thing can collapse, and then in two person-hours of labor, what was once almost a living thing can be made not to exist. How effortless to break things, how hard to make them; how impossible to make something important last. But maybe that's why the builder builds, just so. Working, the impossible seemed a reasonable goal.

He knew he was thinking about death, though. A thing can die in no time; so can a person. He shouldn't stop to think, the Junior Whale Wrecker realized.

"Can you feed me?" Rick looked a bit sallow. "Got any sandwiches?"

"Sure," Avi said. "Just let me finish here." He pointed at three piles of rubble.

"Can't wait," Rick said, as he bolted for the kitchen. "I'll help myself."

Avi waved, sure—"Bread in the drawer, and some ham in the fridge!"—and went back to sweeping, Maureen's trash can mostly full. Time to rent a dumpster, put his feelings in it.

His body would benefit from the physical labor, his arms already tired. Work and sweat, and maybe he could lose his cook's flab, too many cream sauces and too much wine before bedtime settled along his waistline. He scooped and carted a few more scoops. Were he asked, he might admit to having a little fun.

Rick returned, mustard on his face, an ice water in each hand.

"You've got—" Avi pointed, a wiping motion, and accepted the offered drink. "Thanks."

"Yep," Rick wiped. "There wasn't a lot of ham."

They lay on the lawn, break time, admired the empty driveway. Silence worked too.

His water tasted great, and was almost gone. "Got a family?" Avi asked.

"Some," Rick said. "Bad marriage, an ex- and a kid."

"And?"

"And." Rick said. "Got any smokes?"

"Wow," Avi said. "That was almost funny."

"Me neither," Rick said glumly, not listening.

Behind the carport, Dolly could be heard snuffling up something, a big dog on the job, hunting little critters.

"Why you doing this?"

The question was bigger than a whale, Avi thought.

"Hm?"

"It's complicated," Avi said.

"Sure," Rick said, his tone flat. "You're the boss."

"No, I mean . . . it's all wrapped up in stuff. My mom left a crazy will, and there's money if I do something like this—I know, I know, it's nuts—but that's not why, anyway. Not for the money," Avi admitted to himself. "You know how in Egypt there are those pyramids."

"No. Really?"

"Don't be like that," Avi quoted Bean. Bean. . . .

"Fine," Rick said.

"I mean, I guess it's like a memorial or something. I didn't really know my mom very well." Avi was silent, and considered his own silence. "She wasn't the best mom."

"No one's the best mom," Rick said.

"I guess," said Avi.

"All mothers are unknown," Rick said.

"Now look who's the fucking Buddha," said Avi.

Rick almost smiled. "Gotcha."

"Yeah, yeah."

"I like it," Rick said. "Your whale. It's like Mother's Day or something. Her whale."

"Yeah," Avi said. "I guess it was just Mother's Day."

"Naw," Rick said. "Wrong month."

Avi wanted more water. Nice day, even if it did begin with the twins and The Camel's batting practice.

"Gotta get a burn barrel."

"A what?"

"A burn barrel," Rick repeated. "Oil drum. For burning garbage. Feels good."

They were silent again. Avi tongued a piece of ice into his mouth. "We're gonna freak the neighbors," Avi said, and crunched the cube.

"Yep," Rick said.

"Yep," Avi agreed. "Probably illegal."

"Naw," Rick said. "I made a call. S'fixed. Permit's in the works."

The final cube crunched, Avi laughed. "A permit? For a whale? Got a friend at City Hall?"

Rick was pleased. Or not. "Friend of. I used to be a volunteer firefighter."

"Cool," Avi said.

"Seven smokes. Maybe eight." Rick lay back in the grass, his ramrod posture somehow intact. "Dammit," he said to no one.

More ease, the pure product of companionship. Avi closed his eyes for a moment, to listen for the whale. "You know," he began. "Whales do some amazing things. I was reading about one—can't remember which kind—that lifts its tail above the surface and swims. Only sometimes, and the day has to be warm, and it's gotta be windy. They go downwind like that for a long way, and then come back, and do it again. It's called sailing. Can you imagine seeing that? Like you're out for a spin in your dinghy and there it goes. A sixty-foot whale going by like that. Then it comes back to the starting spot and does it again."

"Why?"

"Dunno," Avi said. "No one knows. . . . But they'll sail over and over. Another—scientists played the songs of one whale, a killer whale, so that another could hear it, and the second whale swam away and hid."

"Moby Dick?" Rick asked.

"No," Avi answered. "I think Moby Dick did something else. Killed the one-legged guy. . . . And there's one type of whale that they've found beached, but it's never been seen alive."

"Never?"

"Nope."

"I'd be like that," Rick said.

Avi didn't know what to say. "More water?"

"Later. So what's with the singing? You can buy tapes."

"Yeah," Avi said. "They're humpbacks mostly. It's probably a mating call, but again, it could be other stuff. Sometimes they sing for half an hour."

"Boy," Rick said inscrutably.

"Yeah," Avi said. "I'd like to hear that."

"Put a CD player in her," Rick said.

"Huh?"

"In our whale. Give her a CD player and speakers. Make her sing. Scare away the other whales."

Our whale? Ours? Avi felt a blast of feelings, proprietary and jealous but pleased that Rick had signed on for the duration. Our whale, Avi told himself, to get used to the idea, a kid being taught to share. He smiled up at the big sky. "We'll see," Avi announced. "Maybe she'll sing a song."

CHAPTER EIGHT

· ·

AGAIN, THE TWINS HAD BROKEN into a man's dream, breaking and entering, a window shattered—only this time the man remembered parts of the dream hours later, snippets that returned to him during his manual labors, the repetitive handling of hammer and broom conducive to recall. In the dream, something shiny had beckoned through broken glass, a gem or a stone; someone had taken a picture, and the splash of the flash had lingered on all it touched, the brightness too much, the colors washed out. Luckily, he had been wearing his sunglasses in the dream, although they had seemed to be working in reverse, light and dark switching places, the mirror black.

He was trying to see the dream. He felt like he would be able to see if only that thing would get out of the way.

"Boss," Rick said.

What was that thing? It was huge.

"Boss," Rick said again. "You ain't moving."

Avi had indeed stopped moving; maybe he had even stopped breathing. But now the dream was truly gone. "I . . ." he began. "Damn," he started, startled. "Sorry. Think I was out of it."

"Epilepsy?" Rick's tone was flat.

"No. Just a dream. Dozed off."

Rick's gaze looked pinched. "Dreams are at night, 'cept for crazy people."

"Yep," Avi said. "I wanted to warn you. I've been having wild dreams. I think it's a thing."

"You should fix that," Rick said.

"Tryin'," Avi said.

"Good. Here we go," Rick said.

"What? We're going?" He was flummoxed.

"Supplies," Rick said, chucking his chin toward a truck arriving. "Avon's calling."

Avi rose to greet his new ignorance, his expertise ended for sure. Gloved hands on hips, he watched Rick take over, the contractor's excitement turbo-charged with nicotine withdrawal. Rick waved his arm zestily; one enormous delivery guy and another guy with a strikingly pointy head de-trucked the bulky purchases, the largest items aglow in their plastic wraps. It took a lot of arm waving, some conferring, some rearranging, some sweaty irritation. The pointy-headed guy swore in a language Avi didn't recognize. Finally, the deliverers drove off into the stinky future, their flatbed belching diesel exhaust, their hernias a little less latent.

There was a huge pile of whale makings in front of Maureen's house, ingredients for a dream feast.

"How about it?" Rick asked.

"Okay." Avi managed.

"It stays there."

"Huh?"

"Think?" Rick said, the single word a complicated question Avi couldn't answer. "Doesn't make sense to move it. Not enough storage. So we start with the workbenches, get the ply layered and glued, make those rings. They'll stand up."

"Then make the beams?" Avi said, catching on.

"Yep," Rick said. "Thread the beams through the rings, got a whale."

"How long will it take?" Avi asked.

"Dunno," Rick said. "Thirty cigarettes for each ring, twenty each beam."

"Funny. You said two weeks."

Rick crossed his arms, his T-shirt bunching above his back brace. "Yeah, for the whole thing. But what's a week in whale years?"

Avi didn't answer. Some whales have ten-month gestation periods. Some whales follow ships, and are as curious as dolphins. Some whales are dolphins. A lost childhood was like a mysterious whale.

Okay, he could do this: excited and nervous, he slid a hammer into a loop on his toolbelt, reached into a pouch and found an industrial razor, the term for which eluded him, not a box cutter but something. With a ceremonial *click, click, click, click,* Avi extended the blade and advanced upon the piles of supplies, those various unmatched parts of his life lying curbside at his late mother's house, everything in ready disarray. This whale would be for Mom, he thought.

"Whatcha doing?"

Avi stopped, the epic moment undone. "Uh . . . workbenches, right?"

"Right," Rick said. "Those." He pointed to where Avi wasn't headed. "There."

"Gotcha," Avi said, sheepish. "Maybe you better go first," Avi allowed.

"Yep. Planning to."

They assembled each of the workbenches in the driveway, ferried the smaller items to the carport, hauled the expensive, easy-to-steal power tools out of crime's way, the remembered admonition probably not what Dad had ever said—"Don't leave your tools lying around"—but there, associated with Dad regardless. Dad was more dead than Mom and missed more deeply but less frequently. Or maybe there's only so much love.

The workbenches looked like a squadron of aliens awaiting rescue by a mother ship. Nearby, Avi and Rick unwrapped and laid out the first six sheets of ply, the tongue-and-groove joinery needed for the bottom so that the assembled sixteen-by-twelve-foot layer wouldn't have to be lifted off the workbenches (too heavy, that), just power-stapled and Liquid Nailed, and then the second big layer could be laid atop, screwed and Liquid Nailed, and then the third. After that the excitement would begin: Rick and Avi would cut into the three-ply ply right there where the three-ply ply lay, cut giant concentric wooden rings, the dream whale made possible at last as a graduated series of huge circles, big ol' donuts to be threaded by sixty-four-foot-long beams, or chopsticks.

Everything had to be translated out of builder-speak, Avi realized. Rick-speak.

Avi picked up a tube of Liquid Nails, a product unfamiliar to him from his high school summering amidst the Anders family, contractors and Swedes, their straight-A daughter a failed objective, her lifeguarding suntan more important than Avi ever could be, all that white stuff on her nose. "Eliminates squeaky floors*" was written on the adhesive's label, the asterisk corresponding to the instructive phrase, "*To eliminate squeaky floors, please follow the directions below." Sensible, the fine print resembled a recipe—"Where sheet butts along joist lay one zigging one-quarter-inch bead"—and might even be one, for mille-feuille. Avi was bemused. It was once someone's job in the front office of a factory in Cleveland to write the copy on the Liquid Nails, and to add a bold print warning to the label, "Do not smoke. Vapors may ignite explosively."

Rick had taken a bathroom break and now returned. He was a tall guy who moved in small ways, everything close to the body. Avi wondered how long the hearing loss had been there, since there was no sign of a speech impediment, and how Rick had responded to being prescribed a hearing aid, proud Rick smoking his way through news of the inevitable as he paced outside the audiologist's clinic. Luckily, the hearing aid worked well, aside from those irritating squeals—or whatever it was that made Rick tap the little plastic escargot and swear—even if the man did have a tendency to tip his head while listening, and favor that side.

Or the hearing aid was a fake, tuned to a crime catcher's station, WFBI. Whoever liked to catch bank robbers would surely be checking in with Rick, dialing up the contractor and leaving a message. Avi would have to run interference, he realized. Bean might be at risk.

"I'da made a sandwich," Rick was upset. "But I ate the bread."

"Gotcha," Avi said. "I'll make us some pasta later."

"I like spaghetti," Rick said.

"Me too. Say, Rick . . . are you a Fed?"

Rick stopped and stared at Avi.

"You know, like the hearing aid's an earpiece and you're a Fed."

"A Fed?"

"Yeah."

Rick smiled, put a hand on Avi's shoulder. "No, Boss. I sure as hell ain't a Fed. I work for you, remember?"

"Yeah," Avi believed him. "So you'd tell me if you were a Fed, wouldn't you?"

Rick thought a moment. "Naw," Rick said. He moved his hand away. "That'd spoil it. But if I were a Fed, I'd make you get a haircut," Rick said. "Feds can do those things."

"Aw, man," Avi said. "Don't be like that."

"Then let me smoke." Rick's teeth were gritted again. "I'm not a Fed," he said again. "Promise."

• • •

Consider the sudden spectacle of a sixty-four-foot-long and sixteen-foot-high wooden whale, the skeleton of which shall rise in the driveway of an ordinary house. The house means nothing, with its yellow vinyl siding and faux black shutters, green grass, a dog in the yard barking at what only she sees— and then the bulky bones of an enormous whale appear, a behemoth whose dreamed gargantuan flippers and fluke wrap around the corner, the wooden mammal so long as to be angled pleasingly at 10°. How small the house would seem then, and how trivial the neighbors' chrysanthemums. The park across the way would look empty, even on a Soccer Saturday. But when it's all done and said, what a moment that shall be, when two sweatily awestruck whale-builders stand in the gloaming and clink flutes of bubbly.

Avi could almost taste the Krug, even here at the end of Day One. Man, he was tired. A whale of a tired. Tiredness was a whale.

"I've gotta have a smoke," Rick said. "I'm dying."

"Can't."

"Can."

Avi was helping Rick pack up his tools. The day had gone somewhere days go, sweated away to sunset. "Need a lift?" Avi changed the subject.

"No shit. Truck's towed. Drop me at the garage?"

"You bet," Avi said, aching to shower and eat and fall down but happy to help.

Avi let Dolly out of the yard and threw open the Toyota's back door. She did two crazy dog spins before launching herself into the vehicle. He rolled down her window, so she could smell every scent, 1000 times what humans smell. Must be fun.

Aside from the occasional *left* and *right*, the conversation between the two men and the dog remained silent. The radio was off, the streetlights had just come on, the sky fell apart in barbecue colors, in embers, the sight more than anything to say. Two men and a dog saying nothing was probably not Avi's and Rick's and Dolly's invention, but somehow the car ride together felt new and unabashed.

The lights of the other cars on the road began to point their way through the streets. Late commuters, Avi presumed, those who started in the morning and drove to work in Raleigh, toiled into the evening, and then sped back to Elsbeth, followed home their own trails of crumbs. Hansels and Gretels, and a dead witch.

He dropped Rick at a service station, Rick's truck parked out front, and waited for the wave that said, *Yes, see ya' tomorrow, truck's ready,* a wave that arrived. Dolly watched as well, her head out the window. Avi waved back, his wave saying more: *Thanks for your help. I had a good day.*

He pulled into traffic on 83, where the streetlights had brightened as the darkness filled in. Avi was exhausted and sore, and a prisoner of his own restlessness; wherever his thoughts went, so went Avi. A certain looseness in his muscles furthered the impression, the tiredness ever-present. He could stop nothing.

This was dreaming, he supposed. He had spent the day trading places with his whale, a whale becoming real.

· · ·

She was standing at the side door, hip cocked, her brown satchel matching the very wide belt that wrapped around her dazzling white tunic over dazzling white pants and very high heels, a so-Parisian scarf knotted around her neck, flaunting a very low opinion of Avi and his late arrival. "You bastard," she said. "My boyfriend."

Avi forced a smile as he approached, but was also glad to see her. Only Mimou would travel all in white and not get dirty.

"Kiss me," she grabbed his shirt. *Hfffff*, she inhaled as she nuzzled his neck. "Oh, I like when you smell so bad."

"Mi—"

She tilted her head to Avi's and kissed him deeply, grinding. She sucked a little on his lower lip, then—*pop!*—released him. "Aha!" she said.

"Hello," he managed.

"Bastard. I am here to leave you!" Mimou pushed him away.

Avi didn't know what to say. He found the house key, opened the door. "Glass of wine?"

"*Oui, merci,*" she said. Then she looked into the kitchen, as Avi switched on the light. "Oh, what a terrible house! Who would live in such a place?"

"*Woof!*" said Dolly, muscling by.

"Uh. Go on, you big doggie."

"*Woof!*" Dolly said, and collapsed by her water bowl to lap away.

"How can I work in this condition?" Mimou dropped her satchel on the floor with a loud thump and threw up her hands. "This is barbarical!"

"Barbaric?" Avi asked, regretting immediately the correction.

"BASTARD! You do not say anything nice to Mimou, there are no flowers, and I AM FORTY!" She started to sniff, sniffle, and finally to cry, or seemed to do so. "I am forty. Mimou. . . ."

"It's okay," Avi said. "I have a good wine."

"A wine," she snorted into a tissue pulled from a sleeve. "I want a glass of wine. What is it?"

"A Tempranillo," Avi said. "It'll be okay."

"You are a bastard," she pouted. "A Tempranillo."

"Yes, I probably am," Avi agreed.

"You think nothing of me. I am nothing to you. You are not French."

"That is not so," Avi said. "You are very important to me."

"Bastard," she twirled away from him, unappeased, and with a flourish removed her big belt, gave it a snap in the middle of the kitchen, and then dropped the belt upon the floor with a dramatic little flick. "It is not so. Give me some wine and show me where is *la salle de bain*. I will make myself pretty for you, and we shall fuck. *Non?*"

"Yes." Avi was relieved, her aria apparently over. "I like how pretty you are now," he added.

"*D'accord,*" Mimou said. "*Je suis arrivée.* Please get my suitcase, it is outside."

Avi knew the order of Mimou's universe. She would bathe, he would shower, they would drink a bottle of wine and nibble on whatever the best nibbles he had bought might be, and then they would have sex—pretty good sex—before Mimou would cook. Mimou, who could look at a cake or a pastry and tell you its ingredients along with their proportions, would make something simple and spectacular. Something with a little sauce or surprisingly nutty, just the right combination of texture and taste, with the wine in mind. It was likely that she had brought good butter.

Or maybe she would want more to drink, a second bottle, and Avi would cook. No matter the post-coital plan, always, before and after, he would be quiet near her, a spectator of sorts, eleven years younger and surprised to be her lover.

He stepped into the backyard to let Dolly out to poop, and sipped his wine as Mimou stomped up the stairs. A peppery enough little red. Again, he reminded himself, he had to get to the wine store. Wine was important. But so was manual labor and muscle ache followed by wine and sex, and having Mimou here on the evening of the first day. Day One, on the high seas of the driveway.

Avi raised his glass. "To you," he toasted his whale. "To us." And then he had a funny thought: "To the Whale-o-seum."

• • •

He might have stayed in the shower for an hour, the water felt so good. The spray seemed a miracle. He wasn't thinking, he realized. It was good not to think. Just as well, too, with a naked Mimou fluffing pillows on the bed.

Avi tried to not-remember: he had kissed Bean.

"Avi, Avi, I am so desolate. I have been so alone, and this place"—she gestured to Maureen's furnishings, but meant her kitchen, as always—"it is not good for you. You must cook! I know, I know. . . ." she turned away from him and muttered something to herself in French, too long a sentence for Avi to follow, ". . . it is your own *Maman*, and you must be a man. But the sadness here is everywhere—and I am forty! What do I have? What is there for Mimou. . . ?"

Avi sat on the bed, put his hand on her knee. "It's okay. Here." Her wine.

"I am forty and you are a soccer mom!"

"A what?"

"Is that not the word? A soccer mom?"

"No," he tried to laugh. Damn, he was tired.

"So what are you? I am forty," she announced as though being brave, straightening up and thrusting out her chin.

"What am I?" Avi repeated.

"*Oui.*"

"I guess. . . ."

"You see! You do not know—you guess."

"What?" He was having trouble following. He had half an erection, Mimou was naked, and he might yet be too tired for all of this, even just to talk.

"You do not know, and so Mimou will tell you. And then we will have sex and I will leave you."

"You'll what?"

"We drink wine and fuck and drink and eat, and then I leave. *À demain.* That is why I am here. I am forty, and you know nothing about life. You are such a boy—*c'est vrai.* You cook and you learn, and I think you will be a good chef and Mimou wants to help you, but now you are a soccer mom. Come to me," she held out her arms. "*Je suis arrivée.*"

"You're breaking up with me?" He reached forward and kissed her, a little kiss, and then moved his hand to her breast. "Really?" Avi was confused. "This is break-up sex?"

"Tomorrow I will leave, and you will not have Mimou again." She shifted side to side, her breast cupped, rubbing herself in his hand. "We fuck and break up. It is French. Here," she handed him his glass. "So when you finish at the *Enstitute,* I will get you a good job—and you will finish and be a chef, *non?* But close the door, your dog, she is hateful. A big American dog has no panache and will jump on me if I make loud feelings. . . . Now kiss Mimou," she added. "I will show you."

· · ·

"What is that?"

They were into the second bottle, a pretty good chicken piccata dinner devoured, Mimou ready as ever to stay up all night. The moon was high, and it filled the sky like something spilled. Avi and Mimou were out back, he was shirtless, but wearing her big brown belt for no reason he could muster, and so tired he could sleep right here, standing up like a cow.

"What?"

"You are building?"

"Oh, that. It's a project."

"Avi. I know it is a project. What?"

"It's . . . it's difficult to explain." He didn't want to tell her.

"Mimou understands." She took a long sip of her wine, chewed it a bit, strolled in the grass, her bare feet wet and almost glowing. "*Mmph,*" she snorted. "You make a gymnasium. For the exercise."

Avi had to laugh, which made him shiver. He followed her into the yard. "No, I don't think—"

"You don't think, you don't think. You should not say that—you say it all the time. A Frenchman, he thinks!" She twirled to confront him.

"I . . ."

"You say that you think and you are much sexier. You see, I know that you are a man and not a boy, but you do not have that French passion. Or you do?" She peered at him.

"I think I do," Avi said.

"You think! You think!" She spun away again.

"It's a whale," he said. "My project. I'm building a big whale."

"A what?"

"A whale. In the ocean, you know?"

"Pinocchio?"

"Yes, Pinocchio," Avi laughed. "Not really," he said.

"It is crazy," Mimou said. "You know, I like its building. *Je comprends.*"

"You do?" Avi sighed. "God, I wish I did."

"You will," Mimou said. "I am forty. We do things and then we understand them, and now when I am forty, I understand things before I do them. You will understand. Mimou is forty. . . ." She shook her head. "*Merde.*"

And with a sudden blast of something inside her, she threw her glass up in the air, the last of her wine splashing up into the moonlight and down into the grass, a gesture Avi knew at once that he would remember always when he would think of her, Mimou in the backyard of Mom's stupid little house, the whale in the driveway in its natural habitat under the moon.

· · ·

A bad morning, last night's drinking unforgiving. What was it with Avi and psycho chicks? When with Mimou, he was not who he wanted to be—which he had realized again last night, but hadn't acted upon. Now he was pissed at her. A boy? Perhaps he was. Dammit. Okay, he admitted to himself, he was pissed at her for saying that.

Rick was in the driveway when Mimou and Avi stepped into the morning glare, her flight three hours off. Avi had offered to drive her to the airport, and had even tried to insist in light of the Homeland Security Threat Level, whatever level it was, but she was having no more of him—a taxi would be fine. First, of course, she had to see his project and meet the man out there.

"Hey," Rick said.

"Hey," said Avi.

"*Bonjour!*" chirped Mimou.

"This is Rick. Rick, this is Mimou."

"*Enchanté,*" she cooed.

"How d'ya do."

"You are—how do you say it—Mr. Fix It?"

"A carpenter?" Avi tried.

"Contractor," Rick said.

"Oh, show me how!" Mimou was altogether too cheery. She dropped her satchel and half-skittered and half-sashayed to the driveway. All in fuchsia this morning, something silky, her outfit matched itself beautifully and nothing nearby, the colors of the whale zone decidedly more industrial. She was one of the classiest people Avi knew who never dressed all in black.

"Boss Man?"

Avi shrugged.

"Gotcha. . . . Ma'am, those aren't toys. Ma'am! Excuse me!"

The hour couldn't have been stranger: Rick gnawed his coffee stirrer, Avi tried to be nice to Mimou and tried to be in charge of the worksite at the same time, but yielding, always yielding. Nothing was accomplished, much to Rick's evident irritation—that is, nothing except Avi's continued surrender to the lover who had just dumped him, his embarrassment nearly fatal but unfortunately not quite.

"Then glue and screws."

"*Comment?* Why two?" She had put on a toolbelt—Avi's—and was swinging her hips so that the hammer banged around her butt. The work gloves had been rejected: no pastry chef wears gloves to work.

"Wood'll spit screws and glue's not enough." Rick tried to steer her out of the carport, clearly fed up with explaining.

Avi took the hint: "Mimou, your flight?"

She resisted them both, and with a twist shook her elbow from Rick's helpful grasp. "Avi. Rick. Am I a person, yes?" She looked at her watch. "*Merde!* My airplane! Avi, quick, call a car! You are terrible, not to tell me. Mimou will miss the tasting!"

He drove her anyway, and quickly, which she had of course wanted from the outset. Glum and irritated, Avi moped behind the wheel, her cajoling notwithstanding, her sexiness expired.

"Avi, you are not like you. What is this cloudy face? How do you say, turn it upside down?"

"Mimou, I just don't want to talk, okay?"

"Okay, we will not talk. You are angry with Mimou. We have had no sex today, yes?"

"No."

"For leaving you! For talking to your friend. You are jealous!"

"No. . . . I mean, yes. . . . I mean, I don't know."

She put her hand on his arm. "My boy—"

"Don't call me that. I'm not a fucking boy."

Mimou's eyes widened. "*Oui*," she said. Her hand fell from his arm. "It is true."

Avi glared at the road, the airport never close enough. He didn't like himself much.

"I come to leave you, and you get macho? No, no, Avi."

"Mimou—"

"I might have to call you again."

"Please," Avi said. "It's just . . . you're great, Mimou, and fun. I'm going to miss you, that's all." A break-up lie.

"Avi, Avi. Of course. Everyone misses Mimou. It is my character. Now give me a kiss with your tongue and I think of you the whole plane."

NINE

· ·

TWO MEN CAN BUILD A LOT OF WHALE in eight days. Twelve enormous rings, two-and-one-quarter inches thick, leaned against each other in Avi's dead mother's driveway, an abstract of their future form. The beams were next—beams that would fill the yard with a huge whale tail. Good thing Mom had a corner lot, location, location.

Avi smiled at the thought. He stood at the edge of the construction zone, and flexed and rubbed his sore left bicep appreciatively. How much of a whale is muscle? he wondered. How much is technically its tail?

"Day off?"

Avi started. "Yeah," he said to Bean as he turned around. "Hi. You're back."

"Hi."

She was wearing another flowing long skirt with shiny things sewn in, and a scooped mauve T-shirt. He was sure that she smelled good.

"How was your trip? Break any laws?"

"Only a few," she nodded. Was she kidding?

"But you knew this was my day off," Avi said, the statement its realization.

"Guess so," she shrugged.

"My Ramona," Avi said, testing his paranoia. "*My, my, my, my. . . .*" He accompanied his poor rendition of the Cars song with strumming.

"Please don't," Bean said. "Yes, Ramona."

Avi stopped. Not smooth. "Ah." He said. "Coffee?"

"Love some," she said. "None of that, okay? I have a slight allergy to white-boy air guitar. At least you didn't suck in your lip."

At the kitchen table, elbow propped, facing off with Bean, Avi considered his approach. Bean was a liar, a bank robber, a New Age goofball, and someone who seemed to be honest about her feelings. What the hell. He liked her—and he hadn't heard a squeak from Mimou since her squeaky departure last week. By comparison, Avi was only a liar, an assistant contractor, a fool separated from his mother's money.

"How's the whale?" Bean's eyes twinkled. "Looks good."

"Getting there."

She thought about that, or maybe she didn't, as she toyed with her spoon. "You know," she began, "I'm here on business."

"I know."

"Right," Bean agreed.

"Right. More coffee?"

"No thanks." She waited. "I can't believe it. You're so much like your mother."

"I guess," he guessed, his tone meaner than intended.

"Really," she said, hands up. "I'm innocent, your Honor. I want the list, and seeing you again, I want to kiss you, and you're a lot like Susan, and I'm not supposed to tell you that? Avi, you don't have to give me the list. I promised you could build your whale, remember? But you're glowing again, and it turns up when I get near you, and that's very, very cool. I mean I can almost see the letters, and I'm not even meditating. Look, no Lotus position!" She waved her hands.

"You want to kiss me?" Avi smiled.

She giggled. "*Mmm.* Maybe."

"I want to kiss you," he said. "I broke up with my girlfriend," he added. "That was a nice speech."

"Ohhhhhh," Bean said. "I heard she dumped *you.*"

"Crap! That Ramona! What the—?"

"Avi, calm down. I'm only teasing you. I hadn't heard anything—just an intuition. But seriously though, if she dumped you, tell me. You tell Bean the truth, or you don't say anything. Silence or the truth. Deal?"

"That's how criminals work?" He sipped, then wiped his mouth with a napkin.

"Oh, I don't know. I've told you the truth, or I've not told you. It's how I work."

"Okay," Avi agreed. "She dumped me. Now can we kiss?"

"No," Bean smiled. "I said I *wanted* to kiss you, but I didn't say I *would.*"

Cool. "So, wanna see the list?"

Bean stared at him.

"*Hmm?*"

"You found it!"

"No," Avi said. "Just thought I'd ask."

Bean laughed. "Susan Junior. How about we go upstairs! It's your day off!"

"Why?"

"Sex, Avi! I'm ready!"

. . .

Avi led Bean to the guest bedroom, unwilling to bring a new lover to his late mother's bed where he and Mimou had last slept together—too many weird feelings to consider. Superstitious or stupid, he thought, but Bean understood, or simply didn't ask.

"Undress me?" she said, and put her arms up over her head.

He bent forward and kissed her cheek. He was glad he had just showered.

"Oh, my," she said, and turned so that her mouth found his, her arms still raised, but then lowered and forgotten.

Bean's lips were soft and firm and pliant: that's what Avi remembered as they kissed. She wore no bra: that's what he knew. Her body had some mass in the hips and thighs: Avi enjoyed her hips.

Well, hell, he enjoyed it all.

In the midst of their slow grinding, and then more active rubbing, Bean reached toward him with both hands, and then stopped moving, his face between her palms. They looked into each other's eyes. He couldn't decide if he liked her eyes more than her nose, and then he forgot again to decide.

Their sex was sweet and giggly. She was funny, Bean the sexy Bean. At one point, Avi lay on top—missionary—but she didn't want that for long. "I'm not very religious," she explained breathily.

When he felt her closer, almost even there, Avi slid down, back onto the bed, so that he could enjoy more of her and move to match her deeper desire. He did so, and he did so.

After a long, decompressing silence, Bean touched his cheek with one finger.

"Miss Bean," Avi said.

"Yesssss," she purred. "Me too."

"Mm-hmm."

"But don't let it do your thinking," she said.

"Mm?"

"You know." She gave him a little kiss. "You have a whale to build, and as of now, we can have sex any time."

. . .

He found Bean sitting on the floor of the sewing room, next to a happily keeled over Dolly.

"It's all banking documents. I don't understand what they mean," Avi said from the doorway. His hair was wet from the shower.

Dolly raised her head and thumped her tail on the carpet.

"That's the point," Bean petted Dolly and looked up at Avi. "Innocent look-ing documents on actual forms and letterhead, all legal until the scheme un-ravels. *If,*" she added emphatically as she picked up a folder. "But it doesn't."

Avi crossed his arms. "Who you stealing from?"

"Banks—not people."

Her T-shirt was taut. He really liked her neck. "So . . . how do you justify it?"

"I don't," Bean said.

"Right. No one gets hurt. Victimless."

Bean turned fully this time, to check his expression. "You disapprove?"

Dolly did: she offered a disgusted *grrr-uh*, which meant *scratching, please.*

"I dunno," Avi admitted. "Do you give it all away, Maid Marian?"

"Are you kidding?"

"Yeah," he had to say. "I must be."

She reached for Dolly again, petted the flopped big dog. They liked each other. With her other hand Bean picked up a piece of paper, one of the Inter-bank deposit tickets over which Avi had puzzled. "This is the key," she said. "Susan Woodley," Bean read the name reverentially. And then, glancing up at the wall of boxes, her tone changed: "Wonder why she kept all this? What was she thinking?" She paused, her expression changing. "Dammit, Avi, who the hell are you to judge me? What do you know about me? You think that being a bank robber is easy to live with? You think that I can sleep at night with the law always on my tail, and that my relatives don't need the neat bundles of cash I leave for them in the dead drop, all under $10,000 of course, and that being able to support seven people, two on disability and another a gambler, is something you can judge? I'm thirty-two."

Avi didn't know what to say. "Sorry?" he offered. "I'm twenty-nine."

"Better be," Bean said. "'Cept."

"'Cept what."

"'Cept I made it up! Get a life, Junior: you may be cute, and all glowy and fun in the sun, but you sure are naive." Bean fell over with a groan and a giggle to lie next to the dog, who got a full rub and rolled to accept, yes, please, nice person. "Willikers!" Bean laughed. "I'm never telling you the truth again! Well, except for the part about my being thirty-two, and my relatives, and Aunt Lin-da on Social Security, and her—what's it called—disadvantaged daughter, Shel. No, that's not the word."

"I'm fun in the sun?" He smiled.

She beamed at him. "Well, I thought so."

"Me too," Avi said. "You too." They gazed at each other, sex-stoned.

"So sell me the list?"

He shook his head. "You know I don't have it. Besides, that won't work with me," Avi said. "I'm not some little boy." He was talking to Mimou too, he realized.

"I don't understand," Bean said.

"Sex," he said. He shook his head, not making sense. "I'm not a slut."

"Fuck, Susan Junior. You could be a *person*." She sat up, Dolly's rub-down done. "I mean, really, that was good sex! Think about all the energy here. Your Soul Diary isn't where you write about your day." She paused. "You and Rick have a whale to build . . . and I'm here for more than the list."

"You are?"

"I am. I saw it written. . . ." She glanced away, blushing. Dolly rolled around on her back and asked for more, *grrr-uh* and *rrr-uh*. "I can't tell you. Anyway," Bean brightened. "I have a life to save."

He was so confused. Avi looked up: the ceiling of the sewing room had little swirls that probably had been hand-sponged into the paint, a decorative touch he had never noticed. Crap, he was such a dope with women he liked. But he really appreciated how clear she made things seem, and how uncomplicated she was for a nutcase—except, of course, for the half-stories that were never explained. Which meant that he'd have to think and feel straight for himself— not a bad goal. He lowered his gaze to look at Bean again. She smiled; she had been waiting for him. "I'll try to be . . . clear," he said. "But what do you mean, a life to save?"

"I have a life to save," she repeated. "You know, silly. Yours."

. . .

Sometime late in the afternoon, Dolly roused from her nap to head-butt Avi, anxious for her kibble, and when served, lowered her great dog self onto the kitchen floor to hug the big bowl while she chowed. As he watched, Avi began to think about cooking: he had made breakfast for the twins, a nice dinner for Bean, and three simple pasta dishes for Rick. Not yet for The Camel—what does a Camel eat? Something indigenous, given her predilections, something *nouvelle Americain*, something more regional than artisanal. Maybe he could forage for some Navaho mushrooms, or harvest and husk corn for pone, or bag a wild turkey and stuff it with cranberries and pecans.

He had made a deal with Bean, over avocado, sprouts, and jack sandwiches at lunch: "You're welcome to look, but if you find the list, it's still mine."

She had agreed. "So long as I get to bid."

"Are you kidding? You can buy it. It's just not finders, keepers." Plus, $500,000 for the orphan fund, he thought.

Bean had nodded, started to reach for her water glass, and adjusted her motion. He could see the neurological deficit, and how she lived with her clumsiness, how she had to take such care, her motions necessarily thoughtful.

"Lovers are," she had said quietly.

"Lovers are what?"

"Lovers are finders, keepers." Her gaze had remained lowered; she had sipped her water. "Even when you're not together anymore. You'll always be lovers."

Now, with the light fading o'er the whale, Bean on her cell phone in the living room, Avi stood in the kitchen and considered dinner. He opened the pantry, saw the ugly cookie jar—and felt flooded by a memory. Avi had worked a paper route, his first job, and one that he hated. But the first naked woman Avi had seen (he couldn't recall her name, Mrs. Up-the-Street) had been on that paper route, Avi probably twelve-years-old. Collecting, a heavy envelope of change in hand, he had buzzed a doorbell and been greeted by a naked woman, her face streaked and shiny. Had she been crying? Maybe she had been drunk.

The naked woman had said, "Oh, it's you."

"Um . . . collect?"

"Ta-da!" She had thrown wide her arms, Mrs. Up-the-Street with breasts.

A naked housewife beset by more than she could say: the memory made Avi sad, and a little horny again. Bean.

He wanted to tell Bean everything, how he would never forgive himself. All of the post-coital melodrama was his: all his self-loathing was basking in the light of sex.

Maybe he should just make a nice chicken dish—he had a package of free-range thighs—something lemony and balanced with cherry tomatoes and baby summer squash, a delicate riff on Sal Ferrar's Northern Italian stewed chicken-and-zucchini, only with a pinch of oregano, Sal the Executive Chef at the Blue Egg ham-fisted with herbs. Avi and Bean could repair to the carport to finish their wine, the whale almost singing.

And then there was a tremendous *BANG!* followed by several violent smaller bangs, and then another *BANG!* and then the side door rattled. What should he do? Avi stepped into the pantry and turned off the light: the kitchen went suddenly fuzzy and dark. He left the door open a crack.

"Sister!"

"Here! Sister?"

"Here."

Crashing into Maureen's kitchen, the henchwomen pushed a huge long bag on a kind of lab cart. They were dressed completely in blue denim: pants, shirts, and matching berets. One blond pigtail each, very Patty Hearst meets Lady Gaga.

From the backyard, Dolly barked, *"Woof!"*

"Avi, what's going on—?" Bean walked into the kitchen, bad timing.

The twins were his problem: Avi stepped out of the pantry. *"Ahhhemmm,"* he cleared his throat.

"The Victim!"

"Hello," Bean said. "What were you doing in there? Are you coming out of the closet?"

"Who's she?" growled a twin.

"You know her, Sister."

"I do?"

One of the twins held a golf club, which she used to point at Bean. "She quit."

"Oh, the quitter. Can I hurt her?"

"Yes," said Snow White, she with the putter. "Soon," she said. She pointed her club at Avi. "I know what you've been doing. What's in there?" she pointed at the pantry.

"Nothing," Avi said. "Cans."

"After I hurt her, can I hurt him?"

"Sister, I told you—we need him for now."

"Right, Sister. You're so clever."

"And pretty?"

"You're so pretty." Rose Red began to twirl: she was definitely Rose Red, the twin who spins. "Like my outfit?"

"Woof! Woof, woof!" said Dolly at the door.

Bean looked scared, but who knew. "What can I do for you ladies?" Avi asked.

"Do for us? We know what you've been doing."

Rose Red twirled once more, stumbled, righted herself, just a tad dizzy, one spin too many. *"Wuuuh,"* she said. "And Manny—tell him about Manny. Oh, goody, goody!"

"Yes, Sister. Victim—" the putter indicated the huge bag on the cart. "We found your Manny."

"You found my Manny?" he repeated.

"Yes, yes, yes! Manny, Manny, fo-fanny."

"Manny's a woman, you know." Snow White winked. Their bruises had faded, or been covered up with make-up. Or the twins were Cylons.

"A woman?"

"Manny's Annie."

"I don't understand," Avi said. He didn't.

Rose Red squatted to peer through the door at Dolly, who was scratching to be let in. "When he's dead, can I have this dog?"

"Yes," Snow White answered her twin.

"*May* I," corrected Bean.

"Not you," Rose Red said.

"Yes," Snow White said. "When he's dead, the dog's yours."

"I'll name the dog Larry. Or Barry. I beat up someone named Barry once; wasn't that the umbrella guy? But when *he's* dead"—she looked at Avi—"who will make me oatmeal?"

"Good question, Sister! The Victim—"

"Stop it!" Avi had to interrupt. He had figured out their gibberish. "You found Annie Morrison?"

"Yes," the twins shouted, just out of unison. Rose Red giggled.

"And?"

"And."

"And!"

"And we brought her here!" She poked the big rolled-up package, which squirmed.

Oh, crap, there was someone in there! "Oh, crap!" Avi said.

"Jesus!" Bean said.

"We're here to nip it in the butt," Snow White said.

TEN

· ·

UNWRAPPED, LAID OUT ON THE SOFA in Mom's living room, still tied up, blindfolded and gagged, a woman in a beige-orange pantsuit lay quietly on her side, one foot twitching occasionally. She looked like an enormous, sad, farm-raised salmon. An Orca would eat a salmon; an Orca wasn't a whale, technically.

"Annie Morrison," Snow White said proudly, as the twins, Avi, and Bean ringed the sofa.

"Shit," said Bean. She took Avi's hand.

"What's *your* name then?" Snow White turned to Bean. "You. The quitter." She pointed with her putter.

"Mi Ha," said Bean.

"Mi Ha?" Rose Red sneered. "That's not a real name."

"Mi Ha." Snow White repeated. "She's the quitter," she added to no one.

"It's Chinese," said Bean.

"I've never seen her before," Avi said. "You've got the wrong Annie."

"Oh, sure," Rose Red said. "Now you tell us."

There was a long silence.

"Never?" Snow White's voice had shrunk slightly.

"No," Avi said. "Who is she?"

"Annie, Manny, pizza pie," said Rose Red. "I'm going to kill . . . *her!*" she pointed at Bean.

"Sister . . . later." The twins exchanged a glance, confused. "So she's not—?" Snow White stopped herself. "But that's Annie Morrison."

"No," Avi said.

"Uh-oh," said Rose Red.

"You blew it," Avi said. "Wrong Annie."

"*Mmm,*" said the real victim, jostling her bonds. "*Uhm-mmm-hm-mm-mm-phmp. Mmmmm-mm! PHMMMMPHHH!*"

"What'd she say?" asked Snow White. The four unbound people stared

118

down at the twins' bound bystander.

"*Umph-mmm-phmmppphhh,*" said Rose Red. She worried the end of her pig-tail.

"You kidnapped her?"

The twins nodded solemnly together, bobble-heads.

"She said that she wants to go home now," Bean offered.

"Ask her if she's hungry," Rose Red said.

"Oh my God," said Avi.

"Are you hungry?" said Bean.

"*Mmm-ppp-mmph.*"

"She's not. She misses her cat," said Bean.

"Sister. . . ."

"Ask her if she knows the real Annie Morrison?"

"Do you know the real Annie Morrison?" Bean had a great deadpan.

"*MMMMM! Phhhmmmpp! BBBBPHHHMPPP!*"

"Nope," said Bean.

"Sister, let us think about this. Twin Power."

"Twin Power!" Rose Red exclaimed, and they strode off together to the kitchen, leaving behind Avi, Bean, a stray denim beret, and a kidnapped innocent.

He let go of Bean's hand. "I'm so sorry," Avi said to the woman. He wanted to untie her, but thought that might be a bad idea, and since he didn't want her to see his face, the blindfold had to stay on too. "They're insane," he reassured her.

"We have to get her out of here," Bean whispered. Green Bean with the green eyes.

"I know," Avi whispered. "And them. This is nuts!"

The swinging door swung once more: "Okay," said Rose Red. "Here's the deal. Sister. . . ."

"We're hungry," said Snow White. "You make us dinner and then we'll take her back to the store."

"Oh my God," Avi couldn't help himself. "Back to the store."

"A good dinner!" Rose Red chirped.

"Burritos!" Snow White squealed.

"I don't want burritos," Rose Red snapped.

"Fine."

"Fine."

"Fine."

"Fine."

"Stop," said Avi. He held up his hand. "I'm not making you anything."

"Ask her if she can wait," Snow White commanded Bean.

"Can you wait?" Bean said.

"*MMMMM! PPPPHHHMMMPPPPH! MMM-MMM-MMM, UMMM-PHP-MMMPPHHH PPP! UUUUUMMMMMMMMMPPPPPHHH!*"

"She says she can't wait," Bean reported. "Because sometimes the cat likes to swat the goldfish in the bowl in the dining room, if the cat's been alone for too long, and she doesn't want that to happen again, so please hurry."

"*Ummph,*" said the wrong Annie Morrison with a slump, her shoulders raised and then lowered, disgusted, her body trussed on her namesake's sofa. "*Phmmp.*" Or not her namesake. On her alias's sofa. Or not her alias's. On the sofa of the dead woman who had used Annie Morrison as an alias.

"Girls," Avi said. "Get her out of here. Take her back to the store."

"I'm going to kick you," Rose Red said. She picked up her beret. "You stole my hat," she wagged the denim cap at Avi.

Why was Avi not afraid? Why did he think that he could handle this situation, rather than call the police? What made him take charge? He was curious, he was irritated; the twins were fucking crazy, which scared Avi, but not enough to keep him scared. He was feeling otherwise; all he needed was Ramona to call so that he could hang up.

Kidnapping was a crime. Bank robbery was another crime. If he called the police, Bean would leave. He liked Bean: he liked having sex with Bean. But he was rationalizing. His heart beat faster. If he called the police, and the whole situation fell to pieces, Avi might not get to finish his whale, the dream incomplete. Bean would leave. He wouldn't get to apologize the right way—that was the answer.

Annie Morrison wriggled. "*Mmmmppphhh,*" she said quietly.

"What did she say?" Snow White asked Bean.

"She said that she liked this joke, it's been a very good joke, but now she's ready to talk to her cat. Her cat is named Bubba."

The wrong Annie, an innocent Annie, Annie of the right name, Annie Got No Gun. Avi wondered if the twins would be able to return her to her life, if this alien abduction would be remembered only by Annie during regression therapy, a tabloid experience. "Crap," Avi said. "Unbelievable."

The dining room window was open, a breeze picking up, rain in the wind, low pressure over the low hills. The rings of a wooden whale stood in pieces in the carport, the animal not yet alive but garaged safely and dry. The wind in the curtain gave a little *shoosh*. Avi noticed that he had left a stray drawing on the marble end table, something too-simple from his Sharpie series. He could see the drawing:

He had to get the drawing to safety. "So, Sisters . . ." he cleared his throat. "*Ahhhemmm*, excuse me. You understand that finding every woman named Annie Morrison might not be a great idea, right?"

As he turned to walk away, Snow White pushed him just a little, a rap on the right shoulder. "Whaddaya mean?"

"Yeah," Rose Red said. "Yeah?"

"No touching. Well . . . it's just that there might be a lot of women with that name." He reached the drawing, crumpled the doodled whale, *c'est la guerre*, and pocketed the paper as he turned back, smooth. He lowered his voice: "And someone might know someone who's a cop. It's mathematically proven."

"Cops are nothing!" Rose Red chirped.

"I'm sure," said Avi. "That's not the point."

"A cop?" said Snow White.

"I once tied up a man with just his arms and legs!" Rose Red said brightly.

"Point is, you probably shouldn't go around choosing every Annie Morrison from the phone book and—"

"Stomping them!" Rose Red squealed, interrupting Avi.

"Right," he said. "There's a better way to do a woman-hunt."

"There is?" asked Snow White. "What?"

"*Hmm*," he pretended to think.

Snow White had been listening, and cleaning dirt from under her fingernails with the assistance of a knife she had either brought or found; the air felt close, the twins gave off an odor, the smell around them a little off, perhaps from all that dirty denim, or maybe from leaky brain fluid. Maybe the twins smelled like sweetbreads.

"What?" Snow White said.

"I dunno," Avi said.

"We could advertise," Rose Red.

"Yeah," Avi said. "That's the spirit. You need a plan."

"Oh, Sister," Rose Red said. "I'm so hungry I could eat my Manolos."

"You're not wearing Manolos," said Snow White. She hitched up her jeans, adjusted her beret, and reached toward Avi with her right hand, the middle finger extended; she jabbed him, once, twice, hard in the chest, said nothing, one finger capable of extreme violence, and spun away on the heels of her combat boots, her pigtail flapping.

"She's my hero," said Rose Red. "Yeah," she added meanly to Avi.

He turned away, and Rose Red gave him a whopping slap on the ass, coach to quarterback, which made Avi start and stumble. "Don't do that!" he yelled at her.

"I'll kick you," Rose Red yelled back.

"I'll kick you harder," he snarled back, in twin-speak.

"Ooh," she said. "Fun." Rose Red wiggled her hips. "Let's kick," she said.

. . .

Would they never leave? He showed the twins the phone book, handed it over gingerly, kept his distance, and pointed out the four Annie Morrisons who lived in the Elsbeth area. Then he showed them the Internet. He showed them the number of hits for the name "Annie Morrison," 809,520, but he wouldn't click on a single one. He repeated himself, and then he did so again: Annie Morrison had to be brought back to the store.

Finally, with their predictably dimwitted bluster, the henchwomen figured out the situation. They snarled at Bean as they carried the still-bound Annie Morrison through Maureen's living room and back to the lab cart in the kitchen, even their nonverbal grumblings violent.

Avi looked down, uh-oh, evidence. On the kitchen floor lay one of Annie Morrison's shoes, a black pump, its heel pad worn, a shoe he picked up and carried reluctantly out to the car. The driver's side windows, front and back, were opened, the twin's mugs framed in the openings, double trouble peering from the darkness of the vehicle. Avi approached Snow White, who apparently always drove and probably got to hold the clicker and kneecap student-chefs with a golf club.

"Victim, we're taking you down," said Snow White.

"Yeah. You tell him, Sister."

"I don't like you."

Avi knew better than to speak. He held out the shoe.

"You're too—" Snow White thought hard, which looked painful. "You didn't cook us dinner."

"I'm hungry!" said Rose Red.

Avi could see the unfortunate, wrong Annie clenched on the car's big back seat.

"Her cat needs her," Avi said. "And the police are looking for you."

"The police!"

"Sister, the police!"

"Cops are nothing." Rose Red seemed unconvinced.

"Hey!" Avi said. He held out the damn shoe. "Don't leave any DNA."

"You're too kitcheny," Rose Red said. "A kitcheny man. . . . I bet he has a funny winkle."

"Oh, Sister! Of course he does. You've seen it," Snow White said with an insane, high-pitched titter. "A lot."

"I want to see it now!" Rose Red sopranoed back. "What's D and A?"

"You've seen it enough," Snow White said again as she glanced at Avi. "You didn't like it."

"Oh, shoot! Okay," Rose Red nodded, instantly grumpy again. And with that, finally, she snatched Annie Morrison's shoe, and the car windows whirred closed, a curtain rising on Avi's haggard reflection in the moonlit, tinted glass as the Lincoln pulled away.

And then Bean drew up in her car, which had been parked around the corner. Her window was down. "Going back to the ranch," Bean said.

Avi's window felt down too; his whale might need windows, he thought, nonsensically. "Own a ranch?"

"No sirree!" Bean's voice was strained. The twins must have scared her. "Ranch is just a dressing."

"That's a food joke," Avi complained. "That's my department."

"Kiss me," she said, so he did.

"Stay," Avi said.

"Can't." Bean's smile looked unhappy.

"Why?"

"Emotional unavailability."

"Oh," Avi said.

"Bye," she said, and so she left.

When Avi stepped back inside Maureen's house, Susan Woodley's cell phone was cricketing on the kitchen counter, a non-stop party; a cell phone he should lose by accident in the garbage disposal.

"Hello?"

"Susan Junior. It is I."

"I who?" Avi toyed briefly with The Camel.

"I.Q.," said The Camel. "I.Q. Camel."

These fucking people, Avi thought. "Yes?"

"The feckless ones have left."

"Yes." Avi was confused. What did "feckless" mean? "So how'd you know?"

"They called me. They told me about their wee error—and that the police were on the way. Nicely done, *El Duque*. So they called me and now I'm calling you. We are all participating in a kind of telecommunications economy, associating via the associative property of telecommunications." The Camel paused. "Am I losing you?"

"Look, I'm tired," he said, plopping down on a kitchen chair, the phone squeezed between his head and shoulder. It's the dinner rush and no one's eating, he might have said. Bean left, he might have said. Go away, he wanted to say.

"Yes, I hear so in your voice. Fatigue does contribute to the deflation of one's sense of self."

"Your name's not really I.Q."

"Very good," she said.

"I have set the reserve," Avi said, closing his eyes. He was sick of the twins.

"Ahhh," The Camel purred, a purring, dangerous camel.

"Eighty thousand, minimum. That's the reserve."

"Eighty thousand?"

"Eighty thousand. By the time the whale's done."

"Eighty thousand for the whale, a whale on the floss."

"What?"

"You *are* tired," she conceded.

Avi opened his eyes. "Not too," he said. "Eighty thousand."

"Susan Woodley and now her son. She won't sell and you won't run. . . . That's a little poem."

The Camel was getting to him. "Well?"

"Well, eighty thousand dollars represents a portion of the list's value, *fer sher,* which doesn't mean you've earned eighty thousand. Eighty thousand," she repeated sarcastically. "Consider the other economies of which we are part, our lives constrained by how poorly real works of value are remunerated. Is a filling in your bicuspid worth more than a sculpture in a public plaza? Is a henchwoman's work—the sisters will be paid as one, in case you've been wondering—more valuable than the Red Cross? And what isn't a politician worth?" The Camel heaved a menacing sigh into Avi's ear.

"I'm getting off the phone," he said. "Eighty thousand."

"We'll talk," The Camel said. "Which is not why I called, *mi amigo,* of course—not to have you set the sticker price while pretending to meet with your manager regarding rust-proof undercoating. I called because I need a favor."

"A favor?"

"Ludicrous and embarrassing though the request must be, indeed, a favor, although it may merely be a suggestion."

"What the hell." Phone to his ear, Avi turned off the kitchen light and headed out to let in Dolly. No stars were there. He wanted to see the stars.

"I need you to ask The Lima Bean a question."

"What question?"

"Ask her what happened in Toronto."

"Toronto. That's it?"

"That's it, *khattam shud.*"

"Fine," Avi said. "Will do. Now go back to your oasis." He hung up.

• • •

He made a mistake. Dinner for one was right—the salad the best part, tomatoes and feta brightened with a decent balsamic—but he was so fuzz-brained he drank two cups of coffee. The guy with increasing insomnia drank two cups of fresh-ground Kona.

Asleep for twenty minutes, then not, then forty, then not, then twenty-five, then not, then fifty minutes, then not at all for an hour and fifteen, then not at all once Avi fetched a drink of water. Who knew what time it was in Greenland, and what time it was for the whales in the water there; since a whale has a longer gestation period than a human, whales should have a different sense of time (if they have any idea of time; if one believes in time), a whale's sense of the Music of the Spheres determined by tides and seasons and hungry baby whales and shifting politics in the pod. Okay, Avi acknowledged, whale time might be just like human time, but perhaps without as deep a sense of the past or as terrified an ignorance of the future. Okay, he admitted further, tornadic in the bed sheets, whale time and human time probably were different. What's a week in whale years, Rick had asked just a few human days ago.

Avi should get out of bed. Another twenty minutes not asleep, then fifteen more went by—and to hell with this, he dressed and went outside, to change it up, as the sleep doctors probably said, or so he believed they said. The light spilled everywhere, metallic on the lawn and on the neighbor's silver Mazda speckled with dew and shiny-dull, like the matte side of a sheet of foil. Avi's whale kept to herself, preferring not to sing, and who could blame her?

He would go for a drive, just Avi alone for what felt like the first time in days, crank some tunes in the middle of no traffic, bop and floor it, the idea a little *zazen*, a sitting meditation in a suspect Toyota in North Carolina. Dolly would be fine snoozing, especially as Avi had covered up the bed pillows just in case she had a butt itch or wanted something cushier for her big ol' bod.

He was trying to talk himself into being awake as opposed to not-asleep.

The car wouldn't start, the car wouldn't start, the car wouldn't start, the car started. The Toyota's balky little bulk felt familiar to Avi, albeit alien to Elsbeth, which was how he wanted it, not to fit in here. With the back windows rolled down for air and luck, he drove along the streets, slick and new; there was nothing but flashing amber where the reds liked to be red. For a while, still in the neighborhood, Avi trailed the newspaper delivery guy, papers flying intermittently from the window of the moving vehicle, and then realized it was a newspaper woman. She had a good arm, and on occasion let flip the news backhand across her body, end over end, local politics wrapped in wire service reports. She was probably The Camel, one hump or two.

Avi was out by the highway when he noticed that he needed gas. Cruising S.R. 252, then exiting under the underpass and over the overpass, looping around to go straight, banking hard out of a turn, Avi aimed his low beams high toward a truck stop—lit up on a hill like a 1950s television set—and followed the lights of the Toyota. So much of his life felt like this: aim and follow, point and click, smile and kiss.

Pulling into the truck stop, he made a wrong turn. The sign for cars was over there, oh well, the arrow pointing toward where cars should park. What a lawbreaker. He zipped along toward the big rigs on the great plain of concrete, drivers dozing in their cabs or flipping through porn mags and drinking, one beer per two road hours as Federally mandated for alcoholic truckers. Between one and two hundred trucks: 1, 2, 2, Avi said to himself, agog with America. He was so tired, he could almost cry. He felt drunk on nothing.

Cattle cars of car parts, giant refrigerators, slatted boxes of doomed chickens (heads under wings), Caterpillars and Ingersoll-Rands chained to flatbeds, unmarked C.I.A. semis. One bright eighteen-wheeler, its color a sticky ochre in the fake daylight, said "Orange Van Lines," the hue and the words so off-key they made a kind of sense. A nighttime sense: things didn't go together at night, they went apart.

Avi saw an opening, steered and aimed his little car between a multi-colored paneled behemoth and a supermarket rig. He felt oddly wistful. He let the little Toyota idle too, dwarfed by the two towering trucks. He leaned forward, arms on the steering wheel, to look up through the windshield: no stars would ever hang above a truck stop, so the too-tall light stanchions watched over all, including Avi's nightmares to come, were he to sleep. Were he to dream: to swing in a dream whale he would have to dream.

The lights were merely on, neither asleep nor awake, which was how he felt, neither asleep nor awake. It could be five in the night-morning. He would park 'n doze here an hour or two, wake to roaring engines, fill his tank, and speed home in time to dole out Dolly's kibble, build a whale, foil The Camel's grand design. Kiss Bean.

She had left hurriedly, but who could blame her. Or contact her: he didn't know how to reach Bean, he realized, a little shocked. Oh, right: her phone number should be on Mom's cell.

He shouldn't leave Dolly home alone all night.

To Avi's left, an anonymous, generic semi; to his right, cans and bottles, freshness locked in. He had not looked too carefully at the rows and rows of trucks. Across the extra-wide parking area, angled neatly as though drawn there, an endless battalion of idling semis could be seen in the artificial glare, and quite often, nestled between them, a small car such as Avi's own, something imported or an imitation of an import. Other insomniacs were here to do battle with their bedrooms, rocked by the rumble of machines, like babies who only slept in cars. And more, the more Avi looked: twenty, twenty-five, thirty, thirty-five little cars squeezed between the snoring big rigs—trucks idling to run the AC. And more, and more, so many trucks, so many cars too. No one was sleeping in his or her own bed, everyone had to drive somewhere else to dream, to be lulled to sleep, everyone tucked in and innocent, no one innocent.

Or all of those other drivers were as awake as Avi, and calmer too, here, hushed by the quiet, seismic, American roar of the big rigs. Lit up like another planet, a planet used as a way station between real planets, a place that might not exist were it not for the allure of its nothingness, the truck stop offered a kind of post-highway, pre-dawn solace to those who needed oneiric succor, Avi included.

He felt bathed by something, a feeling that rode in waves. Feeling was a whale, too.

To Avi's left, the driver of the multi-colored paneled semi swung wide a door and then hopped out, found footing and planted himself upon the ground. Avi watched: boots and jeans and a pork-pie hat. One step for trucker kind.

Avi nodded; the trucker tipped his hat.

Avi rolled down the window. "Hey," he said.

The guy was gritty, reddishly mutton-chopped, beer-bellied, long in the saddle or the tooth, and he looked a little sad, although he might have made Tom Waits sing. "Hey." The trucker spat a good squirt from a chaw, leaned back against his rig. "S'late."

"*Mm-hm,*" Avi said.

"You nightie much?"

"*Hm?*" Avi didn't understand. "No."

"First time, then, eh?"

Avi nodded.

"S'called nightie. What we call it. The cars—" he ticked his chin. "Those are nighties. All the stops are full of 'em. More all the time. S'like the Depression or something, eh?"

Avi thought he understood. In the little cars tucked between the rigs, dome lights on, the non-sleepers, he and his compatriots, were nighties in the nightie night.

"Had a talk with a nightie two days back, a gal, she was in insurance, had three, four kids. She'd come out here and park and knit. . . ." The trucker looked at Avi, spat again. "You knit?"

Avi smiled. "Naw."

The trucker smiled back, gap-toothed, looking suddenly younger and a bit worse. "I knit. It works. Got hats and sweaters—" he gestured toward the cab. "Lotsa scarves saved up. . . . Whatta you do?"

Avi thought about that. Build a whale? "I cook," he answered.

"S'okay," the trucker approved, spat. "Someone's gotta eat it. But too much arranging for me."

Yes, that was true, Avi thought, the trucker's insight born of someone who lived alone. "Yep," Avi said. "Sometimes people like it," he appended, whatever that meant.

"Got a family?"

Avi thought about that: he would have liked to have had siblings. But maybe here, in lower gravity on the moon, everyone was family. "Not really."

"Sad. I've got five and one," the trucker said proudly. "Eleven more squirts from each of us five. Five and the gay one. One hauls too. Outta Spokane."

Avi nodded; he hadn't really followed.

"My dad died," the trucker said. "The cancer." He spat.

"My mom died," Avi said. "Car wreck."

"Faster," the trucker said.

"Yep," Avi said.

They were both quiet for a little while. The trucker spat again, hitched up his jeans, going somewhere but undecided too, with nowhere to go. The dirty light sizzled, as it would eternally.

"What was the last thing you said?" The question arrived whole.

"*Hm?*" Avi had drifted away. "What do you mean?"

"To your mom. What'd you say to her, ya' know, *before?*"

Avi nodded. "The last thing. . . ? I'd have to think. On the phone, maybe two or three weeks before—"

"On the phone," the trucker caught himself interrupting.

"We were talking about . . . school? No, my job? I had had a bad shift."

The trucker spat, didn't speak. "Fucking job," the trucker finally said.

"Fucking job," Avi said.

"And I think . . . maybe I said something about my dog. I think—" and now he remembered it clearly. "She and I were talking about my dog, something my dog did when I was at work. How my dog doesn't like my fucking job either."

The trucker smiled. "Good one," he said. "That's rich."

"You?"

"Aw, shit," the trucker spat. "Politics. Pops liked his guns, and me, I'm a *60 Minutes* guy. Helps," he said for no reason. "*60 Minutes* and Rush."

"Limbaugh?"

"Yes. 'Cept he's a fool. But ya' gotta have his shit too, or you're like outta balance. Like your load shifts and you slide out. Gotta be balanced, just in case. . . ."

Avi was trying to follow, but had no room: he was overcome with his mom's voice, the anecdote of Dolly digging in the ficus while Avi double-shifted, his last conversation with Mom. He drummed on the steering wheel, to come back, keep himself present, not be rude. It had not been a good conversation, he realized bitterly. He had merely filled the space with words.

". . . Nighties don't get it all, even if they're kinda road people, you know?

S'weird, but I think the drivers like the nighties."

"Yeah?"

"Yeah," the trucker spat. "Fucking job."

"Fucking job," Avi said.

"My dad didn't like my brother. The gay one."

"Sorry," Avi said.

"He's the best brother," the trucker said. "But you know right away."

"Yeah," Avi said.

"Took a boy to the prom, was all over the Web, made folks crazy. Now he's in sales. Industrial. Good at it, too." The trucker's mutton chops were kind of munching, the chaw being worked. "You got a gal in Kalamazoo, or—?"

"Naw," Avi said. "Maybe," he corrected himself. "I think so," he said.

"Sounds good," the trucker spat and smiled. "Whattabout your mom?"

"Hm?"

"She have a boyfriend?"

Ahead of them, across the wide lot, a truck rattled into gear and pulled out, which allowed Avi time to pause, as he and the driver watched. "I don't think so."

"Dayton," the trucker said about the departing truck. "I won't say I like that Carol." The trucker poked up his hat at the front, a one finger poke. "But she wasn't happy at Pop's funeral, gotta admit. Didn't leave her much."

"Carol."

"Pop's gal. A cosmologist. She has a little suitcase she opens up in your living room, all that make-up. Has a nasty pooch, some kinda yapper." The trucker sure was chatty.

"Gotcha."

The trucker worked his chaw, then spat twice. "When she die?"

Avi counted. "About a month ago. Little more."

"Whatcha do?"

"Hmmm?"

"Truckers, we have a thing, you know? We do funerals, or whatcha wanna call 'em. Not in a cemetery though." He spat, wiped his mouth with a bandana from a back pocket. "Do it our own way. Honor our own."

They were silent some more.

"Guess nighties might do that too, soon enough." The trucker chuckled. "Seeing how, and all."

"Guess so." Avi smiled. "Seeing how."

"Fucking job," the trucker grinned.

"Fucking job," Avi nodded.

"Well, she's all yours, nightie. Do something for her."

Avi was doing something for her.

"See ya', then," the trucker tipped his hat, spat, and began to walk off. "And get a haircut."

"Hey!" Avi called out, craning a bit through the open car window. "Hey! What did you do?"

The trucker turned from where he had walked away, maybe fifteen feet. "Me? For Pops?"

"Yeah," Avi said.

"Had a race," the trucker said. "Lost it. Bet a dime." He tipped his hat again. "Pops woulda liked it."

. . .

He made himself go see. Where the road curved and curved back again one hundred yards or so later, two blind spots could be found, each blind to the other. Avi knew roughly where the place was, but he hadn't gone to look. Now he drove past, pulled over and parked, and then walked back in the high weeds along the soft shoulder.

It was almost full dawn, the colors roaring and the babiest birds frantic, the sky cracked open more than anything else, and if Avi hadn't been so exhausted, the light might have been beautiful. He felt old and incapable and wrong. Nothing he did had any meaning.

Mom in the kitchen flinging a wet sponge that caught him square in the chest with a flat *splat*—she might have been mad at Avi or just joking; Mom reading on the front stoop as she waited for Avi to come home; Mom shaking down a thermometer, the word "mom" in the word "thermometer," she liked to say; Mom's voice softly sobbing over the phone when Avi called to tell her Dad died; Mom's cookie jar and aliases and secrets; Mom asleep in a track suit on a chaise lounge; Mom's prescriptions in the medicine chest; Mom with a pat of butter rubbed in small circles on her burned wrist; Mom just standing there in a starchy brown polo shirt with the collar up; Mom not there as though cut out of a snapshot.

Mom had died here. Not that Avi knew which of the two blind curves she had taken too fast, or which tree she had hit.

The trees were ordinary.

Death was ordinary.

Avi felt a surprising resolve breaking through the surface of his grief. He knew himself to be crying—he had a napkin or a tissue in a pocket—but something else was happening too, neither a plan nor a decision, just a possibility, something that felt willed, and a release.

It was dawn at the side of the road, the traffic had begun again, the dewy, stringy grass had scrawled silvered, cryptic secrets on his shoes and jeans, and aloud, Avi said, "Bye . . ." gulping for air and innocence and freedom, as though he himself were rising through himself, to be at last in his own body. Just standing there, choosing, he had fully breached the surface, thrown his heaving body up, out of grief, through the viscous unconsciousness of twenty-nine years, and into good, wet air, and for no one reason and every reason possible.

"Bye, Mom."

A Tale of a Whale

ELEVEN

· ·

AVI WAS FINALLY ASLEEP, the blanket and sheet perfect . . . then some-one pounded on the kitchen door, Dolly barked, and the sunlight slammed through the blinds. Wow, what a headache he had. Fucking job, Avi thought, the conversation with the trucker and last night's roiling roadside emotions still present. The pounding got louder. He tried not to yell, for fear of explod-ing. "Coming already. . . ." Jeans and a T-shirt. "Coming, dammit!" He grabbed socks and boots, bounded down the stairs.

"Where you been?" Rick leaned on the doorjamb. He had a wan and hungry look.

"You're a mess," Avi noted. "Come in. Coffee?"

"You look worse, Boss. I'll make coffee."

"No, that's okay—really, I've got it. *Buh*," Avi waved off his helper's help. "What time is it?" He looked at Rick. "You all right?" Avi asked.

"Up all night." Rick pulled out a chair and flopped himself down. "Ate three foot-longs. You?"

"Didn't sleep either," Avi said.

"Sucks," Rick said.

"Sucks."

"You look worse," Rick said. "It's eight."

They waited for the coffee like two guys with fifty cents between them and the bus cost a dollar. At last, Avi served. They sipped. Avi handed Rick a bottle of aspirin. Then Avi slumped face-first onto the table, his cheek flat on a cloth placemat.

"Sure you're okay?"

"Aw, it's a long story," Avi demurred, his words smushed too. "Started when I was born. . . . Wanna take the day off?"

"What?" Rick said.

"You heard."

"No," Rick said. "Stay on task. Target acquired."

"Target acquired," Avi repeated. Too bad—days off were good for nooners. Rick gave his hearing aid a little tap.

"You should have that checked," Avi sat up. "That thing's no good." He waved toward Rick's ear, sipped again. "Plus, you're a Fed."

"Not," Rick disagreed. "Yep," he agreed with something else. "Can't fix it, though. Insurance," he said by way of explanation, then tapped the device again. "Damn thing. . . . Okay, c'mon. Let's go." He slugged back the rest of his coffee and stood up. "Work'll fix ya'." He laid a hand on Avi's shoulder.

"Work," Avi repeated. "She's calling." He chugged too, then hauled himself up, standing and teetering. "*Woah.*"

Rick narrowed his narrow gaze. "She is. Know whatcha mean."

"Yep," Avi said. He wished he could finish his thought. Mom had died, and Avi had sacrificed his mind for the good of whale kind.

On the flattest ground available, the two men lined up all nine of the Stanley 3-in-1 workbenches. The tongue-and-groove ply followed, sheet after sheet, Liquid Nailed and staple gunned, a long flat runway, eight sheets in all, sixty-four feet long. It took hours and hours, and then it took another hour, that last one worse, one too many. Then the two men stood back to see.

"*Hm,*" Rick said. He bit his fingernail.

"*Hm,*" Avi said. "Oops. Forgot—" he reached into his toolbelt. "Try these." He handed Rick a bundle of coffee stirrers. "Nabbed a bunch."

"Thanks. That's gonna be heavy." He munched a stirrer.

Avi agreed.

"Lighter cut in strips," Rick said.

"Still not light," Avi added.

The guys stood guy-ishly there.

"Damn," Rick said. "Crazy."

"It's your design."

"It's your whale."

Avi thought about that. "Yeah," he said. "I guess. Yours too, though."

Maybe Rick was pleased, munchity munch.

"You were married, right?" Avi changed the subject.

"Was. Bad scene."

"What was her name?"

"Is," Rick said. "Delia."

"Delia. When the marriage worked—"

"For ten minutes." Rick's deadpan stayed dead.

"For ten minutes. . . ."

"You have a kid, right?" Avi returned to the conversation, or to the part that had been aloud.

"Girl. Sarah. Goes to State."

"Nice," Avi said. He wondered if Bean had gone to college. "Okay," Avi said. "Two questions. . . ."

"Shoot twice."

"Right. One, do you think you trusted your wife? I mean, is that even possible or what? And"—he made a V, two fingers' worth, the Victim, Churchill stepping off the plane—"two, do you think that she could love you and leave you—I mean, is that just some bullshit women say, like I love you but I'm leaving your sorry ass?"

Rick hadn't budged, but he looked suddenly ill.

"Rick, man. Just try one of the questions. . . ."

"Dunno what women say," Rick said. "Where I live, trust is better than a promise."

"That's it!" Avi exclaimed, and clapped his hands. "Exactly! That's what I mean!"

"Boss," Rick said warily. "Not good."

"It is," Avi said. "She's full of promises—they all are—but trust, man, that's the thing."

"Christ," Rick said. "I need a cigarette."

"Sounds right," Avi said. "So I met a girl. She's named Bean. But she might be named Mi Ha, I think."

"Mi Ha," Rick said. "Nice," Rick said. "Met her, 'member?"

"Right. She . . . I . . . she's okay."

"Gotcha," Rick said. "You don't trust her. For one, she's got a couple of names."

"Right. Can't decide what I think of that."

"You've got a coupla names," Rick said.

Avi didn't know what to say.

"Smoking would help," Rick said.

"Yeah, but it kills ya'," Avi said. "Kills ya' dead."

"Worth it," Rick said. "I'm dead without smokes."

"Mi Ha," Avi said.

Rick was mournful.

"Do guys who build houses talk like this, I mean, during their breaks and all?"

Rick almost smiled. "When they smoke they do," he said. "When they don't smoke, they stab each other with screwdrivers."

"Funny," Avi said. "Aren't you a riot."

"Yep," Rick said. "Then they use nail guns."

"For an addict, you've got an okay sense of humor."

Rick glared at Avi.

"Gotcha," Avi said. "Feeling just a wee bit sensitive?"

"Shut up."

"Uh-*uhhh*. Don't say shit like that. Christmas bonus, remember?"

Rick munched hard on his stirrer. "Okay, smart ass. Break's over. Got an hour or so before sunset."

The second layer of ply was easy to place and hard to secure, leverage less than ideal for the screw and staple guns. Small disagreements between the two men didn't help: dog leg or no dog leg; degree of curvature the three-ply beams would allow; whether the beams were beams, strips, or battens; what the skin of the whale might be.

They worked until light began to leech from the sky—and so, the third layer of ply would have to wait, as rain looked to be moving in for a visit.

Avi liked to think that he could smell rain on the wind with a chef's sense of smell, but not today, his exhaustion a bludgeon to his senses. All he wanted was to pack up the tools and take a ridiculously long shower, the kind his mother used to yell at him about a billion years ago.

"Tarp it?" Rick asked.

"Just thinking that," Avi lied. He had tried to talk to Rick about Bean? Crap, Avi thought.

"Tarp 'n tape."

"Gotcha."

"I'm hungry," Rick said. "Let's tarp it and eat."

"Cool, man," Avi said. "I'll cook."

At the kitchen door, Avi kicked off his boots, peeled off his socks, and stepped inside: Bean stood there looking freshly scrubbed, her short hair spiky-wet, a big strand of multi-colored glass doodads around her neck, funky plastic beads joggling. She had on a little red tank top, spaghetti straps, and yet another sweeping spangled skirt. La Petite Bean with the green eyes. She was talking into her cell, she smiled at Avi, held up a finger, just a sec. "I see, yes. No. . . . Yes. It doesn't matter which account, but don't use the Smithers name. Right. Right. No. Yes. Look, gotta go, I'm with a client. Bye, Daddy-O. Love ya'." The call ended, she turned and give Avi a quick kiss, just missed his lips. "Hiya."

"Hiya," Avi was pleased.

"Annie, Annie, fo-fanny," Bean said.

"Crap," Avi said. "That was unreal. Was that your Dad?"

"Not my real dad. The man who raised me. One of my dads. . . ." She gave a little shimmy. "C'mere," she said.

They kissed, *wahoo*. Avi liked Bean.

In trooped Rick. "Hi," he said. "Sorry," he said.

"Hi." Bean blushed, and hurriedly let go.

"Didn't know we had company, Boss."

"Me either," Avi smiled to himself. "You've met, right? Rick, Bean. Bean, Rick." And with a quick turn to the fridge, he fetched filtered water from the chilled carafe and held up the pitcher, a question for Rick, who nodded yes but had to want beer. "Just make yourselves comfy, I gotta take a quick shower, and then I'll rustle up dinner." He poured, delivered the glass to Rick, then wordlessly asked Bean if she wanted some.

"No thanks," Bean said. "Whatcha rustling?"

"I like ribs," Rick said. "Or burgers."

"I'm a vegetarian," Bean said.

"You eat meat." Avi was amused. He poured himself another glass of water and chugged half. "Can't trust you at all."

Bean laughed. "It's an authority thing," she admitted, and winked at Avi.

"My daughter's a vegetarian," Rick said.

"Fine." Avi replenished the pitcher and opened the fridge. "But let me take a shower." He smelled.

"Where's Dolly?" Bean said. "Do you think she'd go for a walk?"

"Oh, yeah. That'd be great." Where was she? Avi gave a Dolly whistle, his tongue tipped to the roof of his mouth. There was no response. He tried again: he hated when she couldn't be found. But then from the living room, she trotted happily. "Good dog." He scratched her ear.

Bean squatted, tipped a little. "Hi, girl."

Like the sociable beast she was, Dolly wagged her way to Bean for love.

"The leash is on the hook over there; use the retractable one for the neighborhood. Plastic bags for scooping—" Avi pointed to the stash of used Ziplocs. "I've gotta shower. That's really helpful, thanks." And to Rick: "Think you can boil some water?"

"Naw," Rick said. "I might cut myself."

"Humor," Avi said to Bean. "Rick's working on his."

"Impressive," Bean said. She snapped the leash to Dolly's collar, who was already a bit doggy gaga, her walk imminent, all those smells, and all those places to pee.

"*Woof!*" said Dolly.

"You should see me be funny," Rick said.

"I'll wait," Bean said. "Bye."

"Bye. . . ." Avi turned to Rick. "Wash first." Then the chef gave the contractor his chopping orders, their roles reversed indoors, laid out a few items from the larder, and put two pots of water to boil—all just to think about while he showered, as Avi had no menu yet. If these people kept coming over, he'd have to start charging, and mark up the wine, too. Criminals and contractors and whales and lovers, oh my. . . .

Maureen's money would pay for Avi's tastes. Or maybe he would spend his inheritance on opening a restaurant, "Avi and Maria's," *Te Deums* on the jukebox, the servers in robes and tonsures, thanks for the moolah, Mom. Or maybe he should turn the whale into a café, serve bacalao and blubber.

Bean was here: Avi would have sex tonight. The thought gave him a surge as he showered, his exhaustion on simmer. But first he had to cook for his nookie, a quick little vegetable root purée, the veggies roasted already, an apple for tartness and sweet, two BLTs for the tobacco-free Rick. and California-style sandwiches (avocado, cheddar, and a zesty tapenade) for Bean. Avi wouldn't have minded a zippy Zin as a complement but didn't have one to offer. Tomorrow he would do a Total Wine run and buy a mixed case.

A pinkie tip of cologne applied judiciously, his hair clean, a nice blue shirt, fresh underwear and jeans, the open-toed dress sandals upon which he had splurged in Santa Monica last year: the togs were selected for action. Something about last night and a good day of work—Avi felt himself to have experienced a kind of spiritual sauna-and-fjord dip, scalded and then dunked in the freezing water. Bean was here. She had kissed him. Man, he was exhausted.

Avi had not meant to eavesdrop, or to be sneaky in any way, but since his sandals made no noise on the carpet and the door was already partially open, he could plainly hear voices in the kitchen—all without entering the room, just by leaning there against the lintel. What he heard was astonishing.

Rick: "*Xiǎojiāhuo, nǐhǎo 'a.*"

Bean: "*Nǐhǎo. Nǐ shuō dé bùcuò 'a.*"

Rick: "*Xièxie nǐ. Nǐ yě shuó de bùcuò.*"

Bean: "*Jīngyú zěnmeyàng le?*"

Rick: "*Tā huó le.*"

Then silence, as either Bean or Rick opened the fridge.

Rick began again. To Avi's ear, Rick's speech sounded as though it were something even he didn't understand, the tones expressive, up and down the scale, squeezed operatically from the voicebox, the contractor's affect at odds with the music his mouth made: *"Sàn sànbù, kāixīn le ba?"*

Bean: *"Kāixīn le. Xièxie le. Jīntiān de yuèliang tōutōu mōmō de xiàngshì yīgè zéi."*

Rick: *"Shì xiàng. Hǎo cǎn 'ó."*

"Ah," said Bean, as both she and Rick sighed.

Avi couldn't stand it; he pushed open the door. "Wow," Avi said. "Hi."

"Hi," Bean said.

Rick nodded.

"He speaks Chinese," Bean said. "Not bad."

"What was that about?" Avi asked. He stepped to the counter, tried to non-chalant his way into the scene, quite freaked, and pretended to consider his vegetables.

"Oh, nothing," Bean said.

"I found beer." Rick held up a bottle. "I'll pour it over ice."

Bean checked out Avi's expression, and apparently saw something she had to fix. "The whale rises, your friend said. It's very exciting."

"In Chinese," Avi said. "You both speak Chinese."

"Sure," Bean said. "It's good for business."

"Have any pretzels?" Rick asked. "China's the future," Rick said.

. . .

Avi did have sex, and so did Bean. After dinner, after Rick trundled to his repaired pickup and hauled his hernia-wear home to his handyman hovel; after Dolly had her romp in the yard with a squeaky chew toy designed to look like a whale, a gift from Bean; after a good forty-five minutes of sharing silence on the deck as the moon didn't part the clouds; after reading in his whale book for forty-five minutes more as Bean skimmed the week's *Elsbeth Herald* and then called her seventy-one dads; after Avi and Bean had gone upstairs together to the picnic room, the blanket spread on the floor amidst the banking documents. Good sex, more kissing. Relatively quick sex, too. After sex, Bean had kissed him on the forehead, washed up quickly, kissed him on the lips, and then left. She wasn't staying the night yet.

. . .

There were daytime choices and nighttime choices: building the whale was a daytime choice, one he had made for Mom. Dreaming, nightie nighting, and Bean—those were nighttime choices he had made for himself.

No, he realized, the break-down broke down; he wasn't stuck in a mind-body problem. The whale was for Avi, the dreaming was for Mom, and any number of daytime choices had nighttime consequences, and vice versa.

It was nighttime, his one true time to think, but unfortunately, also his time to sleep. At least he could trot out the cookie jar and pretend to have fond memories of shit he didn't recognize. Avi sat at the kitchen table and stared at the goods, his whale guide there too. Then he changed his mind, fetched Maureen's cell phone from the counter, and started trying all the numbers, because they were there: of the nine anonymous names in the memory, he reached only two with voicemail and recognized neither voice. The other seven numbers reached no one. Susan Woodley might have had friends, but they had apparently thrown out their phones when she died, or they were just too busy robbing banks or being dead themselves.

$500,000 was a lot of love. Avi suspected that he had loved Mom only $25,000 or so, and that she had known, and that was why she had placed such a crazy condition on his inheritance, to make him prove to her posthumously that he had been joking all these years. He didn't appreciate the gesture. Not that being underappreciated had seemed to matter to his mother, Avi suspected, given her separate daytime and nighttime choices, walking out on her family like that. Here, gone, like that.

Once, shortly before she left, he and Mom had been to the grocery store together, Avi brooding over something inconsequential, the trip meaningless but the memory sharp, and connected with her departure soon thereafter. In the middle of the Produce aisle she had scolded him, and Avi had responded in kind, all kindness abandoned. "You don't care," he had yelled, the young teen gratified by the look of shock on her face. "Avi . . ." she had protested. "I do." But he had been right, which had made his accusation mean—she with her knuckles whitening as she steered the shopping cart, and he lagging behind to check out—a comment to regret when she had proved his words true.

True words from long ago seemed meaningless when faced with fate: what did it matter that Avi had been right, and was still right? The whale was on the way, and would be right. The whale would matter more than hindsight.

Hey, the calculator on the cell phone worked.

Sixty-four feet long, the strips Avi and Rick had cut were longer than ten Avi Heyers lying down. These strips equaled approximately sixty-four size 11 and ½ sneakers laid heel to toe, ninety-six Reuben hoagies from Weinstein's Deli (Dad's fave, and probably what killed him), 192 beefsteak tomatoes lined up on fenceposts to shoot, *pop, pop*. The strips would be as long as the blow is high from a 100-foot-long blue whale.

Through all the reading he was doing, and he had more to read, to know enough about whales, the blow from her blowhole seemed to Avi one of the most magical of whale phenomena. Fifty, sixty, sixty-five, maybe even seventy feet in the air, the blow of a large female blue—female whales are routinely larger than males—might be visible ten miles away, and must be a sight to behold up close.

Page eighty-three. Weighing as much as 200 tons, of which 10% could be blood, a female blue was a remarkable swimmer, and even more so a diver; a whale could dive straight down, thousands of feet down toward the sea floor, and slow her heartbeat to seven or eight beats per minute. To keep from getting nitrogen poisoning, given the atmospheric pressure changes such a dive would entail (as a result of her great length, a blue whale can experience three different PSIs at once, just by swimming straight down) whales developed a remarkable circulatory system, a complex skein of veins and arteries, *retia mirabile*, or "wonderful nets."

She has a wonderful net inside her body. When he came upon that information, Avi paused. A wonderful net: he wanted to be caught there.

More reading: Bean had found a copy of the Bible among Maureen's things, another surprise to Avi, and shown him the Book of Jonah. Jonah, who fled from his God, booked passage from Joppa to Tarshish, and volunteered to be thrown overboard when a storm would not abate; Jonah who was then swallowed by a great fish appointed by the Lord, and who spent three days in the belly of the great fish until vomited ashore; Jonah who, while in the belly of the great fish, remembered the Lord, "when my soul fainted within me. . . ."

"The thing about the Bible," Bean had said, "is that it's like humanity's Soul Diary. But it's just too literal," she had added, her expression furrowed. "Faith's too literal for me."

Avi didn't know much about faith, even though he had his beliefs: fresh ingredients, sharp knives, doing right, and the human capacity for love despite an equally human capacity to deny love, thanks, Mom. A man makes his beliefs out of the best local produce, Avi might say, if asked and feeling witty, Alice Waters his necessary angel. So while Jonah's trial in the belly of the great fish spoke to Avi, whale man to whale man, Avi's desire to be in the belly of a wooden fish that he himself had made, and to swing from its rib, sacred though the desire seemed, had little to do with faith.

Memory, sure: the whale and the dream of the whale were closer to memories than to beliefs. Without childhood memories, he would have to make his own. A whale could be a childhood memory.

He unfolded a piece of paper from the cookie jar.

• • •

Dear Mo,

The first couple of years, I had fun. But I never liked it the way you did. Now you're stuck and there's nothing to do.

I wish you had told me. I might have been able to help. You need help, but you never liked my helping you, which means you won't now, and I know that.

I'll raise our son. You tell him what you want, I won't.

Love,
Todd

• • •

Oh, fuck, Avi thought. Dad had been a bank robber too.

TWELVE

· ·

DONE, THE STRIPS WERE TOO LONG to be stored anywhere, so they were hauled on wheels and laid in the backyard, where Dolly had been enjoined not to chew them apart, good dog. The disks—like the kinds of enormous forms one sees driving by on the highway, mysteriously chained on a flatbed semi—were ready, awaiting only Avi's and Rick's decision regarding the cut-outs. Should the strips, when made into battens, go inside the disks or outside? Where should the cut-outs and framing brackets go? The two men had agreed that they couldn't decide, the advantages and disadvantages of each option apparent, the decision related to weight-bearing but also aesthetics—which would be stronger and nicer?

Rick had begun to communicate a little. He wasn't shy, exactly, just a man for whom talking seemed an expense. In their various conversations together, Avi had learned about the contractor's ex- and her disastrous temper, that his daughter Sarah was studying dance, much to her father's boastful horror, and even a little of what Rick thought about, and how he boxed the world to keep it organized. The guy had his own way of holding on:

A man is what he does.

Work works.

These days, more children are older than they were.

These days, more adults are babies than they were.

People in charge are people who don't do anything.

Be happy. Worry.

Promises mean nothing.

Have an Exit Strategy.

Plan for someone else planning for the worst.

And once, more cryptically and alarmingly, when Avi had dropped a beam on his foot and sworn, Rick had responded under his breath with the imprecation, "God kills."

"Crap, crap, crap." Avi had hopped around the yard. "*Owwww!*"

Rick had stopped measuring and marking a piece of ply, and looked up, his eyes boring into something Avi couldn't see.

"Crap. . . ." Avi had plopped himself down and bent the offended leg to remove his work boot and massage the perp. "What'd you say?"

Rick's silent look had been tight, full of years of something. "I said God kills."

"Whoa," Avi had said. "Crap." He had rubbed his foot. "That's serious."

"Yep," Rick had said.

"Who'd God kill?" Avi had asked.

"Too many good men," Rick had said, the phrase military, the line delivered through gritted teeth, as when a wartime chaplain fingers a dead kid's dogtags, the dialogue as dated as the flick.

"Whoa," Avi had repeated softly to himself. 'Nam, he had concluded, trying to guess Rick's age: fifty-five, sixty, sixty-five? Not sixty-five. Fifty-eight, a Boomer for sure, a guy who had learned Chinese in school, or worse, at Langley. Target acquired. But he wasn't a Fed, he had promised.

And then, "On both sides," Rick had added, unprompted.

Another time, in a stunning, quick conversation in response to a meaningless aside about some newspaper article Avi had read, Rick had stopped sawing, lifted his safety goggles to wipe underneath, and seemed to look into the distant past. "I don't read much," Rick had said. "Learned late," his unfocused gaze unwavering.

"Sorry," Avi had said. "That's a drag."

"Naw. It's okay," Rick had said. "Do okay."

"Yep," Avi had offered.

"Yep," Rick had said, safety glasses back in place.

Now, standing in front of the whale while Rick went into the house to take a leak, mid-afternoon a week later, Avi shook his head at the memory of the bug-goggled contractor handing Avi the instruction guide to the Sawzall—"Study this," Rick had said, his expression that of a man who learned late in life to read.

"Hallo?"

Avi turned around, startled. "Hi." Standing before him was a dude in a bright blue suit that looked to be slept in: the guy even looked slept in, if that were possible.

"I am Sascha. Is Russian. Across the street?" He pointed at his house.

"Right," Avi remembered. "We met at—"

"The funeral, da. I am sorry for your loss. She was good." The two men shook hands. "You build some-tink?"

Avi had to laugh. "Yes, I build something. I—" he caught sight of Rick at the side door. "We . . . are building a big whale."

Sascha looked at Avi, at the whale, and back at Avi before exploding in laughter. "A vhale! A vhale! I have always vanted a vhale! It is on grass but not—how do they call it?—the pink flaminko!"

Avi laughed along. "No," he said. "It isn't."

"I vill enjoy this, I tink." Sascha's laughter eased. He extended his hand once more. "I see many possibilities. Thank you. Thank you, sir." He turned and walked back across the street. "Thank yoooouuuu," he sang the last word.

"What was that?" Rick had arrived.

"Guy across the street," Avi said.

"It begins," Rick said.

"Hmm?"

"It begins. Heard a rumor from a buddy. You're gonna have visitors."

"Visitors?"

"Press too."

"Press?" Avi hadn't considered the prospect.

"Especially"—Rick might have smiled—"when the crew comes in the morning, and we raise her."

"In the morning? Tomorrow?" Avi's heart stopped, started, tripped, bumbled, skidded. He wasn't ready, even though he knew they were close, had known they were almost there. The whale . . . tomorrow. . . .

Rick smiled; really, he did.

"I . . ." Avi said. "Tomorrow?" Avi said. "Tomorrow? I better call Markins," he said quite calmly, impressed with how calm he was.

Or Mom, he thought. Or Dad. Avi should call all the dead people.

• • •

Later that day, Markins leaned against his car and crossed his arms. To make him feel better, Avi crossed his arms too. He had taken off his toolbelt to shake hands, who knew why.

"A whale," Markins said.

"A whale."

"Because you dreamed it."

"I did."

"Will it swim?"

"Ah, no. Well, I don't think so."

Markins reached into a pocket, not there, another pocket, found a hankie and mopped his forehead. It wasn't hot enough today to do that, Avi thought.

"Um, I . . . I think. . . ."

Avi waited; he had uncrossed his arms. Markins crossed his arms again. Avi crossed his arms again. This was kind of fun.

"I hadn't planned to move her," Avi said.

"Her." Markins reached into his suit and found a notebook and a fountain pen.

Avi didn't have a prop. Damn. So he took the lead, stretched his arms upward, came back down, hooked his thumbs in his waistband.

Markins didn't follow along. Avi liked him more.

"She," Avi said.

"She."

"She."

"Mr. Heyer, is she your late mother?"

"Mr. Markins, certainly not."

Markins scrawled flamboyantly in his notebook, lots of elbow.

"She'll be finished soon."

"I see."

"Shall I call you?"

"No," Markins said. "I'll be stopping by. I shall want to see this . . . um . . . she. But I won't wait to alert the executrix."

"The what?"

"The codicil stipulates a secondary affirmation of the terms. I'll let the executrix know that we have an opportunity in the making. It might take some time to get us all here together."

"Right," Avi said.

"A whale," Markins said. "I see." He shaded his eyes, despite facing east.

"A whale, Mr. Markins. Really big."

· · ·

The trail, a path beaten to usefulness by Elsbeth High's cross-country runners, wound downhill, meandering first through a stand of birches and then pulling up short at a stream, and then, four stepping stones later, continuing up the hill and over, then down again, to the scum-pond that Dolly loved. Luckily, the mudder's paradise was in the opposite direction.

The day had held up magnificently, a pretty day, the woods silvered with evening light, the angle of incidence just right to tip the leaves atop the canopy. Dolly had stuck her block of a head into a decaying log, and was probably rousting some poor varmint. "Dolly! Quit it," Avi hollered, surprised by his own voice in the stillness, and then surprised again by Dolly's obedience as she trotted off happily to another rummaging adventure.

They had reached the birches, a place that felt softened. Trees were cool that way. A smattering of hair cap moss, atop an odd lot of alluvial rocks, seemed to glow where it caught a slant of late light, pesto green. To his left, Dolly barked at and flushed a bird who flew through the stand of birches indignantly. Leaning into a tree, calm, Avi turned only his head to watch, amused by what the bird couldn't know: Doll-Doll was the best dog, a mutt with a dash of retriever, but since she was afraid of hunting, there was never anything to retrieve, the big delightful wuss more likely to run away if confronted than to fight.

Now she was hankering to leave the glade, and would have left for the pond already if not for her person hanging out. She had snuffled her way through the birches and woodsy matter, and abandoned the joys of a snout-full of humus for the promise of the pond; now she galloped toward Avi, and stopped to spin and bark, "Woof! Woof!" which he translated easily, to *Let's go, let's go. Dude! Pond!*

On the other side of the stream, on the rise, stood a different kind of grove, second-growth trees, the original stand fire-razed, a blaze probably left untended by some party-happy teen.

Dolly was already in the pond. She splashed about, took a huge lapping slurp of the disgusting water, and then just stood there, up to her belly and chest in the stinking brew. "Yes, you're horrible," Avi told her, to which she responded by barking twice.

He had towels in the Toyota to rub her down, but only after giving her a good soaking from the outdoor tap at the stadium, not quite mudding but part of Dolly's dream date, nonetheless. She loved every part of this ritual, the anticipation burned into the synapses of her monocular imagination, each act necessarily in order, almost causal: the car ride, the walk, the pond, the toweling off, the car ride. Happiness was a series of irrefutable facts in her dog brain, every fun event made more so by the next.

While Dolly splashed and waded through the pond—startling the occasional frog, who would leap for the water—Avi eyed a nearby bank of grass, the incline less severe and the foliage markedly smoother than elsewhere. A lover's spot, maybe, flattened by late adolescent gropings, but comfy enough, a good place to lay himself down to rest.

He plucked a stem of fluffy brown weed, and stuck the twiggy part in his mouth, very Tom Sawyer. The thought made him give a little huffing laugh as he sprawled on the soft, cool grass. Maybe Mom was also named Becky Thatcher. Maybe Maureen wasn't her name either. But Mom was actually a bank robber. And Dad had been too, earlier in their marriage.

And maybe Avi was nuts to be nuts for a nut, a woman whose homunculus wasn't so homonkey, who believed in Soul Diaries and auras and had too many names, a woman who had worked with Mom robbing banks, who spoke Chinese and who was spangly when dressed and when naked, and who liked Avi too. They had even had sex a second time, so the first time couldn't have been so terrible.

"Dolly—" Avi called his dog, who, for once, came running.

L.B. were initials, Bean a nickname. What was Bean's real name? What was her last name? Where was she staying? He would ask Mi Ha if she knew.

Avi didn't want to be the guy who couldn't handle the truth.

He had brought a plastic bag filled with the contents of the cookie jar. He had checked for additional evidence of criminal activities or family scandals but found only pictures and notes, mementos of a lost life. For some reason, she had saved a label from a box of mothballs, a piece of cardboard that she had apparently cut out, the smell long gone, that was good. The meaning of the mothballs label had died with Mom.

He watched the sun go down. Memories were like the light, a lost language.

The Farrington Lake photo made sense, as did Avi's school picture from 4th grade, both stashed in the cookie jar. Less knowable were a photo of Dad wearing underwear—God, really?—on his head, a rotting cork from a wine bottle, a turquoise Navaho-ish earring that had no mate, and even a little note that said "Bring the mountain," all of these stories dead as Maureen.

Which of the unintelligible scraps of paper and clipped labels and loose buttons would have only made sense to Susan Woodley, which to Annie Morrison? And what the hell had been Dad's alias—Rick Morrison? And if a woman could be a golf widow, could a man be a bank-robber widower?

Dolly had found a great, hard stick to chew to bits; she flumped next to Avi, her paws and legs black with mud, already stinking up the car and not even close to it. He put one hand on her head, scratched her right there, watched her thoughts go slack with good lovin'.

He thought he heard something rustle in the trees to his right. "Doll?" Avi asked his dog. She kept closed her eyes, no one there, her expression said. So he kept scratching.

Twins, Avi suspected. Ramona Pill. The Camel. Bean, even. Damn them all, he had work to do, decisions to unmake, people not to see, a house to empty, a new life to live, a funny ending to invent for his blockbuster of a great wooden whale.

Not yet, he decided; first this. Avi with his mother's cookie jar, Dolly with her stick.

THIRTEEN

· ·

THE HOURS WENT BY, indifferent to Avi. It was tomorrow: that's what a dream felt like, when it threatened to come true. But it really was tomorrow— midmorning, so said the clock—and this insanity Avi watched wasn't part of a dream. A crowd of men of various sizes and shapes bounded from three vans, a flock of menacing fellas, each loosely trussed in an orange safety vest atop a matching prison jumpsuit. Holy shit! What was happening? Convicts? The men looked badass; they squinted at suburbia and lined up to shake Avi's hand. The first four stepped forward double-time, adorned with identical neck tattoos and apparently in a cult, and one after the other they pressed the flesh with their sponsor, Avi the Dreamer, the dream today not his own.

"Williams."

"Williams."

"Williams."

"Williams."

Prison break, he wanted to say, but what could he say? Convicts? This was the whale-raising crew? "Rick. . . ." Avi managed to call to his friend who stood by the whale parts, that deserter. They were all named Williams?

Then three more: "Carlos," "Deuce," "Jung."

Next, from Van #2, came "Big Daddy," a tiny guy.

Next "T. T."

Next "Jimmy. . . ." The name was greeted with laughter from the two men behind Jimmy. "Shut up." Jimmy turned to the two who had laughed. "Assholes," spat Jimmy as he shuffled away. "Assholes," he turned to explain, the expletive squeezed through gritted teeth. He was a tall, scrawny guy made scrawnier by scraggly facial hair.

"I'm The Deke," said one of the men, amused, a wide person. "He's the Devil. Don't worry 'bout him."

"The Devil?"

"That's Jimmy," said the guy behind Deke, as he stepped up to shake Avi's

152

hand. "Calls himself Jimmy but we call him Satan. On account of the Bible. He's born again. Makes him crazy," he laughed. "I'm real glad to meetcha. This is fucking cool."

"The guy's called Satan?" Avi asked no one in particular, since no one in particular answered.

Rick had returned from hiding. He scratched something on a clipboard, shrugged his shoulders, enjoying himself.

"I'm Main," The Deke's friend said.

"Main?" Avi said. "That's your name?"

"M-a-i-n. Momma had four kids," Main said. "I'm the fifth. Fourth and Main was where she lived."

"Oh, crap," Avi breathed.

The Deke and Main moved on, Avi aghast.

"Mizzo," said the next guy. "Like the soup."

"Uzi," said another.

"Uzi?" Avi said to no one. "Like the gun?"

"Shit!" the guy piped. "Like the actor. You know."

And finally the men on line #3 stepped forward from Van #3. . . .

"Shoe Glue," said one.

"Tom the Wire," said another.

"Rick?" Avi asked Rick.

"I've got 'em," said Rick, making a show of a check mark. "Check."

"Roberto," said another. "Peaches," he corrected himself with a soft smile.

"Peaches," Avi repeated, and shook the hand of a man named Peaches.

"H. P.," said another, a guy so out of his element he might have been a Martian, clearly white collar, even in prison garb. "Pleased to meet you."

"H. P.?" sad Avi.

"A moniker. Computers." H. P. waved a hand. "Nice place."

"Oh, crap," said Avi. "A nerd."

"Hay-soos," said an Asian guy, his pronunciation Hispanic.

"Hello," said Avi, shaking hands.

"Rick," said the last guy. "Like him. Rick." He jerked his head at Rick.

"Rick?" Avi turned to his contractor. "What the hell?"

"Identity theft," the old Rick said.

"God," Avi said. "Where'd you get them?"

"I'm pals with the warden," Rick the contractor and Avi's former friend averred. "No one's a killer. Promise. You need a crew."

"I can't believe this," Avi said.

"They'll behave," Rick said. "What, you're a liberal?"

"Where's Itchy?" Avi asked. "Where's the Unabomber?"

"Don't be like that," Rick said, quoting Avi quoting Bean.

Then the drivers turned off their engines and got out of their vans—Henry, Rick's flashy buddy in a fancy suit; along with two grim, huge men, one X-ed with a bandolier—guards who stationed themselves on the sidewalk, ever vigilant. Of course, their handy shotguns were even more convincing than their demeanors or get-ups. Two men on the sidewalk with shotguns.

Live shotguns. Shotguns shoot people.

"Boss?" Rick said with a wink to Avi. "S'okay. Don't pick a fight."

The convicts milled about on the lawn in posses of twos, threes, and fours, some smoking, served Rick right, each one casing Maureen's little house, nothing secure, not even Dolly, who stood quizzically in the backyard, her nose jammed between pickets.

"That your dog?" said a nearby Williams, neck veins throbbing decoratively as part of his tattoo.

"A dog," someone said.

"Yeah," said Avi.

"I've got a dog," said the Williams who had spoken. "Checkers," he said wistfully.

Nixon? Avi thought. Nixon had a dog named Checkers. Avi tried again. "Help?" What the hell would he make for lunch for twenty-five? He'd have to cater.

"Okay, okay," Rick hollered in firm fashion. "Listen up, people. Si'down."

No one listened, no one sat.

"Rick . . ." Avi hissed again, "this isn't going to work."

"Shh," Rick hissed back. "Okay," he hollered again. "I'm talking here. . . ."

This time it worked: they sat, but not for Rick. Instead, all intransigence was countered by Henry, who had stepped silently to the front of the throng and pointed at the offending offenders, you and you. Henry, resplendent in gray pinstripes and black wingtips. Henry, who had yet to speak.

"Wow," Avi whispered to Rick.

"Yep," said Rick. "That's Henry. . . . Ready?"

"Oh, sure," Avi said. He threw up his hands. "What the hell." At least Bean wasn't here, and Mom and Dad were safely dead.

Rick showed Henry the simple plan. First, in places marked already, four holes would be dug while a fifty-pound bag of Sakrete was being mixed in the wheelbarrow, holes that formed a graceful line, a ten-degree curve along fifty feet of lawn. Then six-foot posts would be stood in each of the four holes, posts set in speckled gray concrete and framed with two-by-fours, marked and leveled with the Johnson post level, just right, hold it, hold it.

Four big posts, against which the raised whale would lean, until the next three posts, on the other side of her long body, were set to keep the beast from tipping or crashing.

Rick assigned, Henry pointed, the world rolled around like a marble in the mouth of the universe.

One Williams per post.

Main and The Deke on mixing and wheelbarrow.

Jung with a hose.

T. T. on shovel.

Satan and Shoe Glue on sponges.

The work began. They dug, they mixed, they poured, they fed the holes.

Avi had to pee, or thought he should. And then, for a time, he could only watch through the slatted blinds of the kitchen door, once he had secured Mom's hatches, deadbolts snapped into place. But when the concrete was poured, my God, Avi had to go out to join his crew—yes, his crew, every one a felon.

The Sakrete was drying. The twenty convicts drank from the hose and smoked and smoked, Rick looking on, yearning, each orange-vested man on Maureen's lawn present by virtue of malfeasance, kept there only by the grace of the signifying shotguns.

Avi did a loop around his whale, an orbit. As he came from behind a whale end, the big Lincoln cruised by, the twins low-riding, bright yellow floppy hats pulled down—in the big Lincoln that kept driving, the henchwomen apparently incompatible with incarcerated crooks, oil and fire.

Avi gave a little half-wave, a gesture sardonic and perverse, hiya girls, hee hee, what's the matter?

The rings were carried to their places and stood up, each great wooden donut pre-measured, notched, and fixed with an L-bracket mount. Eleven graduated rings, the central three and the final three—under the belly of the beast and under her tail and what would be her fluke—on flat bottoms that Rick and Avi had sawed clean, for balance. Were there enough men? Avi wasn't sure. But the rings were standing, the whale in a place that he had dreamed, so long that she curved around the yard, sinuous for her size.

Avi's heart beat faster than his thoughts could carry him.

They had planned first to attach the beams to the three largest central disks that six men now held upright, two per. At Rick's signal, translated by Henry into a directive, the other ring-holders laid down their smaller circles and fetched one of the enormously long beams. Five men to a beam, sixty-four feet long: they backed up, negotiated a turn, banged into a tree, backed up, stepped forward, swung wide the final thirty feet with each man taking tiny steps, almost tiptoe.

Seated in the grass, H. P. scribbled furiously with a chewed pencil.

By the carport, either Uzi or Mizzo, actor or soup, Avi couldn't recall which, lurked suspiciously.

Rick pointed. "Left, left, left, left—right, right—left, left, left. Okay! Hold it."

"Stop," said Henry.

The beam was poised along the length of what would be Avi's whale.

As they had decided, Rick would climb the ladder to the top of each ring, screw gun at the ready for when the men raised the beam into place.

As he had no choice, Avi would stand there and try to remember to breathe.

. . .

The shape of the whale filled the lawn. Through the shape of the whale, through the open form of its rings and beams, the world looked different, the neighbor's trees and houses framed anew and brilliantly saturated with color. She herself, Avi's whale, had yet to become a whale, but looking through her had already rearranged what looking meant.

And more than her shape, her mass: the whale was huge, as whales are, beginning near the driveway and curving ever so gracefully in front of the house and along the street, much longer than Maureen's house and half as tall. She made the house and trees and park look like a little kid had stuck them there for effect.

She rose, Avi's whale, and what he had never anticipated was that her silhouette alone had the capacity to change what he believed, to remake his desires. He had never thought her possible, in the same way one never really believes love possible until it has already come to be.

And still the whale creaked, despite being clamped and fastened at her joints, her complaint a clear warning to a man whose earlier, ill-conceived whale had collapsed. Even Avi could see and hear the need for increased structural integrity.

He felt fortunate to identify the problem quickly, after only two of her six long beams had been raised and fixed. But Avi's good fortune lay not in the insight with which he diagnosed the engineering dilemma; instead, with a complex problem to solve, he was fortunate to have a distraction from the roiling and burbling feelings that flooded his chest and clouded his vision.

Avi sketched madly with Rick while the convicts took another break—as two of the sneakier offenders were herded back into their gaggle with a look from Henry and the wave of a gun muzzle. Avi and Rick traded drawings in the Composition notebook, what to do: cross-beams were needed, or lodging knees; blocking had to be mounted inside the joinery at the whale's crucial junctures.

"She's a little arthritic," Avi said. "How about this?" He showed Rick a drawing:

"Naw," said Rick.

"Wait, how about this?" Avi grabbed the notebook and tried again.

"Better. See?" Rick made a quick correction.

"Still wrong," said Avi.

"Yep," said Rick.

So it went, the two men like a pair of Modernists inventing Modernism; Rick and Avi traded brains, their sketches almost each other's.

"Yo, yo," said a convict, tapping Rick on the shoulder.

Rick raised one hand, not now.

"Shee-it," said the convict, shuffling away.

"Wait. . . . There. That'll work. Got it," Avi said.

"Yep," said Rick. "And—" he drew one more line and labeled the picture.

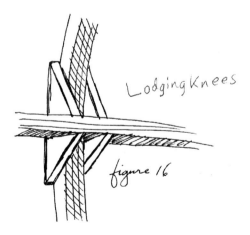

"Figure 16?" asked Avi.

"Lucky number." Then Rick, the Chinese-speaking, detoxed ex-smoker, pal of the warden, arterially-clogged carnivore, co-builder of a whale, and increasingly mysterious not to mention curiously resourceful employee, smiled. Not a broad grin, but curled enough at the corners of his mouth to constitute a look of happiness, his eyes crinkled smaller, his pupils like little black stars.

"Damn," said the smiling contractor, his first big smile ever.

"Amazing," said Avi, amazed by his compatriot.

"Damn," Rick repeated. "Henry," Rick looked up, called out. "Supply run."

Rick made a list of the supplies needed to secure the beast athwart, requisitioned Avi's credit card, revved a van, and deputized three convicts and a guard, let's go. The other jailbirds flocked by the two remaining N.C. state vehicles, sprawled in antisocial attitudes, heads cocked or lolled, their comportments defiant. Someone rapped badly, beat box and console noises sputtered. Cards were pulled from a pocket and riffled.

These were his men. Avi felt a fondness for them, still a liberal: he went inside and stirred up two pitchers of lemonade-from-concentrate, grabbed a stack of Solo cups, and returned to his comrades.

"Got any gin?" Main laughed, as Avi poured him a cup of pink brew.

"Hearts," said Satan, holding up his cards. "We're playing hearts," he said.

"Moron," said someone. "Gin to drink. To get smashed."

"I shall be redeemed," said Satan. He pointed skyward in a gesture of sanctimony, then furrowed his brow and lowered his hand to point at the troublemaker. "Asshole."

Avi poured the lemonade, worked the crowd, and sneaked himself a cup before the drink ran dry; then he left them to their remaining guard and the dapper Henry, and to the empty promises of whispered schemes, recidivism a *fait accompli*.

He looked at the convicts where they lay. Could these men be redeemed?

Could Avi? Hey, he had built a whale, almost.

He put down the empty pitchers and approached the half-finished mammal, loathe to get too close just yet, for fear he might suffer the experience incompletely, an acolyte neither ready nor worthy. Avi squatted by the frame, just beyond arm's length. The beams curved, canted around the corner, a suburban leviathan, a wooden whale making its own ocean of the lawn and the trees and the street.

A raucous semi-ruckus sounded near the vans, the convicts about to kill each other. Avi glanced over, to where the guard was wading into a scrum, and watched the pushing resolve into chest thumping and threats, cards scattered on the lawn. Wasn't there a scattered card game in *Through the Looking Glass*? It seemed possible that he, in his way, was an Alice. "Go ask Alice," Grace Slick had sung to the turned-on and tuned-out, a song Dad had always liked. Dad, who couldn't carry a tune and loved to sing.

Dad, who had said to Mom that he would raise their son; their son, who was raising a whale.

Avi wished he could look up through the frame of the beast and see his future happiness, not only that imminent moment—this evening perhaps, or tomorrow morning, so soon—when he alone would hang and swing in the whale, but also beyond. Bean might be there, in a future he couldn't see, at least for a while, or she might not. There would be money, of course; he would inherit the wind, find and sell the list, and use all the cash to open a restaurant in Taos or Sedona, a gentleman chef catering to the well-heeled alternative universe, his Trustafarian clientele chowing greedily on Avi's famous jicama salsa.

Yet all he could see was the present: despite wanting the clouds to resolve into augury, the clouds were clouds, beautiful in their quick motion through the high sky, but only clouds. To see a dream life, Avi would have to live it.

No, that wasn't true: he could see some of the past mixed into the present, imagine Maureen squinting out her kitchen window at the clouds Avi could see now. There, on her lawn, was a whale: what would she have thought? He had never really considered what Mom had seen, or thought, or felt. What had Mom loved?

· · ·

Rick returned with the supplies, boards and blocks ready for installation, and work resumed, the inmates reorganized into squads, their cooperation improved. Near Avi, at the edge of the driveway and the head of the whale, as the crew swarmed over the wooden beast, stood the silent Henry, who had taken off his suit jacket; with a dash of panache, he wore a pair of red braces. A muscular and trim man, maybe in his forties, Henry stood with the pride of someone who looks good.

Avi scratched his unshaven chin, sheepish.

But the whale: steadily, as though powering motionless through the brine, she began to add mass, to imply life.

One beam to go. Rick had returned with two additional ladders, and now three of the convicts were perched on high along the long, curved length of the beast. They fastened the L-brackets, slotted a beam, and passed along the screw gun—run down the line by one of the Williamses—bantering, laughing easily. Their orange vests seemed apt, the flashes of hazardous color a reminder of an incalculable danger.

The yard filled with the sounds of the conscripted, who seemed to have figured out that the assignment was a plum. No one sweated much and few swore. To be out of their cells and working with their hands . . . Avi understood. He looked around. A crowd had gathered across the street in front of Sascha's house, probably other neighbors. There was Sascha, clutching a cocktail in a rock glass. Avi waved, and Sascha lifted his drink, a toast. Avi wondered if he could have a mimosa. Waiter?

"What now, Boss?" Rick gave a side-to-side wiggle to adjust his lumbar brace.

Avi shook his head, dumb.

"You okay?"

"Yep," Avi said, the voice surely someone else's. "Nope," he confessed.

"Yep," Rick agreed. "She's something. Where's the book?" Rick took the Composition book from Avi, and found the design. "Here," he pointed.

Avi cleared his throat, as though that might help. "Yep," he said, choking up.

"Boss?" Rick squeezed his face a bit to gaze at Avi, the tall foreman checking on his incompetent superior.

"I'm okay," Avi gathered himself. "Let's brace her."

"Naw," Rick said. "Not yet. Raise her, drive the wedges, set the poles, and then."

"And then," Avi repeated. Again, he had to gather himself. He stood. "Okay," he said. "Ropes."

"Ropes," Rick agreed.

"The strain won't rip her apart?"

"Dunno," Rick said. "Don't think so."

"All that pressure on her body. Like being at sea for her, I'd think," Avi said quietly. "Seawater. Waves."

"Yep," Rick said. "I imagine. What about the bottom?"

"The bottom?"

"Gotta line her. Just remembered. Concentrate," he said nicely.

Avi tried. He considered the problem: the chance of rain, the moisture that would rise with the dew and dawn, the bugs, the house at the foot of three big hills, all that runoff. "Yep," he said. "Swimming pool stuff?"

"That vinyl we talked about." He flipped through the notebook, found the page in the plans. "Here. Canvas pieced on top. Her skin."

"Yep," Avi said, imitating Rick.

"Gotcha. I'll get it all. You hang."

Again a supply run was planned, convicts pressed into a mini-gang—and shortly thereafter, nicely pre-arranged by Rick or Henry, news to Avi, pizza arrived, ten pies in all, the delivery kid so happy with the huge order that he looked as though he had just been kissed for the first time. Sprawled across the lawn, once more in their posses, the inmates broke the morning fast, their poses non-violent for now. Avi ate two slices, almost in the crew, a tree at his back: the pizza wasn't bad, the sauce salty but fresh enough, and he was hungrier than he thought. He got a little blob of tomato sauce on his shirt.

By the time Rick had returned, Avi and the prisoners were getting restless.

"You ready?" Rick wandered over.

Avi nodded, scrambling up, the spit-damp napkin with which he had scrubbed his shirt useless to clean the stain. "Did I pay for that lunch?"

"Yep," Rick said. "S'in the budget. Labor."

"Gotcha," Avi said. Thanks, Mom.

"You bleeding?" Rick asked.

Avi laughed. "Pizza."

"Got a smoke?" Rick asked.

"Rick, man . . ."

"No, really," Rick implored. "See. They're smoking. It's after lunch."

"Rick," Avi said. "Look. Let's raise her."

"Fine," Rick said glumly. Then he gnashed his teeth a little, a smoker's gnash.

Another half-hour, or an hour, or a year, Avi's adrenalin wouldn't allow him to keep time—but by then, however much later it was, the men were organized and ready. Six ropes, three inmates to a rope, everyone wearing work gloves that had mysteriously appeared from one of the vans, courtesy of the State Pen. (Or so Avi hoped, his credit card still in Rick's pocket.) Two convicts manned each heavy plastic, triangular block. Looped around the intersections of ring and beam, the ropes were slip-knotted by Rick, who apparently had had some nautical training too. Perhaps he had been a midshipman in the Chinese navy, and he probably even knew how to say *midshipman* in Chinese, or better yet, *I dreamed a big wooden whale was out my window.* . . .

Six ropes, eighteen men. They adjusted their gloves, suddenly less chatty, expectant, eyes on Henry who waited for Rick's signal. The signal came, Rick to Henry, who wordlessly lifted his hand, the ropes lifting in response, the scene tightening. . . .

One, two, three, *pull*. Their labors had the aura of a Cecil B. DeMille epic, the identically dressed convicts exhorted to man their ropes—one, two, three, *pull*—and hold steady the unbelievably heavy folly of the Emperor. One, two, three, *pull*. Slack was drawn up, tethers tightened, men dug in their prison-issue heels, clouds blocked the sun, and the light seemed to flatten.

One, two, three, *pull.*

The whale groaned, rolled up on her side a few feet.

One, two, three, *pull.*

Pull, you bastards, pull, Avi thought with fiery glee.

One, two, three, *pull.*

One, two, three, *pull.*

"And hold it," Rick said, and Henry held up his hand.

They held. She was aloft, on edge. She swam on her flank through the air of Mom's yard.

"Wedges!" Rick called, and the men who held them didn't hesitate, running to the beast to slip the huge plastic triangles under her belly.

"Hold it," Rick said.

Avi wanted not to cry.

"And down. . . ." Rick crooned slowly. "Steady," Rick said.

"Steady," Avi whispered.

Henry's hand came down slowly and the men on the ropes walked up their lines, fist over fist toward the whale as she groaned once again and rolled down a few inches—maybe eight or ten—to settle. If a great inanimate wooden beast could sigh, she did.

"There," Rick said. "Okay," he called. "Now!" The inmates released their ropes, and the whale held.

The whale held.

Almost at once the inmates returned to their error-filled lives, the guy named Shoe Glue engaged in a pushing match with a dude whose name Avi couldn't recall.

"Hey!" Avi called loudly. "Quit it."

Shoe Glue stopped his antics, stared at Avi. "Fuck."

"That's enough," Avi said. "Three posts go in, while we tack the vinyl to her belly, then the wedges come out. Dig and pour," he added. "Then upholstery."

Henry pointed to a few of the men, and work resumed briskly with a kind of low melody. Even Satan looked less glum.

Avi felt in charge at last, for a few minutes anyway, as there she was, awaiting her posts, the open fencing or pen in which his whale would soon blissfully lie. He could almost touch her or step inside her, climb the tallest ladder available, the tallest beam ready to be swung from, but he had decided to wait to swing, at least until the sun went down, and for his wonderful crew of awful people to go back to jail, which meant that he would have to wait until nightfall, as the vinyl skin, lodging knees, battens, and plating all had to be installed first. And the concrete needed time, Avi remembered, one-half hour to set and eight hours before it could be walked upon, so said the instructions on the bag. Eight hours—that meant tomorrow at the earliest. He corrected his vision: for now Avi could look, but he could not swing.

He would call everyone. He would Google all his ex-girlfriends, email everyone at the Blue Egg, call Markins, come to the swinging. To the hanging, he thought nonsensically. Look what I made, he would say.

He realized that he had turned away, if only to breathe. In Maureen's fenced yard, relentlessly curious, Dolly paced, the excitement too much, her dog-day disturbed. She had dug a hole where the fence met the carport, to try to get under and join the fun. What a good girl.

Doll-Doll was barking, and Avi wandered over to reassure her. "It's okay, good girl, it's my whale, it's okay. . . ."

"*Woof, woof, woof, woof!*"

He reached through the fence to scratch her big head. She leaned into his hand.

"Boss," Rick said.

Avi jumped. "Ah! Gotta stop sneaking up on people!"

"My ex- said that," Rick said. "Damn, you're tense."

"She was right."

"Boss," Rick leaned on the fence. "We're working through dinner. More pizza?"

"Now you ask," Avi said with a little laugh. "You've got my credit card," he forced a chuckle. "Sure, but something else. . . . So . . . how is it that they're here? How'd you get them?"

"Community service," Rick said. "Work detail."

"Gotcha," Avi said. He turned around. "It's all a party." He gave a chuck of his chin to indicate the neighbors. Six people sat on Sascha's front steps and watched the whale and the convicts, cocktail hour in Elsbeth. "And the cops? They're gonna lay off? No one's gonna put me in a cell with Satan?"

"Can't help with the neighbors. Town's good."

"'Cause you called someone."

"Yep."

"Your pal the warden."

"Yep. The game warden. The Coast Guard."

"And what about the newspapers and TV?"

"Boss, they're yours."

"They're coming," Avi realized. "Don'tcha think?"

"Yep," said Rick. "All the beat writers smoke."

"Yeah," said Avi, not paying attention anymore. "The whale's gotta be hers. I'll tell them it was Mom's dying wish. You think?"

Rick narrowed his gaze. "No. Don't," he said sternly. "Never."

"What? Don't? I mean, why?"

"No lies. It's ours. She's yours."

"I guess," said Avi.

"No lies," said Rick, adamant and matter-of-fact—then he quickly tapped his hearing aid. "People ask, you tell 'em."

"But you're lying to me," Avi said as he turned to face his contractor, the statement so clearly true that Avi surprised himself by not having said so sooner. "You and your hearing aid. . . ."

Rick said nothing.

"And it's weird, because I trust you. I mean, I trust that your lying is in my best interest, you know—not that I have any idea why. Or how. I mean . . . dammit, I think you're trying to help me. That's why you're here. Crap, I mean look—" he waved his hand at the whale and the whale raisers.

"I am here to help," Rick said. "Trust that."

"Good," said Avi.

"Good. So trust me all the way," Rick said. "That's what trust is. Not a little trust, but all. For the whale."

Avi thought it over. "Okay," he said. "For the whale." Then he extended his fist like a home run hitter, and Rick met the gesture with his own, a fist bump between whale-building friends or a presidential couple. "How do you say *fist* in Chinese?" Avi asked, but before Rick could answer, Avi said, "In whale song, it's *ooooooaaaaaheeeeee*."

The singing had been too loud. A clump of convicts nearby stopped for a moment, looked at Avi.

"Sorry everyone," Avi waved. "Orgasm," he explained.

FOURTEEN

WHEN HE LET DOLLY OUT for her morning pee-'n-poop, and kept her company in the dewy yard, c-c-c-c-c-offee in hand, Avi noticed a Channel 6 news van parked in the street. He got a better look: a broadcast tower rose from the vehicle, the adverts on the van's side promising swift and sure reporting, THE TRUTH BE TOLD. Ten seconds of the truth, Avi suspected. Just the tip of the truth-berg.

Crap, he had been spotted.

"Rick! Rick Woodley!" The reporter was cute, even with make-up finished with a crème brulée torch. "Rick! Channel 6, 6 News in the Street. Do you have a minute?" She skittered on her heels to the picket fence, trailed by a cameraman.

"*Woof,*" said Dolly half-heartedly.

"Nice dog," the reporter said. "What is he?"

"A she," said Avi. But then, because the response was snarky, he added helpfully: "She's a mutt."

"I always think that dogs are boys. Do you have a minute?" the reporter repeated.

"Sure," Avi said, feeling guilty for being rude. He opened the gate, stepped out.

"Rick, I'm Hannah Cara Papadopoulos, Channel 6, 6 News in the Street."

"That's a name," Avi said. "I'm Avi."

"Avi?" She turned to gaze quizzically around. "Is Rick inside?"

"That's me," Avi said. In his mental mirror Avi checked his kit, examined his caboodle: freshly shaved, a reasonable shirt.

"Got it," she said uncomprehendingly. "Do you mind if we roll—" The camera was already filming, the light mounted above the lens shone brighter than daylight, the question lay moot. "We're here with Rick Woodley. Rick, you're up to something. What's the story?" She walked to the whale, trying to turn Avi around so that the wooden behemoth would be in the shot as a backdrop.

"What are you building?"

"It's a whale," Avi said. All but the upholstery, he wanted to add.

"Gosh, that's cool. It's big," she said. "So what's the story?"

He had to admire how Hannah Cara Papadopoulos had made herself so erotically inert, her pompoms traded in, her evident cheerleading skills professionalized, human interest her assigned bailiwick. Maybe she was still a cheerleader, more so than a reporter? The news was entertainment, of course.

"It's a project . . ." he offered. "I'm . . . it's a kinda work-release project."

"So the prisoners are involved?"

"They're the point," Avi lied. Sorry, Rick.

"But why a whale? Does it mean something special? Is it art?"

With a small sweep of his right hand, he gestured. "Does it look like art?"

"Maybe," she chirped. She could be twenty-one; she could be thirty. "So why are you building a whale? C'mon, Rick, you're not much of a story yet."

"It's . . . it's . . . rehabilitation."

She shook her head and signaled to her cameraman, then turned to frame a parting shot, her hair perfect. "So there you have it," she said into her mic. "What Rick Woodley, one citizen, is doing to address jail crowding, and to help men who need help. For Channel 6, 6 News in the Street, I'm Hannah Cara Papadopoulos. The truth be told. . . . And . . . out," she gave the cut sign, the camera's glaring light switched off. "Rick, that wasn't good."

"Sorry."

"How about we try again? Will the prisoners be here today?"

"Soon," he admitted, unfortunately.

"Good," she reached forward, and shook his hand. "Call me Hannah," she said.

What else would he have called her, Avi wondered. "Rick," he said. This was going to be more fun than he had thought. He would have to work on his spiel.

"Hannah." She gave him a funny stare.

"Rick," Avi said again. "And now if you'll excuse me. . . ."

. . .

It takes a prison, Avi thought.

The real Rick showed up in his pickup, the three white vans arrived and parked. Were the inmate-campers singing "100 Bottles of Beer on the Whale"? He stepped outside to greet his crew, and there was the reporter: with a snapping of fingers, Hannah Cara Papadopoulos bade her cameraman to film, and did another swiftly tiptoed teeter across the grass.

Sascha sat on his front stoop. Avi waved across the street, and Sascha waved back. He was munching what looked to be a pastry from a paper bag—maybe cookies from one of the Elsbeth Moravian bakeries.

"*Hellloooo,*" the reporter half-crooned and half-cooed. "Hannah Cara Papadopoulos, Channel 6, 6 News in the Street."

In the cab of his pickup truck, aghast, Rick waved frantically to Avi, no reporters. Avi shrugged a Rick shrug, a happy non-apology.

"Hellloooo! Gentlemen, would you like to be on TV?"

The response was extraordinary. With one exception, the inmates covered their faces as they de-vanned, and as though through a media gauntlet, hustled themselves into an imagined courtroom. If they had been wearing jackets, the prisoners would have pulled the jackets over their heads. Johnny Cochran would have been proud.

The one exception was Satan, who stepped forward to greet the telecommunications universe. "Hiya," he half-chortled.

"Hello, there. Hannah Cara Papadopoulos, Channel 6, 6 News in the Street."

She and her cameraman almost skidded to a stop. The reporter seemed winded, or purposefully breathy. "Hannah Cara Papadopoulos, Channel 6, 6 News in the Street."

"Jimmy Stewart," said Satan.

"Jimmy Stewart?" She nodded seriously, inquiring.

"I'm adopted," said Satan.

"Well, then," she spoke into the lens. "This is Hannah Cara Papadopoulos with Jimmy Stewart. Can you tell me about this whale you're building—or if you don't mind saying, what are you in for?"

Satan smiled. "You're all going to burn in hell," he said. "Soon," he added, the sibilant whistling through a gap in his teeth.

"Ah, I see. . . . Thank you, Jimmy. And out," said Hannah Cara Papadopoulos. And then, "We're filing, Rodney," she added to her cameraman. "Set the uplink."

"Fuck," said Rick, somehow approaching from the other side of the whale.

"Yep. Gonna be worse." Avi squeaked a little by accident. "Didn't *you* warn *me*? Man, you might wanna try a disguise."

"Shit," said Rick. "She smoke?" He tapped his hearing aid. "Morn," he said, his tone shifting.

"Morn," said Avi. "Shall we?"

"Fuck it," Rick said. "Yep."

"Fuck it," Avi echoed.

This morning, Henry wore a chocolate brown suit, the fabric flowing where it hung on his substantial physique, a soft pewter tie and a creamy, button-down pinpoint Oxford. When he approached, Avi noticed that the suit was pinstriped, the shoes wing-tipped once again. Henry had it going on.

"G'morning," Avi said.

Henry nodded.

"Nice duds."

"Windy Oaks." Henry actually spoke.

Avi didn't understand. He smiled to cover his confusion. "Windy Oaks," Avi repeated. "Henry," Avi said. "How you doin'?"

"Splendid," said Henry.

"Splendid?"

Henry gave a wide smile. "It's a whale," he said. "It touches me right here in my feelings," he put a hand over his heart. "It's very moving."

The guards were different today, as were a few of the prisoners, among them a pair of motley miscreants who would look dirty even if freshly showered, scrubbed, and standing in an operating room. Those two would have to pee outside, Avi decided. So much for being a liberal.

Rick and Avi planned their attack. The whale needed some final carpentry—for the battens and lodging knees to be secured and the L-braces to be checked— and then the vinyl and the tenting could be applied. A couple of hours at most, the builders of the whale figured. Right, Avi tried to say. His breath seemed to be holding itself again.

The work began, right it was, as Channel 6 filmed and all of the bright morning became a sun-splashed blur. A chat with Sascha, Dolly racing along the fence line, Bean on the phone—see you soon—and Avi and his whale. His feelings were in his hands, his dream was in the whale, the whale was in his chest, his eyes were open and unseeing, her eyes were open and unseeing.

But one image burned into him: three inmates, each on ladders perched along her length, the geometry a kind of music, the giant Os and long beams and the triangles of the ladders impossibly beautiful and Pythagorean. From ten feet away, Henry threw a hammer to a man atop the nearest ladder, and the hammer never tumbled in the air, its head perfectly aloft, flying upright, silent and lovely.

Then pizza arrived and was devoured, soft drinks instead of lemonade, and Avi waved Sascha over for a slice. What was going on at Sascha's? Avi kept glancing across the street, where more neighbors had congregated, eight or nine now on the Crimean Steps, everyone always apparently drinking something, mint juleps or Sex on the Beach. There wasn't enough pizza to feed Russia, just like throughout history.

One, two, three, *pull*. The whale was in her braces, moored and reinforced; on the lodging knees, fresh ply had been laid in the belly of the beast, a narrow subfloor, but wide enough for Avi's needs.

Oh, Bean. Thank God.

"Hi," she said. She wore a little poofed skirt with crinoline or something, and shoes that might have been dance slippers. Jingle earrings, a tie-dyed tank top. She dangled a bottle of something delightful in one hand, and had a little gift-wrapped silvery package in the other.

"Hi," Avi said. He had to kiss her. He did. "You look great."

"Thanks," she said. "What's with them?" She gestured with the champagne toward the news vans.

Vans? Dammit, Avi thought. A second van had arrived. . . . "It's a whale," Avi said.

"Oh my," she said. "So this is your crew?"

"They're convicts," Avi said.

"Of course they are. Now what?"

"Now?" Avi hadn't figured out *now* for a number of hours. "Now?" He paused. "Now she gets her skin. Then we'll put on a show." He had a thought. "The TV reporter doesn't bother you? You're not . . . worried?"

Bean laughed. "About? Oh, I see," she nodded. "No, I'm not worried. There's a difference between robbing banks and *getting caught robbing a bank*."

Avi laughed, his chest tight. "I'm caught," he confessed. "By all this." He swept his hand dramatically, then felt self-conscious. He lowered his voice. "By you," he said.

"Oh, aren't you sweet," Bean said. "That's good, 'cause I'm pregnant!"

"You're what? Oh, Jesus! How the hell—"

Bean was laughing at him. What was so funny? "It's a girl." Bean laughed harder. "You're such a sucker," Bean said. She tilted her head upwards. "I want to kiss your cheek," she said. And so she did.

"You're not pregnant," Avi said.

"Condoms? Susan Junior? Remember, you were there. . . ."

"Right," Avi said, trying to play too. "I seem to recall—what's your name again?"

"Oh, cute," Bean punched his shoulder, not hard. "Aren't you the romantic."

"Mi Ha," Rick said from nowhere.

"Damn, Rick!" Avi was startled. "Stop sneaking up!"

"Can't help it," Rick said. "I'm in silent mode."

The three of them stood there for a moment and admired the crew's labors, the convicts perched on ladders, the bottom and top fabrics laid out on the lawn for measuring and piecing, the guards with shotguns, the media not quite thronged.

"Nice day for a whale," Avi said to Rick.

"Now can I smoke?" Rick asked.

"Here," Bean said. "I think I've got some in my purse. . . ." She rummaged.

"You do?" Rick became a little bug-eyed. "A cigarette. . . ."

"Naw," Bean said. "Just fooling!" Her voice was sing-song. "I don't smoke!"

"Shit," Rick said. "That's mean."

Avi laughed. "I knew I liked you," he beamed at Bean. Then he put his arm around her. "We're pregnant," Avi boasted to Rick.

. . .

The prisoners had gone back to prison, the neighbors had gone back to the neighborhood. The whale was on the lawn. The TV people, all spiffy in their on-air duds, lifted by their facelifts, clamored for comment, microphones an *attaque simple*, more TV people than Avi had noticed before.

"Mr. Woodley, over here."

"Mr. Woodley, Mr. Woodley!"

"Mr. Woodley, what's the whale for?"

"Rick?" said Avi's new friend, Hannah Cara Papadopoulos. "How about an exclusive."

"Rick," another reporter picked up the first name. "Tell us what you're going to do. Why have you done this?"

Avi raised his hand to say *wait*, and then, purposeful, he turned his back to the cameras and strode so that they would follow him to the whale, straightening his shirt as he walked. "I've got a prepared statement," he demurred. Avi didn't, but when he arrived at his very own whale, he laid one hand on her almost-breathing frame, and with the other hand removed the receipt for the pizza delivery from his pocket. Why not, Avi thought. Then he gave the piece of paper a formal kind of snap, and pretended to read from the page; the No Bullshit Rule didn't apply to the Fourth Estate, of course.

"Ladies and Gentlemen. Citizens of Elsbeth. Last fall, in consultation with the authorities, I began a project, the goal of which is to offer constructive rehabilitation, um, opportunities to men in jail, to people who might knife each other if someone in the TV room changed the channel from their favorite soap to the news." He smiled, irony delicious. "What you see is the beginning of . . . the start of the early returns." Avi snapped the little piece of paper once again, then refolded it, done, so there. "I've created a foundation with monies I inherited, and this is our test case. It's called What Has Anyone . . . Left—" he faltered. He couldn't find the right E-word. "It's called the W.H.A.L.E. Foundation. The "E" is for Ever," he added nonsensically. "Tomorrow, when the tenting has been applied, the Foundation will have finished its first project. You can speak to our lawyer if you would like details; he's Jack Markins here in town. And . . . and that's all I have for you. Oh, yeah, the website's almost live, and soon you'll be able to find out more, www.housewhale.com. Streaming video," he offered, the absurdity escalating. "Tweets. RSS. Our Board of Directors . . ." he began, but didn't know where to take that idea. "Um . . . thanks you," he said. "Each of you. My brother thanks you."

"But Rick, why a whale?"

"What's going to happen to it?"

"Have you ever built a whale?"

"Did your mother want this?"

"Good people," Avi interjected, the final question too personal. "Have some faith. For the past two days, these poor, lost men have built something with their hands rather than count ceiling tiles. I call that success. Now if you'll excuse me, it's late and my dog would like her dinner." Avi began to walk away, and felt one camera light go out and then another. The story would be on at six, he supposed.

Trailed to the kitchen door by Hannah Cara Papadopoulos, he let himself exhale; Rick could be Avi's fake brother.

"Oh, c'mon, Rick. We're all friends here. Off the record—" she waved to indicate their distance from her cameraman. "What's the poop?"

"No poop," he said. "Wysiwyg."

"Wysiwyg."

"Yep," Avi said. "That's foundation talk."

"I see," she said.

"There's a bee in your hair," Avi said, because there was.

"A bee! Where?"

"There," he pointed.

"A bee! A bee! A bee! *Roddd-nnneeeeeyyyyy!*" She skittered across the lawn in a stiletto-heeled, tiptoed dash, a million panicked little girl steps.

"Sorry," Avi said to her absence. "There was a bee there."

He opened the door. In the kitchen, Bean sat mostly naked on the counter, her party dress poofed around her waist, her earrings like silver curlicues, her smile knowing.

"Hey!"

"I was hot," she said.

"Damn," he shook his head. "You are hot," he added stupidly. "I mean . . ."

"Wanna kiss?" she held up the champagne bottle by its neck.

"Okay," he locked the door behind him. "Where's Rick?"

"Gone. I got you a present."

Avi stepped forward into her embrace, her legs locking around him, and they kissed, a light and wet kiss, her lips a lovely little piece of fruit. "I like presents," Avi said. "But we'll need to save some champagne. For Rick. For tomorrow."

"Rick, Rick, Rick," Bean said. She kissed him again.

"The reporters are right there . . ." he tried to finish saying.

"Yes," she said. Kiss.

"Bean. . . ."

"*Mmm?*" She drew back, licked his upper lip.

"I . . ."

"I know," she said. She reached back on the counter and found her bra. "I just wanted to get you all worked up." She moved her hand to rub his crotch, the erection in his shorts. "When you're turned on and you can't talk, you say the cutest things."

Avi could bullshit but not talk. He pulled away, although moving away from a naked Bean couldn't have been dumber. "I have too many thoughts in my head!" He laughed, straightened his clothing. "You, the convicts, the media. Did you see those people across the street? It's like a scenic overlook, or something. I mean, God!" Avi paused, Bean so tempting. He turned to peek out the side door blinds. "You know, those guys did a good job raising her. She's—" he faltered.

"She," Bean said. "I like it." He turned back. The bra was on. Phooey.

"She," Avi said. "I'd like to move some stuff to the whale. For tomorrow."

"Okay," Bean ruffled her hair to spikiness with some kind of gel.

"I like when you do that. Do that again," he asked, although he stayed across the room.

"Do what?" she said. "This?" With both hands, she spiked her hair once more.

"It's like a librarian," he said. "Miss Bean."

"Wow," she smiled. "Kink. Miss Bean, would you come help me in Reference?" she cooed, her head tilted.

"Oh, man. I'll be right there!"

Bean laughed. "You're a weirdo," she said. She slipped her top back on. "Cute, though. . . . So what goes in the whale?"

"Right," Avi told himself. "The whale. . . . The table and chairs. And my camping pad, and some blankets and pillows. Not for tonight," Avi told himself. "For tomorrow night. And some stuff . . . of my mom's," he said, the last phrase hard to say.

"Got it," Bean said. "Let's do it," she said.

Dolly peeked in through the back-door screen, her stare blazing, telepathy a dog's best friend.

"Oops. Gotta feed Dolly."

"I'll be happy to help," Bean said. "When I'm done with the card catalogue."

"Oh, crap," Avi said. "Miss Bean, can you help me? Please?"

Let back inside, Dolly stamped her feet and huffed, miffed to wait for her kibble—and so Avi fetched a big frozen soup bone to thaw for her as an after-dinner mint, even though a whale-day early. When she saw the bone, she began to whine and dance, and to salivate so strongly that she sneezed. Nothing like a satisfied customer. Maybe "Avi and Maria's" restaurant should have an attached doggie diner.

The first item hauled to the whale was the cookie jar, which Avi was glad to lug outside while Bean went to the bathroom, Maureen's ugly jar not sneakable. Backing out the door butt-first, and then swinging around to face the imminent dusk and the newly risen beast, the behemoth's silhouette darkening, Avi felt like he was carrying some kind of ceremonial object, a big ol' bowl of personal history lost and untrue, her Soul Diary. He felt like an ancient priest.

But Mom was the source of all things whale, Avi realized: he was here for her and not for Dad. Dad who was dead longer, Dad who had remarried and re-divorced, Dad who would call or not, Dad who was easy to like. Grieving for Dad was finished, Avi knew, nothing too complicated, each of those feelings smaller than a whale.

Mom, who was hard to like and harder to love . . .

Bean helped with the table, which had to be turned and maneuvered, two legs out the door, angled, and then the other two. Then Maureen's best: four chairs, the good china, bedding, and some strings of party lights, paper Japanese globes of many colors. An extension cord for the lights to connect to an outlet in the carport. Six candlestick holders, all different, and six different colors of tapers: white, red, steely gray, blue, yellow, and something kind of watermelony red. A good tablecloth, heavy and elegant, that Avi had been surprised to find in a chest, along with the dark blue cloth napkins and the teak napkin rings he almost remembered. Mom's funky salad tongs

He wanted flowers but had nothing fresh. So Avi took down from the shelf and brought outside Maureen's copy of the *Webster's 9th*, the pressed flora too delicate to carry free of the dictionary, then laid the pretty, dried blooms on the white cloth, very nice, as though they were floating. Bean approved. She finished making the makeshift bed on the plywood floor—in the whale's belly, really, but tucked into the tail too—and then lay there, the cutest bank robber ever to lie in a wooden whale.

Avi ducked under a beam and turned back toward the house. He wanted Dolly's bowl.

A horn honked. Around the corner squealed a multi-colored, paint-speckled van, splashed with colors as though from a giant brush, flick, flick. The van drove up on Maureen's lawn, and parked with a mechanical groan and a couple of engine ticks right there on the grass, holy crap, get off the lawn.

"Man! Whale Man!" Swinging wide the driver's side door, a nattily dressed older guy—seersucker suit, his ponytail done up in an orange Scrunci—hopped to the ground. "Sorry 'bout the parking job. Man . . . oh, wow. Cool," the guy said. "Man, it's like so real. The energy. . . ." The new arrival skipped reverentially to the whale and put his hands high above his head, palms toward the beast, ready to receive something. "Wow. Listen."

Could he hear the whale too? Avi wondered. That would be weird, and a little awesome.

"Man . . ." he lowered his voice to indicate Bean, his finger waggling excitedly. "You've got, like, *a virgin*." He began to walk toward Avi's whale—too close.

Bean lifted her head, gave a little wave. Avi's visitor waved back.

"I'm sorry," Avi played goalie. "You can't go in there."

"Oh, yeah, I can't go in there!" Pony Tail Guy stopped just short of stepping inside. "It's like too holy! Should I bathe or something, Whale Man? Like will you hose me down, or dunk me, and then I can? Please? Got some water from the Ganges? Man, it's like—"

"I'm sorry," Avi repeated. "She's not open to the public."

"She," the worshipper murmured. "*Wuhhhhh.*"

"It's a figure of speech," Avi said, regretfully.

"*Sheeeee,*" the visitor gave a full-body salaam. "*Sheeeeee.*"

"I'm sorry," he repeated. "She's not open to the public," said Avi Heyer, Whale Man, as he escorted the visitor back to his van. "You need to leave."

Led away, curiously acquiescent, bowing as he revved his engine, the goony acolyte peeled out in reverse, barely looking where he was driving, his tires tearing a double strip in Maureen's lawn. "I'll be back, dude!" he yelled out his window. "Whalie whale!" he shouted.

Avi felt too weird to stay in the whale, especially now that she was furnished, although he didn't know why, and he was too hungry for talk therapy. So they went inside, where he and Bean had a salad supper, good cheese, excellent figs, and a bottle of wine, a Rioja he didn't really like after the second glass. But he did like Bean, and so they invented sex, and then later, they invented sex again before she didn't stay the night.

Bean who wouldn't stay. If he were a bank, she would have stayed.

· · ·

It was a new day in human time, but the same day for a wooden whale. A prison van arrived and seven convicts alit slowly, each outfitted once again in a drab jumpsuit and a lovely, Day-Glo, government-issue vest. As the little parade began, Henry emerged from his truck to keep watch, along with the guard-with-shotgun. Everyone behaved seriously, except for Avi, who had begun to feel himself in charge, *sous* to no one. He greeted his crew heartily, "Good morning, fellas! Deke, Peaches, Williams, Williams, T. T., Satan—"

"I'm Jimmy Stewart," said Satan, gaunt and irascible.

"Oh, right," said Avi. "Satan. And someone new. My, my. Who's this?"

Satan snarled at Avi, but Deke laughed. "This here's Abdu," Deke gestured toward a pencil-mustached felon.

"Pleased to meetcha," Avi said as they shook hands. He felt so capable he puffed up for the news crews; the whale, the jailed, the congregation, and the philanthropist all caught in the camera's crosshairs. Three news vans already. . . .

"Hola," said Abdu.

"Spanish?" said Avi.

"He's burning in hell," said Satan. "All of you are."

"But not you," said Peaches, "'cause you're not a fornicator."

"Unnatural acts! Crimes against nature!" Satan raised his voice, one finger pointed toward the sky, an imaginary Bible clutched to his chest. "Kneel before your savior!"

"All right, already," said Deke. "You wanna get us pulled? The job's sweet, you fuckhead. Pizza, 'member?"

"*Fornicator*," whispered Peaches gleefully.

"Gentlemen. . . ." Semi-encircled, Avi addressed his unchained gang. "Over here," he motioned. "Got a lot to cover," he punned, in charge.

If asked, Avi would have had little reason to explain this morning's mood, which seemed a kind of giddy bravado, but he knew better than to question happiness. The whale was about to be a whale, and the assistant had taken control of the situation at last. The assistant also, apparently, had a case of the sillies. After just a few minutes on the lawn, the prisoners seemed to have been infected with Avi's mood. With the exception of the dour Satan, they bantered and guffawed as they awaited their next assignment, apparently willing to be filmed this time, or bade not to run and hide. The newsies jabbered into microphones, the broadcast towers towered over the scene, and for a split-second, with eye-blinking and a gasp, Avi panicked, the media vehicles like a fleet of whaleboats ready to harpoon his plans.

But then he gulped, calmed himself down. Work works, he told himself, quoting Rick. Be happy. Worry. . . . So where was Rick?

Avi instructed, the prisoners listened—until Peaches exclaimed, "Oh, honey, I got this!" a delighted incarcerated seamster let loose upon a naked whale. "Costumes I can do." Two-fisted, Peaches grabbed a tape measure and a pair of pinking shears from a box, and snapped the blades open and shut, *snap, snap, snap,* which elicited the disapproval of the shotgunner, who waved his gun.

"That's what he's in for," whispered Deke, Avi's latest new friend. "He did the Schwingle uniforms. Conspiracy."

"I see," Avi whispered back, although he didn't understand.

"Hallo?"

"Sascha!" Avi exclaimed. "Comrade!"

"Comrade?" Sascha asked. He looked a bit cross.

"It's just an expression, my friend. How's the party?"

"Da, da. Is a party." Sascha's face brightened. "I vant to ask you a little some-tink, yes? For my little knees."

"Your knees?"

"Knees! Knees! My sister's gurl."

"Oh, yes. I see. Your niece. . . ." Avi eyed one of the cameras trained on him, the on-air talent voicing over.

"Da, da." Sascha wore a polo shirt, brown and green stripes and a white tab collar. In one hand he had a glass of O.J., (maybe). "You could sign this?" He held out his other hand. The photo was digitized, probably downloaded, cached somewhere, and now printed on photo paper. Avi talking to a convict, other convicts on ladders working on the whale, a time stamp, maybe even the pizza delivery kid. . . . "Sign it here—sign Vhale Man. Is vhat you are called in Siberia."

"Siberia?" Avi picked up the pen wedged under Sascha's thumb, and signed "Whale Man."

"Siberia! Is the best joke! Russians call the Internet 'Siberia.' All Russians like that joke—" Sascha indicated the friends on his stoop, perhaps ten people altogether this morning, each with a glass of O.J. (maybe), each of whom waved and lifted up a libation, and suddenly shouted in hearty unison, *"Pust' sbudutsya vse tvoi mechty!"*

Avi laughed. "Sascha? Vhat vas that?" He could feel an accent coming on.

"Is the plan," Sascha smiled. "Everyone yell together. Works perfect! *May all your dreams come true.*"

"Thank you, Sascha. You're very kind."

"Vhale Man," Sascha clicked the heels of his sneakers and returned to his side of the Iron Curtain.

"Mr. Woodley!" one of the TV reporters yelled.

Avi waved, not now. Where was Rick? Rick should be here. And Mom.

· · ·

The on-air talent for Channel 3—The Faces You Know, The News You Don't—was a coiffed white kid probably twelve years old, his hip-hop shirt bright pink, the pre-teen perspective profound. But others had come, too, in the course of the stunning morning. As Avi rounded up the convicts, he took a gander: on the devil's strip stood a hippie dippy family mummified in yellow and green head-to-toe tie-dye; when they saw Avi, they genuflected in size order. Nearby, an older woman with a long, gray braid wore a spangled bed sheet on which a map of the cosmos had been affixed in glitter and drippy Elmer's glue, the fabric of the universe; and next to her, a shirtless guy in overalls, a big bald guy, just stood and stared, seemingly fresh from laying brick, mortar fingerprints printed on his thighs where he liked to wipe. Avi did the math: five members of the Granola family, the space chick, and the giant tradesman, plus Pony Tail Guy. That made eight pilgrims. How many pilgrims does it take to declare a whale a national shrine? He smelled sandalwood.

Pony Tail Guy had dug up Mom's lawn. One of the news vans had tried to pull into the driveway and clipped a noncombatant bush and the news crews' cables were everywhere, the whole scene a hazard. Avi's whale might be in danger—hell, Avi was. He would have to defend himself and his whale. But first, or last, or finally, he would have to cover her.

And then the big Lincoln parked behind Channel 3, and the two henchwomen appeared. The twins had returned incognito: they wore drab blue baseball caps and blue nylon jackets on the backs of which were written "W.H.A.L.E." with masking tape. They had dyed their hair mousey brown, put on Ray-Bans. Both women carried gym bags, and each had acquired a nightstick.

This could be fun, Avi thought. The twins couldn't touch him now. Roll tape, he told himself.

"Victim," said one twin to Avi.

"Sister," said Avi, twinkling. For effect, he leaned against a tree, happy as a soufflé.

"Hey!" said the other twin. "You don't know us!"

"Shhh," said the first twin. "We're hiding. The Camel sent us here to hide."

"Hiding?" asked Avi. "Where?" He looked around.

"Yeah," the second twin giggled. "You don't know us!"

"Shhh!" repeated the first twin. "It's a disguise. We're spies."

"What?" said the nearby Deke.

"Who the hell are you?" A twin glared at the convict menacingly.

"It's okay," said Avi. "He's with the band. Well, fine, sisters." They might actually serve a purpose. "You're needed on the front line." Avi gave a chuck of his chin to the news crews. "Can you keep those people from getting closer?"

The twins looked at each other and tried to process Avi's question. "We can hit them!" said one of the twins brightly.

"Well, no, you can't . . . but you can push them," Avi said.

"Pushing's no fun."

The other twin tried to help: "We could push them into things."

"Well . . . no," said Avi. "You can't."

The dimmer twin pouted, clearly Rose Red.

"How about you push them if they come too close. *And* . . ." He tried to think of something else. "Pizza for lunch."

"Pizza!"

"Pizza!"

"Pizza tastes good!"

Deke had come to stand closer to Avi. He gestured at the henchwomen. "Holy shit. Twins. Bet you can't eat just one."

"Behave yourself," Avi told Deke. But the prisoners were all staring, and so, in a louder voice, he took control. "Okay, that's enough, people. Spit spot. Let's get this baby diapered!" He was having fun. He turned back to the twins. "And try not to be mean, 'kay?"

"'Kay!" said the first twin, probably Rose Red.

"Sister," Snow White admonished. "He's not our boss."

"*Ohhhhhh.* Right. You're not the boss of me!"

"Me either. So let's go push those people," Snow White said.

Rose Red smiled. "Dear Sister. You're so clever."

"And pretty," said Snow White.

"Holy shit," repeated Deke. "Just for fifteen minutes. . . . I'll take one."

"You scare me," said Avi. "No."

"Ten minutes?"

"No."

"Let me help with the fabric!" said Peaches, who had joined the little party. "Hi, girls."

Work began at last on the skin, the whale measured for her suit of many tents, the upholsterers handing up and down their measuring tapes, open spaces in the wood cross-hatched with molding strips to reinforce the nylon and the netting. Watching the convicts clamber over the whale's big body, and haul and hand around the moldings, Avi was reminded of *Gulliver's Travels*, the Lilliputians mounting the snoring adventurer, their tiny ropes crossing and criss-crossing his chest and legs.

Peaches, with the assistance of T. T., worked one panel ahead of the others, measuring and then cutting fabric while the moldings were being attached, then moving to the next gap. After each panel was prepped and handed up to be spread and snapped over the frame, the staple guns came out, one per Williams. They tacked the edges of each panel, followed by the more delicate job of stapling tent cloth to molding, to reduce wind-flap, a task that required two workers, one inside the whale to support the frame and the other outside to staple.

The upholstering went slowly and well, the system systematic, like line work in a good kitchen. The news crews filmed, the twins stalked the perimeter, and Avi became more and more managerial: you two with me; this goes here; no, not there; here, hand me that, would ya'; wait, wait, wait, it's puckering.

Where was Rick?

The penitents gained in numbers, too. When Avi took a break to walk the length of the whale, he saw them in the park, behind some newly installed police barricades, flimsy barriers really. The park looked to be filling up—what the hell?

A portable toilet was delivered. Avi was taken aback. A toilet? First the fork-lift lowered the poop booth, and then he had to sign for the delivery; on the receipt was a little note: "With complimentaries. Sascha." Avi tipped the por-table toilet delivery guy five bucks and waved across the Urals to where the émigrés were drinking themselves into a stupor on the stoop. Sascha lifted his drink in response. The Russians must be Mafia, Avi thought. None of them had a job. Only *maffiya* would know where to get a Porta-John, or even think of sending one as a present.

"*Prost!*" Avi shouted to Sascha, the sound swallowed by the hum of the vans.

Rick and Avi had chosen the upholstery to be even-toned, the gray-green tenting whalish—which looked good, as the panels had a kind of muted marine drabness reminiscent of more murky depths. Figuring out the netting had proven trickier. Eventually, Rick and Avi had chosen to tack tent netting upon her back, to keep the sky visible to whosoever stands inside her belly, and to append weighted sheets of tent fabric that could be thrown over her in case of rain—a maneuver that would be made with difficulty, Avi had argued. The sheets would be secured to each of her sides, strapped tight or even Velcroed. The solution was imperfect, but more precautionary than permanent.

Nothing about her was permanent, Avi supposed—and then he had a pang of anticipatory regret. At some point, she would have to be dismantled, which he wouldn't want to see. So maybe he would hire the twins to strike the set as he sped away.

"Rick! Hannah Cara Papadopoulos, Channel 6, 6 News in the Street." She advanced upon the scene, slinking in polyester, her face epoxied into a smile that meant nothing, a star of every lawn.

"Hi," Avi waved.

"Rick, it's beautiful," she said. Rodney the cameraman hoisted his camera, and on snapped his light.

"Walk with me, my child," Avi said. He turned a corner around the whale's tail, and began to stroll quickly along her flank.

"Gee," said Hannah Cara Papadopoulos to Avi, as she grabbed a hold of his shirt so as not to fall.

"Yeah," said Avi. "She's coming along." The whale was enormous, taller than he by far and long, longer, longest. She was lying the length of Mom's lot and filling her yard, and bending slightly around the corner, and . . . singing, he wanted to say to someone, maybe to a mental health professional? He could hear the subsonic, subdermal, *sub rosa*, submarine song that he had carried for weeks in his songbox, in the dreams he dreamed while asleep and awake.

The whale was singing . . . she sang. . . .

"The whale's so beautiful. . . ."

"Thanks," Avi said. "I didn't—" But the thought never arrived in words, for just at that moment the final panel was affixed to the side nearest Avi, one whole side a closed shape, part of her body suddenly done.

The moment had sneaked up on him, as good moments do. The convicts cheered, lowered their arms, posed like workers in a WPA mural, socially real. The whale was a whale.

Avi was stunned: she sang, it hurt, and he gulped back something that might have been tears. Now in his ear, or in his chest, or everywhere in him, the whale sang. "She is," he finally managed. "Isn't she?" He stumbled slightly, out of the grasp of Hannah, put his hand on the beast—maybe near where her heart would be.

The whale was a whale.

"She sure is a honey," said Hannah Cara Papadopoulos. "Are you ready? Let's do this. And . . . we're live in five, four, three, two, one. . . ."

FIFTEEN

· ·

THE CROWD HAD GROWN substantially by mid-afternoon. Now a cara-vansary jammed the street around Maureen's little house and Avi's bespoke beast, tailored as the wooden behemoth was in her natty outdoor fabrics. At least the twins kept the nosy newsies from approaching, and the wonderstruck pilgrims seemed happy to occupy the park, the sundry whale watchers en-robed in various garish outfits and apparently besotted by the goings-on. For the second time, Avi went to see: the pilgrims knelt or sat cross-legged three deep in rows, and gesticulated in ways meaningful only to themselves. Avi nodded, said hi when greeted. Then he turned back, crossed in front of a black van decorated with renderings of guitars and skulls, the headlights skulls, the side panels tagged with a scrolled name, "Better Than Abstinence."

A horn honked. Rick had arrived, driving a red pickup, a Toyota with a de-cent-sized cab, the dealer's sticker proudly affixed to a window. Avi wandered up the street to the truck. Nice truck. He ran a hand over the pretty paint on the hood as the driver's side window slid down with an electric silence.

"Rick, man. Where you been?"

"Out," Rick said.

"Nice truck," Avi said, admiringly.

"Thanks," Rick said. "It's yours."

"What?" Avi said.

"Yours," Rick said. "A trade-in. On your credit card."

"Shit," Avi said. "You can't do that!"

"Did."

"You're kidding?"

"Not," Rick said. "Got tired of all your moaning. Leased it."

"It's mine?" Avi said.

"Yep. You sit here," Rick swung wide the driver's door and half-climbed and half-slid his long legs over the stick shift to the passenger side, the move not so easy.

"You're kidding," Avi could only say. But he got in, and began to touch the dashboard and the wheel, slowly and with pleasure.

"Course you gotta go back. Sign and say yes. If you're keeping it."

"You're kidding," Avi said, not listening. There was a CD player.

"Better spend the bucks," Rick said.

"What?"

"The money," Rick said. "She'd want that."

"I'm driving," Avi said, and he made a sound somewhere between a hum and a purr, maybe a *pummmm*, followed by a *parrrrummmmmm*. "It's great," he breathed, pretending to check his mirrors. "Cool. Thanks, Rick! This is so cool."

One tiny corner of Rick's mouth turned upward. "Sure."

Avi wanted to drive, to cook dinner, to swing from the whale, to be here with his friends, to lie on a makeshift pallet and stare up through the whale's ribs at satellites and stars, the astro-jewelry. He wanted so many things he felt like nothing would be enough.

"Let's eat." He reluctantly turned off the engine, ran his hand once more over the dash. "Cool truck. . . . Man, I can't believe you did this! Rick! Dude . . . wanna beer?"

"Earned it," Rick said

Avi laughed. "It's just a beer. Or two. Or champagne."

"Beer," Rick said. "Saw your brother," Rick said.

"You what?"

"Saw your brother. On TV. They did a stand-up on your brother."

"A stand-up?"

"Here, lock it. Yeah, a stand-up. That's when the reporter stands up."

"Gotcha," Avi said. "But I don't understand." He had to keep touching the pretty truck.

"You're the Whale Man," Rick said. "He's the brother of the Whale Man. His nose didn't look so good."

Avi was stunned; he had invented his brother only yesterday. "His nose," he managed to say. "I don't have a brother."

"Busted," Rick said. "You said you did on TV. Now you do. Some guy on TV pretending to be your brother."

"Jesus," Avi said.

"Not Jesus. Jesus had no brothers."

More importantly, they headed back to the whale, the goony circus, the media onslaught, the 24-hour Russian Happy Hour, the twins working security, the convicts lolling. "Look," Avi said to Rick.

"I see. She's something," Rick said.

"We did it," Avi said.

"Rick! Rick Woodley! Rick!" The media folks began to get less folksy as they swarmed at Avi. "Rick, what now? Rick, a comment? C'mon, Rick, give us a story—Rick, Rick, Rick, Rick. . . ."

Avi waved, okay, while the real Rick turned to slink into the house. "Meet-cha," Avi said quietly. "I'm cooking, and we're eating in the whale."

Rick nodded.

But first it was time to go public again. "Okay, okay!" Avi said. He could see Bean—she was pretty good at silent mode too—standing by the fence, petting Dolly through the pickets. Bean gave a little wave. "Let's do a press conference. I've got a statement. . . ." This time, he snapped open the receipt for the Porta-John. What the hell kind of gift was that? Holy crap, Avi had to smile. A poop booth! A truck! People were beginning to donate; Avi would need to glad-hand receipts on W.H.A.L.E. letterhead; he needed nonprofit status.

Cameras were ready, mics were jabbed, dishes rotated to zap satellites, re-porters flipped open their flippy notebooks, viewers on couches all over Amer-ica and in various foreign principalities moved not at all. Beside the whale, Henry gathered his cadre of convicts into a bouquet of convicts for a photo-op.

"Ladies and gentlemen," Avi began. Was he news or entertainment? "On be-half of W.H.A.L.E. I am pleased to say that our work here is done. These brave men—" he gestured toward his crew, and then feigned reading aloud. "These brave men have taken it upon themselves. They are ready to build themselves new lives and to voyage upon the Sea of Responsibility. W.H.A.L.E. has given them back their—" he stumbled, tried again. "W.H.A.L.E. has given them back their hands. With hands instead of crimes, these brave men will sail into the sunset."

Wow, that was bullshit. Avi looked into the lights. "Thank you," he said. "No questions." He turned to leave.

"Mr. Woodley! Rick! Rick Woodley! Rick!"

And then a voice he recognized cut through the din. "Mr. Woodley, do you think your mother's at peace?"

Avi stopped, spun. He was staring into the eyes of The Camel, and into a microphone. *Bonk!* She faked a stumble, and whacked Avi with the mic.

"Oh. Sorry. Did I get you?" she asked, and smiled. The Camel was dressed in a blue pants suit, her hair a hair-sprayed helmet. "Mr. Woodley, I'm Annie Morrison, Associated Media. Do you think your mother's at peace? Will you move on with your life now? Do you have *a list* of what W.H.A.L.E. will do next? Have you talked with your brother? Mr. Woodley, do you have any words for your viewers?"

Avi took a deep breath: crap, crap, crap, crap. "I . . . I think my mother's at peace, yes. I'm ready for what happens next—W.H.A.L.E. is ready. That's all I have to say."

She wasn't going away. And who the hell was Avi's new brother?

• • •

He didn't know what to do. Poor little Avi, who lived in a shoe—he made a little limerick as he stood in Mom's kitchen and considered his options. Really, though, he did know what to do: the whale was a whale, the convicts were convicted once more and had been shuttled home to C-block, the media and the wacko worshippers continued to broadcast and worship, respectively, and Avi had a feast to prepare, dinner for three.

Prep was easy, a little chopping, dicing, grilling, broiling, sautéing. Nothing challenging in the sauce department, only drawn butter, but freshness and quality ingredients from the list Avi had given Bean. She was a bank robber, but also a pretty good grocery fetcher.

Bean sat and chatted, Avi stood and cooked and almost listened, and Rick asked to take a shower, proud that he had a change of clothes at the ready, a button-down shirt that might have been ironed three years ago. Dinner! When everything was ready, Avi wanted to ring a bell or flash the lights. Instead, the three diners sneaked into the backyard, and around through the side gate to slip into the whale. Once there, Avi knew their silhouettes would be visible— just like in Plato. The whale was a Republic, too, although Avi suspected that he was mixing up his Plato.

Party lights strung, Avi up on the ladder, so close to the beams and to his dream that he began to hyperventilate; extension cord plugged in, the lights made merry. Then the candles were lighted so that the table glowed.

The night had fallen, but not here.

The three diners stood tall in the whale, a bit stunned, in size order, left to right: Rick with his bottle of beer, Avi with Bean's lovely gift of Perrier-Jouet, Bean with two champagne flutes still sticky with price tag glue. Avi popped the cork, admired the smoke, gave special silent thanks to the Comité Interprofessionnel du Vin de Champagne, a benediction taught to him by Mimou. Then Avi poured, and Bean raised her glass.

"*Lái, gān yī bēi.*"

Rick nodded. *"Lái."*

"What did you say?" Avi asked.

"A toast!" Bean said. "Allow me. *Zhù nǐ wànshì rúyì."*

"Hǎo," said Rick.

"I like it," said Avi. "Sounds cool." He closed his eyes for two seconds, and then opened them. "Chin chin!"

Oh, the music of crystal to crystal. Oh, the gods' gift of champagne. Amen for viniculture, and for the vine that survived phylloxera. Blessed was delimitation, the seat of all surety. Blessed was the sun, the grape, the sugar, the mousse, the cork; champagne, champagne. Blessed was the Taj Bistro's sommelier, Serena, who had given Avi a very, very personal lesson in champagne.

Avi drank, and it was good.

Bean glanced at Avi, smiled at Rick. *"Tā zhīdao ma?"*

"Zhīdao shénme?"

"Nǐ lái zhèr ná míngdān." Bean's gaze was steady.

"No." Rick almost smiled. *"Wǒ bùshì lái ná míngdān de."*

Bean gave a little chuckle, a hollow noise. *"Zhēnde ma? Nà wǒ yěbùshì,"* she laughed, this time genuinely.

"What?" said Avi, mostly unable to care. Champagne had such tiny bubbles. "What did you say?" He shook his head and its bubbles slightly.

"Oh, nothing. Just Chinese," said Bean.

"Now I get it," Avi said. "Hey," Avi said. "Guys." His fake brother was in trouble: Avi had a new problem with which to obsess. "I don't have a brother."

They talked about it, as they spread their meal in readiness.

"Keep the brother," Rick said.

"Definitely," said Bean. "This looks delicious." She patted Rick's hand. "Rick wants his steak. . . . So what's your brother's name?"

"I don't know. I mean, I don't have a brother."

"Got it. But a brother's a diversion," Rick said.

"Daniel," Bean said. "Like in the song. Name him Daniel. May I have some of that lobster?"

Almost *al fresco*, their nice dinner in the belly of the beast felt Old Testament-style, the pin-pricked sky through the screened skin of the whale full of knowledge and faith. Granted, the champagne buzz might have contributed to his cheeriness, but here were Rick and Bean, Avi's friends, and they too seemed to seize upon the moment as a new moment in their lives, communal affection and gaiety the signs of a deeper satisfaction. Avi and Rick had built a whale sixty-four feet long and sixteen feet high: they were having dinner on a plywood floor in a plywood whale's belly, absurdly. If Avi could get the money from Markins, and save his imaginary brother from The Camel, then life might actually be what it seemed, a dream.

If Avi were a whale, he might only hunt langoustine. He dipped a final piece of grilled lobster tail into drawn butter and bit into the firm flesh, life, a big bite out of the Great Chain of Being. He had become a food group, he mused. He wiped his chin with his napkin. But something was wrong. He should have made a little salad of baby greens. He wanted a cheese plate, an earthy piece of something unpastureized, a palate cleanser, just a tiny wedge of Humboldt Fog and maybe a plum.

Or better—Avi had an inspiration. Why not sell the list to The Camel, any old list? She wanted a list, she would get one, and if the list weren't really a list, so what? He could . . . sell her an unsolvable puzzle, encoded gibberish that looked enough like a list to warrant a big payday and buy everyone's safety. Proactive gobbledygook. Whale Man was ready to party.

A libation, this time silent: Avi raised his glass and tipped it slightly, allowing some bubbly to spill from the flute, down his hand and arm, and onto the floor. Bean watched, Rick chewed his filet mignon vigorously.

"Very Shinto," Bean said. "To her," eyes shining.

"To her," Avi said. To Mom.

"*Hm?*" Rick said.

"I was thinking about my mom," Avi said.

"She would have liked this," Bean said, wide-eyed.

Rick waved his fork, more at Avi than at Bean. "Think?"

"I do," she answered.

"Me too," Avi said.

"Our whale." Rick looked around. He was done eating, and he pushed back a bit from the table.

"Yeah," Avi said.

Dinner devoured, bellies round with food-joy—but then someone yelled "Victim!" It figured, Avi thought.

One, two, their fists and faces clenched, the twins stood just outside the whale. "Victim!" one snarled. They had changed clothes again. Now they were dressed in big boots, two-toned tights, matching pink babydoll tops to top off the crime, and they had done something strange to their hair, or to each other's, which seemed to be knotted into two nubs atop their heads, like the beginnings of horns or radio dials.

"You!" One twin pointed at the three well-supped friends.

"Me?" The diners answered almost in unison.

"No, you!" The other twin pointed.

"Him?"

"Her?"

"Him?"

Bean, Rick, and Avi might have been the Three Stooges, or just lesser-known Magi.

"No, *him!*" Twin One pointed at Avi.

"Couldn't be," murmured Avi. "Yes?" he said more loudly.

"Telephone!" Twin One thrust Avi a cell phone; he took the bait.

"Hello?" Avi said, purposefully holding the device upside-down. "Hello?" He held the phone out and shook it. "Hello? It's broken. . . ."

The twin was enraged: she grabbed the phone, turned it, and re-thrust.

"Ah . . . hello?" he said.

"My, my, the diligent Susan Junior. You have been busy, have you not? Tell an incognito Camel all your secrets."

"Hello," Avi said.

"Is now a good time?"

"For what?" Avi asked. He felt so bratty, the glory of champagne. He had a plan.

"No, no, my friend. I mean the question morally: is now a time that is good? Are the remains of your repast, and the promise of the future, *good?*"

"I don't understand," Avi caught Bean's eye. She winked. "What do you want?"

"*Moi?*" said The Camel, amused as always by herself. "I want what I cannot have, for that is the nature of wanting—as God wants of Abraham. Kierkegaard," she added.

"The list," Avi said.

Rick dropped his fork and leaned over, his hearing aid right there near Avi's ear. "Damn," Rick said from mostly under the table.

"My friend, my simple friend . . ." The Camel cooed. "The list is what I may and can have. What I want is otherwise."

"Well, *sheee-it*, little lady," Avi said. "Come and get it. I got your precious list and if the price is right, dang. Come on down, now that we're all here, one big happy family—" and with a flourish, he pressed End.

"Sister!" said a twin. "He can't do that!"

"I will rip off his ears," said the other sister, agrowl.

"No, me! I get his ears!" said the other, other sister. "Mine!" she hopped in place. "I'll make an ear belt!"

"Oh, Jesus," Bean exhaled. "Girls, chill."

"Do not hang up on me again," said a voice not on the phone. The Camel stepped into sight, to be flanked by the twins, formidable despite her reporter's disguise.

"The Camel," said Bean.

"The Lima Bean," said The Camel.

Rick found his fork and banged his head.

"Rickie?" Another voice trilled from another direction.

Avi turned to see: on the other side of the whale, *sans* cameraman, stood a pouting, barefooted Hannah Cara Papadopoulos poured into a red dress as she twirled her shoes by their straps, a pair of red spiky things. She still looked sexless, although she seemed to be straining to twinkle at Avi.

"Who's this?" Bean said. "Wait. You're that reporter."

"Hi," said Avi, politeness the least he could offer.

"Everyone stay calm," said Rick.

The Camel stepped inside the whale uninvited, her presence profane. "To what radio station are you listening?" The Camel asked Rick. She leaned closer to him, and mouthed loudly, "Is it classical?" her gesture a parody of over-reacting to a deaf person.

Rick didn't answer. Bean reached over and touched her fingertips to Avi's arm.

"Sister, it's a disaster!" exulted a twin.

"Someone's going to die!" crowed the other twin. Now they too were in the whale.

"The list," said The Camel. "And you sit there," she said to Rick. "Watch him, girls," The Camel said. "Behold! *Murder on the Orient Express*, redux. Don't we love Poirot? Just dial Trafalgar 8137, and Miss Lemon will answer."

One of the twins snarled at Rick. In response, he laid his hands on the table, calm and clear-eyed. Rick was in control of something, but Avi couldn't tell what.

"The list," said The Camel. "Now."

"The money," said Avi.

"The reserve is agreed upon," said The Camel.

"I'll pay it," said Bean.

"You must know," said The Camel. "Competition is my milieu. A rage for victory provokes my most ardent actions."

"I beg your pardon?' said Avi.

"She likes to win," said Bean. "She's quoting Carnegie again."

"Ah, The Lima Bean," said The Camel. "Forsooth, a rival."

One of the twins, for some sudden unfathomable reason, punched the other, hard, on the shoulder. The punched twin punched the puncher back. "*Oof!*" a twin exclaimed, and both twins giggled.

"Girls. . . ." The Camel lifted up her hand. "We're on business." The three baddies inside the whale seemed like anti-whalies.

"Rickie?" said Hannah Cara Papadopoulos to Avi, the misnomer of her affection. "Can we have a personal moment?"

"No!" said Bean. "You're out of your league, babe. No moments."

"Rickie?"

"Oh, come on in," said Avi.

"Come on in?" said Bean.

"No, that's not what I mean."

"Come on in?" Bean repeated.

"We're all grown-ups here," The Camel said. "Distinguished by our various sensibilities, some limited, to be sure. Plus, *Schadenfreude.*"

"Would you like a glass of champagne?" Avi offered The Camel the empty bottle.

"Well, how gracious. Alas, I have no taste for French Diet Sprite."

Philistine, Avi thought. "Fine," he said.

"Have you any Chocó drink? Or perhaps a fresh egg cream?"

"I like champagne," Hannah Cara Papadopoulos said in a little girl voice. "Rickie?"

"There's beer," Rick said. He made to rise.

"You just sit there," The Camel said to Rick. "Girls."

The twins came around the table to stand on either side of Avi's contractor.

"What's this about?" Rick said.

"You promised I could hit him," one twin whined.

"Did not," said the other.

"My nunchucks are in the car," the first twin said.

"Nunchucks!" the second twin said. "Sister!"

"Girls," The Camel said. "Straighten up and let your comportment be threatening."

"She talks funny," muttered one twin.

"She does," Bean agreed.

"Now, the list," The Camel began again. "Susan Junior, shall we concentrate together? Choose a point in space, and allow that point to become you. Like this." Her eyes went out of focus.

"Oh, c'mon," said Bean. "Not that trick."

The Camel blinked. "Dear rival, if I were you . . . I would be you, and thus miss being me," she smiled dangerously. "And I would miss me so."

"Talk, talk, talk," Bean mimed vomiting.

"Punch her!" one sister squealed.

"Quit it," Avi said. "That's enough."

"Children," The Camel added. "Would you each like a timeout?"

"Enough!" Avi raised his voice. "All of you. Quit it. I would like you all to leave my whale."

In a different wooden whale on another planet in another galaxy—on a planet, say, where a Whale Man with a dream got to rule the waves—Avi's wish might have been heeded, his allies, antagonists, and suitors agreeable. There, Avi would already be alone, swinging on high, as the two moons of the planet Whale slid one behind the other.

Instead, he smelled smoke. Had he left the stove on? "Do you smell smoke?" he asked Bean.

She turned to Avi. Her face was set, her smile tight and her green eyes clear. It took a moment for his question to register. "Smoke?"

"Smoke?" one twin said.

"Smoke?" The Camel lifted her face into an imagined wind, gave a big sniff.

"Smoke?" asked Rick. "I'd like a smoke."

"Something's burning," said Avi. " A lot. Fire!"

"Fire!" yelled Hannah Cara Papadopoulos.

"Fire," said a twin, pointing at Avi.

"Fire!" Avi stood up, upending his chair, pushed past The Camel and out of the whale, and sprinted into the yard where there surely was a fire. But he saw only the news vans and a few straggly worshippers and his new truck. Maybe the whale's tail was on fire—Avi quickly did a loop around her, checking, checking, seeing nothing, smelling plenty.

He tried inside the carport, confused by the shapes of things that weren't things, smelled smoke more strongly, but the carport was fine. He ran outside again and around the back to the garden gate, into the yard, looked in the bushes, saw nothing. Where was Dolly? Sometimes, she would go upstairs to nap after dinner. He turned to look up at Mom's house—and just as he did, something inside the house made a loud popping sound and there, he saw flames rage in an upstairs window. Where was Dolly? "Dollllyyyyy!" Avi called. He reached the kitchen door, stopped. His mother's house was on fire, how could that be?

Dolly barked.

"Dolly!"

Dolly barked *inside the house*!

He shouldn't have opened the door, too late, as a combusted gust of fire blew Avi on his ass, smoke and ash flying, the kitchen already almost devoured by the blaze, a nasty, perfect line of flames searing a path between the crappy old fridge and the scarred linoleum countertop. "Dolly!" Avi called. He rolled over and stayed hunkered down as he scrambled inside. "Dolly!" He hollered, sucked in a wad of smoke and hot air, and gasped at the violence of what he inhaled. Avi covered his mouth. "'*ollwa!*" came the sound of his voice through his hand. Where was she? He couldn't hear her.

Another smell was in the kitchen, a fulminating, angry tang. Crouched, Avi the chef smelled the smell and he knew—the accelerant volatile, the malice of the thing—that someone had torched the place. He knew for sure, because there was a gas can in the middle of the floor.

Dolly, where was she? He had to find Dolly.

Engulfed, beginning to choke, and peering into the smoke, Avi couldn't tell if he might make the living room. But nothing would happen until he could breathe—so back outside skittered Avi for a gulping big breath, already dizzy, his lungs contracting, his face scalded. She couldn't be in the house; she wouldn't survive. He coughed, then called her again, "Dolly!" She would run, for sure.

And again he thought he heard her bark from somewhere inside. A panicked bark! "Dolly, I'm coming!" In a furious kind of crab crawl, spread and half-sprinting, Avi launched himself as low as he could get through the conflagration, burning and cutting himself, uncaring. She was his Dolly.

The living room was a little better, the smoke bad but the furniture still there. Flames licked the stairwell and poured up to the second floor. Avi covered his mouth with his arm—no, wait—he ran to the downstairs bathroom, where fire chewed into the shitty paisley wallpaper, and as he opened the door the window blew out, which amazingly made breathing more possible for just a moment. Grateful, he huffed in a deep, hot gasp and then grabbed a hand towel and soaked it and wrapped it around his head, eyes open and mouth covered.

He would climb those stairs.

The cell phone in Avi's pocket vibrated. Not now.

He had burned his arm; something had slashed across the back of his neck.

At the foot of the stairs he spied another upended red plastic gasoline jug, and another vicious line of red and orange flame, only this time cutting up to the second floor through each carpet riser, the crackle and the rumble like the sounds of war, right here. The world was sucked up by sound. He couldn't hear himself, nor the sirens he wished for and knew would not arrive in time, an unbelief, nor could he hear the dog who would need to be carried to safety, each of them singed.

Up the stairs, bounding two steps at a time, up and up, to the landing where the upstairs was almost gone, the flames larger here and meaner, the darkness of their devastation laced with the violence of their light. Sparks spat and sizzled, hot embers criss-crossing and sizzling against the wall, zinging like artillery fire, and the ceiling light gave a pop and blew to pieces, glass in Avi's hair.

He opened the wet towel mask to yell, but coughed instead. "Dolly!" he rasped.

She would bark. She should bark.

Something groaned and cracked in the spine of the house, a new and horrible noise, something that presaged collapse, the taking of life.

Dolly.

Avi had to go, he knew it. He had to get to safety.

Dolly.

And then, beside him, a form, a figure—not a dog but a person.

A firefighter, a person, oh, help, where was Dolly?

Not a firefighter. Rick. He gave a thumbs out sign, we're going. "Get outta here!" Rick managed, with another thumbs out—just as a beam swung free of its moorings in the ceiling, a flaming sign launched toward the two men, and just in time Rick gave Avi a push backwards, the timber crashing between them with a brilliant, smashed hiss.

Now Rick was on fire! Avi lunged forward and swatted an ember from Rick's shoulder, *ow, ow, ow,*

"Now, Avi!" Rick holler-coughed. "Go! Follow me!"

Now and now, it had to be, the deciding was done. So he grabbed the back of Rick's shirt and let himself be led, skudding on his backside twice as they took the sizzling staircase down, Dolly, Dolly, Dolly, Dolly. . . .

The living room was no more. They were trapped, he and his would-be rescuer, in a box of fire, the walls consumed with rage, the carpet mined, smoke searing their lungs. Avi felt a tug on his shirt, this way, as Rick picked up an end table and shielded them both, moving forward and creating a path, then mightily throwing the now-burning table through a window—which exploded with an enormous shattering roar, the fire sucked into the night, seeking fuel, a deadly race.

One, two, they stumbled to the sill.

Rick's arm wasn't working. Avi helped, Rick first, climbing in slow motion out of the house—until Avi gave him a push from behind, the contractor crashing into the dark.

Avi waited for his friend to roll away, felt fire on his body and could wait no more, then dived, hands over head, into the safety of a prickly shrub.

Dolly. Dolly, oh, Dolly, oh no.

· · ·

It was later. In the lit-up disaster, the lights from the news vans on full blast, the world shone. Help had arrived. Firefighters had deployed, their squawking walkie-talkies unintelligible; an ambulance spread wide its back doors. Everywhere were people in uniforms, men strung along the houseline. But the fire had become too many alarms too soon, Maureen's house a goner. Gone.

Avi had been sitting on the lawn. Now he was tended to, half alert, he and Rick upright on matching gurneys, Rick making sure of Avi, Avi making sure of Rick, each with an oxygen mask, thumbs up. There were too many people, the living and the dead.

He watched the roof collapse, flames shooting higher than the house had been.

There was someone checking him over. A nice face, round.

The cell phone thrummed again absurdly. Avi dug into his pocket to press TALK.

"Avi, where are you? Are you all right?"

A voice on the phone. Whose voice? He pushed aside his oxygen. "Mom?"

"You're all right, God damn you! Avi, oh my God."

"Mom, is that you?'

"Avi, it's Bean."

It was Mom, no, it was Bean. "You're not—" He couldn't speak. "You're Bean." He coughed. "Dolly. . . ."

"Dolly's safe, it's all right. It's all right. She came running out of the house and into the street and I grabbed her. . . . I'm walking toward you, I think I can see you. . . ."

And the relief poured in, and Avi began to cough and cry.

"Oh, honey. It's okay."

"Dolly . . . Bean . . ." Avi rasped. "I thought you were my mom." Then he knew. He gulped, the good air painful. "She's alive, isn't she? Bean? My mom's alive—she must be, I'm sure—she's gotta be alive."

"Oh, Avi. Oh, God. Don't." Bean was standing by his side, holding out her arms, Dolly there too, his Doll-Doll, who jumped on her bestest friend and licked him good. "You jerk, you stupid, silly jerk," Bean was crying as she kissed his face, the unleashed oxygen mask in the way. "Oh, God. You dumbass."

"She's alive," Avi insisted through a cough. He hugged Bean, hard and forever. He wasn't done, Mom had to be alive, he hadn't apologized. "She's alive."

The Whale Is the Message

SIXTEEN

· ·

HE HAD SUFFERED a smattering of burns on his chest and shoulders and a more serious burn on his right hand, a cut on his neck, and a bump on the head bumpy enough to warrant a hospital stay. Maybe the bump on the head had been good for him, Avi thought grimly. Maybe he would be sensible at last. Avi lay back in bed and brooded. The whale was a whale, but his hand hurt too much to swing inside her. The doctor had been clear on that subject when asked directly—no way you do anything physical until the headaches end and the burn stops weeping. The same doctor had wanted an autograph from Whale Man. Holy crap, Avi thought. His burn was weeping.

Hospitals suck, but they're better than morgues. Still, Avi felt punished: six times already the Xeroform gauze was rewrapped (to keep the burns moist, an antibiotic embedded in the fabric), thrice the same candy striper bubbled into his room, each time with a new distraction (a crafts cart, flowers and balloons from an unnamed friend, and copies of *Cosmo* and *Field & Stream*). The food was horrific, the entrée always presented around something gelatinous: gummy applesauce, gummy applesauce, mealy tapioca, gummy applesauce, cups of pabulum all. At least the television stayed off, so that Avi could keep from seeing himself jump from a burning building *ad infinitum*.

"Hey." Rick edged into the room, his arm in a light blue sling.

"Hi." Avi sat up, waved his swathed right hand. "Rick. Glad you came by."

"I . . ." Rick began, and stopped.

Avi's turn: "Let's not shake." He used his unscorched flipper to indicate Rick's sling. "Your arm okay?"

"Yep," Rick waved the soft cast. "Hairline. Doesn't hurt."

"Glad to hear it. You know . . ." Avi started. "Thanks. For getting me out."

"Nothing," Rick said. "You did it. You pushed me clear. Thanks back, Boss."

"Well, you're welcome. All for one, right?"

Their chat was strained, overwhelmed by the specter of the unspoken.

But Bean, thank God, she came to call each of the three mornings, cheerful and loyal, full of reports of sweet Dolly's antics in the care of the bank robbing Lima Bean. Bean, Bean. Bean with the green eyes. Although she never offered him more than a perfunctory peck on the forehead, and wouldn't stay long. She looked wild-eyed, pinched, and out of place—and at last she admitted her fear of hospitals, a kind of cataplexy born of some unmentionable childhood trauma, her phobia instantly excited by the sharp scent of the cleaning agents in the long, white corridors.

"Auntie Cissy," she said, by way of not explaining her sudden exits.

"Emotional unavailability?" Avi blundered.

Bean's eyes widened. "Limits," she said.

"Boundaries," Avi said. "Truthiness."

"That's it," Bean said. And then she recoiled as though from her own thought. "I'm leaving." She picked up her purse. "I'll call you when you're nice. Be nice."

Bean would leave, Avi told the ceiling. She was even better at it than Avi.

• • •

A portly arson investigator came too, on the second day. "You're a lucky, stupid man, Mr. Heyer," he said, hat in hand while standing in the doorway of Avi's room. "You went into a burning building, *A*; and you went upstairs in a burning building, *B*; and the building burned to the ground, *toast*. And you lived. Fires burn up," he added.

"I know," Avi said.

"It was arson," the cop said, flipping open a notebook and clicking his ballpoint twice, stopping to look at the point, and then one more click.

"I know," said Avi. "I smelled it."

"The accelerant." He scritched a note. "I'm Chun," he said, pointing to his nametag. "Officer Chun."

"Pleased to meet you. It was gasoline."

"Yes. How do you know that?"

"I saw the cans. I smelled it."

"Saw. . . ." Chun narrated his note. "Smelled . . . good thing you're stupid," the investigator added. "Good thing you had people with you the whole time, all those alibis. That'll clear the claim. You're off the hook," he said. "Get it?" he quipped, still not smiling. "Hook? Hook and ladder? That's a firefighter's joke. Get it?"

"Firefighters must be funny people," Avi offered.

"Oh, they are," Officer Chun said. "Used to be one," he gave a belly laugh. "It ain't just chili and chrome. I know one guy, he swears like a racehorse."

He what? When Avi failed to respond, the investigator began again, pen poised: "Do you have any idea who might have done this?"

"No," Avi said right away, but slowly, his lack of confidence surely apparent. Or yes, he had a few ideas as to who might have torched Maureen's house; or no, he had none, since all of the likely suspects were with him at the time, all the players each other's alibi. Only Ramona Pill hadn't been in the whale—but Ramona didn't seem the firebug type, and she didn't have anything obvious to gain from the fire. Oh, sure, out of malice The Camel might have hired Johnny Flame to light the blaze, but Avi believed that she wouldn't have incinerated her invaluable list, whatever had been on the list, wherever the list was in the house. The $80,000 list that now was gone.

So who burned down Mom's house? What the hell?

If Mom were alive, she might have burned down her own house, except that it was her own house, and it was all her stuff, so that didn't make any sense either. Plus she was dead, and dead people don't make insurance claims. So maybe Avi's new brother, Cain, did it.

. . .

On the third afternoon of Avi's confinement, a phone call came.

"Avi? It's a fire? You have burned the house of your *Maman*? I see the picture on the newspaper, and your whale. *Formidable!*"

"No, no," he said, the immediate futility of the conversation apparent. Why had Mimou called now? A nice gesture. "The house burned, that's all."

"*Oui, oui.* Such a puny kitchen. The whale is good. You and your Mr. Fix-it, you do a wonderful thing. It is—how do you say—what is found in the soul. But tell Mimou you are okay? Do you save your knives?"

"Yes. My knives are safe in D.C. But I lost the copper pan you gave me. . . ."

"Oh, the Breton copper! I am sad," Mimou said. "I crank the Def Leppard for you."

. . .

Convalescence overrated, concussions an ER doctor's ploy to cover his green fees: a patient's job was to ignore all medical advice in favor of ill-advised behavior. So at two in the morning a fed-up and insomniac Avi slipped from Ward 6, hailed a drowsy cabbie, and directed him to the charred ruin of Maureen's manse, where a great wooden whale loomed over all. "Um . . . to the whale," Avi told the driver, the house number and street name momentarily forgotten.

"Yeah, yeah!" the hack said. "That whale that guy built. I know someone who . . ." The driver's mouth ran like the meter.

Even when a man knows what to expect, surprises are possible. The bouncy taxi turned the corner and arrived in the little suburban dell where Mom's house used to be—only to find the intersection lined with cables and light stanchions, the park jammed with snoozing, whale-worshipping well-wishers, wackos congregating in the darkness and dew. "Here," Avi said quickly, the circus in town. "Right here. Close enough." Where were the cops? Who ran this popsicle stand?

He was furtive beyond all furtivity. Hunched, Avi semi-jogged as he slipped from tree to car to van to tree, back to car, Ninja-style. He counted seven news vehicles along the curb, and one Haz-Mat truck. But there *sheeeee* was, his very own whale—and surreptitiously, no one wiser, least of all himself, he slipped into the beast once more, where at last he could lie afloat on a pallet, hug the cookie jar, and gaze into the rafters.

The doctor was probably right, damn him: Avi's headache banged away, and his hand would have to heal before clutching the beam to swing, swing, swing.

In the belly of the whale, at what might be her center of gravity, he lay. In a dry breeze, with a small sudden gust, the tarp on the whale's tail rippled, the sound a kind of plasticky snapping. The charred house and the surrounding yard smelled sour and sharp, a smell he didn't like. His hair and his clothes would need to be washed every day; the whole place stunk. Apparently, a fire didn't end when the flames went out.

The trucks nearby hummed, an over-hum distinct from the whale's inaudible own. Everything he saw seemed portentous, signs and symbols. He had lain in the hospital bed and wrestled with what to do, and now he stared up into the rafters of the whale and wrestled with what to do. He was almost thirty.

There would be plenty of money from the will's codicil and the fire insurance: if Avi left now, he could cash out, cash in, and leave all this behind. He would call Markins, get the executrix to visit and approve of the whale, and Avi would move forward, invest in his own place in a chi-chi neighborhood in Eugene—even if a restaurant called "Rick's" might be too *Casablanca*, serving couscous five ways, couscous not his idiom. But he could design the joint, one far from this mad crowd, a place with panache. He could hire Rick to be headwaiter, give the front a little discipline, the frou-frou clientele stumped by the contractor's military mien—sit up, cut your hair, finish your food. Bean could cook the books.

No, he couldn't leave yet. Too often, he told himself. He had left too much behind too often. He had, by going back into the burning house, promised himself something.

"Hi," said a little voice outside Avi's whale.

Avi propped himself up on an elbow. "Hello?" he said to the darkness.

"Hi." She stepped into sight. She was wearing khakis and loafers and a kind of windbreaker, regular person clothes, but a brightly colored scarf too, tossed over one shoulder with a dash of Princess Grace. "May I come in?"

"Sure," said Avi, surprised.

"Neat whale," said Hannah Cara Papadopoulos, as she stepped into the whale.

"Why, thank you," Avi played along.

She approached the bed. "May I?" With an open palm, she asked to sit.

"Please."

"I . . . I wanted. . . . Did you get the balloons? I so love balloons." She sat.

"I did," Avi said. "They were from you? Thanks."

"I didn't write a note. Is that all right? I'm a journalist."

Avi was quiet.

"Do you lie down and look up? Is that what you do when you're here? Is that the point? May I?" She didn't wait for an answer: Hannah Cara Papadopoulos lay down. "The stars are so beautiful," she said. "They're like bits of sugar."

Why not? He lay side by side with Channel 6. The truth be told.

"I . . . I wanted to say I'm sorry about your house. And"—she might have been crying—"your mom. . . . I think your whale's beautiful. It's just such a beautiful thing, and not just because you're helping those poor criminals. . . . I think. . . ." Her hands fluttered.

Avi waited a long time. The stars did look like sugar. "The stars do look like sugar," he said.

"I hate my life," she said.

"What are you doing here?" he asked, his own directness a surprise.

"I'm sorry." She sniffed a bit grossly and gave a goodly chuff. "That's okay. I mean, it's not your fault. You built a whale."

"I see," said Avi. He didn't.

"After Rodney slept with Sally, I wanted to kill myself. That fucker. But now I can't sleep, and then you built this beautiful . . . *whhhhhhhaaaaallllllle*." She cried more fully, her bawling loose and hearty. "Don't you see? I'm the *whhh-hhallllllllle*."

"What?" said Avi.

"I'm so *ffffffaaaaaaattt*," she cried.

"Oh, no you're not," he said. "You're pretty."

She sighed again, rolled onto her side to look at Avi, checking something out, the bed a hard cloud beneath them. "You think so?"

"Sure," Avi said. "You've got nice hair."

"Really? You think so? Carlos says that. Carlos is Hair at the station—not that he cares about anyone but the anchors. . . . You like my hair. . . . I'm glad you like it. . . . But I'm not the whale—*snort*—because I'm *fffat*. I'm the whale because it's what I *fffffeel*. I . . . I'm sorry, I'm not making any sense." She touched his arm lightly and chuffed again, her whole body involved.

"You are making sense," said Avi. "It's the first thing you said that I understand," he added. "Promise. I feel like that too."

"I knew it," she said. "I knew it," she said more softly, relieved. "I knew . . . I knew it, I knew. . . . Will you hold me?"

"Um. . . ." Avi was a little interested. What kind of holding?

She rolled onto him abruptly and began to kiss Avi's face wetly, planted kisses all over, her cheeks shiny with tears. "*Mm. Mm. Mm.* Come on. I'll show him. *Mm.* Come on. *Mm. Mm.* . . ."

"Wait, what?"

She pulled up her upper body so that she could see Avi and answer; her crotch pressed onto his. "Nothing," she said. "Oh."

Now Avi was confused. On the confused scale of one to ten, he was a fourteen. "I . . . I can't do this," he said. Her body felt pretty good. "Please don't," he made himself say.

Hannah Cara Papadopoulos gave him the stink eye. "*Hmph*," she said. "Why?" When he didn't answer, she *hmphed* again and rolled off. "You're not very *n-n-n-nice*," she said. She was crying.

Avi said nada.

She had rolled onto her back. There was a silence big as a whale.

"Th-th-thank you," she stammered softly.

They lay there and stared at the stars. The whale rocked them, or didn't. After a long while, after not speaking again for what seemed a very long time, with a soft exhalation Hannah Cara Papadopoulos fell asleep, her breathing its own metronome.

• • •

He sat up: he had slept until dawn, sleeping out under the stars and inside the open frame of the whale. He needed a fix, a *caffè e latté* on a platter served *en whale*. Flopped on the bed next to him, both arms above her head, doing the sleep-wave by herself, Hannah Cara Papadopoulos snored lightly. He could leave her here, go out for everything bagels.

"Whale Man! Whalie whale!"

Pony Tail Guy was wearing the exact same outfit as last time, oh no. *"Whale Man!"* Pony Tail Guy hissed. *"It's me."*

"Shhh, I know," Avi said, and pointed to the sleeping Hannah Cara.

"Yeah!" Pony Tail Guy stage-whispered. "Cool! You've got *another virgin!"*

Avi rose slowly. *"Shhhhhhh,"* he put his finger to his lips.

"Whale Man, the energy is like, wow. You and whalie whale and the virgins. It's so . . . Tantric!"

"Shhh," Avi repeated as he stepped through a zippered opening in the tented sidewall. "Let's go back and talk to your friends. They miss you." He put his unburned hand on Pony Tail Guy's shoulder. The guy smelled like old cinnamon. Avi cleared his throat. "Have you eaten yet this morning? You really should take food with your meds."

Pony Tail Guy went home and the media slept, God bless 'em. With their painted wagons lining the street, just as daylight began to smear the land lightly, the media dozed in their prime parking spots, secure from the advance of other media folks. All but the Haz-Mat truck—which Avi noticed now, the silhouettes resolving into a kind of burnished gray, wasn't a Haz-Mat truck at all but an RV.

Then the RV's door shushed open hydraulically, and down the little stairs stepped The Camel in tennis whites and a cap that read *Hoover Dam Rescue Patrol.* "My friend," she said. *"Caro mio.* Good morning, Sunshine. Do you see what we have in common, our American-ness, so much brio?" With a Broadway sweep of her hand, she indicated her recreational vehicle. *"Ecce, homo.* I too have a whale."

"Very nice," said Avi. "Big."

"Yes," The Camel agreed. "Scale is a function of a national imagination, don't you think? That, and topography. Have you ever thought about how long it takes to drive across each state in the Union? And consider tiny Belgium, by contrast. What a wonderful country America is, so free of itself, so unclaustrophobic, so open." She paused. "Agoraphobic? No. Agoraphilic."

"Hi?" Avi reminded her that he was standing there.

"Oh, yes, hello. *Ahoj kamarade.* Shall we conduct an exit interview? I think that such a conversation is in order."

"Exit?" Avi said.

"Yes, exit," The Camel said. She stepped aside; the open door of the RV beckoned. "Please enter. Dare you speak with me one last time, now that your mother's list is no more?" She smiled, her malice agleam. "What could The Camel possibly want?" Her smiled changed again. "You look needy: I can surely help. Coffee?"

. . .

It's your thing, do what you wanna do. I can't tell ya' who to sock it to. The syncopated squeals of the Isley Brothers popcorned from mini-speakers inside The Camel's RV, the music in keeping with the softly lighted décor, industrial steel-and-black office furniture, 1982 SoHo loft meets Office Max. "My demesne," she said with a wink, as behind her the door closed mysteriously.

"How'd you do that?" Avi asked, surprised. His burned hand throbbed.

"Magic," The Camel said.

"No, really."

She held up her right fist and curled open her fingers to reveal a tiny clicker in her palm. "Silicon Valley," she said. "My place is wired, as your geek might say. Shall we?"

He sat in a narrow chair at a glass-topped table, knees together, Avi pleased to nurse a good cup of java to rinse away the sock mouth, sip a good brew with a hint of something smoky. Were there designs in the sepia-tinted glass? They looked like little Aztec figures.

"You're impressed, I can tell," said The Camel. She sat too.

He wasn't. "Of course," he said.

"I knew you would be." She scootched up in her seat, almost prim, hands on her knees, her tennis togs bright white. "*Ach,*" The Camel exclaimed. "Are you feeling overestimated? Quite a happenstance, don't you think, for there to be a blaze when all of the interested parties were accounted for? And you—" she gestured toward his bandaged hand. "With your wittle mangled paw. Is Rickie Wickie's paw unhappy?" she crooned, her tone a parody of everything decent. "Such a fire, too, a chemical extravaganza, *poof!*" The Camel paused, and then gave herself a mock-smack to the forehead. "Dante! I should have offered you Dante, and then we could have had a chat. Now that's a fire! Don't you think that Dante was the first modern writer? How could any reasonably educated person think otherwise. . . ."

She adjusted the ball cap that had been struck askew by her mock self-abuse. "*Bien sur.* But now, at last, Camel to Susan Junior, with those meddlers removed, I would like the list. You have done your filial duty, and your mother is at peace. I heard you say so. Very moving," she winked—and the lights dimmed.

"Stop that," Avi said.

"More unnerving than the uncomfortable chair?" She smiled a thin, mean smile.

"I don't have the list," Avi protested. "I never did. Really."

"*Really?* Ah, my little lettuce, but you do, you have always had the list. In fact, I am of the belief that you alone have always had the list. And the list is what I want."

She bared her chompers fully—and then she winked again, and a disco ball in the center of the room began to spin and glow, bubbly lights thrown everywhere. Now Avi realized what figures danced in the tabletop glass: they were camels. "How can I deliver what I don't have?"

"Well, think, dear. The list was never in the house—we looked—and so it has always been elsewhere, the Space-Time Continuum being what it is. Good grief! Isn't this just your little conundrum?" The Camel reached forward and put her hand on Avi's knee, pat, pat, then gripped harder, her small hand capable of surprising strength.

Not this guy! Avi grabbed her hand and squeezed.

"*Ow!*" The Camel feigned shock. "You hit a girl."

"Did not," Avi said. "Don't touch me," he said. "There's no list."

But now she was angry for real: The Camel stuck out her lower lip, her eyes ablaze. "You shouldn't have done that. You have forced me to be firm. You have forced my hand, no?" She smiled to herself. "The list, please. Shall we say soon, sooner, soon-ish? A week? And of course, to secure my investment—"

"Forget it, I'm outta here," he rose to go. "You've got nothing on me."

"Susan Junior, Susan Junior. . . ." The Camel crooned as she leaned back, away from the table. "Shall we talk about Bean? Shall we discuss the future of dog-kind? Shall we talk about your long-lost brother?"

What? Avi shook his head. "You leave them alone!"

"I shan or I shan't," she said. "Information is power." The Camel smiled. "Sit," she told him. "Just like Dolly the canine. Or stand. It matters not." She almost snarled. "However, I shall say once more, and only once: the list is in your possession and must be in mine within seven days. 'Provide, provide . . .'" she intoned. "That's from a different poem. Not Dante." The mastermind sighed, her comment to herself, the conversation back inside her head once more, where the crazy people lived. "What criminal enterprise do you know of that operates with as much clarity as this?" She thumped the glass table hard, Avi's coffee cup jumping with surprise in its saucer. "Clarity, my friend! Clarity!"

• • •

"Mr. Woodley! Mr. Woodley! Rick!"

The media was awake, earpieces locked and loaded, armed to the Blueteeth. Avi hadn't even fully stepped out of The Camel's RV, he had just been threatened, and now there wasn't room to move. Standing on the stairs of the vehicle, above the cameras and the crews, with a clear view of the worshippers and the site of the fire, he nonetheless could feel the power of the moment, every act a headline.

"Whale Man, Whale Man, Whale Man. . . ." The worshippers were awake too, and had begun to chant from across the street. What could Avi do? A chant has its own little motor. A police barricade was only as good as its wood, like a whale.

As the noise rose, the clutch of reporters pressed forward, crisp and greedy in their ironed-on beauty. They turned, told their cameramen to pan—get the crowd shot—and came back to assault Avi, stick mics stuck in his face. "Rick, what now?'

"Mr. Woodley, give us a comment."

"Rick, where are you going to live?"

Avi had yet to descend, to de-RV. "People, people," he began, but the clamor barely ebbed. Behind the news crews, he could see a homemade sign bouncing up and down: FREE THE WALE. A worshipper had escaped from the park, not a good sign.

"People, please. . . . I have a prepared statement. I—"

"Rick, who burned the house down? Rick, the report says arson. Rick, what will happen to your foundation? Rick, what are your plans? Rick—"

"PEOPLE!"

"Rick," squeaked the junior reporter with the cowlick, the kid from Channel 3. "Could you tell the boys and girls what we should be when we grow up?"

Oh, crap, Avi thought. Whale Man as yogi. And as though the crowd knew, the chant rose, louder: "Whale Man, Whale Man. . . ."

"People, I am very distressed." He had to improvise. Avi waved his burned and bandaged hand, the motion borrowed from presidential motorcades. In response, the media bevy settled into recording mode, with close-ups of his bed-head, probably. Even the worshippers across the street seemed to hush. "The loss of my mother's house is a great blow . . . but W.H.A.L.E. swims on, through the rough seas of . . . um . . ." Avi lost his metaphor. "We're not drowning yet," he tried again. "You can't just harpoon this whale," he added cheerily.

"What he means to say—" A hand clapped on his shoulder as a voice came to Avi's rescue. The Camel had arrived, she who had threatened him, no fair. She stood above and behind him on the stairs of the RV, and with a firm grip she eased Avi to one side. She had done a quick change into a crisp, green pantsuit, and wire rimmed glasses that made her look unrecognizably secretarial. She brandished a smart phone. "What Mr. Woodley means to say is that W.H.A.L.E. welcomes all challenges. Of course we grieve for the loss of the family home. But remember, those poor prisoners—the men who built this whale—have had worse lives than any of us. They're just unfortunate people. They're not you and I. Happily, we're here to help prisoners everywhere, those men and women incarcerated wrongly or rightly. W.H.A.L.E. is here to facilitate their rehabilitation, and to assist the penal system. Thank you, that's enough for now."

"But Mr. Woodley, what about your followers?" The inquiring reporter pointed his mic at the congregants in the park. "What will you say to them?"

"I . . ." Avi began . . . and stopped.

"Mr. Woodley will say to them that the whale is theirs," The Camel offered. "He will walk among them, and he will welcome them all to W.H.A.L.E. Where they will all be welcome," she repeated herself. "Everyone has a home with W.H.A.L.E."

"I will?" Avi couldn't help himself. The situation was out of control. "They do?"

"Twice each day, Mr. Woodley will join whoever comes to the whale in a meeting of minds and hearts and souls and emotions and—"

Avi elbowed The Camel pointedly. Enough.

"Right," she said. "I'm sorry, but these sessions will be closed to the media. They're private," The Camel added. "For Mr. Woodley to do his job, I'm sure we can expect your full cooperation."

"Yes," Avi chimed, "just me and the people." He looked over the heads of the broadcast crews to the motley maniacs. Was that Pony Tail Guy waving both arms? "Just Whale Man and the whalies," Avi said. "Just regular folks."

". . . Until, at the very least, Mr. Woodley's unfortunate brother is returned to safety."

"Daniel?" Avi said.

The Camel gave two thumbs-up to the cameras and stared meaningfully into the electronic universe. "Daniel, we care. We're praying for you, son."

"Daniel?" Avi repeated.

"Whale Man, Whale Man, Whale Man, Whale Man. . . ."

SEVENTEEN

· ·

RELEASED TO HIS DIMINISHED RECOGNIZANCE, running a gauntlet of cameras, Avi arrived back in the company of the whale, the burned maternal abode, a purty little red pickup parked just down the street, no dog in the yard, and 200 or so new best friends. Who could fault them their affections? Even from behind the police cordon, occasional coppers at ease, the crowd of wackos could see that they weren't so wacko, and that the whale was deserving. Avi stood on the dry shore, admiring. Ay, Captain, she was an awkward beauty, she was, hacked and hewn out of a suburban and domestic Elsbeth. Wooden, mammalian, phantasmagorical, upholstered, ramshackle: a hybrid intermediary between Mom's world and two others, the world of dreams and the briny deep.

Perhaps it was The Camel's high-test coffee he had knocked back, but his heart raced. Damn Camel, he thought. She had set him up, he realized. By promising viewers everywhere that Whale Man would receive penitents twice daily, she had made sure that Avi couldn't leave town. By assigning herself the role of W.H.A.L.E. spokesperson, she had found a way to keep watch. Could she really believe he had a brother? Rick had been right; a fake brother could be useful.

Avi felt as though a moment had passed, though: he might have denounced The Camel as an imposter, but now he couldn't, now that her lies had mixed with his.

Across the yard Officer Chun stomped through the charred ruins and gave a hearty wave. "Don't mind me," he called. "I'm just finishing."

"*Woof!*" said someone Avi loved. "*Woof! Woof! Woof! Woof!*"

He was jumped on, he was dog-licked, he was head-butted, he was pawed. "Hi, hi," said Avi. "Oh my God, hi. Dolly wolly. . . ." He squatted. "Dang, I missed you, Doll," he scratched her ear. She stamped her front feet. "That's better. . . ."

"Hey," said Bean.

Avi looked up. "Hey."

"*Woof!*" Dolly said. *I like Bean too, but scratch me,* her woof meant in Doggish. Her whole body wagged.

"She's here?" Bean asked, her question taking in the RV.

"I've got a week," said Avi, and he rose to give Bean a kiss.

"*Woof! Arruuu,*" yodeled Dolly.

He had missed her too. "Yes, Doll, I know." With his right hand, Avi scratched Dolly's big head, right across the flat part on top, which made her eyes squinch.

"That figures," said Bean. "She's done waiting." Bean touched Avi's arm lightly.

"*Rrrrrroooouuuuuu. Woof! Woof, woof!*"

"Hence my deadline." Avi let his left hand drift down to Bean's right, and took her soft, small fingers in his.

"Hence. You've been listening to her talk too much. Hence," she shook her head.

"Hence. She threatened me."

"I'm not surprised. Hence. Forthwith."

"But I don't have the list." He and Bean began to stroll and talk, so easy. He took the leash. "She said I do have it. I'm confused."

"I've thought about that," Bean said. "It occurred to me too. The list is in code, and it's some place obvious where your mom meant it to be found. That's how she worked. That's what she taught me. She used to say, "What good's a secret if no one finds out?" Not that I ever understood, I mean, what good's a secret if it *is* found out? Anyway, the list was never just in the house."

Avi was silent. Mom's house used to stand there, and now it didn't. "But everything burned," he said.

Bean gave Avi's hand a little squeeze. "Do you miss her?"

"No," he admitted. "Or yes. I don't know." He wanted to change the subject. "The whale . . . she . . . she seems to be a freak magnet."

"I see," Bean giggled. "That's so bizarre."

"*Rrrruuuu,*" grumbled Dolly. She head-butted Avi's leg.

"Yep," said Avi. "The twins are around somewhere too."

"They're trouble," said Bean. "Hey, are you hungry? Wanna get something?"

Avi laughed. "You're always hungry," he said.

She swished in yet another spangly long skirt. "High metabolism."

"I'm glad," he kissed her. "'Cause I like it. A chef's girlfriend and all that."

"Girlfriend?" Bean wrapped her arms around his lower back, and squeezed closer, groin to groin. "Would you like a pony with your fantasy?"

Avi laughed. "Miss Bean, we're probably on TV!"

"You know," Bean said, "I called the hospital early this morning." She paused, still in his arms, her smile slightly different. "You weren't in your room."

"I . . . I slept here," he said.

"Here? Where?"

"In the whale." He was embarrassed. "The bed," he added, in the hope that his offhandedness would suffice—no need to mention Hannah Cara Papadopoulos.

"Were you. . . ? Okay." Bean apparently decided something. "Okay, Susan Junior, Whale Man. You slept here," she told herself. "First night in the whale."

Avi tried to laugh. Her body felt good. "Wanna know something else?" he said, and ground a little against her. She had such a great smell. "I like being your boyfriend."

Bean blushed, almost to the tippy tip of her cute little nose. "Thanks," she said. "Me too. I mean, I like it too."

"We could—" Avi began to make a suggestion.

"We're on TV," Bean reminded him.

"Right," Avi said.

Hannah Cara Papadopoulos had returned to her kind. He could see the cameras trained on him, the masts of the broadcast trucks aiming their microwave transmitters into satellited skies. "I've got to do something," he realized as he spoke: "I need to walk around in there—" he chin-chucked toward the charred house ringed with yellow Police tape. The fire investigator had apparently left. "I want to see."

Bean released him from her embrace. "Go," she said. "I've got calls to make." She kissed his scruffy chin, held out her hand for the leash once more. "I'll take Dolly into the whale," she said. "Meetcha there . . . then we'll go eat? My, you're such an interesting boy," she said. "Your Soul Diary is being rewritten, Avi. There's all this new information—I've never seen so many changes in colors. It's like—"

"I'm a man, not boy," Avi said gently. "I'm a man. If you don't mind, I don't like being called a boy. I don't feel much like a boy anymore," he admitted. "Doll, you go with Bean."

"Woof!" said Dolly.

"Man," Bean said. "That's cool with me, boyfriend. My Whale Man," she sparkled, her lowered timbre delightfully suggestive.

Avi walked around the near side of the whale, turned away from GF and K-9. Luckily, he was obscured by the whale's flank—because if he hadn't been, the cameras would have panned, the crowd would have swiveled as one to see. "Hell," he said to Bean, who was probably out of earshot. "I'm everyone's. Looks like I belong to everyone now. And I'm talking to myself. Listen, see? Crap."

· · ·

Avi crunched and wended among beams variegated by the fire's violence, monstrous chunks of wood thinned to blackened, brittle uselessness. Ghastly, really, the fire had achieved another stage of being—the fire had become a smell instead of a flame. Dank sulfur, dowsed carbon, putrid ash, and the left-over tang of one substance altered by force into another. Avi's nostrils stung, and the odors filled his quick, short breaths. He tried to step carefully; tiny, unsafe, insubstantial forms crunched underfoot. The smell made his eyes tear again. Maybe it was the smell.

He kicked a piece of something colorful. He was standing where the dining room used to be, below where the spare room used to be: the upstairs and downstairs rooms lay charred together underfoot.

The thing he kicked was painted and scorched and unrecognizable. *Crunch. Crunch.* Avi stepped toward the kitchen area. He began to kick clods of soaked, extinguished embers until his foot stubbed on something more solid. No way he was digging around in there. . . . Instead he kicked some more, kicked free a metallic object, some kind of box he didn't recognize, the handle half-off. It all was crap, Avi thought with a glum smile. Just crap.

He kicked and his foot went through the thinned metal, got stuck. He shook his foot free. There were no secrets inside, burned or otherwise. The box might once have been a toolbox full of fishing tackle. The box might have held family photos or a dictionary. Wait! Avi had a happy thought, an idea. . . . He could still make up a list, make up a code, sell both to The Camel, and pocket the $80,000 plus, Bean bidding to drive up the price. That could totally work. Or not. Or could. Good show, Susan Junior, wot, wot.

The burned remains of the house looked like the moon. Back to kicking, Avi breathed deeply, the sour stink of the fire icky. The list and the code would take some planning, to insure plausibility.

The whale. The whalie whale. He had lost the house but found a place to stay. Avi would sleep in the whale, make do with minimal domestic items from the house, downsized by calamity, use Sascha's Porta-John as needed, buy a coffee pot, new shoes, a basket full of expensive toiletries, and some underwear. Why not for a week be the Whale Man to the max, everything his followers could hope? He had made himself a home in the whale—the idea was cheesy enough to inspire a grin, and might even warrant the entrance of orchestral music, soaring strings to accompany the cartoon light bulb. Oh, Whale of Mine. Oh, Immensity!

A man in a whale with a plan is a dangerous man, Avi decided, newly pissed off.

. . .

Breakfast at a diner with Bean, pancakes and syrup, Dolly waiting in the pickup, Bean spilling her juice. Bean and Avi sat at the linoleum four-top and read the newspaper like a married couple who had forgotten their anniversary years ago. He peered over the Local section, checked out the picture of the whale, read the coverage, Rick Woodley and his foundation, the tragedy of the good deed. The burn on his hand felt tight.

"What?" she said. She folded her section of the paper, a page of battle zone obits, but had a little trouble doing so, her coordination apparently not so ho-monkey this a.m.

He hadn't said anything. "I didn't say anything." And then Avi seized the opening: "You know, we haven't talked about it." He took a deep breath.

"About what?"

"Well, not *it* it," he said. "It. The fire. You know."

"About your mom." Bean looked at him. "You don't mean the fire, you mean your mom."

"Hey," he exclaimed. "C'mon, Miss Bean. Can't I have one thought to myself?"

"You believed I was your mom. On the cell."

"I . . . I believed. . . . I *thought* that she might be alive. I thought so then," he added. He lowered his head to stare at the silverware. Forks were odd inventions: maybe they were knives once. "I know she's not."

"It's a nice idea, Sailor," Bean said. "Sorry."

"Sailor?"

"Oh, you know. *The sailor went to sea, sea, sea.* For some reason, I've been singing that song." She sang a line: "*And all that he could see, see, see was the bottom of the deep blue sea, sea, sea.*"

"I loved that song when I was a kid," Avi confessed. "I wish . . ." he began. Bean waited.

He took a deep breath, looked up. "I wish that I had known her the way you did. I'm jealous."

"I know," Bean said. "It worries me."

"It does?"

"Yes." She smiled uncomfortably, ducked her head, sipped her coffee. "I'm worried that's why you like me. That you want more of her. But I don't have more. I don't have what you want."

"That's dumb," Avi said, and regretted saying so. "I mean, I'm worried that you're only after the list."

"Gee, thanks."

"Sorta," he said. "Well, not really. Not anymore. So will you tell me about Toronto?"

"Toronto. *Ahhh* . . . she told you. The Camel. She must have told you to ask me."

"Yes. Do you want to tell me . . . Bean?"

"I . . . I did something I'm not proud of. Your mom didn't like it. I . . . she hadn't really forgiven me, I don't think." Bean raised her gaze to meet Avi's. "It wasn't a betrayal, exactly. The RCMP were close. I had to get out of there. People depend on me."

Avi thought he understood. "You left her there?"

Bean nodded.

"And the police?"

"The RCMP. They almost caught her, but she got out. It's different in Canada."

"A different country," Avi said, and then tried to make light. "All those Canadians. All those mooses and taxes."

"*Mm,*" Bean said, lost in the memory.

"I'm supposed to be angry?"

"Maybe," Bean admitted. "I'm ashamed of what I did."

"You're ashamed of how you treated my mom? You should try being me." He paused. "I haven't told you. . . . I . . . I mean, now that we're confessing." He looked around: a diner was like a church for a lot of people. "Okay," he exhaled. "So, when she left, I was fourteen. And my dad . . . he couldn't handle anything, and he felt so awful, and there were lots of chair days, when he didn't move. I . . . I told him a lie. I thought it would help. I told him that she had been having an affair, and that I had discovered it."

"Oh, Avi."

"Yeah, that was bad." He toyed with the salt shaker; there were grains of rice inside. "But I made it worse. I never . . . I mean . . . I didn't." He stopped, and raised his gaze to make eye contact with Bean. "I never let him know it was a lie."

"Oh, Avi," Bean said, "you were just a kid."

"I know. But my whale is . . . it's kind of . . . anyway, I owe her an apology."

"God, that's awful."

"What?"

She tried to smile. "That you think so. Your mother left and you should apologize?"

Avi thought about Bean's comment. "Yeah, I guess. Sometimes shit's just awful, don't you think? That's why its ours."

They talked and talked, ordered and mostly ignored a desiccated piece of crumb cake. Mom this, Susan that, the whale, Rick, the money, The Camel. Bean's smile sizzled. Damn, Avi was losing it.

". . . I didn't know about you," she was saying. "About us, and all this, and . . . she had talked about you, but how was I to know? In your Soul Diary, there's a kind of—I don't know what to call it. Let me try to explain." Bean wiggled forward in her chair. "It's like this. In *my* Soul Diary, what I've learned to read about myself—remember, I told you about balakweneo meditation? It's so cool. I'll teach you. Anyway, in *my* Soul Diary I found . . . *after* Toronto, that a person who matters to me is not the same as the individual." Her look was searching; Bean wanted Avi to understand. "I know it's confusing. It's that I'm not what I do. I can make a mistake and not *be the mistake*."

Avi was quiet for a moment. "I think I understand."

"Oh, good!" Bean was serious and excited. "We'll see," she added.

The waitress drifted by, coffeepot in hand. "More coffee?" she asked. Shift change, Avi noticed. Her nametag said Rorie.

"Thanks," said Avi, and held up his cup. "Rorie."

"Are y-y-you . . . aren't you that Whale Man?"

Avi nodded yes.

"He is," Bean said. "Please. A little." She held her coffee up with two hands.

Rorie topped up their cups. "I have to . . . I want to say . . . oh, Lordy! You're doing a great thing, and it matters. To all of us here in Elsbeth. It's really . . . it's not only me . . . it's my kid . . . he's not so schooly, you know?"

Avi smiled.

Rorie kept going, the words tumbling upon themselves: "He's fifteen. Sixteen next month, and he doesn't have a dad. Which is a good thing, mind you; that man wasn't enough to spit on. But my boy, he's cutting out all the pictures from the paper. Every day he's printing out pages and pages from his computer—my word, I don't understand where he gets this stuff—but they're about you. Your whale. He's got them on the wall."

"A whale wall?" Avi said gently.

Rorie the waitress laughed—she had a tinkly, wonderful laugh.

"Wow, you've got a great laugh!" Bean said.

"Thank you!" Rorie said. "A whale wall. That's a funny, hon. I'm encouraging his interest. But in small ways, you know? It's so hard with a teenager: if you say you like it, he stops. It's the first time in a long time that he's been interested in anything, bless his heart. Maybe . . . maybe he could meet you—we were going to drop by. I mean, if that's good for y'all's schedule?"

"I'd be happy to," Avi said. "Please bring him by. I'll look for you. What's his name?"

Rorie laughed again, her laugh like having a good breakfast at a diner all over again. "Oh, I would be obliged. His name's Jerry. You're a dear."

"Jerry. That's my uncle's name." Avi wished he could stop lying.

"It is?" Rorie was very excited. "We're kissing cousins! I'll tell my Jerry. We could be relations!"

· · ·

He had to park a block away and walk in with Dolly, Bean off to do more errands. So Avi arrived at his own private Yasgur's farm. Whalestock. He was incognito, hidden under Bean's City Grocery baseball hat, a loaner, his matching cap lost in the fire.

As man and dog passed yet another newly arrived network truck, the mast on the truck's roof rose with a wheezy whir—with the help of a young woman atop the vehicle, who would shake the thing whenever it got stuck, to make it go. He could see inside, where a hairsprayed reporter sat at a console and fiddled with a wireless transponder as he tapped on his earpiece, the guy calling to someone unseen, "No IFB. No IFB." A cameraman, camera in one hand like an enormous, clunky pocketbook, stood next to the truck. He gave Avi a little hiya smile.

"What's IFB?" Avi asked.

"Dunno what it stands for," the cameraman laughed. "It's how we hear. Nice dog."

"Thanks," Avi said, and moved to walk on. Rick had IFB.

"Dogs are good people," the cameraman said.

A few hundred yards further along felt like a few hundred years, the cars lining the street, more news vans nosing their way into position, masses of whale-wishers encamped in the park, the police stunned. Avi didn't want to face them all just now, and so he crossed the street—"C'mon Dolly, let's go bite Katie Couric"— just in front of Sascha's house. On the inclined lawn from stoop to sidewalk, Sascha had erected a party tent inside of which a dozen or so people milled about a TV on a table tuned to "The Price is Right." Sascha was on the edge of his crowd of guests, dressed in a track suit, just a bit of bling away from stereotype. Sascha's guests shouted numbers at the television and hugged each other.

No, not that way. Time for a little sprint, Avi told himself—and so he took off suddenly, urged on Dolly, and headed for the safety of the whale. Maybe he elbowed that guy from CNN, maybe not; the referee would have to decide.

At the door to the whale, the tent flaps along her flank pulled down—like shades, so that no one streetside could see in—Avi and Dolly arrived. Home free.

• • •

He spent all day catching up on nothing. He read a boring novel, some mystery about mountaineers in Spain that Avi saw through on page thirty, not Hemingway's Spain—and anyway, Avi hadn't liked Hemingway much, with all those characters posturing. Everything meant something in Hemingway.

Regardless, it was going to rain, and the whale worshippers were going to get wet, and Hemingway didn't write much about rain, or so Avi seemed to recall.

He kept his head down, the media barrage less dangerous that way, the concussion not so jarring, the brain-jar not so dangerously vitrified, the mullite content low. By dinner time, Dolly at her kibble, the weather was predictably uncooperative, as weather always was (hail or glare, weather didn't care), the whale room dry despite a warm, strong rain that rode the sky from the west. Avi was hungry for something. His poor circumstances had led to a grumbly tummy, only his tummy wasn't the source of the grumbling exclusively. He had lain in his whale all the livelong day, but now he couldn't; well, he could, but he didn't want to lie there longer. The Camel had promised: he should go meet his fans.

Avi felt strange, unrecognizable to himself, smaller in the downpour, the lawns quietly gulping, the news crews taking shelter under their logo umbrellas and inside their comfy trucks until a few of the newsies saw him emerge and head for the worshippers. Scurrying into action, the journalists clipped on their clip-on equipment, straightened ties and blouses. The story was walking: the story was doing a meet-'n-greet. By the time—really just a minute—that

Avi reached the outskirts of the encampment, he was trailed by four cameras and crews: cameramen, stick mics, coiffed talent, and Avi in the blazing glare of mercenary gossips.

The crowd in the park had tents and beach chairs and sterno and portable DVD players. They had conquered Maureen's neighborhood, nearer the whale to thee. The crowd had filled all the open spaces. The open spaces had closed. Who among them had a dead-end hobby, who had not paid taxes, who carried a weapon, who was a part-time troubadour and puppeteer, who had seen a UFO in Uzbekistan upon the latest harmonic convergence, who had left a husband or wife at home to bring an ailing grandparent to be whale-blessed, who didn't know why she was here, who had wallpapered over Eminem posters with whale pics and misquotations, who had no short term memory, who had messaged a therapist and quit therapy, who had brought the nieces, who had abandoned all electric appliances, who was running for office, who was running from whom, who was running to what? Who among them was a hunter and who a gatherer? The crowd had selected its own society. Whale City.

He had done this, made it so. He and his brother, Daniel.

The park must have been five acres, complete with a trickly stream and a baseball diamond, the soccer pitch a toddler's idea of big. Now on the fields of play there were aisles and an occasional vendor. Soaked, his poncho lost in the fire, everything so fucking biblical, Avi could only see dimly through the rain. He hadn't bothered with a hat, not wanting to ruin Bean's loaner. He stepped closer, entered the home of the frayed. Immediately, the crowd knew him, and many rose to greet Whale Man, to smile and touch his dripping sleeve. An old lady under an umbrella, grandmotherly with the exception of her coat (festooned in slogan-bearing buttons, including one the size of a dinner plate that read "LOVE A MONSTER"), offered him a treat from a Tupperware tub. "Chocolate chip Wookie Cookie?" she asked. "They're gluten-free."

"No thanks." Avi worried that he had hurt her feelings. "Well, just one. . . ."

She beamed. "I've got my own website," she said. "Four hundred hits a day."

The cookie tasted like an eighth grade social studies textbook. He feigned a second nibble, the cameramen jostling behind him (the aisle not wide enough, which helped), as Avi wandered deeper into the throng. Two more campsites later, he came upon a family huddled under a tarp, happily playing Sorry, the kids in matching rocket-ships pajamas, the mom in an apron, the dad in a misbuttoned cardigan. The dad even puffed a corncob pipe, June and Ward go wooden whale watching. The father drew in his smoke thoughtfully and waved paternally to Avi, who waved back.

"Evening," Avi called.

"Evening," the dad called.

"Tough weather," Avi said, feeling the drag of his sagging clothes.

"Mommy, is that—"

"Hush, little one," the mother said quickly. "Yes, it is."

"She's a beaut," said the dad.

She, *Sheeeee*. "Thanks," said Avi.

"Oh, thank *you!*" the mother exclaimed.

The father reached over and patted his wife's hand. "Yessir," he said. "You've given us a lot to think about. Do you imagine this rain will end?" He peered up toward the sky he couldn't see.

On Avi wandered along the path between the congregants, a narrow avenue formed by sociability, people assembled in common cause, with mutual affections and outpourings, and he realized how natural the crowd seemed, how organic its organization, and whether they were wackos mattered not. On the right, under another tarp, crouched a woman in a red sari, behind whom two children in baseball uniforms, a young boy and girl, pounded their gloves, narrating into the night an imaginary World Series, play-acting each of the roles: pitcher, catcher, batter, ump, color man. Moving on, Avi came upon a large potted plant in the care of three barefoot college-aged women dressed all in black, hair dyed fuchsia and violet, kohl upon their faces, who skipped in the rain in a happy circle, a rubber tree their Maypole. He stopped to watch, as they skidded like Keystone Kops to a stock-still halt, and gaped at him, astonished.

"Whale," said one.

"Man," said another.

"Whale Man," said the third.

"Hi," said the first.

"Hi," said Avi. "Gotta go," he added. They were mudders too, kin.

"Bye," all three said, awestruck.

"Bye."

Everyone knew Avi; he had never been so popular. He walked on, to be hugged by Pony Tail Guy, whose campsite seemed a cardboard box, and then to be given a tiny gift-wrapped present the size of a walnut by an older woman who began to laugh and cry at once; and on Avi wove through the crowd, maybe three hundred weak but seeming strong, each person basking in the glow of the whale, something in each person touched by the most personal gesture Avi had ever publicly made. He couldn't believe what he felt, which was what they felt, everyone so grateful for Avi's whale. He hugged the huggers back with gusto: he wanted to cook for them all. They had become part of his dream, a part he had not dreamed, but they had dreamed something too, all dreamers meeting in Dreamland, and the whale was theirs.

He turned a corner in the encampment and gazed up the next aisle, where a Coleman lantern and the various flashlights of the whale watchers winked ahead in the rain, each beacon corresponding to at least one whale-worshipper, beings with individual feelings, each a universe. Three hundred seemed a low number.

On he walked, to shake both hands of a professorial type, a fifty-ish short man dressed in black jeans and a French-cuffed shirt, an artsy dude, his glasses designed and his head shaved. They shared a wordless exchange, Whale Man and a stranger whose silent gratitude communicated a glint of an introspective life.

And on, Avi met a young couple eating cold cereal and huddled in lawn chairs under what looked to be an enormous beach umbrella, she far along in a pregnancy, and he in a grease monkey's coveralls. On a whim, Avi slipped into their shelter and joined them, squatted on the muddy ground. He wasn't going to get wetter or dirtier, really, but he would have to figure out where to shower—although as soon as he considered the problem he knew the answer, that he could shower at the truck stop.

"Hi," he said.

Behind him two cameras got good angles, two lights atop two cameras trained to brighten everybody's business.

The girl couldn't talk, flustered and frozen, her spoon mid-air, one Cheerio stuck to her bottom lip. "*Aah,*" she said.

"Hi," the boy said.

"Thanks for coming," Avi said.

"Sure," the boy said.

"*Aah,*" the girl said. With her spoon-free hand, she pointed at Avi.

"When's the baby due?" Avi asked.

"Inna month," the boy said.

"A month," the girl managed. "Whale Man."

"Yep," Avi said. "So if you don't mind my asking, what brings ya'?"

"*Aaaah.*" The girl had lost it again.

"I . . . Jas here, she wanted to come," the boy said.

"*Aaah . . .*" she said. "Whale Man. Jasmine."

"For the baby," the boy said. "Saw you on TV."

"Right," Avi said. "We're all on TV." He nodded to the cameras. "Well, thanks. Thanks for coming." He stood up; one knee creaked. "Gotta go," he said. "Good luck with the baby. Take care," he said.

"*Aaah,*" Jas said. "Whale Man."

And on, down the lane, in rising awe of the worshippers' feelings, Avi walked and talked, receiving small offerings—including a VOTE YES ON PROP 39 bumper sticker from a young local politico, who whispered that she had ditched her handler and campaign manager to see the whale. "Call me crazy," she dared him. Her robin's egg blue suit was spackled up the pant legs with red mud. "It's just the most unique of whales," she said. "You're bringing hope to the hopeless," she intoned sincerely, a prisoner of her platitudes.

"Thanks," said Avi, abashed.

"Thank you, young man," she said, the difference in their ages negligible. She turned and smiled to the cameras, gave a V sign for Valium.

And on, wet from the rain, who cares about the rain, he suddenly ducked between two tents, ditched his tail. Behind him, Avi could hear a reporter shout, "He's gone—we've lost him."

Whale Man was finally alone, sort of. It felt good.

Avi was careful, he kept his head down and headed toward the periphery and back across the street where the makeshift township ended and suburban life began again. But there was a Channel 6 tent edging onto the devil's strip: the lights shone upon Hannah Cara Papadopoulos seated on a camp chair, unnaturally orange tonight in her make-up. A small crowd had gathered, and Avi slipped into its ranks. He was soaking wet, rain the Number 3 disguise in every secret agent's closet. He bent his knees to be shorter.

"Yes, Xavi," Hannah Cara Papadopoulos said into Rodney's camera. "It's been a day of love and gratitude here in Elsbeth, as the people—" she turned to indicate the park behind her, "—the people keep arriving. I think we can call it the beginning of a drove. But now although it's raining hard, no one seems to be leaving. There have been two buses from Mississippi, I hear. There's a small group somewhere of lapsed Amish gentlefolk." She checked her notes. "Plus the Over-the-Hill Foundation. The Mayor has come too, and the Sheriff. We're expecting a call from the Governor's mansion. And Xavi, the police have decided not to intervene. An exclusive source inside Elsbeth HQ told me that someone got an email from someone, and the police are taking a wait-and-see approach apparently, as the park has become a quote-unquote People's Property, whatever we're to make of that. Xavi, it's not a reporter's job to guess.

"But of Rick Woodley, let me say this, Xavi, and I speak as an objective journalist trained at the University of Missouri's prestigious journalism school. I was taught not to become involved. But the man whose mother has died, whose inheritance has burned to the ground, who's done more than local officials for the state of felons in North Carolina, this brave man, whose brother has been kidnapped by parties unknown. . . ." Was she feigning tears? Avi didn't know whether to hope so. "Rick Woodley has disappeared into his whale, where apparently he now lives. As it should be, Xavi. We have all been drawn here. The man people call Whale Man has earned his whale.

"Live from the Elsbeth whale, I'm Hannah Cara Papadopoulos, Channel 6, 6 News in the Street. The truth be told."

EIGHTEEN

. . . .

THE RAIN LET UP. Restive in the belly of the beast, de-concussing just a tad more, Avi reread a few chapters in his whale guide, napped fitfully, and hoped to dream, dreaming itself a Whale Man's research. He felt world-whipped, his only change of clothes dry but not particularly clean. He made two drawings, the better one pocketed:

He was foodless in Gaza. So this time, incognito as himself, the Whale Man left the whale, Dolly sleepy enough to stay, her leash tied to a table leg, to be sure.

"Rick! Over here. Rick!"

"Rick, what's the foundation going to do with all the money?"

"Rick, Rick—"

"Whale Man!"

Avi waved his good hand. A small podium had been erected in the far corner of the lawn, near The Camel's RV. He could see her grinning there—and there he went, planning his Exit Strategy.

She put one hand on his shoulder; she hadn't said a word, a fucking miracle, that. Avi stepped to the microphones. "Good evening. Glad the rain stopped," he said. A few reporters nodded. "W.H.A.L.E. is in the process of setting up a PayPal account for donations."

"Rick, what about the Sausalito whale? What about the New Harmony whale? What are you saying to your copycats?"

Oh, crap! Avi smiled. "The Elsbeth whale is the only official whale recognized by W.H.A.L.E. But the Board of Directors has begun negotiations with prisons nationwide, and will consider all applications for—" he faltered.

"For whales," The Camel chimed.

"For whales," Avi said. "It's a big ocean, people," he added.

"Rick, there's talk that the Elsbeth Town Council wants to promote the whale, and that they've applied for 501(c) and want to proclaim Elsbeth "Home of the Whale." Are you for or against this?"

Avi paused.

The Camel leaned in to the microphones. "Isn't the Mayor the one who closed the no-kill shelter?" she asked innocently.

That got the reporters clamoring, "Rick, Rick. . . . Whale Man. . . . Rick. . . ."

"Enough for now, people," Avi said. "I'll hold a press conference in the morning."

"Rick," said Hannah Cara Papadopoulos. "Rick—"

Avi interrupted her. "On second thought," he said. "With the advice of the Board of Directors, I've decided to speak to one member of the media only. You can pool your video, if you like." He turned to Hannah Cara Papadopoulos; he could remember her body atop his, uh-oh. "You're it," he said.

"I am?"

"Yes, you." Avi said. "We'll talk in the morning." He raised his voice, "That's all, people. Goodnight and good dreaming. Swim well," he said. Avi hopped down from the podium, The Camel's hand on his back—scary—and turned from the nosy newsies. His truck was parked a block away, his dinner warming under a heat lamp somewhere in a strip mall. Wow, did he need a shower. But to get there he had to push his way through the crowd—which included, newly gathered around the news makers, a passel of tie-dyed vagabonds, one of whom was obviously the late Jerry Garcia.

To the truck, to the same diner, where the chef-in-training ate a bad burger, the flat, gray patty clearly tenderized by having been twice run over by a motorcycle. Condiments didn't help, but they at least masked the meat. He didn't see Rorie, her shift over. He didn't dare try the pie.

Avi better leave town soon, and find himself a good kitchen and buy himself a decent set of All-Clad and some good olive oil—quick, before someone got hurt.

It was later and early still, maybe eleven, by the time he shopped for toiletries in the Toilet aisle of PharmaWorld, and blindly in the refrigeration section for just a little decent cheese. Nothing was open, or he would have gone to Jockey Village for jockeys.

The Whale Man drove back down S.R. 252 to the truck stop while his whale slumbered elsewhere, Avi less a nightie tonight than a muddy do-gooder. The same enormous light stanchions lit up the same parking lot, identical and dissimilar trucks idling prehistorically as though extinct, the cars filled with the curiously insomniacal, nighties in their cars slipped between trucks in the canyons of commerce. This time, the scene seemed inevitable and sensible, the disenfranchised everywhere, like some kind of 21st century *Grapes of Wrath*.

Swarms of suicidal insects buzzed each photovoltaic node in the sky. The nighties, exhausted and awake, bodies crooked to look up, watched the tainted colors glow, the light towers ringed with bugs; the truckers not yet in dreamland drank or chatted. Avi parked between a brown semi emblazoned with a trumpet and a bright red moving van—grabbed his new towel, another purchase from a wrong store—and went across the lot to shower at the truck stop.

He showered badly: for two dollars in quarters, the water ran too hot and out too soon. He shaved, peered in the foggy mirror.

In his own little lorry once more, nightie in the nightie night, Avi became aware of the vague relationship between the enormous semis and a whale, no matter that an eighteen-wheeler would seem small when next to a whale. Both the trucks and the whale inspired awe, their size magnetic, real and true. The wacky worshippers apparently thought so too: they were drawn to Avi's whale to find solace in the grandeur. He understood the impulse.

All of the truck stop at night seemed part of a real dream, if that were possible, experienced awake by people who should be sleeping, and who often did sleep in their cars, at least for a few hours, once they got here.

The whale was real. A lie was a real story.

Avi let himself exhale. The whale was beautiful, she should attract the reverential, she did deserve TV coverage, she would learn to swim. She was longer than a house and almost as tall, her tail slightly and delightfully angled, and she lacked only a fluke atop the caudal peduncle, a jaw, and eyes. Would he give her an eye or two? Maybe not: she was a dreamed whale, not a stuffed animal. As for baleen, he had yet to decide if she were *Odontoceti* or *Mysteceti*.

"Whatcha got there?"

Avi looked up. The voice came from the cab above: a young woman in a Greek fishing cap had stuck her head out the passenger-side window of the truck. Above her, the sky threatened again. He had the whale book and a copy of the *Elsbeth Herald* open on the seat.

"It's the local paper," Avi said, not lying and not telling.

"I do Jumbles," she said.

"Jumbles," Avi said. "Those puzzles."

"Yes," she nodded. "Is there one in there? Can I borrow it?"

He looked through, struck Jumbles gold: "Sure," he said, and got out, to hand up the paper. "It's all yours."

"Thanks!" She was excited. "So how long you been a nightie?"

"Not long," Avi said. "What are you hauling?" he asked, both to be sociable and not to talk about himself tonight.

"Don't know," she said. "I hitched a ride."

Avi leaned back against his pickup to get a better look at her. She might have been eighteen, maybe. "Running from or to?"

The young woman was silent, although her expression furrowed, distress evident. "From," she finally said. "To," she changed her mind. "Dunno."

"Gotcha," Avi said. "What's your name?"

She didn't answer. But then her face brightened: "Tomorrow I'm going to go see that whale guy."

Avi's breath caught. "What guy?"

"You know, it was on the news. That guy had all those prisoners build a whale, and they're going to give him an award. Public service. . . . But—" she faltered. "I wanna see the whale." She gave the door a little thump with her hand. "I hear it's big."

"It's big," Avi said softly.

"It is? You've seen it?"

"I have," Avi said.

"What's it like?" She glanced back into the cab, and satisfied with what she saw, opened the door and lowered herself to the pavement, her long legs taking a long time to reach solid ground. "What color is it?"

She was very tall and thin, blond and dirty. Under her cap, her hair lay in dreds or what looked to be botched cornrows. She wore a long-sleeved shirt-dress that seemed to be mis-sized, or maybe her hips were. "What's it like?" she repeated. "Hey, mister. . . ."

Avi realized that his silence had been too long and a little rude. "Sorry," he said. "What's it like?" he echoed. "I think it's female—"

"I knew it!" she gave a little hop, and clapped her hands. Oh, Lord, she was so young to be on the road.

"And she's . . . kind of gorgeous. In a plain way. She's gray and green and she's big. Bigger than the house that burned. Her belly skin's really tough."

"The house that burned down, right? They burned him out. That's the worst thing ever. So Whale Man is living in the whale?"

"Right," Avi said. "'Cept I don't think it's so awful. I . . . *he* told someone that he had never liked that house."

"But it was his mom's. All her stuff burned up."

"Yeah," he said. "Only I think he likes the whale—I mean, wouldn't you?"

"I would," the hitchhiker cooed. "I'm going to build one some day. . . ." Her gaze wandered inward.

"When you get home?" Avi said quietly.

"Yeah," she said. "Home," she said. She began to cry a little.

"It's okay," Avi said. He reached forward to hug her, but she flinched. "Really, it's okay." People around him were becoming so emotional: maybe he was emotionally contagious.

Crying now more fully, she let herself be hugged, a runaway in the arms of Whale Man, a homeless teen held by a guy living in a big wooden whale. He held her lightly, standing together in the bright wash of the truck stop lights, together sucking fumes, surprised by the situation, his shoulder wet with her tears. He felt useless. "I . . . you might. . . ." Avi pulled back, so as not to seem a pervert, and with his thumb wiped a big tear from her cheek, the embrace over.

She laughed.

He was relieved not to be hugging her. "Look for me when you get there," Avi said. "At the whale."

"But . . . why?" she sniffled. "Do you know Whale Man?"

He had to shake his head. "I . . . that's me. I'm the guy. Whale Man."

"You're not Whale Man," she teased. "You're Clark Kent."

Avi said nothing: his steady gaze was his word. A teen was such an interesting combination of a little girl and a grown woman. He dug into a pocket and handed her one of his two new drawings, not the better one, he saw, having mis-pocketed:

She stayed quiet a long time, checked out the sketch, and glanced at the sketchy guy. "Okay," she said. "You do *look* like the guy on TV. Is it you? Really?" She laughed. "I think you're right! I believe you. You're Whale Man. Can I keep this? It's like your autograph."

"Yeah."

"*And* you're a nightie. How cool is that?"

"Whales, trucks, trucks, whales—" Avi shifted left, right, left as he spoke. "See?"

"Okay," she said. "So you built the whale . . . why?"

"*Woooohh,*" Avi exhaled, his arms raised, who knows. "For the prisoners, right? Work-fare or rehab or whatever you want to call it."

"Whale Man," she smiled, and wiped her nose with her sleeve. "That's not true. You're not answering the question. How come a *whale?*"

"Oh," said Avi. His gaze wandered unseeing. "How come a whale. Mom died—"

"Yeah," she interrupted him. "They said that on the news. Sorry."

"Thanks. So Mom died and in Mom's will there's lots of money if I do something crazy. But then . . . I had a dream about it. It's from a dream."

She scowled. "It's for money?"

"It was," Avi admitted. "It's not anymore. Or maybe it never was."

"I *thought* you were cool!" The teen gave another little hop and clapped her hands. "I love whales; they're the best," she said. "Don't you?"

Avi had said too much already. "So . . . let me ask you a question. What's the appeal? I mean, why do you want to see her?"

"Oh, man." She crossed her arms and gave herself a little rocking hug. "You understand. It's like, perfect. Some guy's mom dies, and he thinks he's gonna get a ton of cash, but he has a dream about a huge whale and builds it *on her lawn*, and then her house burns down, and he has to live there. And the dream, like, just takes over! Shit, man. *You gotta live in the dream!*"

"But you didn't know it was a dream."

"Did too," she smiled.

"Did not," he smiled back, paused. "And you can't tell anyone. . . . You seem so lost," he added, because she did, and to change the subject again. It was something Bean would say.

Avi's comment made her cry again, sorry.

After a long moment gathering herself, she nodded and agreed with something she had been thinking. "You're the Whale Man," she said. "Whale Man. I can't believe it's you."

"Me either," Avi said. "Sometimes it's like someone else built her, and everything's going to just float away."

"Whale Man."

"It's okay," Avi said. "I didn't do it," he said for no reason. "I'm getting outta Dodge anyway."

"You better not," she said. "People care. You're Whale Man."

"Right," Avi said, although he didn't agree with the Sit-Rep.

Then she leaned forward and kissed his cheek. "Thank you, Whale Man." She gestured broadly, happy again, and in a high soprano she intoned, "For people like me. For children everywhere. For the dreamer in all of us. . . ."

"Shut up, please," Avi laughed. "Please." She was so young to be a runaway.

"Be true to the dream. For the birds in the sea and the fish in the air—"

"Oh, shut up. Please."

"Whale Man," she said, serious once more, her moods too quickly shifted to be just happy. She paused, stilled, lowered her arms, the parody over. She was quiet for a long moment, with a new thought, and then she exhaled, a halting breath. "Oh, Whale Man, what's going to happen to me?"

NINETEEN

· ·

AVI SAT AT A TABLE in the whale. He laid his mother's copy of *Webster's* 9th next to his Composition notebook. In the notebook, amidst the whale plans and awful drawings, he had copied the words that ran atop the pages where the flowers had been pressed: clemency/clockwise, escape/estimate, *missa cantata*/mob, thimbleful/Thorazine. Some of the nine words seemed apt (clemency, escape, mob), while others were not so. But everyone around him could use a shot of Thorazine, and maybe Avi most of all.

"Knock, knock."

Bean was at the tent flap.

"Come in," Avi said. "Hiya."

She joined him in the belly of the whale. Dolly rose from her new bed and galumphed to greet her friend, Bean, Bean, Miss Bean.

"Hi," she came over and kissed him. "What's that?"

"Dunno," Avi said. "It might be something. . . ."

"Words and letters," Bean said. She rotated her tan City Grocery cap to wear backwards, so that the embroidered slogan faced forward, *no belly achin'*, and peered over his shoulder. "It's a list. You smell nice."

"Thanks. Maybe it is," Avi said. "Could be. List of what?"

Bean took a step back. "I . . . Avi, if I tell you, you'll be involved. Legally."

"I'm involved already."

"Not that kind of involved." She returned his look with a smile.

"There's got to be a key," Avi said. "The list is in code, right? What's it a list of?"

"Oh, Avi . . . please don't ask."

"I'm asking," he said.

Bean looked pained as she considered his request. She was wearing her designy bracelet, a checked short sleeve top, a wide Concho belt, and a skirt he had seen once before. Not so coordinated and very Bean.

"Avi. . . ."

"Please," he said.

"I . . ."

"Bean," he said. "It's me. Avi."

Silence. She was thinking hard. Then, finally, she said, "Fine. Okay. I knew you'd want to know. But this is a stupid move. . . . It's a list of nine names. Your mom's the tenth. It's a list of the women who left The Camel's employ. You see, she trained them well; they could leave and create new identities and not be found. Your mom was their inspiration."

"Mom was—"

"They're working in banks and doing what we do. They're doing their jobs, and not working for The Camel."

"They got out," Avi said.

"Sort of," Bean said. "It's like a velvet revolution."

He considered the tale. The explanation almost made sense. "And you don't know who they are?" he asked.

"No," Bean said. "Not anymore. They're all using other names."

"But you left before all this began. And now you want the list to . . . contact all these women and help them? Or hire them? Or get a piece of the action?"

"In a way, yes to all of that," Bean admitted. "I want what they want—freedom from The Camel. My rights." She turned away, her turn hiding something.

"That's ridiculous," Avi said. He didn't believe her. "What's your cut?"

Bean laughed. "My cut's always negotiable. Until my emotions get in the way." She turned around, approached the table once again, and reached to touch him, missed, corrected her gesture, there. She tucked his hair behind his ear; that spot on his neck always gave Avi a little shiver.

"I see," Avi said. He still didn't believe her. Why was she lying? "How 'bout this, then. Your emotions are in the way. My emotions are in the way. You don't get the list. I don't have a list and I'm not going to find one."

She looked at Avi intently. "Oh, Susan Junior . . ." she began.

"But neither does The Camel." He didn't see a way out, except for this. "I'm going to make up a list. In code. I'm going to sell it to The Camel—and let her try to crack the code. But there won't be a code, because I'll make it up. And we'll all be done." He lowered his gaze. "You and me."

"Done?"

Avi exhaled. "Here," he indicated. "Sit, Miss Bean. It's like this: Rick once said to me that you have to have an Exit Strategy. You know? You need to know how to get out. So I'm going to get out. I talked with Markins—"

"Who's that?" Bean interrupted. She sat.

"Oh, yeah. Sorry. That's Mom's executor. He's waiting on some expert to come see the whale, and if it's approved, he'll process the will. He's optimistic; he saw a story about me on TV. And I'm looking at $130,000 from the insurance for the house. I'm getting out. But I need an Exit Strategy, and I need your help. This is just too insane—" he nodded toward the congregants out there. "I'm a flipping cult."

Bean laughed. She was sad.

"Bean, Miss Bean. I can't give you the list. I don't have it. This isn't it. And from what you say, I shouldn't give the list to anyone anyway. It's . . ."

"It's dangerous," Bean said. "Your plan. The Camel's not stupid."

"I know," Avi said. He thought some more. Her eyes were grayer today, but still green. "She scares me too. But the way you describe this—the list—it seems like it's Mom's wish. Mom never sold the list to The Camel—and she didn't sell it to you either. I don't know. . . . Mom did this, and now I have to finish it." He paused, and then he had another idea. "So I'm going to get her arrested." He was improvising. "The Camel's going down, dude."

"You're what?"

"Yep," he said. "That's the other part of my plan. I'm going to set her up. And I need your help."

A ruckus outside ended the conversation—what the heck was happening? Avi and Bean lifted a side flap to see. Along the row of news vans, which included The Camel's RV, one of the twins was running to aid the other; a tug-of-war had commenced between a cameraman and a twin, each with a hold on the camera, feet squared, and shouting. The twin was dressed in black jeans and a black shirt that had "Concert Security" appliquéd on the back.

"She's gonna break something," Avi said.

"Let 'er," Bean said.

What a great silent movie, the noise swallowed by bigger noises. Meanwhile, the second twin arrived, clambered up a the ladder on the side of the cameraman's van, and began to attack the broadcast mast, ripping wires at the base, all the while filmed by various crews below. On occasion she would pause for a moment, put her hands on her hips, do a hootchie-cootchie move, smile for America, and then return to her rampage.

"Oh my God," said Bean.

Cops began to yell at the twin on the truck and both twins looked up—like predators interrupted at a kill, their jaws bloody. They yelled to each other, probably "Twin Power," and then the twin atop the van jumped to the ground.

They took hands, consulted, and ran.

The cameraman stood, mouth open and then clamped shut. He pointed at the top of his van, then he looked down at the mangled remains of his livelihood, then he pointed toward the street where the twins had just sprinted away, and then he pointed down at his ruined camera. Finally, he buried his face in his hands. News 10, The News The Other Guys Don't Tell You, was crying.

"It's a rough life in Whale City," Avi said.

"You're not kidding," Bean said. She let the tent flap fall. "Boyfriend," she said. "The Camel's not to be underestimated."

"I know," said Avi. "But neither am I."

"I . . . You have to know, I'm no wimp, Boyfriend. And I'm not giving up."

"I didn't think you would," Avi said.

"Your mom wouldn't have given up," Bean said.

"I guess," said Avi. No fair, he thought.

"Trust me," Bean said.

But that was precisely the issue, Avi supposed. Could he trust Bean? Was anyone in the Republic of Whale trustworthy? Avi himself wasn't telling the truth anymore, the lies of Whale Man beamed to the world by satellite. Avi wondered what his friends in D.C. were thinking of Brother Daniel? Of W.H.A.L.E.?

"I'm going out there," Avi said. "Gotta make the rounds."

Bean was silent.

"Gotta go, dear. I'm off to the office. Give us a kiss then, luv, will ya'?"

"Avi. . . ." Bean put her arms up around his neck and conferred upon him a good grinder and an open-mouthed wet kiss, tongues electric. "Don't forget me when you're famous," she joked.

"Wow," Avi said. "You'll have to keep reminding me. Just like that. I'm very forgetful."

"Did you pack your lunch? Do you have your milk money?"

"Bean. . . ."

"Wait," she said. "Hold on. I lost something; . . . it's here somewhere." She dropped her right hand and pretended to rummage in the pocket of her skirt—just an excuse to rub his crotch. "Yep, I found it." Then Bean stopped, and handed him a fistful of nothing. "Here. Here's . . . sixty-one cents. Buy us a condom. Choose a pretty one this time, okay? One with daisies."

Avi smiled. "Okay!"

"Sex in the whale," she said brightly.

"You got it," Avi said. "Whale positions. Sperm whale," he said. "Whale oil."

. . .

On his way to meet his fans, Bean and Dolly minding the whale, the sky blue, the charred house blackened and stinky, the motley maniacs at a low roar in full regalia, Avi could see Sascha—who came running, a cigarette between his lips, his heart a Soviet tank.

"Vhale man," Sascha said.

"Hi."

"This arrives." He had an envelope. "Post doesn't know the address of the vhale," Sascha laughed.

Avi accepted the envelope; it was addressed to him at his mother's street address, in what might be his mother's handwriting. Oh shit. . . .

"Vhale man?"

Avi was silent. Something didn't make sense. "Sascha, tell me the truth. Are you really Russian?"

Wow, Sascha could laugh. "Russian? Russian?" His accent changed. "I'm from Long Island," he said. "But I majored in Russian at Wesleyan, graduated *cum laude*. Did my junior year in Moscow." He peeked back at his party tent and revelers. "It's a business venture," he said. "Four of us are investing. . . . It's a lot of money," Sascha said. "You von't say anythink, Vhale Man?"

"I won't. If you tell me your real name."

Sascha laughed. "It's Mario."

"Mario," Avi said. "My name's Avi. Avi Heyer. Pleased to meet you."

"Avi."

"Sascha, can I step inside your house for a moment? I'd like to read this. . . ."

"Of course! Sascha's house is diplomatic immunity," Mario said nonsensically.

"Great," Avi mostly whispered. He looked down at the handwriting, yes.

. . .

Dear Avi. If you are reading this letter, it means that something bad has happened. I have given my lawyer instructions to mail you this letter two months after my death. If you're reading this letter, I'm sorry. I hope we had a chance to say good-bye.

I'm not who you think I am. So much of my life has been a lie, I'm not even who I think I am. I'm sorry for how this has affected you, and for having to keep you so far away from me. I'm your mother! But I've had to love you from a distance, because . . . it was safer. Maybe not right, but safer. Your father never understood.

There's a lot of money. A lot of it came from various banks, and then I invested and tripled my earnings! You would be proud of me. I've been robbing banks since before you were born. I've left you the money, and it's all cleaned up. I did this so you could have the life you want.

I left you the money and I wrote into my will that you had to earn it. I know, this isn't the nicest thing to do, but I think it's right. You have to earn the money by doing something extraordinary. I expect great things of you! Maybe the money will help you see how your life isn't always what you choose—and that you can choose to have other lives instead. I think that for all of your moving around, you've not been very courageous about your life.

I can't explain all the details, because other people are involved, but some things you should know. I'm part of a lapping scheme. I've been part of a few. That's when someone takes some money, and then takes more to cover up the first theft. It goes on like that, always covering up for yourself, taking more and more. It's addictive! Want to hear something funny? I did this for four years at one bank, and because I always had to cover for myself, I never took a vacation. So the bank promoted me—and then named me Teller of the Year. They gave me a free trip to Hawai'i, which I had to take! But I took it only when someone else joined the ring and could cover for me. Then I came back and quit! They were so surprised.

There are others like me, ten of us who worked for a woman named The Camel. I hope to God you haven't met her. She's not to be trusted. And you can't give her the list of our names! She'll be relentless, along with an FBI agent named Henry Toulouse and another person named Linda Barnes, who goes by Lima Bean, and who was the go-between between The Camel and my network. The network I was in. But we all got out, the ten of us in The Camel's network, and now everyone wants to know where we are, and they all want to know our new names. If I'm dead The Camel's likely to be around—she'll want the list of names. But don't trust her! Avi, I hope you haven't fallen for one of her tricks already—I know how you believe people so easily! At least The Camel's easy to spot, she stands out. That Henry Toulouse, I don't know what to say about him, he's a nice man but he doesn't talk a lot, and I decided a few years ago not to trust him. How can you trust someone who doesn't talk? You know your mom, I'm a talker, and talkers trust talkers, it's how I fell in with The Camel in '95. As for Linda Barnes, she—

. . .

The letter ended there, torn in two. Avi looked in the envelope, disbelieving, where was the rest?

What the fuck, he wasn't courageous? If that's what she thought, he would just . . . he would . . . he smiled, and knew that his smile must be big. Damn dead Mom. He would have to go and build a whale, and prove her wrong.

"Our work here is done," he said aloud to Sascha's empty living room—no people, no furniture, no art, just a pile of what looked to be Persian rugs. "Time to buy a ladder," Avi said to the whale in his dream.

. . .

Avi was too warmly dressed; he slipped off the hood of his hoodie—oops! Mistake!

"Rick! Rick! Rick Woodley!"

"Whale Man, Whale Man, Whale Man!" Across the way, in the park behind the police barrier, someone in the crowd noticed too. Did that guy have binoculars? Crap! The chant was beginning.

The media mustered quickly, and the reporters came running.

"Mr. Woodley, what are your plans?"

"Mr. Woodley—"

"Rick, over here. Jackson Lily, News 9—"

"Rick, why are you living in the whale?"

"Rick, do you have a comment on the arson report?"

"Rick, Emma Jess, *Animal Planet*—"

Avi stopped, and turned to face the onslaught. "What report?"

"Rick, over here. Harve Chesser, Ph.D., News Wagon. The arson report? You've been cleared. Do you have a comment?"

Avi paused. "I . . . I have nothing prepared to say. I just want to say . . . whoever did that must be a sad person inside." Avi gestured toward the burned house, the scorched brick of the chimney all that was left standing; he tried to offer a shot of the bandaged burn on his hand. "See that house? Helping people rehabilitate themselves presents no danger to anyone." He mustered a fake break in his voice. "What could such a person be thinking? W.H.A.L.E. is just trying to help the . . . people who need help." He rubbed his owie for the camera.

"Rick, Rick— what are your plans? Is there another whale planned?"

Avi shrugged, who knows.

"Okay, that's enough. That's enough!" The Camel arrived and waded into the scrum, her timing impeccable; she had on another business suit, this time red with black piping, some college's colors. She wore a colorful string of huge wooden beads around her neck. "Rick's going to have a sit-down with Channel 6 tomorrow at eight, aren't you, Rick? Prime time," she almost purred.

At the edge of the crowd, Hannah Cara Papadopoulos's hand shot up. "That's me!"

The chant was louder: "Whale Man. Whale Man. Whale Man. Whale Man. Whale Man. Whale Man. Whale Man. . . ."

"Right as . . . a whale," Avi raised his voice. "Eight o'clock tomorrow, I'll be chatting with Hannah Cara Papadopoulos of Channel 6, 6 News in the Street. I'll have a few announcements to make then, concerning W.H.A.L.E. I'll have a *list* of items prepared," he winked, just to see The Camel's expression.

The tiniest corner of her upper lip twitched. She got the message.

"Whale Man. Whale Man. Whale Man. Whale Man. Whale Man. . . ."

"Rick, but Rick!"

"Rick!"

"People, people. There's nothing more to say." Avi held up his hands, hold-up style. "W.H.A.L.E. has been in contact with local and federal authorities. We're wrapping things together. But I'll talk about it all tomorrow, when—" he faltered. "When it's tomorrow."

"That's it, that's enough. Thank you, everyone," The Camel crowed. "Thank you, ladies and gentlemen. Thank you, Rick Woodley." She smiled a nasty smile at Avi. "We're all looking forward to hearing you speak, Mr. Woodley. I'm sure your list will be fascinating."

Across the way, the whale worshippers in the park were all excited, buzzing like bugs in a dish. "Whale Man. Whale Man. Whale Man. Whale Man. Whale Man. Whale Man. . . ."

Avi nodded *ciao* to the media, and turned to give the worshippers a nice wave—and a roar went up. Oh, crap. He would have to go over there. He gave another wave, Whale Man on the way. Avi ducked under a surprised camera-man's never surprised camera, then stepped into the street and walked toward the park, where Pony Tail Guy and Grandma Wookie Cookie waited eagerly.

Hannah Cara Papadopoulos and Rodney trailed Avi like his own little duck-lings. Make way, he wanted to shout. Ducklings!

"Whale Man, Whale Man,. Whale Man, Whale Man, Whale Man, Whale Man, Whale Man, Whale Man. . . ." As Avi neared the chant changed—and then became louder, and not just because of physics.

"Back off!" Hannah Cara Papadopoulos told another camera crew. "He's mine! Rodney—" Rodney swung his camera around to cut off the other crew's line of sight. Hannah Cara Papadopoulos added, "We're live."

Avi kept walking, Whale Man walking. Tomorrow at eight, Avi thought, he would be on national television, cool. He would prepare the fake list, plan his Exit Strategy, pack Dolly's kibble in an ol' kibble bag, slip the keys into the pickup, and then deliver The Camel's goods right in the open, the fake list broadcast to our Armed Forces via the Armed Forces Radio Network. That should shock the mastermind's shit.

Oh, yeah. He would also stand the ladder in the whale, to climb and then swing once the interview ended. Good plan, Avi thought.

No, wait. He still had to buy a ladder. A couple of Sascha's rugs might be nice too, to give the whale a homey feel. How could he rent the whale unfurnished? Really.

Now that was a funny idea: Avi would build whales and rent them to wackos nationwide, Whale Man landlord. And Rick would help build, and procure all the necessary variances. But where was Rick? Avi would have liked to say goodbye to his nicotine-starved, not-so-deaf contractor, who hadn't been named in Mom's letter—just to consult, to see what the Feds would want Whale Man to do. . . . What a crappy assignment: help the klutz build a whale, poor Rick.

"Whale Man, Whale Man, Whale Man, Whale Man, Whale Man, Whale Man, Whale Man. . . ."

But Bean . . . what to tell Bean? And maybe more important, what to ask?

Hannah Cara Papadopoulos cut in front of Avi. "Rick, before you meet your guests, is there anything you would like America to know?"

He had to stop, there in the middle of the street at the nexus of it all. "Yes, Hannah Cara Papadopoulos, Channel 6, 6 News in the Street, The Truth Be Told. . . ." Avi was stalling. What the hell. "I would like to say . . . W.H.A.L.E. believes in the principle . . . that words aren't deeds. A man isn't always wrong. Believe what you build. And . . . and that's all. . . . Are we off?"

Hannah Cara Papadopoulos gave Rodney a cut sign. "We're off."

"Okay, good," Avi said. "You can join me in there—" he pointed at Whale City. "But no questions. I've got work to do."

"Thank you," Hannah Cara Papadopoulos beamed. "I don't know how. . . ."

"It's nothing," Avi said. Crap, all he could do was make these wackos happier, despite himself and without trying. "I mean, you're welcome."

• • •

At Avi's request they congregated on the soccer field in the occupied zone, a tent tented here, a folding table unfolded there, someone's bonfire from last night still sizzling. Was there anything to stand on? He was handed a plastic milk crate labeled "Asia-Backstreet," a remnant of record collecting. He turned it over and stepped up. The worshippers liked it: height worked. They gathered and jostled politely and hushed a little.

"Hi, people."

"Whale Man!" a few people in the crowd shouted, a poor attempt at unison.

"Try again—hi, people!" Avi raised his voice.

"WHALE MAN!"

"That's better," he laughed. "Can everybody hear me?"

"I can't," yelled someone from the back.

"Yes," yelled another voice.

"No," another person piped.

"Right," Avi said. "I'll try to speak up. Sit, everyone. Find a patch and sit. I thought we'd have a town meeting. Clear as much space as you can—find room for your neighbor."

The injunction succeeded, as the crowd responded with camaraderie, fellowship, jocularity, and minimal bursts of turf envy, a U.N. But with more worshippers than room, a lot had to be done before everyone could be accommodated.

Whale Man was nothing if not patient. Patience was a whale, too.

He gazed at his new friends. Working their way through the wackos, the young pregnant couple edged forward, the husband's hand marital on her shoulder, her smile beatific. Jasmine, Avi remembered. Jas. He waved at them, and the husband returned the greeting, the wife gave a shy nod. "Does anyone have a chair for Jas?" asked Avi.

A chair appeared, pretty much presto.

"Hi," Avi said to the future mother of a person.

"Hi," Jasmine smiled as she lowered herself onto the chair.

She might never get out of that chair, Avi thought. She looked ready. "How do you feel?" Avi leaned down to ask.

"*Wuh* . . . I'm okay," she said. "It's soon," she smiled. Her hands were on her belly, pregnant woman style. "That would be good."

Avi nodded. The crowd still hadn't settled down completely; he could wait. Three or four rows deep, he saw Pony Tail Guy. Avi tented his fingertips together—*salaam*—and gave a tiny bow, a greeting returned by PTG and six or seven of the people nearby. The Friends of Pony Tail Guy. FPTG.

"Whale Man," said someone to Avi's left.

He turned to see Rorie the waitress, still in uniform, accompanied by a teen-aged boy who was clearly her son. "Hi, Rorie. You must be Jerry," Avi said. He stuck out his hand, shake.

The kid shook hands wimpily. His hair hung straight in front of his face. He looked like the love child of a Scrubbing Bubble and an ear of corn. "Yeah," Jerry said. He nodded a lot. He wore all black.

"I hear you like whales," Avi said.

Jerry held out a pen and a poster of *Sheeee*, a picture he had made or maybe just bought from Sascha. "Uh. . . ?"

Avi accepted. "Sure," he said. "Now you listen to what your mother says. She and I are very good friends." He signed "Whale Man" with a flourish, elbow flared, and then handed his handiwork to the teen.

Rorie beamed. Jerry nodded, speechless. They turned to go. "Sorry we can't stay. I'm double-shifting," she said. "*Thank you*," Rorie mouthed over her shoulder.

Avi smiled. Not a bad gig, he supposed, making pouty teens less pouty.

"Whale Man." Someone tugged on Avi's pant leg. "I think we're ready."

The crowd had crammed in, maybe a few hundred strong as they pushed back and back, cleared more space, tried to sit, community a form of compression. Avi looked them over and admired their fortitude. And their insanity. The motley, cheery, marginalized, needy, spiritually bereft were all here—all followers of a sort, looking for something they saw in the whale.

There was Bean, way at the back. She gave a little wave. Hi, Bean. Dolly too.

A big white bowl of caramel corn was being passed around among the folks up front. Avi liked caramel corn. "May I?" he asked. The bowl was handed up—to Hannah Cara Papadopoulos, who stood nearby. Gingerly, she helped herself to a handful and then offered the bowl to Avi. Yay, Avi thought, taking some. Maybe he could ask for an offering of caramel corn every day, to be delivered of course by a different virgin.

Munching the treat gave him another good moment to consider his approach. What to say to the gathered? They came to the whale . . . because an orphan built it? Because Mom's house burned? Because building a whale was such an insane thing to do? What could it represent to all of these different people—to each, the whale must mean something different. What could it mean for there to be a real Whale Man, live, in person? He should find out. "I . . ." he began, and then stopped. He had caramel between his teeth. "Excuse me," he turned away for a sec, covered his mouth with one hand, and with the other tried to jimmy free the offending sugary grout. Got it. He turned back. "Ladies and gentlemen, boys and girls. . . ." No, he corrected himself as the crowd hushed. Too circus. "Hi, everyone," Avi called.

"WHALE MAN! WHALE MAN!"

"Please," he said. "Thank you," he said. "Hi, everyone."

"Wait," said someone to Avi's left. "Here." He was handed up a cordless microphone. "Test, 1, 2, whale," said Avi. His voice filled the air.

The crowd laughed.

"Hi," Avi said. "I just want to say . . . I'd like to thank all of you for bringing such *energy* to the whale. I mean, can't you feel the electricity?"

The crowd cheered. "Whale Man," they called. "Yeah!" They whistled, they clapped.

Avi dug it. "I can feel what you feel," he said. "And I know that you can too. Living in Whale City—"

"Whale Man, I love you!" a guy called out.

It was like a concert. Too bad Avi couldn't sing—but maybe he would be pelted with panties. "Thank you, thank you. . . . People, this isn't about me, it's about you. Each and every one of you. In each and every one of . . ." the thought went nowhere. Avi tried again. "In your hearts, there's a whale. And you know it." He looked down. A woman in the front row was crying. She had curlers in her hair, under a bright green scarf—no, wait. She was a *he*, with curlers in his hair. "But I want to hear from *you* today. Today is your day. I'd like to hear your stories, how you came to Whale City, what we as a society here—because that's what we are, good people, we're a society—how we can help each other." He turned to the guy who had handed up the mic. "Can this work? Can I walk around?"

"Whale Man," the guy said. "It's who I am."

What? "Cool," Avi said.

So the stage shifted, the podium emptied: Avi hopped down to amble into the crowd evangelically. "Please, stay seated," he said into the mic. "I'll come to you." He didn't want to tread on any fingers, or put his foot through a picnic basket, so he tiptoed, he sidled; the Whale Man stepped carefully into the beach blanket bingo of the whale worshippers, to help them find their voices.

"Hi," said Avi. He pointed the mic at a young guy's face whose green polo shirt had the collar turned up, prepped-out.

The guy leaned forward into the mic: "Hi. I'm Gary, I'm not from Indiana."

A few people tittered politely. "Why are you here?" asked Avi.

"I . . . I'm here because . . . I just lost my job. I didn't like my job, but I've never been fired before. You know?" Some polite applause ensued. Nearby, a number of people nodded. Then the guy grabbed the mic. "It's like something was taken from me. But then I saw your whale on TV, and I thought, it's just like math: minus one, plus one, you know?" He moved to return the mic. "Oh, yeah," the guy said. "One more thing. I like whales," he chortled. "Here," he handed the mic home.

"Thank you, Gary," Avi said. He turned to look, as hands in the crowd went up, everybody calling to the teacher, me, me, me, pick me. Avi spun around. Hannah Cara Papadopoulos was standing right behind him. "And you, little lady?" He aimed the mic at the reporter, now that was funny.

"I . . . " She blushed. "I'm here because of Rodney," she said. She took a very deep breath, and looked over at her cameraman a few feet away. "Rodney, I love you."

"*Awww,*" said the crowd. "Kiss, kiss! Kiss her!" someone hollered. Rodney had his camera by his side, his jaw dropping open. She rushed to him; they kissed.

"Yay!" yelled the crowd. "Whale Man!"

"Aren't they cute? Let's have a round of applause for the media folks in love."

And on he went, skipping some people who ducked away, drawing out others wanting to be noticed by the inquiring Whale Man, a man of the people who was running for nothing. One woman said that her daughter was sick— Whale Man of Lourdes, Avi supposed—another claimed to be an oceanographer, although the aluminum foil hat said otherwise. Two older men, holding hands, had come to celebrate their anniversary. A very well-dressed red-headed woman in her thirties said, "*Ik was een walfis,*" whatever that meant. The bricklayer from last week, the dude in the overalls, shirtless again and covered with mortar marks, took the mic from Avi and said, very quietly, "You built this. It's important. You're building. . . . I don't like to talk. . . ." Avi patted the guy on the shoulder, there, there.

And more, until he arrived at the back of the crowd, and found Bean, Bean, Bean, and Dolly so happy to see him she gave a full body wag. Avi petted his dog.

"And you," Avi smiled at his girlfriend. "What brings you to Whale City, pretty lady?"

"Pretty lady," she said softly. Then she accepted the mic. "I've come because of Whale Man. I'm here to save him. His Mom sent me."

TWENTY

. . . .

"TELL ME," AVI SAID. They were back in the whale, standing across from each other, not too close. "What's true and what's a lie."

"I—" Bean started but stopped.

"Linda Barnes," Avi said.

"Oh, you're good," she said. "But really, *I like Bean*. And you can still call me Miss Bean."

"Go on," Avi glanced at Bean sidelong.

"May I have a sip?"

There was a bottle of Ozarka water on the table. Ozarka? Avi reached for the water and handed it to Bean.

"Thanks. Okay, what's true and what's a lie. That might be too big to handle."

"Try," said Avi. He sat at the table to encourage her.

Bean exhaled slowly, her cheeks puffed, "*Puhhh*. All right. I don't want the list, except to destroy it. To keep it from The Camel and the FBI. Your mom sent me half a letter—I got it three days after she died. She asked me to come to Elsbeth, and to keep an eye on you, and to get the list, and to mop up."

"Aw crap, Bean—"

"But she told me not to tell. I couldn't tell you anything! She . . . she knows me. *Knew* me, sorry. There's $50,000 for me if the list is destroyed. I . . . I'm sorry."

"You're here for the money."

"Avi, please. The moral indignation doesn't suit you. I always said . . . I mean, is there any difference that I'm here for the money from your mom instead of the money for the list? You believed I wanted the list to *make* money with. Wouldn't that be *worse*? All those people who don't want to be found. . . ."

Avi's hands were on the table. He turned over the burned one, looked at the bright pink skin. Burns hurt. "Greed-wise, yes, I guess so. But you lied to me."

"Yes," Bean said. "I lie a lot. Don't trust me." She lowered her gaze.

"Okay," Avi said. "I won't trust you." He asked for the water bottle back from Bean, took a sip.

"Okay," Bean said. "Can I trust you?"

Avi thought about that. "Maybe," he said. He had lied to her plenty, that was the truth. "Maybe not . . . no," he finally said.

They didn't know what to do or to say.

"This is new territory, Miss Bean."

She smiled, oh, that smile. "Yes," she said.

"I . . . I think. . . ."

"Yessss. . . ?" Bean came over and sat too, Ma and Pa Whale.

"I don't know. It's too mixed up to say. I probably love you." There, Avi said it.

"Oh, Avi," she said. "You're a fucking jerk."

"Bean!"

She laughed, her head thrown back. "Probably? What the hell is that—probably? I mean *probably* I . . . I mean . . ." She stopped. "I can't do this," she said. There was a long and then a too-long pause, and then she began to cry. "Avi, you can't. Don't. You don't know me, you can't trust me—*I* can't trust me." She was crying quietly and hard. "It's not the money, Avi, it's *getting* the money. I . . . can't explain. You shouldn't love me."

Those were big tears. Avi handed her a shop towel. "Sorry, I don't have any tissues," he said. "But you do too, you love me. I can read it in your Soul Diary."

"You can?"

"Yes," Avi said. "I see it. It's right there. Silly," he teased.

Bean wiped her face. "Oh, Avi," she gave a little gulp as she spoke.

"What are we going to do?" Avi said. "I don't trust you," he said.

"You shouldn't." Wordlessly, she asked if she could blow her nose into the towel.

"*Ew*," Avi answered. "Go right ahead."

She did so. *Eww.* Again, they were speechless. Avi waited.

"Oh, Avi. . . ."

"Miss Bean," he said. "You have the prettiest eyes," he said. Her eyes were even greener from crying.

"Oh, no I don't," she said. "They're contacts."

"They are?"

Bean laughed through her tears. "Of course not! See! You're just such a sucker. Everyone lies to you, and you want to believe what everyone says, and so you do. It just seems so simple to be you. But it's . . . open . . . it's . . . I . . . I've never known anyone like you." Bean lowered her gaze again. "Oh, Avi, I'm pregnant," she said.

"Yeah, right, you tried that one—"

"No, really I am. Avi. . . ."

He took a deep breath. "Bean?" He was stunned.

She laughed again. "See! You're such a sucker. I love that about you. In my business, no one believes anyone. It's all so horrible." She wiped her nose on the shop towel.

"Bank robbing," he said.

"Yes," Bean said. "Whale building," she said.

"Yes," Avi said. Then he had an inspiration. "Okay, so give me the news. Henry—the guy with Rick—he's FBI."

"Of course he is."

"And Rick?"

"Avi, I'm just not sure. He's new—I never met him. But whoever he is, he's good. I had people check. The legend stands up. Ramona doesn't even know who he is."

"The legend?"

"Oh, it's a term. It means that his story's good—you know, airtight. There is a daughter, he did some time in the Navy, he might be with the government, but I really don't know. Did you ask him?"

"Sorta," Avi said. "Well, not really. I mean, he said to trust him."

"Heard that one," Bean said.

"Me too."

"Avi . . . what are we going to do?"

They were silent again for a long moment. "Have sex?" He smiled at her. Damn, her eyes were gorgeous. Nice lips too, great nose.

Bean laughed. "Oh, boyfriend. Of *course*. I'm not wearing *pan-ties*," she cooed.

"You're not?"

Bean laughed. "I am too!" She laughed harder. "At least right now. . . . But I like having sex with you, and I like . . ." she looked around. "I've been think-ing. . . . I mean, here would be a good place to have sex. Don't you think? We should fuck here." She looked at the bed.

Avi nodded vigorously. It was the middle of the day, the whale's tent flaps were down, Dolly was napping, the town meeting had gone well. Quiet sex in the whale, he thought. Snap, he thought. Jonah never had no sex in no whale; Pinocchio wasn't old enough. Avi would be the All-Time Sex-in-the-Whale

Master of the Deep. He laughed.

"Good joke?" Bean asked.

"It all is," he said. "Crap, look at what's going on—I mean out there. But you and I . . . we should *definitely* have sex. And then we've got to come up with a plan, and get the hell outta Whale City."

The sex was slow and meaningful, all quiet on the media and wacko front. At one point, Avi thought that Bean might be crying again—but when he turned to see her face, she smiled. At another particularly charged moment, Avi opened his eyes to see Dolly's big head just a few inches from his own, *right there*, smiling a dog smile that fogged his senses with humid dog breath. "Doll," Avi had gasped a little. "Go lie down."

"I am lying down," Bean had whispered.

"Yes," Avi had said, his wit gone.

Dolly had barked very loudly, and then licked his forehead and one eye.

"Crap, Dolly. Go lie down."

"*Hhhhhrrrrfff*," Dolly had said.

But then, later, all done, Avi was hungry and ready to shower—damn, the lack of a decent shower sure made a post-coital dude feel pungent. "I need a shower," Avi said. He sat up in bed: the whale looked different from down here.

"Yes." Bean was curled in the sheet, one leg and her hip exposed. "*Mmm*," she said.

"I need dinner."

"Avi . . . later. . . ."

"Yes," he said. "C'mon," he gave her butt a playful pat. "Help me buy a ladder. C'mon, then I'll take you to my favorite truck stop. Food!"

"Fine," she said. "Soon," she sighed sleepily.

"C'mon, c'mon. Up and upsie."

Avi roused Bean further, slipped on his jeans and a shirt. He and Bean agreed to meet up the street at the pickup. Should he lock the house? He had to chuckle, glancing around. Only the cookie jar meant anything. Ready, though, time to go, through the tent flap and into the trenches. Avi and Dolly exited first, to attract and deflect the glare.

"Rick! Rick!" He was noticed right away.

"People. . . ." Avi called loudly as he raised his hand. Dolly sat, good dog.

"Rick!" The media advanced, almost at a run.

"Rick, what do you think about the Mayor's comments?"

Avi waited a little longer. He hoped that Bean had escaped. Maybe two minutes of face time with America would suffice for Bean to slip from the whale, duck down, fish for her keys, harpoon. . . . Avi was a bit sex-stoned. And starving. He could eat a tarpon, or a tarp.

Five or six mics came at him, too many capped teeth gleaming whitely. He looked at the world around: the sky was kind of an undecided color, Avi noticed, neither blue nor gray, the dusk wishy-washy tonight. The burned house smelled less. Maybe Avi was upwind. "I'm sorry. The Mayor? I . . . I'm not sure what you mean," Avi said into the jabbing microphones. "*Ahhm,*" He cleared his throat. "Excuse me," he said.

"Tommy Blue Heron, First Action News. Rick, earlier today Mayor Taniscopani said, and I quote, 'The whale represents all that Elsbeth, North Carolina, can be. Our plan is to move the whale to the town square and set up a whaling museum. There were whalers off the North Carolina coast in the 19th century—'"

"That's not happening," Avi said.

"Rick!"

"Rick!"

"Rick, what will you do?"

"The whale's not his. It belongs . . ." he waited for the drama to build. "It's not a government whale. It's not a town whale. It's not a North Carolina whale. The whale is a people's whale. Those people," Avi gestured toward the park. "Ask them what should happen to her."

"Rick, Rick!"

"Sorry, folks. Hunger calls." He waved, backed up, turned to leave. "Dolly, come," he pulled the leash.

"Rick! The Mayor's here, he's in the park, he—"

"Sorry! Folks, you need to show some respect. Tell the Mayor that when I get back, I'll buy him a drink. We'll talk then." And then to be perverse, Avi raised his bottle of Ozarka water, his hand covering the label. "Whale Water. It's all a Whale Man wants, and it's all a whale could want. Available online and at your friendly grocer . . . for a drinking experience to dream about. Whale Water is the water for you." Avi gave a big smile into the cameras, hoisted his bottle and chug-a-lugged a good chug; he let some water slop down his chin heartily. "*Ahhhhh.* Swim with the best, dream what you dream. Whale Water."

· · ·

He was standing in painting supplies, the paint mixer rattling as though with emphysema. Bean had left to use the store's facilities.

"Let me help," said Rick.

Avi spun on a sneakered heel, his Chucks squeaking. "Rick! Dude!" He reached forward to hug his friend.

"Boss Man," Rick recoiled. "Don't do that."

"Rick," Avi said.

"It's a store," Rick explained.

"I know that."

"What are you doing here?" Avi asked. "It's good to see you." Avi still smelled Bean on his skin, a smell he liked—but should a guy mind? He had never known what to think of that.

"Waiting." Rick looked closely at Avi. "How're the burns?"

"Better," Avi said. "Your arm?"

"S'okay."

"Where you been, man?"

Rick narrowed his gaze even further than it should go. "Can't say."

"Can't say," Avi repeated. "Huh. . . . So, Rick . . . I . . ." Avi surprised himself, he couldn't ask. Being a sucker, Avi realized, had more to do with how a sucker felt, or whether the other person's lies could be construed as friendly. "I'm buying a ladder."

"How big?"

Same Rick! "Fit in the whale, stand on, reach the top. Inside." Avi tried to calm himself down, to speak Rick-speak.

"Twelve-footer. Aluminum or fiberglass?"

"Let's look."

"Yep." He took a toothpick from his shirt-sleeve pocket. He held up the toothpick. "It's like the patch. To quit smoking. . . . Ladders're over there." He pointed with the toothpick, and then took off down the aisle toward the back of the store.

"Huh?" Avi hurried to tag along. Hadn't they had this moment together before?

"Latest thing. Toothpicks. For quitting smoking. They're laced."

"Wow," Avi smiled.

"Whale's done. Haven't smoked. You owe me money," Rick said.

"Crap," Avi smiled a bigger smile. He broke into a carny's patter: "Yessir. Cash on the whale head. Step right up. Small, unmarked bills."

"Not funny," Rick almost smiled.

Avi laughed. "Right," Avi said. "I . . ." he thought about how. "I'll get an advance on my VISA. Come by tomorrow night, and I'll have the money. I'm giving a press conference—"

"I know," Rick said. They turned a corner and arrived at the ladders. "With that reporter. Watch your ass, Boss. She's not what you think."

"No one's what I think," Avi said, and tried to make his gaze look telling. "But she's okay. So, hey—maybe you want to join us for dinner? Tonight? Bean and I are just about to get a bite to eat, maybe—"

"Not a good idea," Rick said. "All the leaders in one place."

Avi didn't understand: was that a joke? Rick was rolling the toothpick between his teeth. "Okay," Avi said. "Tomorrow, then. Which ladder?"

. . .

Avi and Bean ate in a one-room Thai place in a strip mall, the food so-so, his *Tom Yam Gai* better than her *Shrimp Pad Thai,* the chicken in his dish particularly nice, and the inevitable after-dinner *Kah-Feh Yen* always a treat. Except for all the caffeine: *Kah-Feh* could keep a Whale Man up all night, or at least for a few hours, following late afternoon sex and a big meal. He would be awake, anyway: more sex would be okay.

Avi wondered, as he and Bean stepped to the register to pay the bill, what brilliant culture had first taken coffee as a remedy for post-coital stupor.

"Whale Man," said a young girl standing by the fish tank. Wow, that girl had an awful do: her hair was spiked and curled, green and red, as though she had combined two bad haircuts, one on each side of her head, and not paid enough for either. Elsbeth clearly needed a new salon, Avi thought; he should invest his Mom Bucks.

The whole wait staff and kitchen crew had suddenly materialized, and lined up almost in size order. The girl put her fingertips together, then bowed her forehead to touch her hands. *"Sawat-dii ka,"* she said. She lifted her eyes to look at Avi. "My mother wishes to thank you," the kid said.

"I—" he was a bit stupefied. "You . . . you're welcome," Avi said.

"Your dinner is free," said the girl. "Our gift. My mother—" she indicated a tiny woman who was beaming at him, 3,000 watts at least. "She would like to give you something else. For the whale."

The mother put her fingertips together and bowed in the manner of her daughter. Bean squeezed Avi's hand and then let go. He followed the mom's lead, bowing too: fingertips, forehead. It was cool.

"Sawat-dii ka," Mom said.

"Hi," said Avi.

With both hands, the mother offered Avi something wrapped in tissue paper. "Please," she said, and then she stepped back.

"Thank you," Avi said. They wanted him to open the present here. He dug into the paper, found a metal thing—one of those Jewish good luck icons, what are they called?

"It's a mezuzah," the girl said. "It's really *old*."

"I . . . I know. I've seen them before. I live in D.C.," he said for no good reason.

"Put it on the door frame. Up here," she raised her hand. "On the right side. Two-thirds up the door."

"I . . . I will. Thank you."

"Wait, though." The girl nodded to her mom, who stepped forward again shyly. "Ma wants to say the blessing. It's kinda important."

Avi held out the mezuzah.

The mom put her hand on his, and then she sang in a quiet voice, *"Baruch atta Adonai Eloheinu melech ha'olam, asher kideshanu bemitzvotav vetzivanu likboa' mezuza."*

Bean had tears in her eyes, Avi noticed. He decided not to look at her anymore for a little while.

"It's got the *Shema* inside," the girl said.

"You're Jewish," Avi said.

"*Duh*." The girl couldn't help herself. Her mother gave her a quick smack on the shoulder. "Uh, yeah. My family's from Phuket. Jews came there in 1641." Then she shifted into recitation mode: "The Jewish people in Thailand have a storied past. The yeshiva there represents the finest example of Jewish persistence in the Diaspora. Thank you," she added.

"Wow," Avi said.

"That's part of my Bat Mitzvah two weeks from Saturday. Wanna come?" She smiled an orthodontic smile.

"I . . . thanks," said. Avi. "I'm not sure where I'm going to be."

"That's okay," she bobbed her head, thoroughly embarrassed by herself. "My name's Suchin. It means beautiful thought. Like your whale," she said. Her head hung low, her hair spiked high and awry.

"That's a cool name," Avi said. It so sucked to be a teenager. "Suchin. I'll try to make it to your Bat Mitzvah, if I'm in town. Can you write down the date and time and the address?"

Suchin lit up. She turned to her mom, and said something very quickly in Thai.

"Please," her mom said. "Please," she nodded happily at Avi.

. . .

In the parking lot with Bean, Dolly whining and staring in the locked cab of the truck, the windows opened an inch, the ladder in the bed and on the roof tied down with tie-downs, Avi had to laugh, his celebrity absurd. "I—" he started to say, then stopped. He walked Bean to the passenger side, to unlock her door.

"*Oooh,*" Bean said. "Manners."

Thai Jews? With his left hand, he fingered the mezuzah in the pocket of his jeans.

"Avi," Bean said. "See? I told you. It's your Soul Diary. It's *visible.* . . . Everyone can see it now."

"Sure," Avi said, half believing. Or maybe three quarters.

Bean hopped into the truck, and was met with big doggy licks and doggy glee. "Dolly, down. Easy," Bean laughed.

Around the truck to his side, the lock popped by Bean, the ladder angled from truckbed to the roof of the cab, aimed high, Avi paused. Then, "Hey," he said to Bean as he opened his door. "I'm not used to mattering," he said. "I don't know how to handle it."

"That's right," Bean said. "Which is why you're so good at it."

"Ah," Avi said. "Dolly, down! Thanks." He started the truck. "I guess. . . . Okay, I wanna show you something. There's a place I . . . I go. Well, I've been twice. Can I show you?"

"Boyfriend," Bean said. "Anywhere. This is a great date."

S.R. 252 to the overpass. Under the underpass and over the overpass. He bore left, ignored the parking lot for cars, headed for the trucks and the nighties and the moonscape of it all. Avi saw an opening, shifted into neutral, glided into the narrow spot, into a walled-in canyon between trucks; he braked, parked, turned off the engine.

"Where are we?" Bean asked.

"Just here."

"Do we get out?"

"Um . . . no."

Dolly stuck her head between the front seats. "*Woof!*"

"Doll, go lie down," Avi instructed and Dolly obeyed. The truck had a good bank seat for a dog. Maybe he should have a whale drawing stenciled onto the back window. A caption too: The Elsbeth Whaler.

Bean was silent. She leaned forward to look up at the huge lights, the bugs frolicking and frying, the trucks idling, the night mostly forgettable above it all. Bean was good at being quiet. Bean.

Avi leaned forward too.

How long did they stay like this? Avi had no idea.

. . .

In the dream, someone was yelling at the dreamer: "Chef! Chef! Your flambé!"

A vendor ticked items off a list: "Carpaccio, radicchio, enoki, wasabi mayonnaise, truffle oil, sesame oil, *fleur de sel*, pork loin, chevre, sage leaves, ice wine. . . ."

"I'll get there, I have to get there. Wait. . . ." The dreaming man tried to move his feet, no go.

"Kumamoto oysters, basil, polenta, chorizo, chick peas, *Sriracha*. . . ."

"Chef! Chef!" Someone new in the kitchen picked up a long-handled fork, winked at the dreaming man, bowed to the AGF, and then flung the fork— which zinged through the air to the ceiling and lodged in a ceiling tile with a resounding quiver, *gazzzoiinnnggg*. The dreaming man looked up: one hundred identical forks stuck in the ceiling tiles. The assistants were flinging forks, a thicket of forks, a shimmery forest, an army; more flung forks zinged and quivered, stabbed the square ceiling tiles.

Rick was on salads, resplendent in kitchen whites. "Could you help me untie this?" he asked, his apron strings knotted in a clump. The forks worried Rick, who kept looking up. He didn't have on his hearing aid.

The dreaming man reached out to help—oh no, his hands were mummified in oven mitts shaped like lobsters, big cloth lobster hands. "My hands," Avi the dreamer said, holding up the mitts. "Look."

"Gotcha," Rick said. From his station, he pulled out a pair of even more enormous gloves, with which he sheathed the dreaming man's lobstered hands. "There. You'll need 'em," Rick said. "The twins burned dinner."

"I knew my ex- would want ganache," Rick said. "It's all gone to hell. They ruined your vegetable medley."

Ick. The colors in the medley were off, too charred to eat. But then, wafting with the acrid smell of smoke, infused with too many wrong colors, the right colors left behind, the dream shifted, the dreaming man's discomfort abandoned for other feelings, mismatched as ever, but differently.

He lay on his back in a field of blowing grasses, browns and greens scratchy and fluffy at once, the day warm and the sun unseen. Something far away smelled like diesel fuel and vinegar. The field felt more like water than land; the grasses moved tidally, pulled by the moon and by the earth spinning below—which the dreaming man could feel, amazingly, the planet and its logic available to him, a part of his body.

As though he were blind, Avi could only feel the rocking of the wind and the grasses. When he tried to open his eyes, he couldn't. So he stopped trying, and when he stopped trying, he felt himself cradled in and by the various rhythms (the shift, the heave, the drag, gravity). He was changed, metamorphosed, he was . . .

Still asleep? Yes. Or only partially. He was being watched.

His face smushed against the driver's-side window, the shoulder strap from the seatbelt digging into his neck, sweaty and drooly and incomplete and out of time, Avi opened his eyes to see Bean staring at him. They were still in his truck, what?

"*Ummm,*" he said. "Hi." His tongue felt like a dust bunny.

"Hi," Bean said. Now she was crying. "You fell asleep. I couldn't wake you, you were too beautiful."

"Bean." He stirred more fully. "Bean, what's wrong?"

"Oh, Avi," she said. Then she dived across the bank seat and upon him, *oof.* "Hold me."

TWENTY-ONE

· ·

HE LAID TWO COPIES of the *Webster's* 9*th* on the kitchen table in the whale, one book his mom's and the other from the bookstore. The reporters were in the street, the multitudes were gathering, the press conference was in a couple of hours, Whale Man in Prime Time, and Avi laid before himself two copies of one dictionary and a good cup of coffee. The new aluminum ladder leaned against a joist, ready to be climbed once the evening's events were concluded. The whale was half-alive, a meeting place for the dead and the living, where Avi's dreams and his memories and the spirit of his mother could commune, grief and joy available, childhood finally over. He was feeling an impending sense of closure, as though flipping to the final pages in an album of family photos.

Now all Avi needed was to swing inside the big wooden beast, back and forth between one part of his life and another, into the past and into the future, finally, to move backwards in order to move forwards in time. To be done here.

He was almost ready to hold the auction, too. He had spent an hour copying random numbers onto a piece of graph paper, one number per box. What stupid, little work—how many boxes were there? Who invented graph paper, for crap's sake? He was filling a second sheet, just in case. If The Camel fell for his ruse, she might try to escape without paying—and then he would say, "Oh, no, Frau Camel, you cannot outsmart me!" and he would flourish the second page, "You see, the code is not complete. Ha!"

If she didn't try to steal the page of code, Avi would sell one *Webster's* 9*th* and one page of copied numbers to The Camel and fake another sale to Bean; if The Camel didn't sic the twins on him.

Avi's hair was still wet. He had just showered at the fake Russian neighbor's, and now he wore his new Chucks, nice jeans, and a mostly violet Hawaiian shirt that Bean had picked out earlier in the day when they met at the mall. He had signed autographs in the clothing store, shaken the hands of the assistant manager and three clerks. Security had arrived, and Avi and Bean had been given a ride in a golf cart through the candy-colored atrium. A posse of senior mall-walkers had chanted "Whale Man, Whale Man, Whale Man," two of the women swinging their purses as though conducting the marching band.

Avi numbered the boxes to finish a row: 7, 5, 2, 2, 2, 4, 0, 5, 1, 6, 5, 6. Then he got bored, and he grabbed another sheet of graph paper.

First, he would draw a whale, he thought. Wait. No.

He started to draw. From memory, badly, he drew a picture of his mom.

The picture didn't look much like Mom, but so what, the whale didn't really look like a whale. The lack of resemblance mattered in a good way, Avi realized: Mom had changed. Mom was a bank robber, Mom was a Chatty Cathy, Mom had three names and hay fever, Mom pressed flowers, Mom knew Bean.

In the picture, Mom's chin was too pointy. She also looked about fifteen years younger than she was when she died. He ran his finger over the drawing, but only over the sweater, not the face, bad luck. "Hi, Mom."

He smiled, returned to numbering the boxes. "Frau Camel," he said aloud, in a butchered accent from nowhere. "You will pay me in cash, no?"

Earlier, Bean had suggested that The Camel was treating Avi the same way she had treated his Mom: threateningly, with respect. Maureen had kept the list, now Avi did so. The Camel could bully and bluster, and even send the twins, but when the gritty turned nitty, she had to wait: he held the list. Made sense, Avi had agreed.

"So you're in charge," Bean had said. "It's your call, Susan Junior."

"I see," Avi had said. "Okay, I'll plan a surprise."

There was a knock on the whale.

"Hello?"

"Get out here," someone yelled. A twin.

"*Cooominnnnnggg*," Avi said. He folded the two pages of numbers, stuffed one sheet into each of his back pockets. The dictionaries could stay on the table for now.

"Hello?" Avi emerged through the tent flap.

The twins, dressed in riding outfits, complete with riding crops and ridiculous black-heeled boots, snarled in jodhpurs and flanked the entrance to Avi's whale, everyone blessed ecumenically by the mezuzah nailed to one of the beast's wooden beams.

"Nice duds," Avi said. "Horse feathers," he said for no reason.

"Feathers! These aren't feathers. Sister, I want to whip him."

"Now Sister, you know you have to wait."

"But I don't want to wait!" Clearly Rose Red, she shook her crop at Avi. "I want to bend back his thumb."

"What do horses eat?" Avi asked.

"What?" said Snow White.

"What do horses eat?" Avi repeated the question.

"Hay?" said Snow White.

"So there you go," Avi said. "You need to get some hay. For the horses."

"Sister?"

"I think he's stupid," Rose Red pouted.

"Is there something you want?"

"I want to put my finger in your eye!" Rose Red squealed.

"No, I mean, is there a reason you knocked?"

"We're your bodyguards," Snow White said glumly. She scratched the top of her head with her riding crop.

"Ah, to get me to the church on time."

"What?"

"Please, Sister, oh, pretty please. Please with maple syrup and marshmallows and candy corn and—"

"Just stop," said Avi. "That would be disgusting. You're embarrassing yourself."

Rose Red said, "You're meat. . . . You can go back inside now. We'll stand guard here. Right, Sister?" The announcement seemed momentous; Rose Red awaited her sister's approval.

"Oh, Sister, I love you," Snow White said. "That was very take-charge. Just like Dr. Orson said."

They hugged. "I love you, too, Sister."

"Hay," Avi said. "Remember the horses." He opened the tent flap and moved to return to the whale, the press conference still an hour away. "The horses will be hungry," he said. "You have a job to do." He hunched a little, lowered his voice. "Our secret password will be *the horses are hungry*. When I say *the horses are hungry*, I want you two to pretend to fight each other. Can you do that for me?"

Snow White smiled. "We don't have to pretend," she said. "I like to hit Sister."

"I like to hit you," Rose Red added. "I love you, Sister."

"I love you," Snow White said.

"And I love you both," said Avi. "Just remember the secret password. *The horses are hungry*."

. . .

"Call, Mr. Woodley," a voice hailed Avi from outside the whale. He was ready.

"Okay," Avi responded. Thirty minutes to airtime, as agreed: he would check out the set, chat with Hannah Cara Papadopoulos, put on a little make-up, clip on a clip-on mic strung under his shirt, the transmitter snapped to his belt. But other details of the plan remained murky. When last he spoke with his pert reporter pal, she hadn't decided—or Network hadn't—whether to do only a sit-down or a walk-and-talk, too. Rodney had lots of tape already, as he had been filming the perimeter of Whale City, interviewing stray acolytes all day, so Channel 6 had options. And this would be Hannah Cara Papadopoulos's big break, she had told him. Once she joined the White House Press Corps, she and Rodney planned to commute, she had said. She had giggled in a little-girl voice.

"I'm so happy," she had declared earlier in front of the Channel 6 van. "Do you think Rodney and I could get married in the whale?" she had asked.

"Well . . ." Avi had demurred, "I don't know about that."

"It's really a chapel," she had said.

"I don't know . . . but . . ."

"Just think of the beautiful wedding video!" Hannah Cara Papadopoulos had piped. And then she had turned toward the van and crumpled slightly. "*Ow!*" she had complained. She had grabbed her ankle suddenly. "I hate high heels," she had winced. "But Xavi insists, and he even wears them. . . . I hate being short," Hannah Cara Papadopoulos had added. "Sometimes I have to stand on a wooden box to go live."

"Sorry," Avi had said. "About the wedding, I don't know. It's—"

"It's too soon?"

"Yes," Avi had said, thinking about their sleep-over.

"Too up close and personal?"

"Yes," Avi had agreed again. She loved to reach her own conclusions. "Exactly. You should put some ice on that." He had gestured toward her turned ankle.

"I understand," Hannah Cara Papadopoulos had nodded as she rubbed her leg, nuptials promenading in her head. "Maybe we can build our own. *My whale*," she had said as she stood up straight once more. "Rodney Fuentes and Hannah Cara Papadopoulos invite you"—she had swept her hand directorial-ly—"to a whale of a wedding! That's it! It will be the perfect video," she had squeaked. "Oh, Rick. You're so . . . inspiring."

But now, flanked by the twins, Dolly left in the whale with instructions to stay, stay, *staaayyyyy*, Avi was escorted to the press area by a head-setted assistant to an assistant. "It's . . . it's right over here. Over there. Gee, I never thought I'd meet someone like you, it's . . .what a treat, I mean; my name's Billy—"

One of the twins gave the kid a bump, elbowed him in the back of the head.

"Hey! That hurt!"

The other twin giggled. "We're Security," she said.

"Don't do that," the kid said. "Mr. Whale? Tell them to stop. *Ow.*"

"Children," Avi said in a mock basso profundo, chin to chest. "Don't make me pull over."

Their little cavalcade wended through the various news vans, stepped over cables, wandered into the street in front of Sascha's place, his lawn packed with revelers—"Vhale Man!" someone there yelled, which inspired a great roar and a tinkly and percussive clinking of glasses—and then the troop arrived at a new, enormous Channel 6 van, and after a little pushing and shoving, the twins were convinced to wait outside.

"I won't go anywhere," Avi promised.

"You better not!" Rose Red said. "If you run away, I'll make you bleed."

Avi was directed to a canvas chair. Various paper towels were immediately clipped to his clothing, and his hair was gelled with something kind of dry. *Wssshhhwssshhh,* cold base was sponged onto his face; *fffssshhhh,* a little rouge rouged the cheeks; *flick, flick,* his eyelashes were feathered; *chchchchch,* his eyelids were lined. But nothing on his lips. He was shown himself in a hand mirror, yes, fine, ridiculous. He felt stunned, although he wasn't sure why. Nerves, maybe.

"Nice shirt," the make-up artist said.

"Thanks," said Avi.

"Fish on it," the guy said.

"Yep," said Avi. "Gift from the GF."

"Had to be," the guy smiled.

Hannah Cara Papadopoulos had asked to film inside the whale, but Avi had said no. Of course, that hadn't stopped her. Once his face was done, and a microphone was clipped near his top shirt button and the cord was run out of sight to the wireless transmitter snapped to his belt, another assistant assistant led Avi to the set, the twins in tow once again. Crap! The whale's innards had been almost perfectly reproduced: the picnic table, the wooden joists and lodging knees, the tenting, and the flooring were all there. A fake whale of a whale that was a fake.

"Hi. Rick!" Hannah Cara Papadopoulos waved from her interviewer's chair. "Hi!"

Avi wandered over to her. "Look at this place. What have you done?"

"You like it." She waved away Make-up. "It was my idea."

"I figured," Avi said. "Looks . . . sorta familiar."

"It's so real," Hannah Cara Papadopoulos said. "That's what TV is. Now, let's chart." She examined a clipboard. "We're going to begin with some footage and voice-over. Then we'll have a surprise. Then we'll say hello to you. Then we'll talk to you here on set. Commercial breaks will be counted down by that woman next to Camera Two. Rodney's Camera One—isn't that the best! Now, you won't have an earpiece, but I will, and I'll be listening to the producer—Xavi, he's the one talking over there with his back to us. He'll tell us what to do during the breaks. We're live, which means the board will run a three-second delay. No bad words, 'kay, Rick?"

"Of course," Avi said. He hadn't followed everything.

"Right. I might ask you some difficult questions," she looked down, her little-girl voice kicking in. Hannah Cara Papadopoulos's body and hair moved as a unit. "Just a weentsie heads-up, 'kay, Rickie?"

"'Kay."

"Right, then. Sign here—" She held out the clipboard.

"What is it?"

"Oh, nothing. A standard release. We're live in five."

The form was two pages long. Whose name should he sign? "Rick Wood-ley," Avi scrawled on the bottom of the second page. "Whale Man," he added in parentheses. He looked up from the document to see a crowd of production assistants beginning to ring the set, people taking their places here in the fake whale belly—and The Camel leaning against a light stanchion. She smiled a bad smile for Avi. In response, coolly, he patted his back pocket. She nodded, her smile unchanged. Behind the dastardly Camel, her henchwomen seemed to be ravaging a single piece of pie on a plate, stabbing with separate forks.

Hannah Cara Papadopoulos crossed her legs, changed her mind, uncrossed them, and then crossed them the other way. "Rick? How do you feel? I'm so glad you're here. We're live in just a few. Now remember to look natural, that's what America wants. Rick, don't be nervous, it's just national television. I'm not nervous. Rodney said—what? Xavi?" She cocked her head and leaned into her earpiece. "Okay! Change is good. Rick, they want you offstage. We're go-ing to do a Jerry Springer, and bring you on with a lead-in. Could you go wait over there with your friends? Here, Jules will give you an IFB so you can listen in. . . ."

• • •

A tiny guy stepped to a standing mic, put a hand over his ear, and opened his mouth: the teleprompter rolled before him and a huge, deep voice came from his tiny mouth: "And now it's time for a Channel 6 network exclusive—our own Hannah Cara Papadopoulos live in Elsbeth, North Carolina, with Rick Woodley, the enigmatic Whale Man, the homeless philanthropist whose generosity and imagination have captured the hearts and attention of people worldwide. Ask not what a man can do for his country, John F. Kennedy once said. Rick Woodley has asked not . . ." The announcer paused, piled on the melodrama, a little cake and five layers of icing. "And let's go right away to Elsbeth and our own Hannah Cara Papadopoulos. Hannah Cara."

She was lit up, sparkly and calm. She looked good, her face somehow more relaxed than when offstage. "Thanks, Russ," she said. "I'm here in what could be the inside of Rick Woodley's whale to tell you a remarkable story, America, of one man's loss and a community's gain. Of hope and hopelessness. Of what we give to one another. I'm here with Rick Woodley, who will join us shortly, and some special guests. After the show, the phone lines will be open, and we sure do hope you call. The number is 1-900-942-5362, that's 1-900-WHALENC. Each call will cost you two dollars and ninety-five cents, and all monies left over will go to W.H.A.L.E., Rick Woodley's foundation. That's 1-900-WHALENC, whale and North Carolina."

She shifted in her chair, lowered her gaze, put on an important face. "I need to tell you, America, that not everything here in Elsbeth is what you think it is. Every day, we Americans face important decisions. Paper or plastic? Raise taxes or ignore the poor? Live with guns or be shot? Toss our empty hairspray cans into the river when we drive across the overpass? Rick Woodley, America, is one of us. He has also faced difficulty, and you'll see tonight how he has chosen. To lead us in this time of moral blight? Just maybe."

Into Avi's back, something poked. "Pow," said The Camel into his ear.

"That's your finger," Avi whispered over his shoulder.

"But first, a surprise!" Hannah Cara Papadopoulos held out her hand to beck-on someone off-camera. "Channel 6, 6 News in the Street, would like to begin with a down-home exclusive. We're here at the base camp for W.H.A.L.E., the mysterious foundation that has begun building wooden whales throughout the country with the help of our nation's worst felons, a new approach to the rehabilitation of criminals. Well, my—" she appeared to have a little epiphany. "I guess that some of these felons might not even be Americans! Isn't that American?" She giggled carefully. "And with us tonight . . ." Hannah Cara Pa-padopoulos turned gradually, one, two, three, four, to keep the lighting keyed. "With us tonight is a young person you all know even though you've never met her. She's a young person you know because you know ten or twenty young girls like her, sixteen-year-olds lost in the craziness of being a teenager in this mad, unhappy world. Only this young girl, sixteen-year-old Samantha B.—"

Out from behind a small mob of assistant assistants stepped a tall young woman. Wow, it was the runaway from the truck stop! She had been cleaned up, she wore heels and a pretty red dress with silly bows all over it. Samantha. She smiled shyly, waved toward Avi.

"She couldn't take it any more, and she ran away from home. Where did Samantha B. run? To the whale, where so many people have run these days. To the enormous and strange whale built by Rick Woodley, President of W.H.A.L.E., on the front lawn of his dead mother's house. But you know what happened, good friends, once the whale was built? A tragedy, America; some monster set fire to Rick's Mom's house, and now Rick Woodley, who was only trying to help, has himself been made homeless, and forced to live inside his whale. So this is the story of lost people in America, America, of runaways and arsonists and homeless dreamers.

"Rick Woodley is here, America, and he will join us soon on camera—and I know that you'll be as excited as I am to talk with him. He's not bad looking either," she blushed, clearly an act of will. "But first, America, tonight we're going to reunite Samantha with her mother and six stepsisters, as soon as her Mom returns from canasta night in the small town of Confidence, Nebraska. Wait. America, this is so exciting—I understand that Samantha's mom is driving up to her house right now! You, America, will be there, with me, Hannah Cara Papadopoulos, Channel 6, 6 News in the Street, The Truth Be Told. As soon as we pay some bills with a few words from our sponsors. So don't go anywhere! I'm riveted, how about you? Back in a flash," she winked.

"And . . . we're out." Xavi walked onto the set, turned to face his crew. "Two-fifty to the feed, people. Hair, Hair! Where's Hair? Hair, take a look, please— she's been fidgeting. . . ." Xavi seemed to be speaking into his headset and to other people at the same time, treble-voiced. "Honey, please leave your hair alone once we fix it, it's perfect. Rodney, stay with Hannah. Angela, let's lead with tape of the fire."

"Bang," The Camel said.

"Put a hoof in it," Avi whispered.

"Now, Susan Junior—"

"I've got your precious list, and I'm selling. You just chill." He turned to look her in the eye. "Tonight's the night."

"*West Side Story*," The Camel said. "I don't see you as Maria, though. No, wait: Rod Stewart."

"God," Avi was exasperated.

"Susan Junior, you're not in charge," she warned. "Forsooth, when the mayhem yields to madness, you best bring your best."

"What's that, *Romeo and Camel?*"

"Why no, you insolent boy," The Camel calmly hissed. "I just made it up."

"Back in ten!" Xavi the producer shouted. "Places."

"I'm not a boy," Avi said.

The TV people scurried about, the cameras trained their invasions upon Hannah Cara Papadopoulos and Samantha B., The Camel leaned back, and Avi turned and walked away. Could he just keep walking? He had a powerful urge to leave, the dream of the whale enough. But he knew that he couldn't: to leave would be to surrender. Instead he wandered about the jury-rigged stage—trailed, he realized, by Billy the assistant assistant. Whale Man had a new minder.

There were monitors on tables, on carts; everywhere Avi looked, Hannah Cara Papadopoulos returned from the commercial break to reunite Samantha B. with her family in Nebraska, thanks to the miracle of television. He stopped to watch. The girl was crying. Even Hannah Cara Papadopoulos seemed to brush back a tear.

"Um . . . Mr. Woodley? You're wanted back on set. They're looking for you. You're on soon!"

Avi took a deep breath. He closed his eyes for a count of three, then opened them again. "Billy?"

"Yessir."

"Do you have a dog, Billy?"

"Yessir. Queen Mab. She's a long-haired Dachshund."

"Does she behave?" Avi asked, not knowing where the question was going.

"When she wants!" Billy laughed. "She likes to eat money. Dollar bills. Change too."

Avi laughed. "I think I'm someone's dog," he said.

"Whale Man? Sir?"

"I feel like that."

"We all do, sir." The kid seemed surprised by himself. "There's always some-one else in charge. . . . But it's only national television," Billy tried to help.

"Right."

"Sir? Really. They're waiting for you."

"Okay," Avi exhaled. "*Woof*," he said to the absent Dolly. "I have a bad feeling about this."

. . .

"Why a whale, Rick?"

The lights were hot enough to caramelize. No whale would be caught above water in lights this bright. "I . . . well, Hannah Cara Papadopoulos, and Amer-ica, a whale seemed so . . . big and mysterious. So friendly. Plus they're hard to build."

"I see. Isn't that fascinating? Rick, what inspired you to enlist the assistance of the prisoners?" She nodded toward a monitor, where they watched footage of his crew: Peaches and Deke laughing and hammering; two of the Williams gang tussling over a two-by-four, Dolly barking in the background; pizza being delivered; all the jump-suited help munching happily. There was Mom's old house. "Could you talk us through?"

"Sure, Hannah Cara Papadopoulos. The whale was too heavy to pick up. My contractor and I couldn't move most of the parts we built, so we left them there. The prisoners—the people you see here—they're doing the hard work. What W.H.A.L.E. asked of them. You see, Hannah Cara Papadopoulos. . . ."

Avi felt himself warm to the task, this wasn't so hard. "You see, building something with your hands is like . . . making your life . . . building your life. These men, they mostly lift weights, and find ways to deaden themselves; they're strong outside but not inside. Then they suddenly get out on parole. We at W.H.A.L.E. are trying to offer them *life*—not life in prison but another life. Don't forget. After tonight's broadcast. 1-900-WHALENC," Avi added.

"That's beautiful," Hannah Cara Papadopoulos. "1-900-WHALENC," she said, her eyes opening wide as she faced Camera Two. "Now Rick, I'd like to . . ."

Avi tuned out for a few a seconds. In the distance, dimly, he could hear a growing noise, a kind of roaring. Something was up.

"Rick—"

"I beg your pardon. Sorry." Avi sat up. "Could you repeat the question?"

"Rick, I said that we need to settle a couple of details. Is it true, for example, that you built the whale for money?"

"I . . . no, Hannah Cara Papadopoulos. I mean, there's money involved, sure. But I intend to give every penny back. 1-900-WHALENC," Avi smiled.

"$500,000 seems to be the figure I've heard. To split with your brother?" Hannah Cara Papadopoulos's smile hadn't changed.

"I . . . yes, that's sort of right. But—"

"And is it true that your name's not Rick Woodley?"

"I . . ." What the hell was Hannah Cara Papadopoulos doing? "I . . . yes, that's technically true. Remember though, you decided to call me Rick. I told you—"

"And is it true that at the time of her death, your mother was wanted for questioning by the FBI? That she may or may not have been a bank robber? That the $500,000 she left you and your brother might be money *she stole from a bank?*"

"No!" Avi stood up. "No! That's a lie! She was innocent!"

"And isn't it true—" Hannah Cara Papadopoulos seemed to be enjoying herself. She gestured with her left hand, and straight onto the set walked The Camel, to hand the newswoman a file folder, turn crisply, wink at Avi, and then stride off.

Hannah Cara Papadopoulos paused meaningfully.

He should go, he had to leave, he—

"Rick, now Rick." Hannah Cara Papadopoulos put up her hand. "Calm down. Sit down, please. Everyone's innocent until we say so. This is America. Now. . . ." She opened the folder and removed a document. "This just in. I have here in my hand evidence—given to me by your former spokesperson—that identifies your late mother's activities. Seems she wasn't so innocent. Rick, is this true?" She waved the piece of paper around. "Isn't it true that *you don't even have a brother* and that the kidnapping of Daniel Woodley is a total fabrication?"

Avi still hadn't sat. His mouth must have been open.

"America, I'm Hannah Cara Papadopoulos live in Elsbeth, North Carolina, with Channel 6, 6 News in the Street. The Truth Be Told. We'll be back after these messages."

TWENTY-TWO

. . . .

THE BEAST SEEMED AT ONE with the darkness, the night grim above the handmade behemoth in suburban dry-dock. Inside, Avi strung up a clip-on Shoplite, clipped the clip to a beam above, plugged in the cord, and splashed light and shadow on his sparse furnishings, surface details effaced by the radiance. The ladder was steady, the dog had been walked: what more could a man want?

He was embarrassed so profoundly he would never be un-embarrassed.

The cell phone trilled.

"Hello?" Avi felt numb. He had forgotten to turn off the phone.

"Rick!"

"Yeah," said Avi to Ramona Pill.

"It's Ramona Pill," said Ramona Pill.

"Right," said Avi.

"Is it safe?"

"Huh?"

"Is it safe?"

"Look, Pill. Why do you always ask that?"

Ramona Pill laughed a high, scary laugh. "Ah, Rick. Good question, mate." She laughed again. "You know, in *Marathon Man*, that's what Laurence Olivier keeps asking Dustin Hoffman, and then Sir Larry does the Nazi dentist thing. *Is it safe*? He drills Rain Man's teeth."

"Crap," Avi breathed. Ramona Pill was mixing up movies.

"He's the White Angel, mate."

"Who is?"

"Laurence Olivier! Rick, join the program already in progress! He's the White Angel of Death. Or should I call you *Avi*. . . ."

"Crap," Avi said again.

"Crap? Wot, wot. But here's breaking news: The Camel's done waiting, and she wants to see you."

"That's not happening."

"Rick, Rickie, Rickles . . . do I look like I'm kidding?" Ramona Pill's tone had a sneer inside. She wasn't a nice person, but who could tell anymore.

"I can't see you," Avi said. "We're talking on the phone."

"Spot on." In the background, wherever Ramona Pill was, a loud engine revved.

"I'm not going to be there."

"Right, luv," said Ramona Pill. "And she's not going to send the twins."

Avi paused: she had already ruined him, but she was capable of anything. He still wasn't sure whether The Camel had killed Mom. "Where? When?"

"In an hour. At the Self-Storage on 252. Just before your favorite truck stop, wot. Come alone."

"Shit," said Avi.

"Bye, *Avi.*" Pill seemed too happy. "I see it's not safe," she laughed. "G'luck, mate. Nice knowing you."

Ramona Pill had hung up: Avi stared at the cell phone. "I'm sorry," Avi whispered aloud, surprised to say so. To himself, he was apologizing. To Whale Man.

He had an hour. He would swing from the beam and then be Whale Man no more; he would sell the fake list to The Camel, say buh-bye to the charred leavings of Maureen's life, drive to D.C., clean out his apartment, skip town, move out and on, be forgotten. He had done it many times: leaving was easy. He would head West, find a job in a decent kitchen, a windowsill his ficus might like, a place to run Dolly, a parking spot for his pretty new truck. If he were lucky, he would live close to a high school mudding field.

He was almost thirty. He was about to inherit $500,000.

No Camel, no whale, no Pill, no dead mother, no fake brother. No Hannah Cara Papadopoulos, no media exposé. No Bean.

Bean. Where was she?

To hell with them all. The kitchen table and chairs pushed aside, the ladder's legs spread into place, upright and unfolded: up there, at the top of the whale, was all Avi wanted, to find purchase with both hands and drop his weight completely into the air. To be the guy in the dream. He would kick away the ladder and then point his toes and launch.

A roaring was in his ears, a kind of blood-borne, tympanic beat, something tidal. He stopped to breathe—then he stepped away from the ladder and dragged the bed nearer to break his fall. No reason to die, Avi supposed.

What else? Dolly lay on her own bed and stared up at him. "Sorry," he said to Dolly. She thumped her tail, rose and stretched at the same time, then put her big head almost into her water bowl and took a long slurpy drink before ambling over to be scratched behind her ears, head-butting her way into being petted.

"There you go," he told her. She deserved a treat for being a great dog. Avi fetched a dried pig's ear from a bag brought by Bean. Dolly woofed, and accepted the enormous, skuzzy delicacy—and then trotted happily back to her bed to munch and crunch the yummy between her front paws, every crumb licked up, two minutes max.

"Good dog," Avi said, waiting for something.

Whale Man. Whale Man. He tried to open his lungs and heart and feelings to the moment, calm down, make all of his senses available only to what was about to happen, steady his pulse. A big whale can slow her heartbeat to seven or eight beats per minute when diving.

On the table, the cell phone chirped again. Fucking Ramona! He stared, willed the thing into silence, didn't answer. The chirping stopped.

What a fucking disaster. On national television, Avi had been shown to be the failure he had always known himself to be, his awful self-image confirmed, burned into the memories of viewers everywhere, each of his little lies turned around by the truth. Then turned around again, Hannah Cara Papadopoulos a flack, Avi her human sacrifice, the whale's true meaning lost to her ambition. Those people had cared! Avi had cared.

He returned to the ladder, nothing in his life in the way: Avi approached the moment once more, wishing hard for peace. Whale Man. Whale Man. His heartbeat beat time, Whale Man, Whale Man. He began to climb the ladder: hand, foot, hand, foot, eight rungs up, one step shy of the top of the ladder, upon which he clearly should never stand, so said the warning label, NOT A STEP. From up here the belly of the whale looked like a little house in which a poor homeless man had spirited a few crappy belongings, including a bed on which his dog now lay happily—not on her own bed, of course.

The cell phone trilled again.

Dolly gave a little half-bark, falling asleep.

Wary of the drop, Avi closed his eyes too, checked himself for vertigo—and finding none, liked what he felt, for a moment being nowhere in space and time. Slowly, he eased himself upward. He would be able to reach the beam from here, once he stood tall—but there was nothing to grab and swing from, he now saw, the raw wooden beam was too wide to hold, and the curved ring awkwardly placed. A design flaw? Crap. Down Avi backed again, to consider the problem. Down the ladder to the plywood floor, where his legs felt a little shaky upon the solid planking.

With a staple gun he could rig something, a loop like an acrobat's strap. A loop before he leaped. But what to use? The loop would need to support Avi's weight, and not shred when his swinging rubbed the material against the ragged ply. A bungee cord would only pop its hooks, the fabric would tear, and down would come Avi, ladder and all.

The cell phone gave its *tweet-tweet* again, and Avi relented. "Hello?"

"Hi, Boss Man."

"Hey."

"Whatcha doing?"

Avi was going to explain, but decided against. "Oh, nothing."

"Yep. Sorry 'bout the news lady. She sure set you up."

"Yeah," said Avi. "You warned me."

"Tried to."

"Told me not to lie."

"Right."

The men were quiet. Friends, Avi thought. "Say, listen, I've got an engineering problem."

"Yep," Rick said.

"Thinking cap on?"

"Yep," Rick said.

Avi began to pace as he talked, the walking connected to the words, roaming in the whale, the world out there irrelevant, to hell with them. He described the problem.

"Gotcha," Rick said. He was quiet.

Avi waited.

"How 'bout an extension cord?"

"An extension cord."

"Yep. You could wear gloves."

"Gloves."

"Cut up a heavy-duty extension cord. You've got a few."

"—and wear gloves."

"Yep. You might have to loop it a few times. Give it some strength."

"Gotcha," Avi said. He was concerned that his balance on the ladder wouldn't allow for too much motion, the cord difficult to loop repeatedly. "Maybe."

"Give it a shot."

"Maybe." Avi had stopped orbiting around his little room; he began to believe. Yes, Rick's idea could work. "That's great—that should do it. Thanks. . . . So, what's up?"

"Well," Rick almost laughed. "What's up," he repeated.

"Yeah, what's up? You called."

"What's up," Rick said again.

"Rick, man. What's up? It hasn't been a good day. I think I need a smoke."

"Not funny," Rick said. "What's up," he said again.

"Come on," Avi said. "You called me, remember? Taking my temperature?"

"Yep," Rick said. "Sorta. It's like this. I'm here with your mom."

. . .

"Avi . . . are you there?"

"Aw, Mom."

"Avi?"

"Mom? What the fuck?"

"Avi, language. Excuse yourself."

He felt tears on his face. He looked blindly around the whale. "Sorry . . . Mom?"

"I know, Avi. *I'm* sorry . . . to have put you through all this."

"Mom?"

"I know, I know. It's okay."

"You're dead."

"Yes, dear. The Camel wouldn't leave it alone, and she was getting close. I had to fake my death, and the list—"

"What?"

"There's no list, Avi. I made that up. It was my hold over The Camel. But you were brilliant!"

"Mom. . . ."

"Don't worry, it's okay. Rick was watching out for you."

"Rick?"

"After I set fire to the house—"

"You burned your own house! Dolly almost died. I almost died! Mom!"

"Yes, I know. But it's all right, Avi, we're all okay. . . . Besides, I never liked that house, it had such a small feeling to it, and the bed in the master bedroom, oh my Lord! It just faced the wrong way, which isn't good for the heart—you know what they say—and I would get such pains and have bad dreams. . . . Anyway, dear, the files had to be burned so that The Camel would suspect they were real files after all. That was the plan. So I burned the house, and you were sensational, and I—"

"What about Bean?"

"What?"

"Mom, what about Bean?"

"Pardon me? I don't understand. Linda—"

"Barnes, Linda Barnes. Mom. What about her?"

"Well," Mom began. "Oh, dear. Rick, honey, I . . ." Mom didn't want to admit something. "Well, then! Out with it!" Mom laughed. "I guess it's secret-telling time. . . . Rick, Avi. . . ." She addressed them both at once, or so it seemed. "I sent Linda to help. Yes, yes, I know, you were there already, dear, but Linda is so reliable. I thought that if you and she didn't know about each other, that might be best, Rick. I'm sorry not to tell you. . . ."

Avi didn't know what to say, or to ask. Mom was alive. And she had sent both Rick and Bean to watch over her son, and told neither about the other. "Mom, why? Why do all this?"

"I told you. The Camel was too close. I had to disappear, and everyone had to believe it, the FBI had to believe it. You had to believe it, or The Camel wouldn't."

"I don't understand."

"Yes, you do. You always say that, and you always do. You've said that since you were three."

Avi paused, and held the phone out, staring at it, the news impossible. Then his mother said something else that he couldn't hear.

"What? I'm sorry."

"You'll get the money, yes? For your whale."

"I think so. Markins seemed pretty confident. There's one more hoop to jump through."

"That's great, Avi. It's your money. I didn't lie about that."

Now he was a mess. "Mom. I love you."

"I know, Avi. I love you too."

"Can I see you?"

"I'm afraid not. Not for a long time. I'm going away until it's safe—or until there's a grandchild!" She laughed again, and then quieted. "Rick will keep in touch, and I'll send word when I can. He'll . . . I'm glad you got to know him. And you worked some kind of magic, dear, to help him quit that stupid habit. Two Heyers must be better than one!"

"Mom?"

"Yes."

She seemed to be confirming what he suspected. She and Rick. Mom had a boyfriend.

"I guess I just need to process. I mean, holy shit."

She didn't correct his swearing this time. "I know, dear. But there was no other way. I was cornered. And now you've freed me. Thank you, Avi. I'm free."

"Holy shit."

"Find a home, Avi. Go somewhere and cook beautiful meals and find someone right."

"I'll try," he said. Bean, he thought.

"Take care, dear. I love you."

"I love you, Mom."

"That's right. Now Rick wants to have a word."

"Bye."

"Bye."

"Boss Man? You okay?"

"No," Avi said. "I mean, yeah."

"Nice whale," said Rick.

"What?"

"Nice whale. It's a good 'un."

"Thanks," Avi said. "And for taking care of me. And Mom."

"Sure," Rick said. "Been a pleasure."

"So let me get this straight—you met Mom . . . how?"

"FBI. I was a field agent. But I took my twenty after I met her."

"And how did you manage this?"

"Right," Rick said. "Contract. Henry thought I'd be helpful freelance, since I worked your Mom's case a few years back. I helped him think that."

"But he doesn't know."

"Nope."

"Is he gonna be around?"

"Maybe. He's hot for The Camel."

"Gotcha," Avi said, although he didn't quite understand.

"Should be okay, though."

"How?"

Rick was silent for a moment. "You'll think of something," he said.

"Gee, thanks."

"I mean it," Rick said. "I'll think too."

"You're very encouraging."

"You owe me money, Boss Man. Pay me, and I'll be encouraging."

Avi almost laughed. "I see."

Now Rick gave a very small chuckle, a miracle. "No, you don't," he said. "Look, it'll be fine. You'll know what to do—ya' done great. . . . Now I gotta go. I'll see you later. Take care, Avi."

"Take care," Avi said, tears welling. "See ya' soon."

He sat and stared and then stood and stared and then paced and then sat and stared. Five, ten, fifteen minutes, who knows. Mom was alive, Rick was with Mom. Avi stood up and stared. He needed only to climb the fucking ladder and loop the loop and swing the swing, a man finishing what a dream started. But oh, crap, his emotions were flying all over the place—Mom was alive!

Rick was with Mom. Holy shit.

Avi trundled out his equipment from the whale's tail, the work gloves in the toolbox too, and took a pair of bolt cutters to the extension cord, two cuts that required muscle, the resulting piece of cord eight feet long. He was sweating a little.

Done, the orange cord tied loosely around his waist, gloves in his back pockets, Avi approached his ladder once more.

"Here we go," Avi told his now sleeping dog.

He climbed two rungs, aware of new tears. He paused to wipe his face with a forearm. Hand, foot, hand, foot.

Mom was alive.

The bed was in place below, the ladder led up to the man's dream, everything where it needed to be, and Mom was with Rick.

"It's like this," Rick had said. "I'm here with your mom."

Hand, foot. Hand, foot.

Mom was alive.

"Find someone, make a home, cook beautiful meals," his Mom had said.

Hand, foot. Whale Man. Whale Man. He had to wipe away his tears once more. Amazing, unreal, life never was what a man plans—and amen for that.

Mom was alive. Avi was almost at the top of the ladder, and then, yes, he was there, extension cord at the ready. He eased himself up, and balanced fairly well on his bare feet on the top rung as he slowly raised his arms, cord in one hand and nothing but air in the other. From here, he could reach the plywood ring and L-bracketed beam, stretch to use his free hand and grasp the wood, fully vertical, he and the ladder.

The ladder from his dream. The whale he had dreamed and built. Mom's whale.

Mom was alive.

With room enough between the wood and the tenting, the heavy-duty orange cord sufficiently stiff to aim, throw, and thread, he ran his cable, pulled the end down and through, and ran it again and again and one last time, three loops should do it, triple strength. He tied it off with a square knot.

He was crying, and ready.

Tugging down on the cord, Avi evened the loops, his balance still good, tears wiped away on his shoulder.

He tested the cord gradually, first with one hand, pulling and letting some of his weight contribute, and then with both hands. He put on the gloves, kept his balance. Gripping the triple-looped cable, he allowed more of his weight to hang, then more, and finally gently launched himself away from the ladder.

He was afraid.

He was happy.

Maybe he had always been afraid, but now he was happy.

Whale Man, he told himself, and then with a good little push he tried to kick down the ladder, away from the bed below, but only made the ladder rock, then sway back into place. A better kick was needed: Avi pointed his toes, regained purchase, and stood there once more, learning.

He took a deep breath.

Avi threw his hips and butt backward, pushed off a little, backwards, and gave in to the strain of his full weight in his arms, the dismount six inches or so away from the top of the ladder; and then, fully in the air, he tucked his legs and swung back again, brought his toes through and tucked his legs for the backswing.

He was swinging some.

Forward and then back, his weight producing his momentum, Avi bent his legs at the knees in a fuller movement and came through extended, toes pointed, and kicked the ladder over, just right, the crash to the plywood below resounding.

Dolly jumped up and barked.

Avi hung there—dangled, really. Then legs tucked and toes pointed, legs tucked, toes pointed, the swing began in earnest, the cord held, the man giving in to the weight of his body, on earth but in space, all he had imagined.

He closed his eyes.

He swung.

In the whale, he swung.

In his dream again, or almost. What he had dreamed, all he had wanted seemed possible this once. He swung; one promise kept.

TWENTY-THREE

. . . .

AVI ANSWERED the cell phone. "Hello?"

"Is it safe?"

"Go to hell," Avi said.

"Now, Susan Junior. Let's not be trepidary."

"Trepidary?"

Ramona Pill paused. "Wot," she said. "Trepidary. Afraid."

"That's not a word," Avi said. "You've been talking to The Camel."

"Is too," said Pill. "Just ask her. Look, mate, don't throw a wrench in the amber."

"That's not the right saying. What the hell does that mean, a wrench in the amber?"—and with that, he hung up. She would call back: that was why hanging up on Ramona Pill was fun.

The phone chirped again. Avi answered brusquely, "What is it now?"

"Don't do that!" Pill might have actually been annoyed. "She's changed the meet, she has."

"God," Avi sighed.

"Get out of the whale and go to the corner of Elm and Wojocowicz, and wait for my call. . . ."

. . .

Get out of the whale: he wasn't so sure. Avi was scared to go out there again, to face his followers and the media horde, everyone devouring, munching on the whale, chewing him to bits, everyone demanding something he had only pretended to have. All Avi had wanted was to build his whale . . . and grieve for his living mom, and kanoodle with Bean, and open a good wine, and make Rick smile, and mud with Dolly, and greet his admirers, and—sure, the truck was nice too, okay, very nice. And yes, maybe he had wanted too much at once, and the God of All Whales was making him pay. Some parts of his behavior had probably been hubristic.

They had gobbled him up and spat out the bones of his lies, Hannah Cara Papadopoulos and her ilk, those inhumans. Admittedly, he had lied a lot, and might have earned this comeuppance. Still, when Avi had fled the fake TV whale for the real fake wooden whale, his fame newly infamous, notoriety in the place of celebrity, the newsies had circled, smelled the fresh kill, howled into their IFBs as though the moon were full, true Elsbeth Jackals. He had been forced to bull his way through the throng, just as he had been forced to bull his way for years through his own unhappiness.

He could blame the broadcast media forever, but really, Avi had done this to himself, his whale a narcotic, fame a second dose. Damn, he had no excuse that worked, no metaphor with which to assuage his conscience. Guilt was a whale, Avi reminded himself. Grief was a whale, too.

But stupidity could be a drug, apparently.

Mom was alive.

He realized that he was completely like his mother: she had left, and taught him how to leave, and he had spent his life leaving, and now he would leave again, and she would leave again, and she would live elsewhere once more in comfortable, happy anonymity. Maybe he would never forgive her, a mother who had faked her death for fifteen years.

Whale Man, Avi reminded himself: he had dreamed the dream, kicked the ladder and watched it fall, hung from the dreamed beam, swung from the past into the future. It was time to snag a bag of oranges and suck a good one, and forgive himself.

. . .

He crawled into the tail of the whale, rolled under the tenting in one corner and out into the darkness, sneaked away from the klieg lights and the rumbles in the jungle of Whale City. Hoodied and anonymous, Avi jogged to the pick-up, the good dog Dolly happy to jog along, her person her very favorite. Then he drove to the meet and waited. When Ramona Pill called back, Avi cooperated—this had to end—and sped down roads too quickly to remember them: left, right, straight, second left, left, straight. He thought he might not be far from the truck stop, but he really couldn't tell. How did Pill know where he was? He never saw her vehicle, and after a while, he never saw any other cars on the road. That sneak.

A card table had been placed in the middle of a parking lot, lit by two blazing lights on stanchions, flanked by two simple bridge chairs, and on the table stood a pitcher of water and two cut crystal glasses. She was waiting for him, her back to the lights, very Al Capone, her silhouette knowable; he intuited that her backlit silhouette would be something he glimpsed for years, the wrong shadow lurking at the periphery of every crowd.

He turned off the engine, got out of the truck, and stepped into the glare, the little pickup left deep in the darkness so that Dolly could sleep.

"Ah, Susan Junior," said The Camel. She made as though to rise but merely gestured to the available chair. "Shall you be West Germany and I shall be East? Here we are diplomatically together, at Checkpoint Charlie."

"What?" Avi approached, and cautiously sat. She couldn't bite him from this distance.

"Of course, indubitably; you are presenting with dissociative symptoms. Were I capable of any sympathies, I would sympathize, sympathy itself a kind of mercy, a lesser state of—"

Avi held up his hand, no more. "Stop," he said.

"Ah." The Camel poured him a glass of water. "Care to be slaked?" She had changed clothes once again; now she wore a sweatshirt that advertised a Garlic Festival. *To Reek is Chic*, said the sweatshirt; there was a comically drawn picture of a ground hog on the front, or the drawing might have been of a Dalmatian. The Camel also seemed to be wearing culottes and clogs, but Avi couldn't be sure. With her right hand, she yanked her own right earlobe a couple of times, and began again: "I'm so glad we had this time together, just to have a laugh and sing a song."

He wasn't going to touch that glass of water. "What do you want?"

"Susan Junior, you demonstrate such deflationary egoism! I thought it not possible."

"Look, you win. What do you want? I don't have the list."

The Camel tented her fingertips, looked down at her hands. "See, how very Episcopalian I can be. . . ? But of course you don't have the list! Forsooth, no list shall be found."

"What?"

"There is no list, my little Gund bear, and there never was."

"You knew?"

"I am nearly offended!" The Camel's feigned indignation rose with the raising of her penciled eyebrows. "Note my mock horror."

"Then why . . . what do you want?" Avi felt tireder and tireder.

"Dear Susan Junior, I want one-half of your payday, what is mine in truth and has always been mine, no matter in whose hands the funds have resided. I want an untraceable deposit into an unmarked Turks and Caicos account in the amount of a paltry $250,000—that's a "quarter mil" for those Americans among you enthralled with slang, and yes, money is a type of slang—or otherwise, I shall bring to the authorities evidence of your dear mother's continued existence." Her fingers tapped each other; the gesture somehow threatened.

"You knew," Avi realized. "The whole time, you knew . . . about the codicil, the money, and you"—he was pretty damn surprised—"you waited for me to get the money . . . for you! So the twins were just—"

"Diversionary tactics. Melodrama. Yes, dear lad."

"So you waited because the money wasn't here yet. This was your plan all along. You knew my mother was alive. Jesus!"

"Do you take me for a block of wood? My word. As Flangoni says in *De Rerum*, 'A beast that crawls may yet still soar.' One must know one's Flangoni. A little obscure, granted, but available to a lay-person, the apophthegms translated, of course. The epigram is a curious form, yes? I have long been taken with its economics. Not that Flangoni compares to Martial, whose—"

"My God," Avi heaved a deeper sigh of understanding. "You played me."

"It is what it is." She sipped her water.

"And now you're blackmailing me. Her—you're blackmailing her, through me!"

"What a tender little shoot you are, dear flower."

"Crap," Avi said.

"Yes. Crap."

They were silent. Around her head, the light made a little corona—a corona of evil, Avi mused. He probably didn't have a choice here.

"So you let me do all of this. . . . You watched . . . my whale—"

"Cute, really."

"Cute?"

"But not the prevarications, Susan Junior: one learns to provide only as needed, and never falsify unprompted. In our industry, cuteness is a hazard." The Camel bared her teeth slightly. "I fear that you will never be your mother's son, and determinedly as the night has proven, rather more of a horse's ass. Of course, you know whereof I speak. *Segue!*" She raised an index figure skyward, then with an open palm broadly gestured to their surroundings. "Look at where we are: the concrete pasture, the paved garden, the macadam Eden, the American future. A parking lot is evenly divided into nation-states, as it should be. Those lines bespeak older times, the Industrial Revolution, the railroad, the Turner Thesis. My God, I love this country's excesses and excuses."

"And what about Ramona Pill?"

"Ah," The Camel cooed with a growl. "She is the unknowable. As such, she resembles the one whale you mentioned—is there not a species never yet seen? The Camel once again pointed her index finger skyward and began to declaim, "Ramona Pill, she lurks yet still." She stopped, and smiled tightly at Avi. "I do wish you would be more helpful when I wax ironic," she said. "Irony is the language of failed expectation, no? As such, I'm speaking to you."

· · ·

When Avi returned to the road, he did so as a tempted man: there was the highway beckoning, the endless strips of open transit a sign if not a portent. But to drive without purpose would be to forfeit his share of Mom's proceeds, which he found himself unwilling to do, even though The Camel would also get a share. Avi's whale had earned its half of the paycheck, dammit.

But instead of fleeing, upon finding his bearings—all larger roads in Elsbeth apparently leading to S.R. 252—he returned to the truck stop to be among friends in the pursuit of interstate solace, the rumble of the diesel engines more like his heart than the systole-diastole of Whale Man, Whale Man.

Between a vibrant, metallic blue eighteen-wheeler emblazoned with the phrase "Foundation Bros." and a pale green eighteen-wheeler—well, pale green in this light—decorated with four nonsensically interlocked triangles underscored by the words "Lick 'n Chicken," Avi parked his cool new truck. He was fuming; the world could not contain his sudden rage. He felt stuck, harpooned. Goddamn Camel, playing him the whole time.

Above the car and the trucks, the night never changed. Avi looked up into the picture-imperfect sky awash with photovoltaic light: he leaned forward to crane upward through his windshield, to make himself too uncomfortable to sleep, not out of penance or from any great self-loathing, but just to process, process. All that had happened to him tonight, the whale and its past, all time moving backward through his mind, the unwinding skein of his memories— he wanted to know everything and to understand. If a man wasn't going to dream, he might as well learn something.

But what had he learned? Not to lie into a microphone.

Or, not to lie to better liars. He had been outclassed as a liar. The one talent he had brought to Elsbeth—thanks, Mom—had turned out to be second-rate. Even his whale was a big lie that no one believed.

· · ·

"Rrrmph," Dolly said from the backseat.

"Rrrmph," Avi answered from the front seat. "What? Who?"

He had fallen asleep, slept while leaning on the steering wheel. There were drool marks on his arm.

"*Woof!*" Dolly said, standing up and glaring. "*Woof! Woof, woof, woof, woof!*"

"What. . . ? Doll, easy. Down, girl," Avi stretched and leaned back to pet her head, and doing so, he glanced over to the passenger side, where a figure loomed a little—a figure who couldn't loom much, because she wasn't very big. Bean.

With her knuckle, she gave a little tap on the window, two, three.

He reached over to unlock the door, but couldn't find the little knobbie, the truck too new to know; then he realized he could unlock the door from his side. He was sleepy, but he could still unlock a door.

"Hi," she said. She climbed into the cab.

"Hi."

"I've looked everywhere," she said. She reached into the back to greet the insistent Dolly, a dog's love forever.

"I . . . I've been here. I met with The Camel," Avi added.

Damn, they were awkward together. Bean had yet to look at Avi directly; Dolly was a good proxy for now, he figured.

"And. . . ?"

"She knew. Everyone knew but me. All along, she just wanted a chunk of the inheritance. There was no list," he glumly added.

"Right. Your mom called me too," Bean said. "Oh, Avi. . . ."

"Right," he said. "You lied to me even when you were telling me the truth."

Bean smiled a very little Bean smile; he had to look away. "That's ridiculous," she said. "I never really lied, I just didn't say. Oh, and I should probably tell you something. I . . . Avi . . . I'm the executrix. Your mom named me. So I'm supposed to approve of your whale."

"Gah, that's absurd," Avi huffed.

"I know." Bean smiled more fully, and a damn nice smile she had. "So I approved. Is that okay?"

"*Rrrrmppp!*" Dolly said, and Bean and Avi laughed quickly together, and then stopped laughing just as quickly, not yet.

"Avi, tonight was terrible. The TV. I'm so sorry."

"Where'd you go?"

"I . . . I got scared. That newswoman knew too much about you. I . . . thought . . . I panicked. I'm sorry."

"You ran," Avi said. "You left me."

"Oh, boyfriend. I didn't leave you. Don't be such a drama queen."

"Don't be such a leaver."

"Don't be such a do-goody."

"Don't be such a felon."

"Don't be so Type B."

"Don't be so afraid."

"Don't be such . . ."

The whole time, trading insults that they meant or didn't, Avi and Bean had begun to lean in, toward each other, until—*POW!* Yes, he kissed his girlfriend, and *POW! POW-POW!* she kissed him back, with sugar and slippies.

"I need you," Avi said, holding tight.

"Oh, Avi. Don't."

"I'm sorry. I don't think . . ." He didn't finish his sentence, it seemed wrong. He changed his approach. "I think," Avi said, "that I haven't needed anyone, or convinced myself that I haven't. I think—"

"Oh, Avi. Look. You're glowing," Bean said. "Can we have sex again, please?"

"In the whale?"

Bean blushed. "I liked that," she said. "And wherever you'd like, really."

"You're so bad," he said.

"I know," she blushed another couple of reds. Their foreheads were doing that little forehead love bump.

"Hey," Avi pulled back just a bit, so that she wouldn't appear to have only one eye. "Does a penis have a Soul Diary?"

"I don't know!" Bean laughed. "Let's find out."

· · ·

Parking was no longer possible close to the whale, so Avi, Bean, and the too-tired, hang-doggity Dolly had to hoof it home from two blocks away. He felt like he was arriving at Whale-a-palooza, a feeling he had experienced before: somewhere up ahead, a roots band would be playing the Star Spangled Banner, and the TV crews would be filming, and Hell's Angels would be thumping gate crashers, and Jas would be giving birth. But as the three of them de-trucked, just one more block before sex with Bean, he sensed something else—there was a ruckus at the whale, the TV lights were blazing, and all sorts of noises, chants and shouts were cascading through suburbia. Wrong noises, Avi thought. Especially for three in the morning.

Dolly barked anxiously, "*Woof! Woof, woof, woof, woof!*"

"What's going on?" Bean said, as they all turned the corner.

"Doll, it's okay." Avi reached down to calm her. Then he picked up the pace. "Let's go," he said, breaking into a jog and slipping on the hoodie hood. "C'mon, Dolly."

The crowd had increased in size. Even from four or five houses away, Avi could see the street and sidewalk filled with whale worshippers and police and news crews. But he couldn't run home: now he and Bean had to weave through a serious crowd, excuse me, excuse me.

Something was wrong. People were shouting.

"Do it!"

"Yeah!"

"Whale Man!"

"Get him!"

And then he was there, he could see the TV vans, their masts erect, the cameramen on top of their trucks like sailors in crows' nests, the media event live and in person, the world their exclusive.

The whale was mobbed. The mob was surging.

The mob surged forward, ebbed back. Surged. The mob was chanting differently, the sound mean: "Whale. Man. Whale. Man. Whale. Man. Whale. Man. . . ."

"It's not safe," Avi called to Bean. "Wait here! Hold on to Dolly!"

He navigated through the worshippers he had betrayed. Would he get to the whale? What could he do?

Avi got closer, and now he was scared.

Something flew into the air—a piece of something.

"Whale. Man. Whale. Man. Whale. Man. Whale. Man. . . ."

He was almost there. He elbowed someone, squeezed closer. Avi could see through the faces of the raging, shifting crowd; and there, bobbing up and down, Hannah Cara Papadopoulos chanting along with the larger chant, "Whale. Man. Whale. Man." Hannah Cara Papadopoulos's fist was in the air, and in her fist was a pair of scissors; her face looked purple, fury and violence were in her expression. Avi didn't see Rodney: Hannah Cara Papadopoulos was decidedly off the air.

"Whale. Man. Whale. Man. Whale. Man. Whale. Man. . . ."

Something else flew into the lighted sky, and the crowd roared.

And something else—it looked like a piece of . . . cloth. Of tent fabric.

They were destroying the whale!

"Liar," someone close to Avi yelled. "Fake!"

"Whale. Man. Whale. Man. Whale. Man. Whale. Man. . . ."

He could do nothing. The whale was surrounded, the police were letting it happen. The TV crews were filming the destruction of the story they had written.

With an awful snap, something in the whale gave way. The crowd surged forward, vengeful and righteous. Another snap, another roaring surge.

It was too late.

Avi backed away. He couldn't watch, it wasn't safe.

And then the whale was flying up into the air—but in pieces, not whole, not in the water, not breaching to breathe. Wood and cloth again, the whale would soon be no more, returned to the dream from whence it came.

"Whale. Man. Whale. Man. Whale. Man. Whale. Man. . . ."

Head tucked further into the hoodie, he backed away. Where were Bean and Dolly? Avi had to find them, make sure they were safe. It was time to leave Elsbeth; the whale was done, her song silenced, Avi's grief once more a dulled, low hum.

"Whale. Man. Whale. Man. Whale. Man. Whale. Man. . . ."

He ducked down, only to feel someone grab him, a hand on Avi's shoulder with a grip that wouldn't let go, someone shaking him.

"Whale Man. Whalie whale. It's me."

Avi squirmed to get away, oh no, they would hurt him. The chant was everywhere: "Whale. Man. Whale. Man. Whale. Man. Whale. Man. . . ."

"Whale Man, chill! I've got you. It's me."

From under the hoodie, Avi looked up at Pony Tail Guy.

"Whale Man, like, now, we gotta go. *Now*, Whale Man. Come on, let's get you outta here."

. . .

They were sitting in Pony Tail Guy's van not far from the whale, the crowd noise growing, a mob in need of de-mobbing, Avi's whale apparently not so easy to tear to pieces.

Avi, Pony Tail Guy, and some woman in a lab coat sat in the back of Pony Tail Guy's van. Now Avi understood why Pony Tail Guy smelled like old cinnamon—because the van smelled like a van-full of old cinnamon. A van decorated with what looked to be expensive electronic equipment, interior design provided by the good people of Radio Shack.

"How long has that been going on?" Avi nodded to indicate the crowd.

"Wow, dude. They're like following the false prophets."

Avi decided not to ask again.

Pony Tail Guy was a little out of breath. "But The Pod's got you now. And your virgin and your sacrificial dog."

"My sacrificial dog—"

"Don't worry, Whale Man." With a jittery gesture Pony Tail Guy pointed toward the woman in the lab coat. "She's a physicist."

"Who are you people?"

"Dude! *Sheeeee!* You gave us what we've been looking for! We're The Pod."

"The Pod?"

The woman in the lab coat spoke for the first time, her clipped tones the work of memorization: "The Pod is a guerilla organization dedicated to the teachings of the Elsbeth Whale. The second whale will soon be finished in Monmouth, Illinois." She curled her pinkie and ring finger so that the other three fingers made a bad "W" and tapped her chest with what was clearly The Pod's dorky secret signal, holy shit. "*Sheeeeee.*"

"You're the copycats," Avi said.

"Hold on, there, Whale Man," Pony Tail Guy said. "No one's sleeping with the fishes here. The copycats did Sausalito."

Avi thought about that—and the other stuff he would never understand, and probably didn't want to understand—and decided to keep going, just move forward. "Right," he said. "Can you get me out of town?"

"Whale Man," Pony Tail Guy said. "In Monmouth *you can hear her!*"

"Dude," said Avi. "Focus."

"I've run the frequencies," said the physicist. "I can't account for it. Not even at 5 kHz."

"What's your name?" Avi asked, hoping she might be saner.

"Sue," she blushed.

"Avi," he said. They shook hands.

"So, can we leave now?"

Pony Tail Guy smiled a big smile. He tapped his ear—oh, crap, that better not be a hearing aid!—and then put his hand on Avi's shoulder. "Three, two, one . . ." he said. With his other hand, PTG made The Pod's secret hand sign.

Bam bam, tink, tink, tink Someone was bamming and tinking on the van door. The noise stopped, and then began again, *bam, tink.*

"That's the signal." Pony Tail Guy slid open the door. "Quick!"

There were Bean and Dolly with two more guys in lab coats.

"Avi!" said Bean, climbing into the van and his arms.

"*Woof! Woof, woof, woof, woof!*" said Dolly.

"Oh, God," said Avi, clutching Bean.

"Whalie whale," said Pony Tail Guy. "*Sheeeeeeeee,*" he said as he gave The

Pod sign to his pals and slid the door closed. "That's it, we're out." He clambered awkwardly over the couple to get to the driver's seat. "Sue, you're on GPS. Whale Man, hold onto your virgin. Hug her." Pony Tail Guy gazed sagely through the windshield and started the engine. "The sea's a bit rough."

ACKNOWLEDGMENTS

Technical assistance was provided by numerous friends and experts in the writing of this book. To the following, *grazie mille*:

Matthew Churchill, Attorney-at-Law
Corinne Duchesne, Foundation Studies, Sheridan College
Dr. Julio Ramirez, Department of Psychology, Davidson College
Dr. Ping Shao, Department of Chinese, Davidson College
Tim Chavis, Pro Desk Supervisor, Home Depot
Dr. David Galef, Department of English, Montclair University
Rudi Gombert, Gombert Engineering
Jessica C. Malordy, Davidson College
Frank Molinek, Davidson Fire Department
Dr. Liza Potvin, Department of English, Malaspina University-College
Rabbi Michael Shields, Davidson College
Dr. Shelley Rigger, Department of Political Science, Davidson College
Special Agent Tim Stutheit, Federal Bureau of Investigation
Dr. Homer Sutton, Department of French, Davidson College
Dr. Mark Willhardt, Department of English, Monmouth College
Dr. Stephen K. Mange, Davidson Clinic
Ashley Warlick, Warlick Enterprises

With thanks to the twins, Bella and Isa; with thanks to Davidson College, The Fundación Valparaiso, and the Virginia Center for the Creative Arts. With special thanks to the crew at WordFarm: Andrew Craft, Sally Sampson Craft, Marci Whiteman Johnson, George Eddy Smith and Mark Eddy Smith. As ever, with love to my first reader and toughest editor, Felicia van Bork; and in loving memory of my mother, Dr. Ellen Parker.

ABOUT THE AUTHOR

Novelist and poet Alan Michael Parker is the author or editor of ten books, including a previous novel, *Cry Uncle*. For fifteen years a book reviewer for *The New Yorker*, Parker has published poetry and prose in *The Believer*, *The New Republic*, *The New York Times Book Review*, *Paris Review*, *Salon*, *The San Francisco Chronicle* and *Slate*. He has received a Pushcart Prize, The Fineline Prize from *The Mid-American Review* and The Lucille Medwick Memorial Award from the Poetry Society of America, among other awards. He teaches at Davidson College and in the Queens University low-residency M.F.A. program.

Other Books by Alan Michael Parker

FICTION
Cry Uncle

POETRY
Elephants & Butterflies
A Peal of Sonnets (letterpress edition)
Love Song with Motor Vehicles
The Vandals
Days Like Prose

EDITED AND CO-EDITED VOLUMES
The Imaginary Poets
Who's Who in 20th Century World Poetry (Editor for North America)
The Routledge Anthology of Cross-Gendered Verse (co-edited with Dr. Mark Willhardt)